Suddenly Engaged

A LAKE HAVEN NOVEL

Suddenly Engaged

JULIA LONDON

Published by Montlake Romance, Seattle

www.apub.com

ISBN-13: 9781477848616
ISBN-10: 1477848614

Cover design by Eileen Carey

Printed in the United States of America

Suddenly Engaged

Prologue

The pregnancy test kits were lined up in formation like a marching band on her bathroom counter. Seven of them in all, one for each day of the week, four digital wands in the back row, three nondigital wands in the front.

Kyra watched Brandi closely as she stared down at the sticks. "You're pregnant," Brandi announced.

"Maybe it's the brand," Kyra suggested hopefully. "Maybe I should try different brands just to be sure."

Brandi gave her a side eye. "You're *pregnant*, Kyra."

Kyra swallowed down a swell of nausea. What was that, morning sickness? Or was she just sick with worry? She couldn't be pregnant. There was no room in her life for pregnant. "Maybe I should try the test in the middle of the night. You know hormones fluctuate at night."

Brandi didn't bother to respond to such inanity. She turned around and walked out of the bathroom.

Kyra reluctantly followed.

Brandi draped her supermodel-thin body over Kyra's secondhand couch, then flipped her blonde Brazilian Blowout over her shoulder. "Did you call him?"

Kyra sank much less gracefully onto the matching secondhand chair. "I've called him, I've texted him. He hasn't responded."

"He's ghosting you. It's those damn destination weddings." Brandi sighed. "Weekend romances are so intense, and then they never work once you're back to real life. You should really avoid them."

Kyra looked curiously at her friend. "It was *your* destination wedding, Brandi."

"You know what I mean."

Yes, she knew what Brandi meant—she should have been more careful. Generally, Kyra was on board with Brandi's advice. They'd met when Kyra landed a job at *US Fitness*, a magazine devoted to weekend warriors. It was Kyra's first real job out of college; she'd been hired on as a junior copy editor. She'd had great ambition when she'd started—she wanted to run her own magazine someday, just like she'd run her high school yearbook, and she saw the job at *US Fitness* as her springboard. She'd worked hard and volunteered for any extra work anyone would give her, and it had paid off—in six months' time, she was promoted to copy editor.

Brandi was a senior editor at the magazine and had seen promise in Kyra. She'd taken her under her wing, told her about an editorial position opening up at the end of the year. When she'd found out Kyra was new to New York, she'd helped set Kyra up with a personal life. She'd made sure to invite Kyra when a group was going for drinks or to join them for a weekend outing . . . if that outing didn't include a thirty-mile bike ride. Kyra hadn't exactly gotten on board with the fitness part of her job.

Brandi had been engaged to Mark when she and Kyra first met. As good-looking and as fit as his fiancée, Mark introduced Kyra to his handsome and successful friends, several of whom Kyra had dated . . . maybe a bit indiscriminately. Why not? She'd been a full-fledged, card-carrying adult, and it was New York! Dating and sex were mandatory recreation for a single woman in New York. Before she knew it, Kyra had morphed into a party girl, and the party girl had lit up like a bonfire when Brandi and Mark decided that they would host a destination wedding in Puerto Vallarta.

"You *have* to come," Brandi had said.

"I don't know if I can swing it," Kyra had responded, thinking of money.

"Kyra!" Brandi had said laughingly. "Since when do you turn down a good time?" She'd been standing over Kyra in her little work cubby, wearing fabulous high heels and a miniskirt that showcased her runner's legs. "You cannot pass this up! It's a chance of a lifetime, and it will be so much *fun*. And just wait until you get a look at the groomsmen." She'd winked at Kyra. "My assistant is looking for a roommate," she'd added as she'd walked on.

No doubt about it—a long weekend in Puerto Vallarta had sounded fabulous.

Kyra had wanted to go, but after a quick study of her bank account, she'd found it wanting. She'd called her dad in Florida to borrow the money for plane fare.

"Puerto Vallarta," he'd repeated gruffly. Kyra's father was a working man and didn't think highly of vacations. "Sounds like a cheap beach hotel."

"It's a town in Mexico, Dad. On the Pacific Ocean. It's supposed to be really beautiful."

"Ocean! Come to Florida. We've got ocean, and it's a hell of a lot cheaper than what you're talking."

"But Brandi isn't getting married in Florida," she'd pointed out.

In the end, he'd lent her the plane fare with a lecture about how he was an electrician and wasn't rolling in dough.

Kyra had booked her flight, had shopped online for two fabulous dresses—one for the party the night before the wedding, one for the wedding—and made arrangements with Lisa, Brandi's assistant, to share a room. And then she'd flown out of the country for the first time.

She'd met Josh at the beach resort where the wedding was held and the guests had stayed. It was a beautiful oceanfront property with three pools and a private beach—all the amenities dozens of twenty-somethings could possibly want. Kyra had noticed Josh, but at first she hadn't realized he was following her around. When she figured it out and called him on it, he laughed and bought her a mojito.

He was an old school chum of Mark's, a Prince Harry lookalike, a charming, dashing man with his tall, muscular frame, his winsome smile, and his ability to make her laugh.

It was embarrassing that she'd fallen so hard and so fast for him. They'd spent three fantastic days and two incredible nights together, and after the wedding she'd flown back to New York with his number in her phone and the belief that love at first sight could really, truly happen.

"What an idiot I am," she said now, staring at the floor.

"You're *not* an idiot," Brandi said. "Well, the part about having unprotected sex was incredibly stupid, but you're not a total idiot."

"Gee, thanks." Kyra couldn't look Brandi in the eye on that one. A condom had not been readily available, so they'd used the old rhythm method . . . except that Josh's rhythm was way off, and he hadn't pulled out in time. He hadn't pulled out at all.

"I get it, Kyra, I do," Brandi said, sounding more sympathetic. "Who would have thought he would ghost you?"

"You had no idea he was like that?" Kyra asked.

"Me?" Brandi asked and shook her head. "I met him for the first time in Puerto Vallarta. He and Mark were college buddies, but they don't really hang out. I saw the same thing as you did—supercute, nice guy, someone you could have a blast with."

Oh yeah, she'd had some fun, all right. Just look at her now.

"But you're definitely pregnant," Brandi continued, "and now you have to pull on your big girl panties, and Josh needs to hike up his big boy briefs, and you two have to talk about this." She glanced at her wristwatch. "I have to run. Will you be in the office Monday?"

"Sure," Kyra said halfheartedly. She hadn't even thought about how this pregnancy might affect her job. She hadn't thought of what she might do if she was truly pregnant. She'd been so determined not to *be* pregnant, but now . . . now she couldn't deny it, and uncertainty began to pound in her temples. What was she going to do? She had options, didn't she? None of which felt like an answer as they flit through her head.

Brandi stood up, pulled Kyra to her feet, and hugged her. "Listen, it's going to work out. Mark says Josh is a good guy."

"Right," Kyra said.

She had a really bad feeling about this. A good guy didn't ghost.

♦ ♦ ♦

That bad feeling only grew worse over the course of the weekend as she repeatedly tried to get in touch with Josh. When he wouldn't respond to her phone calls or texts—even after she tried to assure him in another unanswered text message that she was not a stalker—she had to resort to drastic measures.

Monday morning, as she walked to work, she built up a good head of steam. She knew where Josh was employed, thanks to some pillow talk, and stopped outside of her office building to call his office.

"May I say who is calling?" asked the woman who answered the phone.

"Kyra Kokinos," Kyra said. "Please tell him it's important."

A moment later, Josh was on the phone. "For God's sake, Kyra," he said impatiently. "What are you not getting? When a guy doesn't respond to your calls or your texts, it means he—"

"I know what it means, Josh," she said, cutting him off before he could utter the indelible *I'm not that into you*. She knew what was up, even if there was a tiny part of her hoping that maybe he'd lost his phone or had been hit by a bus and had been in the hospital all this time. How could she have been so wrong about their connection? "What part of important do *you* not get?" she shot back. "I wouldn't have called you at work if you had just responded to a text or two."

He sighed. "Look, Kyra, we had a great time in Puerto Vallarta. Fantastic. But this is—"

"I have to tell you something, Josh," she said angrily. She was suddenly shaking. As in might-pass-out shaking. She sat down on a bench. "I'm pregnant."

That was met with silence. Cold, hard, empty silence. And then, "Is it mine?"

"What? *Yes*, it's yours! What do you think?"

"How can you be sure?" he asked, sounding a little frantic.

"Are you kidding me right now? For one, I can count. For two—"

"Kyra—you have to get rid of it."

Kyra didn't know what she'd expected him to say, but it definitely wasn't that. There was no *how are you feeling*, or *what do you want to do*, or *let's meet to talk*. Just a very firm *get rid of it*, spoken so decisively that it made her stomach twist.

"Look, there is something I didn't tell you in Puerto Vallarta," he said, his voice low.

Now Kyra's stomach fell to her toes. She instantly assumed disease or drugs or something that meant she was carrying a mutant in her. "Oh my God, what is it?"

"I'm getting married in a couple of months."

Those words didn't register at first—they confused her. "You already met someone?" she asked. It had been six weeks. How had he met someone, proposed, and already set a date? Was that even possible?

"Yeah. I mean, a long time ago. This wedding . . . it's been planned for a while."

The fog of confusion began to lift from her brain. The asshole had been engaged while he was hitting on her in Puerto Vallarta. "But you were sleeping with me."

"Only twice."

"Only *twice*?" she shouted into the phone. "Like that makes it okay? When does it become *not* okay, Josh? Three times? Four times? What kind of douche are you?"

"Jesus, don't freak out, Kyra."

"Too late! I'm freaking out! I don't sleep with guys who are with other women, Josh! I don't help guys cheat! Oh my God, I don't believe you—I honestly thought we had something," she said, railing at herself for being so dumb. "We had so much fun, and I thought it could be real, and you gave me every reason to believe it *could* be real, and *you* said you'd pull out, and then you didn't! Did everyone *know*?"

"That I'm engaged? No, no," he said, sounding miserable about it. "I haven't seen Mark in a while. He sent me an invitation with a plus one, and I . . . I figured it was one last good time before I got married. So I didn't mention it."

"That's insane! Who does that?" she exclaimed. That's how blind she was—she had never once considered that he wasn't being entirely truthful with her.

"Stop shouting! Where are you, anyway?"

"Honest to God, have I learned nothing?" Kyra exclaimed to the sky, ignoring the woman who pulled her son closer as they hurried by. "All the sex education in the world, and still I had unprotected sex!"

A man passing by gave her a sharp look.

"Don't judge me," Kyra snapped at him. "You had to be there!"

"Who the hell are you talking to?" Josh asked, sounding worried now. "Will you please calm down? I know, that was wrong, and I regret it, but it was great, and *you* were great, and it felt good, and I just . . . I just sort of lost myself," he said.

"Great," she said. "You just sort of lost yourself and now I'm pregnant." By Josh, the guy who was engaged, who just sort of lost himself.

But she couldn't put the blame all on him. She had been there, too, just as lost. *God, what am I going to do*? She supposed she'd been hoping that Josh would have some miraculous answer for her. But he was just making everything so much worse.

"Kyra? Are you there?"

"I'm here," she mumbled and sighed heavily, the weight of her situation really beginning to sink in.

"You have to do something," he begged her. "If you don't want to get rid of it, then put it up for adoption. I'll pay. You don't have to worry about that, I'll pay."

It? It wasn't an *it*. "I can't believe you," she said, her voice shaking right along with her gut now.

"Look at it from my perspective. Liz and I have been together for two years. Two *years*. The wedding is planned, our life is planned. You'll ruin her life."

"What about *my* life?"

Josh was silent. "I don't . . . I don't know what to say."

Neither did Kyra. She hung up on him. She had in mind to hurl her phone into the Hudson, but she was two blocks away. She stood up and started walking. Marching, striding, desperate to reach the river and throw that fucking phone to the other side. She'd be late to work, but she didn't care.

I have no one to help me. Her mother had been gone fifteen years, taken from their lives by brain cancer. Her dad—oh Jesus, he'd be pissed, and he'd be no help. And what about her job? Brandi said she was in line to get the editorial position, but that job required long hours and had deadlines that sometimes kept staff in the offices all night.

Kyra somehow reached the river without knowing how she'd crossed the streets, but here she was, staring down at the undulating current as the river flowed merrily along.

She knew nothing about babies. She didn't know how to have one, she damn sure didn't know how to take care of one. And what kind of money was she looking at? Diapers cost a lot, didn't they? Her insurance sucked, and she didn't have any money in the bank, because hello, she'd spent it on that damn trip to Puerto Vallarta. How was she going to pay for this?

Maybe Josh was right. Maybe she should abort it. What was she supposed to do, bring a baby into this world whose father didn't want him and whose mother couldn't afford him?

Kyra's breath began to grow short. She braced her hands on her knees and bent over, desperately trying not to hyperventilate. *"You can't have this baby,"* she whispered to herself. *"You can't. You can't."*

It was several moments before she managed to catch her breath. She slowly pushed herself upright and shook her head, trying to clear the muck of so many jumbled thoughts. She dug her phone out of her bag and punched Brandi's name on the contact list.

"Brandi Jenkins," Brandi answered after two rings.

"Brandi . . . I talked to Josh."

She gasped. "You did? What did he say?"

"I don't . . . I—" She paused, rubbed her forehead. "He's engaged."

"*What?* Since when?"

"Will you go to Planned Parenthood with me?" Kyra whispered.

She heard Brandi's breath catch. Her friend said nothing for a moment. "Oh, *Kyra*," she whispered. "Of course I will."

Chapter One

Seven years later
July

Leave it to a female to think the rules did not apply to her.

The little heathen from next door was crawling under the split-rail fence that separated the cottages again. Dax, who already had been feeling pretty damn grumpy going on a year now, wondered why she didn't just go over the fence. She was big enough. It was almost as if she wanted the mud on her dress and her knees, to drag the ends of her dark red ponytails through the muck.

She crawled under, stood up, and knocked the caked mud off her knees. She stomped her pink, sparkly cowboy boots—never had he seen a more impractical shoe—to make them light up, as she liked to do, hopping around her porch several times a day.

Then she started for cottage Number Two, arms swinging, stride long.

Dax watched her from inside his kitchen, annoyed. It had started a week ago, when she'd climbed on the bottom railing of the fence, leaned over it, and shouted, "I like your dog!"

He'd ignored her.

Two days ago he'd asked her, fairly politely, not to give any more cheese to his dog, Otto. That little stunt of hers had resulted in a very long and malodorous night between man and beast.

Yesterday he'd commanded her to stay on her side of the fence.

But here the little monster came, apparently neither impressed with him nor intimidated by his warnings.

Well, Dax had had enough with that family, or whatever the situation was next door. *And* the enormous pickup truck that showed up at seven a.m. and idled in the drive just outside his bedroom window. Those people were exactly what was wrong with America—people doing whatever they wanted without regard for anyone else, letting their kids run wild, coming and going at all hours of the day.

He walked to the back screen door and opened it. He'd installed a dog door, but Otto refused to use it. No, Otto was a precious buttercup of a dog that liked to have his doors opened for him, and he assumed that anytime Dax neared the door, it was to open it for him. He assumed so now, stepping in front of Dax—pausing to stretch after his snoring nap—before sauntering out and down the back porch steps to sniff something at the bottom.

Dax walked out onto the porch and stood with his hands on his hips as the girl brazenly advanced.

"Hi!" she said.

She was about to learn that she couldn't make a little girl's social call whenever she wanted. There were rules in this world, and Dax had no compunction about teaching them to her. Clearly someone needed to. He responded to her greeting with a glower.

"Hi!" she said again, shouting this time, as if he hadn't heard her from the tremendous distance of about six feet.

"What'd I tell you yesterday?" he asked.

"To stay on the other side of the fence."

"Then why are you over here?"

"I forgot." She rocked back on her heels and balanced on them, toes up. "Do you live there?"

"No, I just stand on the porch and guard the fence. *Yes*, I live here. And I work here. And I don't want visitors. Now go home."

"My name is Ruby Kokinos. What's yours?"

What was wrong with this kid? "Where is your mother?"

"At work."

"Then is your dad home?"

"My daddy is in Africa. He teaches cats to do tricks," she said, pausing to twirl around on one heel. "*Big* cats, not little cats. They have really big cats in Africa."

"Whatever," he said impatiently. "Who is home with you right now?"

"Mrs. Miller. She's watching TV. She said I could go outside."

Great. A babysitter. "Go home," he said, pointing to Number Three as Otto wandered over to examine Ruby Coconuts, or whatever her name was. "Go home and tell Mrs. Miller that you're not allowed to come over or under that fence. Do you understand me?"

"What's your dog's name?" she asked, petting that lazy, useless mutt.

"Did you hear me?" Dax asked.

"Yes." She giggled as Otto began to lick her hand, and went down on her knees to hug him. "I *always always* wanted a dog, but Mommy says I can't have one now. Maybe when I'm big." She stroked Otto's nose, and the dog sat, settling in for some attention.

"Don't pet the dog," Dax said. "I just told you to go home. What else did I tell you to do?"

"To, um, to tell Mrs. Miller to stay over there," she said, as she continued to pet the dog. "What's her name?"

"It's a he, and his name is Otto. And I told you to tell Mrs. Miller that *you* are supposed to stay over there. Now go on."

She stopped petting the dog, and Otto, not ready for the gravy train of attention to end, began to lick her face. Ruby giggled with delight. Otto licked harder, like she'd been handling red meat. Frankly, it wouldn't surprise Dax if she had—the kid seemed like the type to be into everything. She was laughing uncontrollably now and fell onto her back. Otto straddled her, his tail wagging as hard as her feet were kicking, trying to lick her while she tried to hold him off.

Nope, this was not going to happen. Those two useless beings were not making friends. Dax marched down off the porch and grabbed Otto's collar, shoving him out of the way. *"Go,"* he said to the dog, pointing to his cottage. Otto obediently lumbered away.

Dax turned his attention to the girl with the fantastically dark red hair in two uneven pigtails and, now that he was close to her, he could see her clear blue eyes through the round lenses of her blue plastic eyeglasses, which were strapped to her face with a headband. She looked like a very young little old lady. "Listen to me, kid. I don't want you over here. I work here. Serious work. I can't be entertaining little girls."

She hopped to her feet. "What's your name?"

Dax sighed. "If I tell you my name, will you go home?"

She nodded, her long pigtails bouncing around her.

"Dax."

She stared at him.

"That's my name," he said with a shrug.

Ruby giggled and began to sway side to side. "That's not a real name!"

"It's as real as Ruby Coconuts."

"Not *Coconuts*!" She squealed with delight. "It's Ruby *Kokinos*."

"Yeah, okay, but I'm pretty sure you said *Coconuts*. Now go home."

"How old are you?"

"I'm a lot older than you," he said and put his hands on her shoulders, turning her around.

"I'm going to be seven on my birthday. I want a Barbie for my birthday. I already have four. I want the one that has the car. The *pink* car with flowers on it. There's a *blue* car, but I don't want that one, I want the *pink* one, because it has flowers on it. Oh, and guess what, I don't want a Jasmine anymore. That's my favorite princess, but I don't want her anymore, I want a Barbie like Taleesha has."

"Great. Good luck with that," he said as he moved her toward the fence.

"My shoes light up," she informed him, stomping her feet as they moved. "My mom says they're fancy. They're my favorites. I have some sneakers, too, but they don't light up."

They had reached the fence, thank God, before the girl could give him a rundown of her entire shoe collection. Ruby dipped down, apparently thinking she'd go under again, but Dax caught her under her arms and swung her over the fence, depositing her on the other side.

Ruby laughed with delight. "Do that again!"

"No. This is where our acquaintance comes to an end, kid. I don't have time to babysit you, get it?"

"Yes," she said.

She didn't get it. She wasn't even listening. She had already climbed onto the bottom rail, as if she meant to come back over.

"I mean it," he said, pointing at her. "If I find you on my side of the fence, I'm going to call the police." He figured that ought to put the fear of God into her.

"The policemans are our friends," she said sunnily. "A policeman and a police woman came to my kindergarten. But they never shot any peoples."

Dax had a brief but potent urge to correct her understanding of how plurals worked, but he didn't. He turned around and marched back to his cottage.

He didn't even want to look out the kitchen window when he went inside, because if she'd come back over the fence, he would lose it.

He'd known that family was going to be trouble the moment they'd arrived a few days ago. They'd cost him a table leg he'd been working on, because they'd slammed a door so loudly and unexpectedly that

Dax had started, and the permanent marker he was using to outline a very intricate pattern on said table leg had gone dashing off in a thick, black, indelible line down the leg. He'd had to sand the leg down and start again.

Naturally, he'd gone to investigate the source of the banging, and he'd seen a woman with a backpack strapped to her leaning into the open hatch area of a banged-up Subaru. She'd pulled out a box, hoisted it into her arms with the help of her knee, then lugged it up the path and porch steps to Number Three. She'd been wearing short shorts, a T-shirt, and a ball cap. Dax hadn't seen her face, but he'd seen her legs, which were nice and long and shapely, and a mess of dark hair about the same color as wrought iron, tangled up in the back of the cap. She'd managed to open the door, and then had gone in, letting the door bang behind her.

Neighbors. Dax was not a fan.

The door of Number Three had continued to bang away most of the afternoon, and Dax had been unable to work. He'd stood at the kitchen sink, eating from a can of peanuts, watching the woman jog down the front porch steps, then lug something else inside. He'd noticed other things about her. Like how her ass was bouncy and her figure had curves in all the right places, and how her T-shirt hugged her. He'd noticed that she looked really pretty from a distance, with wide eyes and dark brows and full lips.

Of course he'd also noticed the little monster, who'd spent most of the afternoon doing a *clomp clomp clomp* around the wooden porch in those damn pink cowboy boots.

Kids. If anything could make Dax grumpier, it was a cute kid.

He'd turned away from the window in a bit of a snit. Of course he was used to people renting any one of the six East Beach Lake Cottages around him for a week or two, and usually they had kids. He much preferred the olds who took up weekly residence from time to time, couples with puffs of white hair, sensible shoes, and early bedtimes.

Families on vacation were loud, their arguments drifting in through the windows Dax liked to keep open.

The cottages were at the wrong end of Lake Haven, which made them affordable. But they were at the right end of beauty—each of them faced the lake, and a private, sandy beach was only a hundred feet or so from their front porches. He'd been lucky to find this place, with its unused shed out back, which he'd negotiated to use. He had to remind himself that his setup was perfect when new people showed up and banged their doors open and shut all damn day.

Dax had realized that afternoon, as the banging had undone him, that the woman and kid were moving *in*—no one hauled that much crap into a cottage for a vacation. He'd peered out the kitchen window, trying to assess exactly how much stuff was going into that cottage. But by the time he did, the Subaru was closed up, and he didn't see any signs of the woman and the kid.

He'd wandered outside for a surreptitious inspection of what the hell was happening next door when the door suddenly banged open and the mom came hurrying outside. She'd paused on the bottom step of the porch when she saw him. Her dark hair had spilled around her shoulders and her legs had taunted him, all smooth and shapely and long in those short shorts. *Don't look*, those legs shouted at him. *Don't look, you pervert, don't look!* Dax hadn't looked. He'd studied the keys in her hand.

"Hi," she'd said uncertainly.

"Hi."

She kept smiling. Dax kept standing there like an imbecile. She leaned a little and looked around him, to Number Two. "Are you my neighbor?"

"What? Oh, ah . . . yeah. I'm Dax."

"Hi, Dax. I'm Kyra," she'd said. That smile of hers, all sparkly and bright, had made him feel funny inside. Like he'd eaten one of those powdered candies that crackled when it hit your mouth.

"I wondered about my neighbors. It's pretty quiet around here. I saw a car in front of one of the cottages down there," she said, pointing.

"Five," he said.

"What?"

He'd suddenly felt weirdly conspicuous, seeing as how he was standing around with nothing to do. "That's Five," he said, to clarify.

"Ah."

"You're in Three. I'm in Two."

He'd been instantly alarmed by what he was doing, explaining the numbering system on a series of six cottages. She'd looked as if she'd expected him to say more. When he hadn't said anything, but sort of nodded like a mute, she'd said, "Okay, well . . . nice to meet you," and had hurried on to her car much like a woman would hurry down a dark street with some stranger walking briskly behind her. She opened the door, leaned in . . . nice view . . . then emerged holding a book. She locked the door, then ran past him with a weird wave before disappearing inside.

Dax had told himself to get a grip. There was nothing to panic over.

He hadn't panicked until much later that afternoon, when he'd happened to glance outside and had seen a respectable pile of empty moving boxes on the front porch and the little monster trying to build a house out of them.

That was definitely a long-term stay. And he didn't like that, not one bit.

He'd managed to keep busy and avoid his new neighbors for a few days, but then, yesterday, the truck had shown up, treating him to the sound of a large HEMI engine idling near his bedroom window.

He'd let it pass, figuring that it was someone visiting.

But it happened again. Just now.

Dax was in the middle of a good dream when that damn truck pulled in. He groggily opened his eyes, noticed the time. It was a good hour before he liked to get up. Was this going to be a regular thing, then? He groaned and looked to his right; Otto was sitting next to the bed, staring at Dax, his tail thumping. "Use the damn dog door, Otto," he tried, but that only excited the dog. He jumped up and put his big mutt paws on Dax.

With a grunt, Dax pushed the dog aside, then staggered into the kitchen. He heaped some dog food into a metal bowl and put it on the ground. In the time it took him to fire up the coffeepot, Otto had eaten his food and was standing at the back door, patiently waiting.

Dax opened the door. He glanced over to Three. The Subaru was gone, and he couldn't help wonder who was driving that massive red truck. A husband? A dad? Jesus, he hoped the guy wasn't the chatty type. *Hey neighbor, whatcha working on over there?*

Yeah, Dax was in no mood for more neighbors or barbecue invitations or neighborly favors. But it was becoming clear to him that little Miss Ruby Coconuts was going to make his policy of isolationism really difficult.

Dax got dressed and went out to the shed to work. A few hours later he walked into the kitchen to grab some rags he'd washed in the sink and happened to look out his kitchen window.

The redheaded devil was hanging upside down off the porch railing of her house, her arms reaching for the ground. She was about three inches short, however, and for a minute Dax was certain she would crash headlong into that flower bed and hurt herself. But she didn't. She managed to haul herself up and hopped off the railing. And then she looked across the neat little lawn to Dax's cottage.

"Don't even *think* about it," he muttered.

Ruby hesitated. She slid her foot off the porch and onto the next step down. Then the other foot. She leapt to the ground from there, looking down, admiring the lights in her shoes. Then she looked up at his cottage again.

"Don't do it, you little monster. *Don't you dare do it.*"

Ruby was off like a shot, headed for the fence.

Chapter Two

Kyra went in silently, like a shark, quietly circling around the two women bent over their wineglasses, sliding in to collect the check so she could get the hell out of here. The women had been at the Lakeside Bistro since two o'clock, giggling and whispering across the table, ordering glass after glass of wine, showing no signs of going anywhere, which meant Kyra had to wait it out until the night shift showed up.

This was not how her day was supposed to go. But when did it ever go as she'd planned? Had *anything* gone as planned since Brandi met Kyra at Planned Parenthood and Kyra had realized she couldn't end her pregnancy? As much as she hadn't wanted to be pregnant, as much as she'd hated that unexpected and catastrophic complication in her life, she just couldn't go through with it. She'd had a breakdown in the lobby instead, and Brandi had gently steered her in through another door—the intended pregnancy door—where they verified Kyra was indeed pregnant, loaded her up with prenatal vitamins, and advised her to visit her OB-GYN.

Everything since had been a struggle. But Kyra wouldn't change anything.

She'd managed to keep her job at *US Fitness* until Ruby was born, but Brandi had warned her, "You know you can't work here anymore, not with a baby. It's too demanding."

Kyra had already figured that out. So she'd taken her paid maternity leave, and when that had run out, she'd handed in her resignation and had begun to look for a job. Unfortunately, jobs were hard to come by when you had a baby on your hip. Kyra was forced to take low-wage jobs where she could get them, then spend all her spare time looking for something better that would pay her enough to live and give her flexible hours so that she could manage with a toddler, then a preschooler, and now a first grader.

After a series of part-time jobs, she'd felt lucky to land a position at a day care, because she could bring Ruby to work with her. But the day care didn't pay the rent, and Kyra had struggled to keep the roof over their heads. When the opportunity for something better had come up in East Beach, she'd jumped at it.

And still nothing was going as planned. Today, it was already almost five o'clock. Her babysitter had said, unequivocally, that she would not stay past six. Kyra would be extremely lucky to get home by then, and then she'd have to try to read boring real estate law while a six-year-old talked and danced and sang around her. Kyra loved her daughter so much, of course she did . . . but that child made it impossible to concentrate on reading her coursework.

She hurried back to the wait station with the credit card and ran it.

Dinner. What was she going to feed her kid? This morning she'd had the idea of spaghetti, and really, when was she going to learn to cook a few things so she'd have them for days like this? She vowed then and there that on her next day off, she was going to do exactly that. But not tomorrow, which happened to be her next day off—she had too many other things to do. But the *next* day off for sure.

At this rate, by the time she got home, made dinner, then gave Ruby a bath and read to her, she'd be lucky if she could study even a page before falling asleep.

With the ladies dispatched, Kyra popped into the kitchen, where the staff was preparing for the evening rush. Megan, the lunchtime sous chef, was still on the clock. Kyra had been hoping for Rob, the nighttime sous chef. Rob never cared what Kyra took from the kitchen. But Megan? She could be a little judgmental. "Hey," Kyra said brightly and wiped her hands on her apron.

"Hi, Kyra," Megan said as she searched a file of papers for something. "You're still here?"

"Late table. Ah . . . I kind of need a favor."

Megan's head instantly came up. She eyed Kyra warily, like she expected Kyra to ask for money.

"Was there any pasta left over from lunch today?" Kyra asked. "This table is so late, and I don't have time to get anything for my daughter before her babysitter leaves, and my kitchen is a little bare." She made herself laugh, as if that was supposed to be funny. As if she were that girl about town who just never had time to get to the grocery store. "You know how it is."

Megan's green-eyed gaze narrowed slightly, because Megan didn't know how it was. Megan was the poster child for organization and perfect mothering. "This is the second time this week," she pointed out. Megan had two girls, and she'd lectured Kyra about children's nutritional needs earlier this week when, in a similar mothering fail, Kyra had asked for pasta. "Kids love pasta," Megan had said in a tone one might use to deliver basic information to an imbecile. "But you have to make sure your kids are getting fruits and vegetables."

"You're right, it's the second time. It's been a crazy week." Kyra smiled, hoping she would not have to endure another lecture about nutrition.

"We're not supposed to give food to employees," Megan added.

"I know," Kyra said, nodding. "But come on, Megan—you're going to throw it out, anyway, and it would be a huge help to me tonight."

Megan sighed.

Why was it that some moms seemed to believe that if you were a single parent, you had no concept of how to do it right? Kyra knew what her child needed—she just couldn't always deliver. If anyone was keeping score, she was guilty of bad mothering on a fairly routine basis—but it wasn't from a lack of trying.

The truth was that Kyra was slightly envious that Megan apparently had time to grind up vegetables and make sure her kids' meals were balanced. She could imagine Megan's kids had their baths by six, their teeth brushed, their hair combed, and were dressed in matching flannel pajamas before seven. They probably had a grandma to fill in on those rare occasions Megan had to work a night shift, and a hands-on father to read charming stories to them.

Ruby didn't have a grandma to fill in. She didn't have a father. She did have a grandpa in Florida who could never hear her on the phone and kept shouting *"What?"* when Ruby tried to tell him something. Frankly, the only thing Kyra's daughter had was a mother who was constantly running behind the eight ball, and today she *needed* that pasta.

"I wish you would find a better alternative than pasta and some store-bought sauce that is full of empty calories," Megan said. But she was pulling a large container off of a gleaming chrome service table as she spoke, so Kyra kept her mouth shut. "I mean, pasta as a treat once a week or so is okay, but . . ." She shrugged. "At least it's not mac and cheese out of a box."

Please. If it wasn't for mac and cheese out of a box, Ruby would be dead by now.

Megan spooned a serving into a to-go container and handed it to Kyra with a smile of superiority, as if she pitied her poor, irresponsible coworker. "Child nutrition is a personal passion of mine."

Whatever. "Great cause," Kyra said, nodding. "Thanks, Megan."

"Hey, maybe we can get the girls together sometime," Megan said brightly. "You could come over for dinner. Chet and I would really like that."

Kyra could well imagine a night at Chet and Megan Bonner's house—a lot of talk about how Megan's kids went to dance class or art class while Ruby did something inappropriate, like eat with her fingers. "Sure, maybe," she said, already backing up to the door. "Thanks again—you're a lifesaver." She whirled around and went through the swinging doors before she got any more mom advice and was forced to punch someone in the throat.

♦ ♦ ♦

At five to six, Kyra drove her sport utility vehicle onto the rutted drive of her cottage. Fern Miller had been very clear about her expectations in babysitting Ruby, and Kyra couldn't afford to screw it up. She grabbed her purse, her bulky book bag with her workbooks for the real estate license she was working toward, the basket of laundry she'd done at eight o'clock this morning at the Spin and Swim Washeteria near the pier, and her favorite sandals, which she tucked up under one arm. The laundry basket was piled too high for her to balance the bag of pasta on it, and she thought perhaps she ought to make two trips . . . but Kyra didn't want to make two trips. Her feet were killing her, she was tired, she was hungry—so she slipped the handles of the bag between her teeth, wincing at the thought of how many germs were probably on that bag.

She backed out of the seat, hoisted everything into her arms, and turned toward the door of her cottage. She glanced back over her shoulder so she could shut the car door with a bump of her butt.

"Excuse me."

A man's voice startled Kyra so badly that she jerked around and dropped the bag of pasta. She tried to catch it, but it bounced off the laundry and landed on the drive, upside down. So did her book bag, which she ended up dropping when she tried to catch the pasta. Her books landed on top of the to-go bag with a thunk.

Before she could do anything but stare in horror over her laundry basket, a dog suddenly appeared, depositing his slimy, overchewed tennis ball next to her feet so he could eagerly nose under her books for the pasta.

"Hey!" Kyra cried at the same moment the man said, "Otto!" and grabbed the dog's collar, jerking him backward and away from the bag.

Kyra lifted her gaze to the man. It was her neighbor, Dax, otherwise known as the guy she'd decided might possibly be an ax murderer.

He picked up the bag, glanced inside, and handed it to Kyra. "Looks like the lid came off. Sorry," he said gruffly. "Ah . . . what do you want me to do with it?"

"Here," she said impatiently, waving the only two fingers she could spare at him from the side of her laundry basket.

He looked as if he disagreed with her solution but slid the plastic onto her two fingers, then bent down to pick up her book bag as well as the two workbooks and notebook that had spilled out. He balanced the book bag on top of her laundry, then tried to tuck the books in around it, but her basket was stuffed. "Just . . . just put them on the hood of my car," she suggested irritably.

The dog, realizing he would get no food, lunged for his tennis ball, then decided to give his coat a good shake. Up until that point, Kyra hadn't realized the dog's coat was wet. "No!" she said, moving backward. But it was too late—she glanced down at her arm, now covered in the spray of dog and lake water.

"Otto, sit!" her neighbor loudly commanded as he slid the books onto the hood of her car.

The dog didn't sit; it lay down to chew its tennis ball.

"I'm sorry," he said to Kyra. "I didn't mean to startle you."

Yeah well, what did you think would happen, sneaking up on a woman looking the other way?

"I was walking my dog and saw you and thought I'd say hello. Name is Dax, in case you've forgotten. Dax Bishop." He stuck out his hand as if he was offering to shake hers, but glanced at her armful of books and pasta and quickly withdrew it, awkwardly shoving it into his pocket.

"I remember," she said, as if she could forget that strange first meeting. "I'm Kyra Kokinos." His weird, almost nerdy vibe didn't go at all with the way he looked. He was a very good-looking man. He should have been a GQ model. Not an ax-murdering nerd. She would bet herself that he was good at sex.

"I, um . . . I was caught a little off guard when we met the other night," he said.

Caught off guard? So when a guy stands outside a cottage looking totally deranged, that's caught off guard? God, she hoped this wasn't going to be one of those *where are you from* chats. She wanted to go inside, pay Mrs. Miller, and kick her shoes off. She didn't want to be neighborly.

His gaze was locked on hers, as if he expected her to say or do something. His eyes were an unusual color of blue—they reminded Kyra of rain clouds. His tea-leaf-brown hair was neatly trimmed, and he was clean shaven. It was kind of refreshing, really—so many men came into the bistro with beards these days. He was tall, too—a couple of inches over six feet. She thought he was surprisingly young to be living in the East Beach Lake Cottages. She had the idea this place was where old people came for the summer.

He frowned lightly. "Okay, well, I won't keep you," he said.

Praise Jesus.

"But I wanted to mention that I've met your daughter."

"Wait, what?" Kyra said, startled. What did that mean, he'd *met her daughter*?

"The girl with red hair," he said, as if Kyra had dozens of daughters and didn't know which one he meant.

"Right, my daughter has red hair." How did he meet Ruby? He wasn't some kind of freak, was he? Wouldn't that be just fantastic, to find the only affordable rental in East Beach only to discover some pervert was living next door? If he was nosing around Ruby, Kyra would go to the owners and complain. She'd go *tonight.* She'd given the McCauleys a full month's rent, and she wasn't going to put up with a weirdo this close to her daughter while she was at work. "How—"

"That's the thing I wanted to mention," he said. "I work out of my house, and she . . . well, apparently she likes to climb fences. Or go under them. And she's really . . . *friendly*," he said, as if mystified by that.

Oh. Well then. Not a pervert after all. Potentially still a nerdy ax murderer, but not a pervert, which was a relief, because of the ridiculously cheap rent. Furthermore, as Kyra had a bad habit of secretly sizing up every man she met as a potential sex partner, she would not like to know she'd pictured this guy as really good at sex only to find out he was a sicko. "Ah," she said, nodding and wincing apologetically. "Sorry about that. I'll talk to her."

"Yeah," he said and ran his hand over the crown of his head as if he was uncertain about the whole thing now. "Cute kid, but, you know, I have to work."

"Sure. Thanks for letting me know. I'll nip it in the bud," Kyra said and smiled as she took a step forward. Would he go now? Please?

"Great. Thanks." Now he shoved both hands into his front pockets. He didn't move, just stood looking at her.

Kyra's arms were starting to ache. "If there's nothing else, I'm going to get these things inside . . ."

"Yep. Right. Thanks again," he said and turned, as if he meant to leave. But he hesitated.

She waited for him to speak.

He didn't speak, just sort of nodded, then whistled for his dog, who was now half under her porch, his butt in the air, his tail wagging. The dog scrambled out and raced after his owner. Kyra watched the two of them go around the fence that stretched between their cottages.

Her neighbor had a very strong and broad back. She wished she'd known someone with a back like that to help her lug stuff when she'd moved in last week.

He paused at his back porch and glanced back at her, as if he thought she might have called out to him. Only then did Kyra realize she was still standing there, ogling him.

She lurched forward and strode for the front porch. She tried to dash up the steps like she was Holly Golightly carrying a Tiffany bag. But she wasn't Holly Golightly, she was a woman who'd worked all day and was carrying too many things at once to save a second trip, and she misjudged the top step. As she tried to catch her balance, her knee collided with the porch railing. *"Ow, ow, ow,"* she gasped and hobbled to the door. She didn't dare look back to see if her neighbor had seen that, and hastily and precariously balanced everything on her knee and up against the wall so she could pull open the screen door. She used her foot to hold it as she fit herself through, then let it bang shut behind her.

She dropped everything onto the worn sofa and leaned over, glancing out the window.

Her neighbor had gone inside.

Kyra sighed. She reached for the TV remote and tapped down the volume as the Wheel of Fortune spun. "Hello!" she called out and started for the kitchen with the spilled bag of pasta.

Fern Miller stuck her head in the doorway between the living area and kitchen, wiping her hands on a dishtowel. "You're late," she said.

"I know, and I'm really sorry," Kyra said. "I had a really late table."

Mrs. Miller waddled back to the kitchen sink. She was a sizable woman who was partial to khaki capris and big, roomy tops in lots of bright colors and patterns. She wore her hair in a halo of silver curls around her face and once bragged she washed and set it only once a week. "Now, Carrie, you know I don't mind babysitting, but my husband likes his supper ready when he gets home. He's going to have a fit." She put the dishtowel down.

Kyra had long since given up getting Mrs. Miller to say her name correctly. "I won't be late again, I promise," she said and hoped like hell she could actually keep her word this time.

Mrs. Miller looked her up and down, as if she were gauging her sincerity. "Well," she said. "Just don't make a habit of it." She picked up her black, utilitarian purse from the tiny kitchen table and slung it over her shoulder.

"By the way, I just met my neighbor," Kyra said. "He said Ruby was over there today?"

"Yep," Mrs. Miller said. "I guess she got into his yard."

Kyra really wanted to ask where Mrs. Miller had been when Ruby had gone over to the man's yard. But Kyra was also afraid of upsetting this apple cart. She needed child care she could afford, and in a town where most people employed au pairs, Mrs. Miller had been the only one to answer her ad on Craigslist. No one else was going to watch Ruby for thirty bucks a day, and that's all Kyra could swing right now. She figured she just had to keep a lid on the situation until the fall. Ruby would be starting first grade, and she'd be in an after-school program and everything would be okay. *Get to the fall, get to the fall* . . . that's what she kept telling herself.

"What was she doing over there?" she asked.

"Who knows why that girl does anything?" Mrs. Miller said with a shrug.

Kyra tucked her hair behind her ear. "Were you, ah . . . outside with her?"

"That girl is in and out all day." She said it accusingly, as if Ruby were at fault for being six.

"Where is she now?" Kyra asked.

"In her room," Mrs. Miller said. "Now, I fed her," she said, gesturing with her chin at the kitchen table and the deflated juice pouch, the empty paper plate, and the half-empty tube of saltine crackers. There had probably been cheese, too, which Ruby loved. Wouldn't Megan lose her mind if she saw this?

"You should get some groceries," Mrs. Miller said.

"Yeah . . . I'm going tomorrow since it's my day off," Kyra said guiltily. But come on, like she'd had time in the last few days to drive to Black Springs to the only grocery of any size in the area.

"She needs a bath," Mrs. Miller said, wrinkling her nose. "She got into mud or something. I hosed her down in the yard, but she kind of stinks."

Hosed her down in the yard? Would it have been too much trouble to put her in a bath? Kyra bit back her irritation. "I'll take care of it."

Mrs. Miller started for the door; Kyra followed her, reaching for her purse on the couch. She pulled out two crumpled bills—a twenty and a ten. "Thank you," she said, handing Mrs. Miller the money.

Mrs. Miller looked disapprovingly at the crunched bills, took them from Kyra, and made a show of straightening them out against her knee. Not only had Kyra run out of time to grocery shop, she'd run out of time to iron the bills. If Mrs. Miller wanted cash every day—and she did, having said, *"What Ed don't know won't hurt him"*—she was going to have to take some crumpled tips from time to time.

"See you Wednesday?" Kyra asked hopefully.

"I'll be here at seven a.m.," Mrs. Miller said as she walked out the door.

A moment later, Kyra heard the truck rumble awake as she stuffed the takeout into the fridge. "Ruby?" she called and stifled a yawn as she walked down the little hallway to the two bedrooms. They were small, separated by a bathroom. Ruby's room had a twin bed with a pink cover. Kyra had decorated the walls with a Minions poster and pictures of flowers and of balloons she'd found on sale at Walmart. She'd bought a small white dresser at a thrift shop and had wedged that under the window. The closet was teensy—maybe three feet long and one foot deep—but it held Ruby's things well enough.

Ruby was sprawled on the bright green shag rug, coloring madly on a pad of construction paper.

"Hey, pumpkin," Kyra said. She stepped over her daughter and sank onto the bed, lying back with her head on Ruby's pillow. She yanked a stuffed dog out from under her back and placed it on her stomach.

"Look, Mommy, I made a unicorn," Ruby said and held up her drawing.

One day Kyra would know what Ruby's talent was, but she felt pretty safe in saying it wouldn't be art. The unicorn was a blob and its horn was twice the size of its body.

"It's beautiful, Ruby. What do you have all over you?"

Ruby rolled onto her side to look. "I don't know."

"It looks like paint," Kyra said. Ruby's glasses were splattered, too. Kyra sat up and leaned down to have a better look. "Where did you get paint?"

"I don't remember," Ruby said. "I'm going to make a dog next. Mommy, can I have a dog yet?"

"Not yet. Come on, you can draw your dog after you have your bath. I brought some pasta." She hoped she could salvage some of it, anyway. "Do you want some?"

Ruby shook her head no. "I'm full."

Fantastic. Kyra had suffered Judgmental Megan for nothing. She bent over to pick up her daughter. Ruby was getting too heavy for Kyra to hold anymore, but sometimes she still tried, unwilling to admit that her baby was now a little girl.

Ruby giggled as they wobbled toward the bathroom and she slowly slid out of Kyra's grip. "You're dropping me, Mommy."

"Because you're getting so big!" Kyra said, huffing, pretending to struggle more than she was. She managed to get her daughter into the shoe-box-size bathroom and started the bath.

Ruby stripped off her dress. Her hair, a vivid and dark orange-red shade that sometimes made Kyra think of garnets, was a tangled mess of curls. Kyra often wondered where that hair had come from. Her own hair was black, thanks to her Greek heritage, and her eyes were brown. Ruby's father's hair had a reddish tint to it, but it had been more blond than red, or at least in her memory that was so. She hadn't seen Josh since conception.

Ruby also had the most amazing blue eyes Kyra had ever seen. They sparkled like the surface of a pool, and in her glasses, they looked much larger than they actually were.

Kyra worked the hair ties out of Ruby's pigtails, then picked up Ruby's dirty clothes when she climbed into the bath and started to play with the red plastic Solo cup, her only bath toy. Another thing Kyra hadn't had time to get for her daughter. She really had to fix that tomorrow. Not only could she not seem to feed her child properly, her child was playing with a red Solo cup in the bath.

"Dax has a dog," Ruby said as Kyra began to wash her. "His name is Otto. He told me not to pet him. But he's really nice, Mommy. He's got brown eyes."

Kyra glanced at her daughter. "His name is Mr. Bishop, and I think he has blue eyes." Definitely had blue eyes. A very blustery shade of blue.

"The *dog*," Ruby said with great exasperation. "His name is *Dax*, Mommy."

"He is Mr. Bishop to you. By the way, did you get in trouble for playing in his yard today?"

Ruby considered the question. "No," she said.

"Ruby—"

"I got in trouble for crawling under the fence and touching his stuff and petting his dog," Ruby clarified. "His dog is *big*," she said. "He likes it when you scratch his ears."

"Listen to me, Ruby. You are not to go into that man's yard again, do you hear me?" Kyra demanded.

"Yes."

"I *mean* it," Kyra said sternly. "If I find out you've been over there, you will lose your TV privileges this week. I don't care how much you want to pet that dog, you do *not* go over that fence."

Ruby didn't say anything. She had turned her head slightly and stared at the white tiles on the bathroom wall as she fluttered the fingers of one hand against the water, as if considering and debating what Kyra had said. That, or she was thinking of dogs.

"Hey, are you listening to me?" Kyra said sternly.

Ruby didn't answer.

Kyra snapped her fingers in front of Ruby's face. "Did you hear me?" she asked again.

"What?" Ruby asked and blinked at Kyra.

Kyra caught her daughter's chin in her hand. "Ruby Ellen Kokinos, do *not* pet that dog."

Ruby blinked. "I didn't *do* anything!"

"Yes, you did. You went somewhere you weren't supposed to go. You have to respect people's things, and the yard and the dog are Mr. Bishop's things, not yours. Wash your face and I'll be back to check on you in a moment." She stood up. "Don't forget to use soap."

"I won't."

Kyra left Ruby—not washing her face, she noticed, but playing with the cup again—and went into the kitchen. She opened the old, white fridge that looked as if it might have been salvaged from the fifties and pulled out a bottle of wine. She uncorked it, removed a mason jar from the cabinet, and filled it to half full. *Wineglasses.* Add that to the list of things she needed to find the time to purchase.

She had a good, healthy sip, and another, then rummaged around the fridge for something quick to eat, landing on the cheese Ruby hadn't completely polished off yet. She went back to the bathroom with her mason jar of wine to get Ruby out of the tub.

It was the same every night—dinner, bath, and the inevitable struggle to comb Ruby's hair while she wailed about how much it hurt but also refused to let Kyra cut it. Brush teeth, find pajamas, read a story—Kyra would say a short story, Ruby would say a long one—and then finally to bed with a bit of tickling and talking about the day. Put up the laundry, iron a work shirt, wash dishes, take out the trash . . .

It was almost nine when Kyra was finally able to sit down at her ancient laptop with her books and her wine, the rest of the saltines Ruby had left on her plate, and the cheese from the fridge. As she nibbled a cracker, she opened her laptop and her notes, looked at the quiz at the end of her reading assignment, and groaned. Sometimes this goal of hers seemed impossible. Sometimes it felt like she couldn't summon one more ounce of energy from her body.

A new career in real estate was a crapshoot, anyway, a pipe dream that was looking totally unattainable at this magic hour. Ever since Kyra had found herself accidentally pregnant seven years ago, everything seemed like a pipe dream.

It was hard to remember the person she'd been then—fresh out of college, working at *US Fitness*. It had been her first foray into adulthood, her first time making it on her own without help from her dad, and the possibilities had seemed endless.

She'd been dazzled by the magazine and the staff of beautiful, toned people. With her dark hair, her olive skin, and a body with more curves than angles, Kyra had stood out as the exotic one and had fit right in.

She shook her head now, recalling how glamorous she'd thought she was. She'd believed she was just like her beautiful coworkers and, for that matter, like all the beautiful people who streamed into New York looking for bigger and better futures.

What a great run, she thought wistfully. Her coworkers were always jetting off to exotic locales for race photo shoots or to follow a new fitness trend and then write the articles that Kyra copyedited. They met up on weekends for "long" runs, whatever those were, and traded passes for spin classes. Kyra didn't run, and the one spin class she'd attended had almost killed her. But she could drink with the best of them, and she was the life of the party at those happy hours.

And then had come one long weekend in Puerto Vallarta, and look at her fabulous life now.

Not that she could possibly conceive of a day without Ruby. It still nauseated her to think she'd considered abortion, and then adoption . . . but when she'd held Ruby in her arms for the first time, she'd felt a swell of love so great that she'd almost swooned with it. No, she wouldn't want to be without Ruby for a moment. She just wished she'd been a little further along in life so they didn't have to struggle so much.

Things had been better since they'd moved to East Beach. She'd found out about this village one day when she'd happened to run into Trace, a guy she knew from *US Fitness*. She had been living in Queens at the time and had gone into the city to have lunch with Brandi on a rare day she had off and Ruby was at day care.

She and Trace had stood on the street corner, catching up. "How's it going with the baby?" he'd asked.

"The baby is six now." Kyra laughed. "We're hanging in there."

"Where are you working?"

"At a day care. For free day care." She laughed self-consciously. She definitely wasn't one of the players anymore. "It's been tough financially, to be honest."

"That sucks," he said. "Hey, I've got a great idea. I'm just back from East Beach. You know East Beach, right?"

Kyra shook her head. She didn't know anything that didn't involve McDonald's or Dora the Explorer.

"Sure you do. Lake Haven," he clarified. "We did that great shoot there a few years ago, remember?"

Kyra suddenly remembered. She definitely knew Lake Haven—everyone on the East Coast knew Lake Haven. That's where rich people hung out in the summer. "Right, I remember," she said.

"So I had dinner at Lakeside Bistro—they have a great chef there, excellent food. They have some openings for waitstaff, I heard. You could make some serious scratch, Kyra."

Kyra snorted.

"I'm not kidding. I dated a girl who worked there last summer. You can make some great money in the summer months," he'd said. "All the fat cats come up from the city to their vacation homes. They drink a lot, they eat a lot, and they tip a lot. You should totally do it. It's not that far out of the city. The girl I dated said you could rent for pretty cheap, too."

When she told Brandi about her chance meeting with Trace, Brandi's eyes lit up. "You should totally do it. A small town would be better for Ruby than your part of Queens."

That was true. And cheap rent sounded really good to Kyra. Brandi was right—Ruby would be starting school soon, and Kyra was leery of their rough neighborhood. Maybe she was wrong, but Kyra guessed that a school district with money like they probably had in East Beach would be better than the impoverished school district where they lived now.

The more Kyra thought about it, the more she agreed—she should totally do it. So one Saturday she'd found a babysitter. She'd taken the train up to Black Springs, paid an outrageous amount for a cab to East Beach, and applied at the Lakeside Bistro.

"Thank goodness you came in," said Randa Lassiter, who, along with her husband, owned the bistro. "We can't find anyone to work the day shift. Everyone wants nights, because that's where the real money is. If you can work days, I can throw a few night shifts your way, and if something opens up there, I'll move you to nights."

She'd explained to Kyra what she could expect to make, and Kyra hardly had to think about it—she'd taken the job on the spot, then had packed up Ruby, who had tearfully said good-bye to her best friend at day care, Taleesha, and had moved to East Beach.

Things were better. But Kyra was determined to make things even better for her and her daughter.

She stood up and returned to the fridge to study its contents. Unfortunately, there was nothing in the fridge that looked even remotely appetizing at this late hour. She glanced at the apples as if they'd hurled a personal insult at her and shut the fridge door. She moved on to the pantry, where she discovered that her package of Oreo cookies had been decimated. She kept them on the very top shelf so Ruby couldn't find them, but there were only two left. *Damn babysitter.* She removed the package from the pantry, grabbed the last two cookies, then walked across the kitchen to toss the package into the bin beneath the sink. As she stood back up and stuffed a cookie into her mouth, a movement outside caught her eye. She leaned forward to look out the window and saw her neighbor carrying what looked like a small table on his shoulder. He put it in the bed of his truck, then walked back to his cottage, his dog enthusiastically trotting behind.

As Kyra munched on her Oreo, her neighbor appeared again with another, identical table on his shoulder. He had one of those firefighter physiques—strong and built for physical work. Not like the guys at *US Fitness*—some of them had been so puffed up they'd looked like a bunch of Michelin men walking around the offices. No, this guy was more natural in his strength, and Kyra found that far more appealing.

He placed the table next to the other one, then went about strapping the two together and securing them with nylon rope. Was he moving? That would be ideal—that dog was too tempting for Ruby. But then again, someone else would take his place, and if they had kids, or a cat, or a parakeet, or floats for the lake, Ruby would be just as excited. And it wasn't hurting Kyra's feelings any to have a bit of eye candy living next door, even if he walked a little on the weird side. That's about as close as Kyra got to sex these days—checking guys out through the kitchen window.

She stuffed the second cookie in her mouth—whole thing, wasting no time—pondering her neighbor when he suddenly looked up and directly at her. *Crap*, had he seen her watching him? Worse, could he see her with a mouth full of cookie? She suddenly ducked down, then bent over and darted out of sight. *Note to self—don't stand at the kitchen window in plain sight while you ogle the guy next door.* The last thing she needed was complications with the neighbor.

Chapter Three

The next morning, with his latest creations secured in the bed of his truck, Dax backed down the drive of Number Two. He glanced at Number Three as he turned onto the main road. There was no pickup this morning, no slamming of doors. The Subaru was sitting in the drive, the loose books he'd placed on its hood still there. There was no sign of life in that cottage, which, in the short time the Coconuts had been there, seemed unusual. Dax wondered if he ought to be concerned, then thought the better of it. If he was concerned, he'd need to have a look. If he had a look, either Ruby Coconuts or her unacceptably attractive mother would come to the door, and there would go his day.

So Dax drove on to East Beach and to the Green Bean coffee shop, where he had a morning joe and a bear claw as he perused the local paper. To say there wasn't much happening in East Beach would be an understatement. This town was supposed to be the place to be in the summer. There were a lot of summer people milling about, but it was Deadsville. And that was just the way Dax liked it. He didn't like traffic or festivals or anything else that brought people down to his beach to leave their trash lying around.

When he finished his breakfast, he headed over to John Beverly Home Interiors and Landscape Design on the main drag. He pulled around back to the service entrance, hopped out of his truck, and rang the bell.

A moment later the door opened and Wallace Pogue appeared. Wallace liked to dress in trendy outfits. Today, he'd rolled his pants up to showcase his bare ankles and wore boat shoes that looked as if he might have found them in the trash heap, dusted them off, and donned them. His pants were so tight and rode so low on his hips it was a wonder he'd managed to tuck in the floral shirt he was wearing. He'd turned the cuffs of the sleeves of said shirt in perfect symmetry, just below the elbows.

"Well, well, well, if it isn't my favorite tall drink of water," Wallace purred and leaned up against the door frame, his arms folded, smiling saucily through red rectangular glasses like Dax was an ice cream sundae.

"Hi, Wallace."

"What do you have for us today, darling?" he asked and pushed away from the door to walk out and peer into the back of Dax's truck.

"End tables," Dax said. He unleashed them, then set them carefully on the drive for Wallace to inspect. He'd made them from wood reclaimed from a demolished train depot and the twisted wrought iron he'd found at a salvage yard.

"Spec-*tacular*," Wallace said, nodding approvingly. "You never cease to amaze me." He winked at Dax, imbuing more meaning into that remark than was necessary.

"Cut it out, Wallace," Dax said dispassionately. They both understood that Wallace had earned the right to flirt with him—and he didn't seem to care that Dax didn't lean that way—because Wallace had almost single-handedly brought him into the custom furniture business.

"You're such a square, Dax," Wallace complained. "You never let me have any fun."

"Square? What is this, the fifties?"

"If anyone is stuck in the fifties, it's you. Whoever would have guessed there were so many black T-shirts to be had on the East Coast?"

Dax glanced down at his T-shirt.

"All right, stand aside, let me have a look," Wallace said, waving his hand at Dax to step back. He squatted down to examine the tables.

Making custom furniture was not an occupation to which Dax had ever aspired. It had been a hobby of his, nothing more. But after his wife had confessed she was leaving him for someone else, and Dax hadn't known how to process that stunning bit of news, he'd turned to his hobby with a vengeance, filling long, bleak hours by making unique pieces. It did not take the pain away, but it did restore his world to an upright and locked position.

Eventually he'd made so many items that he began to show up at weekend craft shows around the tristate area. He'd hoped to unload some of the stuff he'd made and make room for more. And it was something to do on the endless weekends. It kept him out of the house, away from reminders of Ashley and everything that had been between them for twelve long years.

He'd been surprised when his pieces sold quickly. He thought maybe he wasn't charging enough, and upped the prices. They still sold quickly. He began to get requests. Dax had resisted at first—he was a full-time paramedic and didn't have time to make custom orders.

But then he'd met Wallace.

He hadn't known at the time that Wallace was a designer of some repute, working on high-end vacation homes around Lake Haven and tony Manhattan apartments. He was just a guy in a pink blazer who had gushed over a dresser Dax had built, distressed, and painted.

Wallace began to seek him out at those weekend craft shows, always looking for a piece to accent his showcase designs, showing him pictures of luxury penthouses where he'd placed something Dax had made. Dax was kind of blown away by it—he'd never imagined anyone would really *like* the things he made.

Wallace had even suggested to Dax how to improve his custom designs. "Too big," he'd say, shaking his head. "The average New York apartment needs that very thing but on a much smaller scale. Aren't you from New York?"

"New Jersey," he'd said. That wasn't entirely true. That was the last place Dax had lived, but he'd come out of the army by way of Arizona. He had no particular affinity for Arizona, either—that just happened to be the place his family had ended up after years of relocating, following his father's corporate promotions for a national company. Ashley was the one who'd wanted to move to New York—she'd had that dream since she'd been a kid, had fond memories of visiting an aunt there. But the rents in New York City were out of the question for them—they couldn't afford a closet in that town. Teaneck was a quiet part of a bustling New Jersey, just across the George Washington Bridge from Harlem, where Dax had gotten a job as a paramedic. Ashley had found work at a health food shop. They'd stumbled into a great deal on a single-family, four-bedroom, two-bath house with a detached garage and an unfinished basement. It had plenty of room for swing sets and sandboxes.

Everything had looked rosy as far as Dax was concerned. He was ready to start a family, ready to be a father. More than ready—he'd wanted children in the worst way. Squads of them. Ashley wasn't up for squads of them, but she was open to at least one, and once they'd felt settled, they'd begun to try for their one. When the natural way didn't work, they'd started the long, grueling process of in vitro fertilization.

What was that saying about the best-laid plans?

Anyway, Wallace was the one who'd suggested that maybe Dax ought to consider moving to East Beach and making furniture full-time. "Trust me, I have clients up and down the East Coast who *adore* this kind of thing," he'd said when he'd bought a hutch Dax had made. "I could keep you busy year-round."

"East Beach," Dax had repeated.

"Oh, honey, *surely* you've heard of Lake Haven," Wallace had said and had hitched his arm around the waist of the young man in his company who stood so loosely that Dax kept waiting for him to slide onto the ground.

"Heard of it," Dax had said with an insouciant shrug. "But I'm not that kind of person."

"Excuse me? And what kind of person would *that* be?" Wallace had asked, getting all prickly on him. "And before you answer, please keep in mind that *I* call East Beach home."

"Rich," Dax had clarified. "I'm not rich."

Wallace had blinked. And then he'd laughed with delight. "The people who live year-round in East Beach aren't rich, darling. It's the summer people who come out to their lake houses to sip mimosas on their decks who are rich, and trust me, your chances of mixing with them are quite slim."

Dax hadn't been sure how to take that. He'd shrugged again. "Nah," he'd said. He'd had enough going on in his life without thinking of a move.

"Well, think about it. We could put your pieces in the shop. God knows Beverly could use some quality custom pieces," he'd said with a roll of his eyes, and his companion had laughed. Dax had wondered if he was supposed to know who Beverly was.

"I'm not kidding around here," Wallace had said. "The things you make? They'd sell like hotcakes. You'd not believe the sort of money those rich bitches will spend on their lake houses." He'd handed Dax his card and said, "Call me," using his little finger and thumb to mimic a phone at his ear.

Well, Dax had thought about it. He'd believed there was no way in hell he'd leave Teaneck to move to East Beach. But then the undercurrent at work had begun to eat at him.

It was a vibe he couldn't quite get a handle on, couldn't quite figure out how to combat . . . until he began to understand that he'd become the laughingstock to a bunch of guys he'd once considered his closest friends. It boiled down to a couple of unwritten rules in the guy code: when someone's wife left him for another man, everyone sympathized. The wife was always the guilty party in that scenario—a slut, a no-good woman who deserved what she got. But when a man's wife left him for another woman, which Ashley had done, it got a little stickier. And when a man's wife left him for another woman who just happened to be a fellow paramedic and coworker, the one person on the team Dax had never really gotten on with, somehow Dax became the problem.

More guy code: if a guy lost his wife to a woman, then there was obviously something wrong with *him*.

Dax didn't buy into that. He'd tried to understand Ashley's point of view, to understand how she had slept with him for all those years when supposedly she'd wanted a completely different set of equipment. He didn't understand it, and he sure as hell wished that she'd landed on some other woman besides Stephanie. Ashley's lover, if you wanted to put a word to it. The sharp-tongued prickly pear in his unit.

The worst of it was that Stephanie kept working beside him. They worked accident scenes and suicides and gunshot wounds, and Dax was so flummoxed by this, so flabbergasted that Steph had no shame, that he didn't know what to do. Had it been another man, he would have known how to settle it—he'd have decked the asshole. But it was Steph, and he couldn't very well haul off and hit her, no matter how desperately she deserved it.

Their awkward working situation soon had guys drifting away from Dax. Some of them sniggered behind his back. A few called him a pussy for continuing to work alongside Stephanie and then proceeded to treat him like one.

And yet Dax stayed strong. He'd given up his wife, but he wasn't giving up his job, too, and they could all go fuck themselves if they thought Ashley and Stephanie could chase him out of town.

But then his poor old heart splatted right at rock bottom the day Ashley called to tell him she was pregnant. She'd continued her in vitro appointments, she'd said. She still wanted one. And she and Stephanie were going to be parents to—*surprise!*—a baby she'd made with his goddamn sperm.

Ashley knew how badly he wanted children. She knew how hard it had been for him to go into some plain office and produce sperm so they could try to have a baby. She knew he would not be happy that she'd left him and was taking that part of him with her.

And really, what *was* he supposed to do with that? Dax didn't know, but he couldn't look at Stephanie's face one more day, couldn't bear the thought that she'd be sitting in for him when his baby was born.

Dax had called Wallace one night half-drunk, wholly miserable, nearly crying in his beer.

"Sweetie, you come to East Beach. I know where you can rent some space." So yeah, Wallace had earned the right to touch Dax's shirt buttons every once in a while and call him *darling*.

And Dax?

He'd been a grump ever since.

He couldn't seem to shake his disgust and disappointment with the world. All he wanted to do was make furniture and take his dog down to the lake for a swim. He didn't want people complicating his existence. He wanted to be left the hell alone.

"This is divine," Wallace said, running his fingers over the artfully twisted wrought iron legs that Dax had fashioned into a tripod. "I honestly don't know how you do it, Dax. We'll take them." He stood up, dusting his hands together. "Well, come in, love of my life, and I'll write a check. Oh, and by the way, I've got a custom design job if you're interested."

"I'm interested," Dax said and followed him inside.

"It's a dining table," Wallace was saying over his shoulder. "They want a farm table with carved legs. They have the wood, too. Naturally, it comes from a barn on the property that was quite historic, but in the way of the pool they had to have, even though there is a lake not one hundred feet from their door. What better way to preserve history than to destroy it and make it into a table?" he drawled. "Summer people," he added with a shake of his head. "Anyway, it must seat twelve. Do you have room to build it?"

"Ah . . . I think so." The McCauleys, the owners of the East Beach Lake Cottages, had been cool with him turning one of the cottage bedrooms into a workshop—with promises he'd restore it when he left—in addition to using the shed out back. They were cool with it because Beverly Sanders, née McCauley, the better half of the John Beverly Home Interiors and Landscape Design shop and Wallace's business partner, was their daughter. Dax didn't know where he'd make this table, but Dirk McCauley had a sizable workshop behind the main house where he lived with his wife, Sue. Maybe Dax could strike a deal with him. "I'll have to speak to Mr. McCauley about it."

"If you run into any trouble there, let me know," Wallace said. "Stay here, and for heaven's sake, don't touch anything unless you've washed your hands. I'll be back with your check."

Wallace disappeared into an office.

"*Helloooo*, Dax."

Dax closed his eyes and prayed for patience. He turned toward the register where Janet, the part-time help, was sitting. Dax knew Janet—he'd met her at the Green Bean coffee shop when she'd introduced herself, sat at his table without invitation, and begun to chat away as if they were old friends while he tried to read the scores of the Little League baseball tournament. He supposed that sort of uninvited chattiness made her good in a store like this, but when he went for coffee, he didn't want a lot of chatting. He wanted coffee.

Janet was a divorcée and was working her way through a list of men she met on Match.com. She liked to keep Dax apprised of her progress. More than once she'd urged him to try his hand at online dating. More than once Dax had refused.

"You are just the person I wanted to see," she said, coming out from behind the register. She had to be in her fifties, but she wore the shortest skirts Dax had ever seen. At one time he'd thought them tennis skirts. He'd found out one morning that they weren't tennis skirts when she'd bent over to pick something up and had flashed her thong panties at him. She had skinny, tanned legs and a big chest that featured prominently in her clothing choices.

The door opened, the bell tinkling to alert the shop that a customer had entered.

"Good morning!" Janet called, switching from predator mode to shop clerk. "Is there something I can help you find?"

"Ah . . . no, we're just looking," came a voice from somewhere near the soaps.

Janet turned her attention back to Dax. "I have a proposition for you," she said in a singsongy voice.

"No," he said instantly.

Janet laughed and flipped the tail of her hair extensions over her shoulder. "You don't even know what I'm going to say!"

"I know that when a woman says she's got a proposition, it's rarely a good one."

"Just hear me out," she said, lifting her hands and her ring-laden fingers, as if she were trying to talk him out of jumping off a ledge. "I have a friend—"

"No," he said, feeling a slight tic of panic. "For God's sake, Janet."

"Her name is Heather," Janet said as if he hadn't spoken. "She's probably about your age, she has blonde hair, and she's a *doll*."

"I'm not interested. When are you going to accept that?"

"So, what, you're a monk? Anyway, she works at the library and she's had the worst luck meeting guys her age. There are just too many retirees in East Beach. And she is like you—she refuses, simply *refuses*, to get on Tinder or Match. But she's really great, and she deserves a great guy, so I told her about you."

"You what?" he sputtered. "*Why?* I've told you not to do that," he said irritably, pointing at her. What did Janet not get about *no* and *hell no*?

"I know you've said it, but I can't bear the thought of you all alone out there in those cottage rentals. You're too cute, Dax, in that sourpuss way of yours, and I don't believe you can be okay with no contact with the outside world."

"First, I am *not* cute." He could feel his face begin to flame. He was a grown man, for God's sake. He was thirty-seven years old. He didn't need her fixing him up. If he wanted to date, and he assumed maybe he would someday, he'd figure it out himself. But today was definitely not that day. He trusted women about as much as he trusted mice to stay out of the pantry. "I *like* being alone."

"Dax," she said, shaking her head, looking at him like he was a raging alcoholic who couldn't admit he was drunk again. "I get that you're a loner, but *everybody* needs companionship. Haven't you heard of those studies that say you'll die years before your time if you don't have meaningful relationships?"

"Good."

"And you will *love* Heather."

"If Heather's so great, why does she need someone to set her up?" he asked and pointed at her again, proud of himself for acknowledging the obvious.

Janet didn't bite. "That's so funny! She wondered the very same thing about *you*."

"Ah . . . excuse me?"

Dax glanced over his shoulder at the interruption, and to his abject horror, he saw his new neighbor and her little girl standing there. Mrs. Coconuts was wearing faded jeans with holes in the knees, a long-sleeved, black T-shirt tied around her waist—he'd be sure and point out to Wallace that there were still some black T-shirts available if he'd like to get in on the fad—and a camisole. Her dark hair was tied in a long tail down her back.

"Hi, Dax!" said Ruby Coconuts.

Dax grunted a greeting that sounded a little like *shello*, a cross between *shit* and *hello*.

"Oh, do you know each other?" Janet asked, lighting up.

"We've met," Mrs. Coconuts said. She looked flushed. She lifted her hand. "Hi," she said.

"Hi," he growled.

"Where's Otto?" Ruby Coconuts asked.

"At home," Dax said gruffly. Did she think dogs were welcome everywhere? "Right where he Otto be."

The kid blinked those big blue eyes at his subtle little jest, then giggled. She was a smart little troublemaker.

"I don't mean to interrupt," said her mother, "but do you have any bath toys?"

"We sure do, hon. Right over here." Janet gave Dax a pointed look. "Don't you go running away on me, sugar."

Not until he got his check, he wasn't. What was taking Wallace so long? How hard was it to slap a couple of zeroes into place and sign his name?

Janet led the Coconuts to a section, and there ensued a lot of discussion about bath toys.

Wallace finally appeared, waving the check in his hand as if he'd written it with quill and ink. "Did Janet tell you about Heather?" he asked, waggling his brows at Dax.

"Not now," Dax said low.

"Oh come on, Dax. As much as I despise her matchmaking attempts, I have to agree about Heather. She is the *one* woman in this pretentious little village who's not trying to get her hands on a rich man." He handed Dax the check. "That makes her perfect for you."

"Thanks," Dax said. He folded the check and slipped it into his wallet.

"I like this one, Mommy!" Ruby Coconuts said.

"Not that one, sweetie," her mother said. "It's too expensive."

Dax couldn't help himself—he looked back to see the kid holding what looked like a purple octopus.

"Thank you, but I don't see what we're looking for here," Mrs. Coconuts said.

"There's a Walmart in Black Springs," Janet suggested.

"Right. Thanks," Mrs. Coconuts said and began to hustle her kid to the front door. "Thank you," she said and glanced at Dax, her gaze flicking over him just before she disappeared through the door.

As soon as she went through the door, Janet whirled around. Dax started moving. "Don't run off!" she shouted at him.

He quickened his pace, headed for the back door.

"At least consider it!" Janet begged him.

Jesus, there would be no end to this. Janet was going to come after him every time he stepped foot in this store. "I'll think about it," he said, hedging his bets.

"Well, don't think too long, baby—you don't want important body parts shriveling up and falling off," Janet said saucily, and she and Wallace laughed like a pair of hyenas.

Dax's face burned. His body parts were all functioning very well, thank you very much, and it wasn't any concern of these two. He made it out the door, but before he could disappear from their sight, Wallace called after him, "Don't be such a crab!"

Impossible.

He got into his truck and sat a minute. He was humiliated that his neighbor had heard those two trying to hook him up with a woman. Like he needed their help. He was going to tell Wallace that he wouldn't make any more furniture for them if they didn't knock it off with the dating thing.

Yeah, that's what he'd do. He could go back to craft shows.

Dax went by the bank, then headed home. When he pulled in the drive, the Subaru was not parked in front of Number Three. Maybe they'd gone on to Black Springs after all. Curiously, the books he'd placed on the hood of her car, per her request, were now scattered in the drive, as if they'd fallen when she'd backed down the drive. How could she miss them? He got out of his truck and stared at the books.

It wasn't any of his business.

He was not responsible for her books.

What kind of person left books in the drive, their pages curling against the gravel? "It better not be like this all the time," he muttered as he stalked across the lawn to collect the books.

He gathered them up, noting that two of them had something to do with real estate. The other one was a romance novel. Personally, he liked a good thriller on those days when he couldn't get much work done. Something with a lot of blood and death.

Dax stacked the books neatly on one of the porch steps, went into his shed to check what materials he had on hand to finish his hutch.

He was in the middle of pounding out some metal inlays when he heard a car pulling into the drive. He glanced out the open door of the shed as the Subaru rolled to a stop. Ruby Coconuts leapt out of the backseat. She had a balloon animal twisted around her head and was holding two round balloons filled with helium. She ran, leaping and twirling, the balloons floating behind her. Otto took notice, too, lifting his head from between his paws and thumping his tail against the floor of the shed, kicking up a lot of dust.

"Stay," Dax commanded.

Otto whined about it, but for once, he did as he was told.

Mrs. Coconuts emerged from the driver's side. "Ruby!" she called, and then whatever else she said, Dax couldn't make out. She opened the hatch of the Subaru and grabbed bags of groceries.

All of them.

The woman was determined to drop something. That was too many to carry; she could hardly wrap her hands around the handles. What was wrong with making two trips? Why was everyone in such a hurry?

He watched as she and Ruby went into Number Three, the screen door slamming behind them. Hardly a moment later, Ruby emerged again with a bang of the door, hopping off the porch and admiring her sparkles, then running to the car to fetch some forgotten item. She returned to the cottage with another bang.

Dax sighed as he continued to sort through a box of scrap metal.

He spent an hour or more in the shed, then returned to his cottage, feeling hungry. It was a fine summer day; he had the windows and screen door open so that the breeze from the lake wafted through his space. He was making a sandwich when he heard the unmistakable sound of pink cowboy boots on his front porch. He leaned backward and turned his head to look across the living room and saw the kid, her face pressed against his screen door, her hands cupped around her eyes, staring into his house.

"Ruby Coconuts? I told you not to climb over or under that fence."

"I didn't *climb* it, I went *around* it."

"Seriously? You're going to get all literal on me?"

"Guess what? We got a watermelon."

"I don't care."

"What are you doing?" she asked.

"What does it look like? I'm making a sandwich."

"It kind of stinks in your house."

That was because he'd been working with some wood oils yesterday, but he didn't feel like explaining that to her. "Where is your mother?"

he asked as he slapped a piece of bread on top of turkey, cheese, and pickles.

"She's asleep. She sleeps a *lot*. Guess what?"

Dax bit into his sandwich, determined to have a couple of bites before he dealt with the pest on his porch.

"GUESS WHAT?" she said again, louder, apparently still unconvinced he wasn't deaf.

"I heard you."

"I lost a tooth! The tooth fairy is coming tonight."

"Great. Maybe you ought to go home and wait on her."

"It's a he."

Dax paused with the sandwich near his mouth and leaned backward again to look at her. Her face was still pressed against his screen. "The tooth fairy is a girl."

"Uh-uh. It's a boy."

Dax moved to the opening to the kitchen. "That's ridiculous. Fairies are always girls."

"There's *lots* of boy fairies. I saw a movie with boy pixies."

"Pixies and fairies are not the same thing. How can you not know that?"

That seemed to stump her, and Dax smugly congratulated himself on knowing the difference between a fairy and a pixie. He took another healthy bite of his sandwich and put it down. "Okay, all right," he said, brushing the crumbs off his hands. "Time to go." He strode for the door, gesturing her away from the screen. "Time to go home and wake your mother."

"I'm not supposed to."

Asleep in the middle of the day with a kid running wild. How many calls had he gone out on where the kid was unsupervised while the mom was smoking meth inside? Well, just two, but still—normal people did not sleep in the middle of the day.

He slowly pushed the screen door open, forcing Ruby back. He tripped over Otto, who squeezed out between his legs to have a good sniff at the kid.

She bent her knees to pet Otto's head. She was wearing butterfly wings on her back, and her hair, a wavy river of red, spilled down between them. "Come on," he said.

Ruby glanced up; her glasses were so smudged he couldn't see her eyes very well. "How can you see?"

"See what?"

He sighed. "Give me those glasses."

"Do *you* wear glasses, too?" she asked as she pulled them off her head.

"No. But if I did, I'd clean them once in a while. Wait right here."

"Can I pet your dog while I'm waiting?" she called after him, although she was already petting the dog.

"No," he said as he returned to the kitchen.

He had another bite of his sandwich, then went to the sink, put a little soap on the glasses, and washed them under the water. He glanced out the window to Number Three. He could see a bare foot hanging over the edge of the porch hammock. Wasn't that nice—she was passed out for all to see.

The list of his neighbor's offenses was getting longer. If he ever had a kid, which, he supposed, he would in a couple of months, he would make sure the damn glasses were clean.

He returned to the porch, fit the glasses on Ruby's head. She tilted back her head and said, "See?" and hooked her fingers into the sides of her mouth and pulled, revealing a gap between two baby teeth. She looked a little like a loon.

"Yeah, yeah, it's gone. Come on."

Ruby whirled away from him, stretched her hands out to each side, and leapt off his porch, barely clearing the last step. "Did my wings move?" she asked.

"Yep," he said. "Just like a butterfly." He put a hand to her shoulder, marching her across the lawn while Otto came along, his snout to the ground, his tail high in the air.

When they reached the porch, Ruby clomped right up the steps.

Her mother didn't move. She was asleep in the hammock, one of her long legs bent at the knee, one arm hanging off the side, her fingers touching the porch. Dax peered at her, curious if she was merely sleeping or dead.

"Mommy," Ruby said and gave the hammock a slight shove.

Mrs. Coconuts didn't open her eyes, but she spoke. Alive, then. "Five more minutes, pumpkin. Go watch TV a little, okay?"

Before Ruby could respond, Otto shoved in beside her and touched his snout to Mrs. Coconuts's face. She shrieked, and Dax couldn't blame her, having been the unsuspecting recipient of that cold snout more than a few times. She came up with a start and tried to catch herself with one leg and arm to the ground, and knocked her daughter backward in the process. "What the *hell*?" she sputtered.

"You said a bad word, Mommy!" Ruby accused her.

She righted herself and blinked upward, her gaze landing on Dax. "What are *you* doing here?" she demanded, managing to get to her feet. "What's going on?"

He stepped up onto the second porch step. "What is going on here is that your daughter was peering in my front door."

She gasped and turned a look of mortification to her daughter, who, predictably, was focused on Otto's ears.

"She climbed over the fence again."

"No, I went *around*," Ruby said unapologetically.

"Around," he conceded. Next time he would be sure to enumerate all the ways she was not to cross the fence line. *Literally* enumerate.

"God, Ruby," Mrs. Coconuts said on a sigh and rubbed her forehead a moment while Dax tried not to check her out. She'd changed from her jeans into cutoffs, and they didn't cover one inch of her very shapely legs. He had mixed emotions about that. He didn't want to like looking at her legs, but he was liking it so much he didn't want her to cover them.

"I told you to stay on the porch, Ruby," she said wearily, as if she'd said it a thousand times if she'd said it once.

"I had to see if my wings could fly," Ruby said and bent over to pick up a marker from the floor of the porch. She skipped to an easel and a whiteboard, where someone had drawn a very colorful collection of blobs, some with arms and legs.

"I am so sorry," Mrs. Coconuts said to Dax. "It's been a long week, and I'm just so tired."

What was that smell? It smelled like wine. Dax looked to his left, spotted a mason jar on the railing that looked as if it contained apple juice. Christ, it wasn't even six o'clock.

She followed his gaze, then squared her shoulders like she was getting ready to give him a one-two knockout punch. "It's my day off."

"Apparently."

Her gaze narrowed. "Not all of us live like a monk," she said.

Oooh, touché. So she *had* heard everything Janet had said.

"Ruby!" she said, keeping her gaze on Dax. "Say you're sorry for bothering Mr. Bishop again so he can go home."

"Sorry!" Ruby said. She was standing in front of the whiteboard with her legs braced apart, as if she were about to attack it. Dax noticed her cowboy boots were on the wrong feet. "Mommy, we could give him a cupcake so he won't be mad," she suggested.

"Nope. Won't work," he said gruffly.

"We could give him *two* cupcakes."

"No," Mrs. Coconuts said. "If one isn't good enough, two is just a waste of good cupcakes. Ruby, you will stay on this side of the fence so Mr. Bishop doesn't get mad," she said, folding her arms across her body.

Sounded good to Dax. He glanced at the kid; she had stilled in what she was doing, apparently studying that whiteboard. Or maybe considering what her mother had said, but given Dax's experience with her thus far, he doubted that very much. She was holding the marker loosely between her fingers and began to flutter them, as if she were trying to dislodge the marker.

"Ruby? Are you listening to me?"

"She is not listening to you," Dax observed.

"Yes, she is," Mrs. Coconuts said smartly.

As if she meant to prove she was not, Ruby dropped the marker. But her hand stayed up, her fingers moving as if she were playing an invisible piano.

"Ruby Ellen!"

Ruby glanced at her hand then, noticed the marker was missing, and looked around for it, squatting down to retrieve it.

"Jesus," Mrs. Coconuts muttered.

"Told you she wasn't listening," Dax mumbled.

Mrs. Coconuts jerked her gaze to him. Her eyes were the exact color of teak, his favorite wood. "*Excuse* me?" she snapped as she pushed a big swath of her dark hair back from her face.

"I'm leaving," he said and whistled low to take Otto's attention from a loose pile of toys. Otto dutifully trotted off the porch. Dax had every intention of trotting off the porch, too, but he was having a hard time looking away from Mrs. Coconuts's eyes now. "Have a good evening." He wanted to say something about her having a pretty good start on one but thought the better of it. She didn't look like she was in a laughing mood.

Dax made himself step off that porch.

"So *sorry*!" she called after him.

Dax didn't think she sounded the least bit sorry, and in fact, she sounded very unsorry. He muttered something under his breath about *sorry* being about as useful as a wooden nickel.

Chapter Four

Her neighbor might not be a pervert or a nerdy ax murderer, but Kyra was beginning to suspect he was a Number One Ass.

Okay, yes, no one knew better than Kyra that Ruby could be a pest, and the kid *had* gone across the fence again in spite of being told more than once she was not to do it. But she was six, and that man was very judgmental, and Kyra did not like judgmental people. She'd had her fill of them, thank you, since the moment she'd gotten herself knocked up and endured all the side eyes as her belly grew.

She was tired of whispered speculation about the sort of person she was. Today was her day off, for God's sake, and she was entitled to a drink if she wanted one, but she hadn't actually had anything to drink! She'd brought the wine out here and set it on the railing, then had made the mistake of lying down in the hammock. The breeze was soft and cool, the leaves of the maple trees were rustling, and the perpetual exhaustion that seemed to surround her every day had crept over her before she could take more than a sip.

She would have been just fine, would have grabbed her forty winks and been back at mother duty, if Ruby had stayed on the damn porch. Ruby was generally pretty good about it, but she just had to have those butterfly wings from the dollar store, and she just had to see if they would fly, and really, who could blame her? What was the point of butterfly wings if they didn't fly?

Kyra looked at her daughter now. She was drawing something that resembled the rock that Patrick the starfish lived under next to the pineapple under the sea. The theme song from *SpongeBob SquarePants* wormed into Kyra's head and stuck there, adding to her disgruntlement.

She glanced back across the fence at the cottage next door. Just her luck to get a troglodyte for a neighbor.

When they'd first moved in, Ruby kept showing up at Mrs. McCauley's house, the big Victorian that sat on the hill just above the cottages. The porch swing had beckoned Ruby, but Mrs. McCauley had understood—she was a grandmother. She didn't freak out when a kid wasn't perfect and didn't do what she was supposed to do. She served Ruby homemade lemonade and sat on the porch swing with her, just talking, until Kyra found her. Mrs. McCauley got that Kyra shoved about thirty hours into every day and was dealing with a babysitter she could afford instead of the good one she wanted.

But then Ruby had discovered that damn mutt living at Number Two, and Kyra did mean the dog. Why didn't the dog's troglodyte owner understand that any animal with a wagging tail, a crooked ear, and a cocked head was like crack cocaine to a little kid? They couldn't stay away.

"Ruby," she said gruffly and swiped up her wine. She paused to drink. "What do I have to do to make you stay on this porch when I tell you to?"

"I'm sorry, Mommy," Ruby said.

"I don't think you are," Kyra said evenly. "Because if you were sorry, you'd stop disobeying me and stop going over that fence."

"I went around," Ruby pointed out.

"Under, over, around," Kyra said impatiently. "Don't do it. I know you like the dog, but the dog belongs to Mr. Bishop, and he doesn't want you over there."

Ruby's chin began to quiver. "I was just testing my wings."

"I know," Kyra said with a sigh. She wished she could explain to Ruby that there were people in this world who were just assholes, and there was nothing you could do about it. "You can test your wings in our yard, on our porch."

Ruby lowered her head, chastised.

Now Kyra felt like a heel. This was the part of parenting she hated—the correcting, the discipline, the whole scene about being responsible and making sure her daughter grew up to be a fabulous adult. It was hard to bust the chops of a six-year-old, and even though she'd intended to study tonight . . . Ruby looked as if she could use a friend. Kyra glanced through the screen door to the clock hanging on the kitchen wall. "Come on," she said, and with a sigh of defeat, she held out her hand to her daughter.

Ruby eyed her hand suspiciously. "Why?"

"Because I feel like playing Candy Land."

Rudy gasped. Her big blue eyes rounded with surprise. "Yay!" she shouted, throwing her arms in the air, and clomped as fast as she could in boots on the wrong feet to the screen door, throwing it open and letting it bang behind her.

♦ ♦ ♦

Kyra couldn't even guess how many rounds of Candy Land they'd played before she'd convinced Ruby it was time for hot dogs—another nutritional fail for her daughter, but come on, they both loved them—and toddled her off to bed a half hour past her bedtime. Kyra spent the rest of the evening picking up the cottage and washing dishes. When she got her real estate license, she was going to get a dishwasher. And a washing machine. And a dryer.

Yep, she had some really big dreams.

This dream of becoming a real estate agent, however—a relatively new dream—was beginning to take firmer root in her head. Kyra had spent so many years making it from one day to the next, trying to hold down a job and care for a daughter, that she hadn't allowed herself to think too far ahead. Or to dwell on the missed opportunities. She had concentrated on putting one foot in front of the other, on constantly searching for a better job with better hours so she could spend as much time with Ruby as possible.

Trace had been right about East Beach—the tips were great. The living was far less expensive than the city. She'd found this great little cottage that she could actually afford, bigger than anything she and Ruby had ever lived in before. She had finally saved enough money for the deposit and first month's rent, and at the beginning of the month, she and Ruby had moved out of the extended-stay hotel.

But that wasn't enough. For a while now Kyra had been seriously considering what was next for her and Ruby. As good as things were going, she knew that with the first cold snap the summer people would take their bulging wallets and go home.

She'd been mulling over what else she might do, how she might earn a decent enough living so that she could perhaps one day move into a real house, but nothing she thought of had seemed particularly viable, given her limited resources and need to be around for Ruby. But then one day, she happened to overhear a conversation between two women at the bistro. One of them mentioned she'd just sold her lake house for $1.2 million.

One point two *million* dollars.

Expensive lake houses surrounded Lake Haven, and it seemed like every other day a new one was for sale or had just sold. Kyra had never thought of real estate as a career until that moment, but once the idea was planted, she'd started looking into it. She found out what the requirements were to buy and sell real estate. She had to take so many hours of coursework and pass a test, but it looked doable.

She'd caught up with a woman who frequented the bistro and who sold real estate around Black Springs. "It's great!" the woman said when Kyra asked her how she liked her work. "Are you thinking of getting into the business?"

"I'm considering it," Kyra said.

"I love it. You can literally work your own hours . . . well, there's a lot of weekend work, because that's when people are out looking for houses, but during the week you can work whenever you like."

Weekend work aside, the idea of flexible hours that would work around Ruby's schedule sounded ideal to Kyra. She next called a company that offered the required coursework and licensing. "If you're smart and you're willing to hustle, you can make a very good living at real estate," the woman had said. "You sound like a real go-getter to me. I think you'd do *great.*"

Kyra had realized that was a full-on sales spin the woman had just given her, but she knew how to hustle. She thought she might be pretty good at it, and she at last decided to go for it. What did she have to lose? Nothing. But she had so much to gain. So she'd borrowed five hundred dollars from her dad for the online course.

Now her only problem was finding the time to get through the course and take the exam. Speaking of which, Kyra glanced at the clock. It was a quarter to ten. She groaned, but she opened her workbook and began to study.

Chapter Five

Ruby was still asleep when Mrs. Miller arrived the next morning. The woman was not the best babysitter in the world by a long stretch, but at least she was punctual. She walked into the cottage with her black handbag over her shoulder, a lunch box in one hand, a big plaid thermos in the other.

"Good morning," Kyra said.

"Morning," Mrs. Miller said and stalked past Kyra on her way to the kitchen. She put her lunch box down on the countertop, opened it, and removed a sandwich and some fruit, which she shoved into the fridge. She turned back to zip up her lunch box and eyed Kyra. "What are you standing there for? Don't you need to go to work?"

"I do. I wanted to ask if you could keep a close eye on Ruby today."

Mrs. Miller's head came up, her expression unhappy. "I always keep an eye on her."

Well, no, she didn't, but Kyra didn't want to argue. "It's just that she's been sneaking over to the neighbor's cottage and he's not happy about that." She winced apologetically, and she hated herself for pretending she was imposing on the woman she paid to watch her daughter.

"That sounds like his problem, if you ask me," Mrs. Miller said with a shrug. She turned away from Kyra, opened a drawer, and took out a spoon. She then opened the cabinet door directly above the drawer, took down the sugar canister, and proceeded to spoon sugar into her thermos as if the conversation was over. And as if she'd bought the sugar. What was that, four spoonfuls?

"Ruby likes to swim," Kyra suggested.

Mrs. Miller snorted. "What kid doesn't?" She looked up and locked eyes with Kyra as she stirred her coffee. "You know I raised three boys. This ain't my first rodeo."

"No," Kyra agreed.

Mrs. Miller didn't say more but continued to slowly stir her coffee, holding Kyra's gaze, her expression clearly conveying that she would not be trudging down to the beach with a six-year-old in tow. They were facing each other like they were two gunslingers standing in front of the O.K. Corral, and Kyra knew she was not a fast shot. She debated insisting that Mrs. Miller do something with Ruby, but she kept coming back around to the fact that she had someone coming to her house to babysit for thirty bucks a day, and she really needed to go to work, and if she drew her gun first, Mrs. Miller might leave her in a bind.

"Anything else?" Mrs. Miller asked, drawing her gun first. "I don't want to miss *Good Morning America*."

Kyra folded. She smiled and shrugged. "Nope, that's it. Have a good day."

She retreated like the coward she was. She picked up her book bag, her perpetually full laundry basket, and her backpack on the way out the door.

The Laundromat didn't open until eight, and her shift didn't start until ten. Kyra decided to swing by the Green Bean coffee shop to take her mind off her babysitter woes and knock out some of her required reading for about an hour.

She had a plain coffee—she couldn't afford the fancy coffees that smelled so good as they went wafting by in the hands of others—and finished up one of the workbook assignments. She was pleased with her progress—until she happened to glance at the clock. "Oh shit," she murmured. It was a quarter past eight. She gathered up her things in her arms, not even bothering to shove her books into the book bag, and hurried out to her car.

Naturally, her car would choose this morning to decline to start right away. It had been acting up lately, and Kyra didn't want to think about what was wrong with it or how much it might cost to fix. She was able to coax the engine to life after a few false starts, then sped off to the Laundromat.

As Laundromats went, the Spin and Swim Washeteria was a small one. There were five washers and three dryers, and Kyra was dismayed to see four of the washers in use this morning. An old man in a heavy coat was sitting in one of two orange plastic chairs, reading a newspaper. How could one man take up four washers? She had her work clothes and the soiled clothes of a little girl who changed no less than four times a day.

Kyra didn't have time to wait; she'd have to use the college kid approach to laundry and shove everything into the remaining washer.

She loaded it up, set it on a short cycle, wincing a little as she thought of the two work shirts that needed some serious attention. Satisfied when the water began to fill the tub, she looked around. There was no other place to sit except beside the man in the heavy coat, so Kyra retreated outside. She figured she had forty-five minutes until the wash was done, and as the morning was beautiful, crisp and clear with a cobalt sky overhead, she decided to take the path down to the lake.

She retrieved her workbook from her car and found a bench, where she sat and finished her reading assignment. She was feeling pretty good about things; this was the most work she'd done on the real estate business in two weeks. At this rate she might be able to get her real estate license before the end of the year.

She kept an eye on the time, and after forty-three minutes, she walked back up the hill to the Laundromat. The old man was still there, but he was now methodically folding clothes from a heap in one of the rolling clothes bins. Kyra grabbed her basket, dumped her wash into it, then moved to the dryers. Two of them were in use. One of them was sitting idle. She opened the door of that one—but discovered it was full of clothes.

She looked at the old man. "Excuse me? Are these yours?"

"Nope," he said without looking up from his folding.

Then whose clothes were they? This was the sort of thing that drove Kyra nuts—people who had no respect for other people's time. People who would dump their laundry at the only Laundromat in town, and a tiny one at that, then go off for a round of golf or whatever. Didn't the idea that someone else might need the dryer ever cross their minds? Wasn't it an unwritten rule of public Laundromats that if you left your wash unattended, the next person up had a right to move it?

Yes. Yes it was.

Kyra grabbed one of the rolling baskets and began to dump the clothes into it.

She didn't hear anyone else enter the facility over the sound of the dryers. She didn't notice anyone else until she felt someone almost at her back and jumped, whirling around—and came face-to-face with the stormy blue eyes of her neighbor, Mr. Bishop. "What are you doing here?" she demanded as she pressed a hand over her racing heart. "Why are you always sneaking up on me?"

"Sneaking up on you?" he echoed incredulously. "I didn't sneak up on you, I walked in like any normal person and went directly to *my* dryer, inside of which I find your head."

She looked at him, then at the armload of damp black T-shirts she was holding. She dropped them in the rolling basket. "These are *your* clothes?"

He didn't speak but leveled a withering look on her.

Her heart beat even faster, trapped between indignation and shame. "Well, I'm sorry, but the dryer was finished and I needed one." Her earlier conviction of being completely justified in removing his clothes was now feeling a little weak.

"You couldn't wait five minutes?" he asked and grabbed the rolling basket, moving it away from her. "I'm sorry that I caught the light on Main, but it was literally five minutes."

"I'm in a hurry," she said and glanced at the clock.

"Oh, you're in a *hurry*," he said. "Then please, allow me to remove my damp clothes from the dryer for you, princess." He kept his dark gaze on her as he reached into the dryer with one arm and grabbed what remained of his clothes. "I'll just wait over there until you're through with the dryer so I can finish my drying."

"No, go ahead," she said, gesturing to the dryer. "You finish."

"Oh, I wouldn't dream of it," he said. "You're in a hurry." He turned his back to her, rolling the cart over to the two plastic orange chairs.

Kyra didn't have time to debate with The Grouch. She threw her laundry into the dryer, deposited her quarters, and started it.

Now she had the problem of what to do while she waited. The Grouch was sitting in the orange chair, his legs splayed in front of him and taking up all available space, his arms folded across his chest. He wasn't exactly glaring at her, but he was not projecting a friendly *let's start over* vibe, either. Kyra self-consciously tucked her hair behind her ear, then ducked—okay, fled—outside.

She stood beside her car; her heart was still racing. She kept checking her watch, waiting for the thirty minutes to pass, and when at last they did, she hurried back inside to claim her clothes.

The Grouch was standing at her dryer, leaning against it with his shoulder. "You're a minute late," he said.

Kyra rolled her eyes. "Okay, all right. I said I was sorry."

"Uh-huh." He opened the door to the dryer.

She grabbed her things and threw them into her basket while he waited. They were damp—she could have used another round of drying, but she wasn't about to ask for more time. When she had fished the last of the things from the dryer, she turned to go.

"What about this?" he asked.

She turned around. He was dangling a pair of her panties from his forefinger.

She snatched it from him. "Are you always so grumpy?"

"Yep." He pulled his basket around and began to stuff his clothes into the dryer.

Kyra made her escape with her damp clothes.

♦ ♦ ♦

Vincent, the bartender, was the only person in the bistro when Kyra crashed through the back door, fumbling with her time card and her apron at once. "Sorry I'm late. There's something blocking the road where it meets Juneberry."

"A food festival," Vincent said. "Didn't you see the notice by the time clock?"

"No."

"You really have to start checking the board, Kyra. Anyway, it's gonna be a slow shift. Hope you brought your schoolbooks."

He wasn't kidding. After Kyra and Deenie, her friend and fellow waiter, set up for lunch service, they mostly stood around, each of them with two tables.

"No one eats indoors on a day like this," Deenie said as they stood at the bar, watching their diners. "Did you see all the food trucks? I wanna go. Let's go when our shift ends."

"Can't," Kyra said. "I've got to go pay the babysitter."

"Come on, Kyra. You never go out. You never do anything."

"That's because I've got a six-year-old daughter at home and only so much money for babysitting."

"You haven't even met my new boyfriend," Deenie said, playfully nudging her with her shoulder.

Kyra couldn't keep up with all of Deenie's boyfriends—she went through them regularly. Of course she did—she was cute and sparkly. Kyra hadn't had a boyfriend since Ruby was born. She'd had a couple of dates, both of them bowing out when they learned she had a daughter. Kyra didn't hold it against them—they were young men, not ready for a family, not ready to babysit. She got that. But that didn't mean she didn't feel a little sorry for herself from time to time. She would love a nice dinner out. She would love to go to happy hour for a drink. She would love to have sex. Just sex. No-holds-barred, no-strings-attached sex.

"Isn't there anyone you'd like to date?" Deenie asked.

Kyra laughed. "I don't know anyone to date. I don't know any guys in East Beach. Well, except my neighbor, and he, as it turns out, is a grumpy asshole."

"Brandon has a friend," Deenie suggested.

Kyra looked at her.

"You could get a babysitter," Deenie said, suddenly excited about the idea.

"Babysitters cost money. And Mrs. Miller won't babysit past six. Believe me, I've tried."

"At least think about it. Phil is really cute."

"Maybe," Kyra said. "But if business keeps up like this, I won't be able to feed my kid, much less afford a babysitter," she said, glancing over her shoulder at their four tables.

"No kidding," Deenie said and went out to check on her diners.

Two hours later, Kyra arrived home with a mere twenty-seven dollars in her pocket. She scrounged around in her backpack and the cup holder for more. She found a dollar in the side pocket of the car door, some loose change in the cup holder she hadn't used for laundry this morning. The lesson here, she decided, was that sometimes it was a good idea to shove all the laundry into one washing machine.

She was still fifty cents short, however, and she leaned over to look under the seat for loose change. She stuck her arm under as far as it would go but touched only dirt and crumbs, some paper, a straw, and one of the thousands of cheap plastic toys that showed up in every kid's meal from a fast-food joint.

She sat up halfway, then remembered she had thrown some change into the glove box. She stretched across the center console and popped the glove box open, and there found one dollar and forty-four cents. *"Yes,"* she said under her breath and gathered up the loose change.

She sat up, shoved her hair back with one hand, then reached for the door handle to open it—and screeched with surprise. Grumpy Gus was standing outside, his arms folded, his weight on one hip, impatiently waiting for her.

Kyra muttered a few curse words under her breath then opened the door, shoving so hard that the grouch had to take a step backward. "You seriously have to stop sneaking up on me!" she said loudly as she got out of her car.

"How am I sneaking up on you when I walk across the lawn in clear view?" he asked calmly. "It's not my fault if you're oblivious to your surroundings."

The screen door slammed, and Mrs. Miller came hurrying down the stairs, her black bag slung over her shoulder, her thermos and lunch bag in one hand. "Oh, by the way," she said, marching toward Kyra. "This guy says Ruby's been next door again."

"Are you kidding?" Kyra didn't know if she was madder at Mrs. Miller or Ruby. Either way, she was starting to feel the jaws of defeat squeezing her over this battle of the fence.

"No one is kidding," Grump said. "Your daughter brought me the breaking news that she pooped twice today." His brows went up, as if that was somehow wrong of her.

"Hi, Mommy!"

And to complete the picture, here was Ruby with paint smeared on her face. "Okay, all right, I'll talk to her," Kyra said.

"I don't want to butt into your business—" he started.

"Then don't—" she snapped.

"But it looks like the talking isn't working."

That remark was as maddening as it was true. "Will you just give me a minute?" she demanded, flustered now. She would really, seriously, like to come home from work and not run into him. "Ruby, you're grounded."

"What? *Why?*" she wailed, already crying.

"You know why," Kyra said and opened the back door to get the laundry. "I've told you more than once you are not to go and bother Mr. . . ." *Grump . . .*"

"Bishop," he muttered.

"Bishop," she repeated loudly. "Go inside. We'll talk about this in a minute."

"Mommy!" Ruby wailed.

"Go," Kyra said, pointing at the cottage. Ruby turned around and ran, sobbing wildly. Or rather, trying to sob wildly.

Mrs. Miller watched Ruby go into the house, then turned back to Kyra. "Got my money?"

"Right," Kyra said and dropped the laundry basket. She handed Mrs. Miller a ten, a five, thirteen ones, and two dollars in change.

Mrs. Miller stared at the change Kyra had put in her palm.

"It was the best I could do today," Kyra said.

Mrs. Miller was frowning when she lifted her gaze. "I don't like change, Carrie."

"It's Kyra," she said impatiently. "Can you please take it this once?"

Mrs. Miller pursed her lips and stared down at the change. "This once," she said curtly, and walked on without so much as good night.

Kyra and Grumpy Gus watched her get in her truck. As the thing roared to life, he shifted his gaze to Kyra and said, "I didn't mean for you to yell at the kid."

"Oh no?" Kyra asked and stooped down to pick up the laundry. "Then what *did* you mean? As you said, talking wasn't working."

He looked uncomfortable. He squinted toward her cottage. "It's just that I work over there, and I've got a lot of equipment."

"Uh-huh. Is there anything else?"

He rubbed his nape and looked at the cottage again, where Ruby's wails could plainly be heard. Which, of course, was exactly what Ruby intended. But The Grouch winced as if those cries pained him. *Amateur.*

"No. Nothing else," he said.

"Great. If you don't mind, I've got some scolding to do," Kyra said and walked on.

She stepped into the cottage, dropped the laundry on the faded couch, and said, "Cut it out, Ruby."

Ruby was lying facedown on the floor. "You hurt my feelings!" she shouted, and cried again.

"I'm going to hurt more than your feelings if you don't stop that wailing," Kyra said wearily. "Come on, cut it out. I've had a long day." She walked into the kitchen, noticed cookies cooling on the counter. She sat down on a kitchen chair and rubbed her face a moment. When she looked up, Ruby had crept to the kitchen door, half-hidden behind the wall, and was peeking at Kyra with one eye.

"Did you and Mrs. Miller make these?" Kyra asked.

"Mrs. Miller let me do it."

"Nice," Kyra said. "Come pick them up and put them on the plate." She stood up, opened the fridge, and began to look around for something to make for dinner.

"I'm sorry, Mommy." Ruby sniffed as she gathered the cookies.

"I'm sorry, too, for yelling at you. But sometimes sorry isn't enough, Ruby. I want to believe you are really sorry. Except that you told me you were sorry before, and that you weren't going over to our neighbor's house anymore. And then you did."

"I didn't mean to," Ruby insisted. "I forgot."

"Well, you disobeyed me. What should your punishment be?"

Ruby looked up, seriously considering Kyra's question. "No TV?"

Kyra folded her arms. "Do you think that's fair?"

Ruby nodded.

"Okay. No TV tomorrow."

Ruby's bottom lip began to quiver.

"Do you think you will remember not to go over there?"

Ruby nodded again.

God, it was hard to look at her little crestfallen face. Kyra knelt down and wrapped her arms around her daughter. "Sometimes it's really hard to be six, isn't it?"

"It's *really* hard," Ruby agreed.

Kyra kissed her cheek, then stood up. She noticed a movement out the window. It was The Grouch, of course, stalking around the back of his cottage, his dog trailing behind him. She watched him pick up some long planks of wood and carry them into the shed. A moment later he appeared again, picked up more wood, and stepped inside the shed again.

"You know what, Ruby? I have an idea. Let's go tell Mr. Bishop that we are sorry. Maybe we can take him some of the cookies you made."

"Yeah!" Ruby said eagerly.

Kyra found some plastic wrap, and she and Ruby packaged a half dozen of the cookies. She twisted the wrap around the cookies like a Tootsie Roll, and then together she and Ruby tied red ribbon on either end. Kyra took Ruby's hand, and with the cookies in the other, they went outside, down the porch, and walked to the fence.

The Grouch had set up two sawhorses and had braced one of the planks of wood across it and was busy sawing away with a handsaw. Beneath the plank lay the dog, his tail thumping on the ground as he watched Kyra and Ruby walk up to the fence.

They waited until The Grouch had finished sawing the plank.

"Excuse me?" Kyra called.

He glanced up. And frowned. And then straightened, eyeing them with suspicion as his dog stood up, stretched long, and then trotted over to the fence to inspect. Ruby immediately dipped down to pet the dog through the fence railings.

"We brought you a peace offering," Kyra said and held up the package of cookies.

"A what?"

"A peace offering!" she said louder. The dog stuck his head through the railing to sniff Kyra's pants, then began to lick them, much to Ruby's delight.

Grumpy Grouchy Gus didn't move, just stood there staring at Kyra. Well, clearly, this had been a mistake. *Try to do something nice and look where it gets you.* "Look, if you don't want it, that's cool," she said. "But my arm is getting tired."

"What is it?" he asked warily.

"Big cyanide tablets."

He looked startled, and Kyra couldn't help but laugh. "They're *cookies*," she said. "Ruby made them today."

"All by myself!" Ruby chirped.

The Grouch began to move toward the fence in a manner one might use to approach a coiled snake. He peered at the package of cookies she was holding. "What for?"

"Don't you know what a peace offering is?" Kyra asked.

"I know what it is," Ruby said. "It's when you say you don't want to fight anymore."

He frowned down at Ruby. "Were we fighting?"

"No."

"What we mean to say is that we are very sorry for being so annoying. Isn't that right, Ruby?"

"Yes," she said, punctuating that with an emphatic nod.

"And we're going to try really hard to do better," Kyra added. "Aren't we, Ruby?" she asked, looking pointedly at her daughter.

Ruby nodded emphatically again, her pigtails bouncing, her eyes big and blue and earnest, and Kyra felt a shock of love for Ruby spark through her.

"Well . . . okay," Grouchy Grump said. "I accept your apology." But he looked uncertainly at the cookies.

Kyra poked him with the package. "Don't be scared. They're not poisoned, I promise."

He gave her a dubious look, but he gingerly took the cookies from her. "Thanks," he said shyly. "I appreciate it."

"Can Otto come and play?" Ruby asked.

"No!" Kyra said at the exact same moment The Grump said no. They looked at each other, startled. And then something miraculous happened. The Grumpy Grouchy Goat smiled. It was a faint smile, and lopsided, but above it his storm cloud eyes lit up like a rainbow. Another shock went through her, but this was of a much stronger and fierier variety. "Well," she said, her gaze on Grump as she groped around for Ruby's hand. "Enjoy. Come on, pumpkin, it's time for us to go."

"Is it time for an adult beverage?" Ruby asked.

Kyra could feel herself color and laughed a little hysterically. "You're a silly goose! It's just time to go," she said, dragging Ruby backward. "Okay, well . . . see you around," she said.

Her neighbor didn't say anything. He watched them go, still looking suspicious. But just as they reached the drive, Kyra heard a low, "Thanks again."

She kept walking, her back still to him, but she lifted her hand and waved to acknowledge she'd heard it, then herded her daughter up the steps and into the house.

"Mommy, what's funny?" Ruby asked, looking up at her.

"Funny?" Kyra asked.

"You're smiling," Ruby said, peering at her as if she were viewing a rare woodland creature.

"Am I? I didn't know that. Come on, let's figure out what's for supper," Kyra said and kept smiling as she returned to the fridge to resume the search for something fast and easy.

Chapter Six

In his kitchen, Dax unwrapped the cookies and tossed one in his mouth—and then immediately spit it out into the sink, coughing. Otto began to wag his tail furiously. "What the hell?" he asked, holding the rest of the cookies up to have a closer look. "That's the worst crap I've ever tasted." Was it a joke? It was all salt and something else, something truly awful.

He glared out his kitchen window. He could see her at her kitchen window, working at the sink. Maybe the kid really had made them by herself.

He bent over, opened the cabinet beneath the sink, and pulled out the trash can. Otto instantly thrust his nose into it. "Get out," Dax growled. "Even you can't stomach these." He tossed the rest of the cookies into the bin, then shoved it back under the sink. When he straightened up again, Kyra had disappeared.

She had some very pretty eyes, he mused. And some perky breasts. Not that he was looking. Well, he'd glanced. He couldn't help but glance because there they were, pointed directly at him in that tight shirt she wore. Not that he was complaining about that shirt, not for even a moment.

But his sudden preoccupation with his neighbor's body parts did cause him to wonder if perhaps he ought to take Janet up on that arranged date. From time to time, he was aware, sometimes uncomfortably, that he could use a little companionship. Preferably the sort that only used two legs and didn't stick its nose into trash cans. The truth was that he hadn't had a date in . . . a very long time.

It was best if he didn't try to count things like that. The passing of weeks and months depressed him. It was like counting the days until his baby was born—his son, his firstborn. He couldn't wait, but at the same time he dreaded it. That was weird, he'd decided, because he ought to feel nothing but joy. And he *did* feel joy—incredible, overwhelming joy. But he hadn't reconciled himself to how he might possibly share that moment with Stephanie, so he dreaded it.

Best not to count the days.

Best to just go in when the time came and deal with her then.

In the meantime, yeah, maybe he'd swing by and see Janet in the next day or two. She'd be beside herself with glee. She would set herself up as the grand marshal of his parade, and Dax would have to deal with that. But when he weighed that against how many times he'd imagined his neighbor naked in the last hour, it seemed the lesser of two evils.

The next morning, he was awakened as usual by the roar of a HEMI engine as it barreled up the drive, followed by the slam of a truck door. Dax moaned, which Otto took as invitation to hop up on his bed and settle in, half on top of Dax. He yanked the pillow over his head, put his back to his dog, and fell back asleep. He had hardly slept at all when he was awakened again by the sound of the Subaru grinding. That car needed work. A lot of work. At the very least a new starter.

It went that way for a couple of days, the morning wake-up call with the cars. The little coconut remained on her side of the fence. Dax saw her outside one morning, following Mr. McCauley around as he tended to some landscaping. He couldn't make out what she was saying, but he could hear her endless stream of commentary, punctuated by the occasional deep voice of Mr. McCauley managing to get a word in edgewise.

The kid stayed true to her word . . . but Dax knew it wouldn't last forever. Otto was the shiny object that attracted that little blue-eyed crow, and she would be back.

The other thing that didn't change was the constant slam of the door at Number Three. He was going to have to do something about that. One morning he walked up to the main house and knocked on the door.

Mrs. McCauley, a tiny little thing with gray hair cut in the shape of a bowl and glasses with pink, sparkly rims, opened the door to him. "Well, hello there, Dax! Come on in! I just made some homemade lemonade. I don't use that canned stuff—too much sugar."

"Thanks, Mrs. McCauley, but I can't stay. Would you mind if I installed a pneumatic door hinge on a screen door?"

"Won't hurt my feelings. Why?"

Dax debated telling her which door he was referring to. "It slams."

"Well sure, Dax, if that's what you want to do. I don't know if we'd want to pay for that—"

"On me," he said.

"Then by all means. Whatever you need to feel comfortable. Now come on in and have some lemonade."

"Thanks, but I have to run," he said and touched the rim of his ball cap before he hurried off her porch. He'd made the mistake of coming in for a slice of homemade pie once and almost never escaped.

Dax motored into the village and over to Eckland's Hardware. Old Man Eckland was sitting in his favorite chair at the window, reading the paper. "Morning," Dax said as he walked in.

"Morning," Mr. Eckland said without looking up from the comics.

A few minutes later Dax was at the counter with his hinge. When he'd paid for it, he headed back into East Beach and turned onto Main

Street. He was pulling into the Green Bean coffee shop when his phone rang. The ID said John Beverly Home Interiors. "Hello?" he answered as he opened the door to his truck.

"Hey, Dax!" Janet said. "Wallace and I are eating in today, and we were just sitting here talking about you."

"Why?"

"Because you're our little project. We were wondering if you'd had a chance to think about Heather."

It was kismet. With one leg out of the truck, Dax paused and rubbed his chin. He thought about Mrs. Coconuts, with eyes the color of his favorite wood and a figure that made his mouth water. He thought about all the things he was thinking and feeling while she was standing at the fence, talking. Like sex. He was thinking a lot about sex and feeling like he wanted to have sex in a very bad way.

"Just listen to me," Janet said.

"Janet—"

"She's *really* cute, and all you have to do is meet her. If you don't like her, if you can't see yourself dating her, then no harm no foul, but Dax, you have to *try*. You at least have to—"

"Okay," he said.

Janet gasped. He could hear Wallace in the background and heard Janet cover the phone, say something to Wallace, then, "Okay . . . *what*?" she asked carefully.

"This friend of yours. Heather or whatever. Okay."

Janet gasped again, this time so loudly and deeply someone might have mistaken it for a stroke.

"Don't get so excited," he said. "It's not that big a deal."

"Yes it is, it's a *huge* deal. I'm proud of you, Dax! I'll get in touch with Heather and set something up."

"Don't go whole hog," he warned her. "I'm just going to meet her."

"Of course, you bet," Janet said. "Hang on."

"What? Why?" he asked suspiciously.

"Wallace is texting her now."

"For Chrissakes, you don't have to do it right—"

"Yes, he does, before you change your mind!" she shouted into the phone. "Okay, it's sent. You won't be sorry, sugar. You're going to *love*—oh, look, she texted right back. She says she'd love to meet you and asks when. *When*, Dax?"

"Jesus," he said, flustered now. He was still getting used to the idea and wasn't ready for the actual date. He thought about when. How long could he drag this out? As much as a month?

"Ah . . ."

"I know when. How about lunch on Wednesday? Just a meet and greet, right? See if you two hit it off, which I totally know you will."

Wallace said something Dax couldn't quite catch.

"Wallace is right. The Lakeside Bistro for lunch Wednesday. He's texting her back."

"Can you guys just take a breath?" Dax demanded, sliding back into his truck and slamming the door closed. "I need a minute—"

"She says that would be great!" Janet chirped. "This is so *exciting*. You know the Lakeside Bistro, right?"

"Yeah, and that's a little fancier than I had in mind—"

"Oh, shush. It's perfect. You've got something to wear that's not covered in varnish and sawdust, don't you?"

Dax gritted his teeth. He was already regretting this.

"She says she is looking forward to it. Dax?"

"What?" he grunted irritably.

"You have made me *so happy*," Janet said, as if Dax had just handed her one of those giant lottery checks for a million dollars.

"You worry me," Dax said. "You're too into this."

"I *love* love, what can I say? Okay, half past twelve, Wednesday. Make sure you wear something nice!"

"Yeah, okay, good-bye," he said and clicked off.

Dax didn't go into the coffee shop after all. He was too annoyed and feeling a little queasy. By the time he reached home, he was feeling positively sick. He'd just agreed to a blind date. A *date*.

He marched up the porch steps and into the house with his door hinge. Otto slid off the couch he was not supposed to be on, stretched long, and trotted over to have a sniff of Dax's bag.

A memory slipped into Dax's thoughts—of the first date he'd had with Ashley. God, that had been a long time ago. He'd been just a baby then, fresh out of college. It had been about four months before he'd gone into the army. They'd met through friends, and man, he'd fallen hard for the girl with the silky blonde hair, the long legs, the toothy smile. He could still recall how hard it had been to summon the courage to ask her out. He couldn't recall what he'd said, exactly, but he'd bungled it, because Ashley had squinted up at him and said, "Are you asking me out, or what?"

He'd taken her to an Italian restaurant, a chain. They'd dined on spaghetti and breadsticks, and then he'd suggested they go to a movie. Wasn't that what a date was? Dinner and a movie?

"I have a better idea," Ashley had said. "Let's take a walk." And then she'd slipped her hand into his like it was perfectly natural, and he'd felt that delicate hand in his, and he'd felt invincible. They'd walked along the canals in Phoenix, talking and laughing and talking some more until they were kissing, and Dax was completely besotted. He could vividly remember how his belly had been filled with butterflies and sparks.

He would never feel that way again, he was certain of it. For one, he'd been young and inexperienced, and love had felt new and amazing and extraordinary. For two, he wouldn't allow it. He would never let himself go like that again, just free-falling into love, because look what could happen. The love of your life could leave you for another woman. The love of your life could take your sperm and make a baby, and you? You were standing on the outside looking in at the life you were supposed to have. You were trying to attend birthing classes and feeling like a fool sitting behind Ashley and Stephanie, and you were trying to read books about the stages of pregnancy and the first year of your son's life, and you were reading alone with a lot of questions and no one to ask.

So what was he doing, meeting some woman he'd never even seen? He glanced out his kitchen window to Number Three. It was *their* fault, those coconuts next door. He'd been perfectly happy making his furniture and living with Otto until they'd come along and he'd been reminded of just how good a woman looked. Just how pretty a woman was when she smiled. Goddammit, he'd been sucker punched.

Dax was mad at himself now, and the only way to get over it was to get to work. He went out to the shed. Otto followed him, then plopped down onto his belly, stretched across the door opening so that Dax had to step over him every time he went back into his house.

He was starting work on a hutch, and that kept him busy for a couple of hours. He never heard the Subaru leave, but he heard the slam of car doors when they returned, and then it began, the slam of that screen door as Ruby Coconuts went in and out, in and out, *slam slam slam*.

Otto rearranged himself at the threshold so he could prop his head against the door and watch the goings-on at Number Three. Once or twice his tail thumped on the wooden floor of the shed, and Dax steeled himself, waiting for a child with blue-plastic-rimmed glasses to pop her head in.

She didn't. Apparently the kid was otherwise engaged in a serious project, because the door was sounding off at a regular clip.

At last, Dax had had enough. He couldn't take it, couldn't bear the tiny start to his heart every time that door slammed. He dropped what he was doing, stepped over his worthless dog, and strode into his cottage. Moments later, he returned to the shed to pick up a power drill, then stalked in the direction of Number Three, going over the fence.

He walked up the steps and rapped loudly on the door. Through the screen, he could see Mrs. Coconuts at the kitchen table. A pile of papers was spread in front of her. She stood up, and he noticed she was wearing cutoffs so short that the interior pockets hung below the hem.

He swallowed hard and tried not to eye her legs as she walked to the door. "Hi," she said.

She had a thick mess of wavy black hair tied in some sort of knot at her nape. No way she could untangle that thing. Dax feared she might have to chop it off.

Ruby's shadow suddenly bounded into view. She had three pigtails today, each of them braided. "Hi, Dax! Guess what? I got some new bath toys. And two balloons at Taleesha's birthday party! Do you want to see them?"

"No," he said.

"My hair is like Taleesha's hair. Mommy did it."

"Fantastic."

"Mommy, can I show him my bath toys?"

"Sure," she said with a shrug, and Ruby darted off.

"Is there something you need?" Mrs. Coconuts asked him, watching him like she expected him to announce something terribly important. *You've just won the Reader's Digest Sweepstakes! You almost killed me with those cookies!* Dax held up the door hinge. She looked at it. She squinted. "Okay, I give—what is it?"

"A door hinge," he said. "Pneumatic."

"Oh-kay," she said slowly, clearly not getting the genius of it.

"I'm going to install it on your screen door."

"Mine? Why?"

"Mommy, I think my bath toys are still in the car!" Ruby cried and darted past her mother, pushing the screen door open and forcing Dax backward as she raced to get them. The screen door slammed behind her.

Dax arched a brow.

"Ah. I see," she said. "I should probably ask Mr. McCauley—"

"Already done," he said, and without thinking, his gaze flicked to her legs, then quickly back up.

"I'm kind of in the middle of something," she said apologetically.

"Me, too," he said. "That's why I need to do this."

The car door slammed. "They're not in there!" Ruby shouted and raced back up the steps, yanking the screen door open and jumping inside. The door banged shut again. "Where are they, Mommy?"

"I don't know, pumpkin. Check your room."

"She doesn't need to go to so much trouble," Dax said gruffly. "I'm not that interested. I just want to fix this door."

Mrs. Coconuts—Kyra—smiled a little lopsidedly. "I'm not that interested in them, either, for what it's worth. But there is nothing I can do to stop her. She's going to show you."

Somehow, Dax knew that. And sure enough, Ruby reappeared with a Walmart sack. She promptly turned it upside down, and out tumbled the contents. Nail polish remover. A box of tampons. Three bath toys attached to cardboard with plastic ties—a pirate, an alligator, a scuba diver. They had nothing to do with each other that Dax could see, and yet there they were, bound to the same thick piece of cardboard.

Ruby went down on her knees and tried to rip the ties open. She was mangling the toys. "Here," he said impatiently. "Give it to me."

She handed the package up to him, and Dax pulled a pocketknife from his pants to cut the plastic ties. Ruby tried to help.

"Honey, calm down. Let Mr. Bishop do it."

"Dax," he said. "Call me Dax. Otherwise I sound like a principal."

"They squirt water," Ruby said.

"Who would have guessed?" he said and freed the alligator. He handed it to her. Ruby turned to one side and held it out, squeezing it. "There's no water in it," he pointed out. This kid was missing a spark plug in the old ignition switch. She didn't seem to hear him at all, but went down on her knees, her attention on the alligator, squeezing it.

Dax glanced at her mother. She shrugged again. He freed the other characters and held up the hinge. "So?"

"So . . . this isn't going to be one of those all-day projects, is it?"

"Nope. Fifteen minutes, tops."

She considered that. "You're not going to get mad if you can't get it to work and throw your drill or anything, right?"

He stared at her, mystified. "Who would *ever* throw a drill?"

She smiled. "You'd be surprised. Okay," she said, gesturing to the door. "Have at it."

She walked back into the kitchen and sat down with one foot tucked up under her. At Dax's feet, Ruby was still studying the bath toys.

"Okay, Ruby Coconuts, you're going to have to move," he said, stepping around her.

Ruby didn't move.

He nudged her with his foot, and she started. She looked up, blinking at him. "They *all* squirt water."

"Well, that's going to be a jolly time for you," he said. "Move it."

He took the door off its hinges and began to install the new hinge. It was mindless, easy work, which enabled him to steal glimpses of Mrs. Coconuts at the table. Well—glimpses of her legs, at any rate. He hadn't realized he was such a leg man until the Coconuts moved in next door, but when presented with the evidence, he certainly was. Now he was trying very hard not to imagine them wrapped around him.

She glanced up and caught him looking at her. Dax felt his face heat. "What are you doing over there, anyway?" he asked.

"Studying."

That was all she said. Apparently she was going to take a page out of his book and make him work for it. "College?" he asked.

"Nope. A real estate license."

"Oh yeah? Going to sell some houses, huh?"

"That's the plan," she said, looking down at a book. "Hopefully some of these mega lake houses around here." Her brow was furrowed as if she was trying to concentrate. Dax took that to mean that she didn't want to talk. But then she said, "I need something with flexible hours, especially now that Ruby will be entering the first grade."

"How close are you?" he asked.

"Hmm?" She glanced up.

"When will you get your license?"

"At this rate?" She looked at her wristwatch. "In about ten years." She smiled. "What about you?"

"I'm not getting a real estate license."

"Very funny," she said. "I mean, what do you do? What's with all the wood and iron and that little shed next door?" she asked.

"Furniture," he said.

"Huh?"

"I make furniture."

Mrs. Coconuts laughed. "Do you think you could give me a little more than that? Like what kind of furniture? And for who?"

"Tables. Bureaus. Hutches. Mostly for rich people." He looked at her sidelong. "The summer people who own those lake houses you want to sell."

"Nice," she said, nodding. "So *that's* what you're doing over there."

"What'd you think?" he asked curiously.

"Oh, I don't know. I had some theories—building crypts. Burying bodies."

Dax stared at her, uncertain what to say to that.

She laughed. "I'm kidding. Well . . . sort of."

Her eyes were twinkling at him, Dax thought. He liked that twinkle. It made him feel sort of twinkly himself.

"You're kind of a mysterious guy," she said. She'd twisted around in her seat, had crossed one leg over the other. Her foot was bouncing in time to the pencil she drummed against a thick, spiral-bound notebook. She wore a happy, amused smile that made him feel a little wobbly inside.

"I'm not mysterious," he said. "Actually, I'm pretty boring." He drilled the last screw in. "There you go."

"That's it?"

"That's it."

She didn't look convinced, and stood up, walking to where he stood. She ducked around him and slipped between the door and him. With hands on hips, she looked up at the hinge, then the door. "It doesn't close all the way," she pointed out.

"Just adjust it," he said.

"Just adjust it," she repeated. "I don't even know what this is, much less how to adjust it."

Dax clucked his opinion of that. Everyone ought to know how to adjust things. Adjustment was part of life. He reached around her, but the hinge was a little bit out of range. He shifted, and she bumped up against his chest, and that mess of hair brushed against his cheek and made his skin tingle. "Here's how you do it," he said, showing her the tab.

"Aha," she said and turned around, looking up at him with eyes the color of warm teak, crinkling in the corners because she was sort of smiling again like she was amused or happy, he didn't know what. All he knew was that something was crackling in him, like a piece of paper thrown into a fire . . . crackling and crumbling and turning to ash. Dax couldn't help himself; he looked at her mouth. He wanted to kiss that mouth in the worst way, wanted it so bad that he was a tiny bit fearful he might vomit with all that want churning in him.

The corners of her mouth turned up into a full-fledged smile, and Dax felt himself perilously close to doing something stupid.

"Thanks," she said lightly, her voice reminding him of a morning bird. "I never knew how much that door annoyed me until you fixed it."

"Yep." He made himself look away and pick up his stuff. "Where'd the kid get off to?" he asked and risked a quick glance at Mrs. Coconuts.

She was still smiling. "She's in her room—can't you hear?"

All he could hear was a buzzing in his ears, Dax realized, due to the manic beating of his unused heart.

"She's singing with her little recorder. She wants to be Katy Perry."

"Well, if you can ever get the singing part of that to work out, she'll be great at it," he said.

She laughed.

"Okay, well . . . see you." He opened the door and didn't notice how soundlessly it closed behind him. He walked down the steps of the porch and tripped over one of Ruby's toys in the yard, which he'd failed to notice right in front of him. Dax had been made deaf and blind by lust.

Okay, maybe not *lust* . . . but something equally precarious.

Chapter Seven

Kyra was surprisingly happy that she didn't have to listen to the constant sound of that screen door slapping shut, but she realized very quickly that now she didn't know when Ruby went in and out. When it came time for supper, she thought Ruby was in her room but found her in the newly planted rosebush beds Mr. McCauley had installed last week. Ruby was burying some of her Little People.

"Why?" Kyra demanded irritably as she dug them up and tried to repair the mulch.

"So someone can find them," Ruby said. That made no sense to Kyra but seemed plainly logical to Ruby's six-year-old brain.

Ruby was in bed now, and Kyra was, as always, beat. She wondered how those single moms with three children did it. She thought about Taleesha, Ruby's friend. Kyra had taken Ruby into the city to attend Taleesha's birthday party today because Ruby missed her so much. They'd practically grown up together in the day care where Kyra had worked. But Taleesha's mother had three more children, all of them under ten years old. And she worked two jobs. Kyra would be dead on her feet if she had to squeeze in another job, and she only had one child.

She helped herself to a beer—cheaper than the bottle of wine she'd really wanted at the grocery store and had put back on the shelf—and turned on the television, intending to watch some mindless reality program. A wavy line cut through the middle of the picture. She tried several other channels and found the same thing. "Great. Just great," she muttered.

She wiggled some of the cords coming out of the back of the television. That didn't work. She pounded her fist on the top of the set. That definitely didn't work, and she nearly toppled the thing over. This was a disaster. Ruby wouldn't notice the line, but Mrs. Miller would not be happy. And if Mrs. Miller wasn't happy, Kyra was not going to be happy, either. She couldn't handle any major purchases right now. It was bad enough her car kept acting like it was going to quit on her, but this?

She sighed, turned it off. Maybe she could pick up some extra shifts, but she didn't want to think about that tonight. She decided she'd have a long bath, maybe finish that paperback she'd been reading. There was nothing like a trip to eighteenth-century Scotland to take her mind off her money woes, nothing that a good Scottish Highlander couldn't cure.

She walked into the kitchen and tossed her empty beer bottle, then moved to the fridge to get another beer. Through the kitchen window, she spotted Dax in his yard, working on that big piece of wood between the two sawhorses. It was getting late; the sun would be going down soon. Didn't he need some light to do that?

She watched him lean over that enormous plank of wood, the size of a small boat. It reminded her of *Titanic* and the door that Rose had floated on while Jack had sunk to the bottom of the Atlantic Ocean, when clearly there was enough room on that door for both of them. Dax sort of looked like a Jack—chiseled. Strong. Handsome. She idly imagined him in that situation, bobbing around the Atlantic Ocean as the ship went down. *He* wouldn't have let go and sunk. No, he would have told her to move over, she was certain of it. It would have been a simple *"Move."* She smiled, amused by that.

He suddenly straightened and looked straight at her window. Kyra gasped and ducked behind the fridge. She had to quit watching him out her kitchen window. It wasn't her fault that he kept working right in her line of vision, but still. She opened the fridge, got a beer, and popped the top, unthinkingly taking a deep drink while she pondered her neighbor.

Really, had she thanked him enough for the new hinge? Sure, she'd said thanks, but she really ought to *thank* him.

Okay, she was not going to do that—she was not going to find an excuse to go over there and bother that man. Or was she? Because it wasn't the worst thing to be neighborly and say thank you. And really, was she *bothering* him? Mr. McCauley stopped by routinely just to say hi and ask how they were doing, and that didn't bother anyone. Then again, Mr. McCauley owned the cottage, and he was probably trying to get a look to make sure they hadn't destroyed the place.

Okay, enough. She'd already sort of said thank you, and to say thank you now would be . . . flirty. Yep, flirty. And she was not the flirty type, even though Deenie had urged her to be more flirty. "You have to at least try," she'd said one afternoon at the bistro when an older guy who smelled like cigars and sweat was hitting on Kyra. "You'll make better tips. And are you really going to wait until you're, like, forty before you date again? Because that's too late. You're practically done by then."

Forty did sound a little too late to reenter the dating scene. Ruby would be eighteen when Kyra was forty. Kyra could well imagine that all the good guys would be taken by then, and she'd be left with those who drove around in old pickups with campers on the back and giant antennas bouncing around on top.

Maybe she should just go and say thanks. Maybe just practice her flirty skills.

She took her beer and ducked into the tiny bathroom, flipped on the light, and recoiled slightly at her reflection. Jesus, had she walked around like this all day? There was a smudge of dirt under one eye, and holy smokes, her *hair*. She drank more beer, then pulled down her ratty hair and brushed it out. That helped, but not enough—she hadn't used any product this morning in her haste to get the errands run, and now it was frizzy. There really wasn't anything short of an industrial-strength makeover that was going to help her.

She reached for a bag tucked on a shelf above the sink—too high for little hands—and brought it down. Her makeup bag, stuffed with half-used tubes of mascara, face cream samples, a bronzer so old that it had caked, and some eyebrow shadow. She found a tube of mascara that looked newish and dabbed some on, then added a bit of blush.

That was better. At least she had long lashes, but that was about the only natural beauty thing going for her. She needed to seriously up her game if she didn't want to die old and alone at the age of forty. Deenie kept talking about going to Black Springs to shop. Maybe Kyra should put a little money aside for that. She could do with some shopping therapy.

Oh, who was she kidding? Right now it was all she could do to pay rent, Mrs. Miller, and the grocery bill. She tossed the mascara in the bag with a snort. Ah, those little pipe dreams of hers. When would they end?

She tried to make her hair look less like a fluff ball and more like a free spirit sort of coif but realized the longer she tried to tame it, the chances of Dax calling it a day were growing.

She returned to the kitchen and looked out the window. He was still there. So was his dog. It was lying beneath that massive piece of wood, its snout in the air and pointed in the general direction of the lake. Kyra opened the window in case Ruby should wake up and call for her, polished off her beer—liquid courage—then grabbed two more beers from the fridge and walked outside.

She had made it to the fence before Dax looked up and saw her coming. He straightened up and eyed her with his usual suspicion as she hooked one leg over the fence, and then the other. As she neared him, his gaze fell to the two bottles of beer.

Kyra hiccupped. "That was involuntary," she said.

The dog hopped up and sauntered over, and stuck his snout in her crotch.

"Otto!" he snapped.

The dog ignored him as he moved his snout down her leg and studied her flip-flops pretty intently, snorting once or twice, before trotting back to his spot beneath the big plank of wood.

"Okay, well, now that's over—" She hiccupped again. What the hell? She could feel heat flooding her face. "Sorry," she said, touching three fingers to her mouth. "I have the hiccups."

"I gathered."

She held out a bottle. "Would you like a beer?"

He peered at the bottle. Then at her. "Why?"

"Why?" she laughed and hiccupped. "You're a funny guy, Dax Bishop. Why does anyone offer a beer? I'm being neighborly, and I want to thank you for fixing that door. It's so much better now."

He nodded and wiped his hands on a dirty towel. "Where's the little coconut?"

"In bed," she said. "I have a window open so I can hear her if she wakes." Did that make her a bad mother? He probably thought that made her a bad mother. Well, she wasn't a great mother, Kyra was the first to admit. She smiled a little self-consciously and managed to choke down another hiccup.

He tossed down the towel. "Your hair is different."

"What do you mean?" she asked and put a hand to it. "I set it free." It was probably really frizzy now. Why, oh, why couldn't she have used a little hair product? And so what if it was a little off-putting? She'd brought the man a beer, for God's sake—that ought to make up for being offended by frizzy hair. "Okay, Dax, are you going to take this or not?" she demanded, dropping her hand from her hair.

"What?" He dragged his gaze from her hair to the bottle. "Sure. Thanks. By the way, I like it," he said, his gaze traveling up to her hair again.

Kyra instantly smiled. "What, my hair? *Really?* Thank you."

He walked around his project and took the beer from her hand, his fingers brushing carelessly against hers. He took a swig of it, nodded as if he approved, looked at the label—Budweiser—then at her again. He took another drink as he studied Kyra, as if he didn't quite know what to do with her. The feeling was entirely mutual. "What are you making?" she asked, stepping around him.

"Table."

She could appreciate a man of few words, but he didn't seem to know how to have an actual conversation. "For anyone in particular?"

"Some clients of John Beverly Interiors." He took another sip. "I make some pieces for them."

"I love that store. I can't afford even their bath toys, but I like to look. So when you said you make furniture, you were talking *furniture*."

"Well . . . yeah," he said, sounding slightly mystified. "What else would I be talking about?"

"I mean high-end pieces."

"I guess."

She was going to need a pair of pliers to have any semblance of conversation with The Grump. Her look must have conveyed how she felt, because he said sheepishly, "I don't know what to call the stuff I make. I just like to make it."

Okay, then. She could go with that. Kyra moved to have a closer look at the big plank of wood and brushed past him, shoulder connecting lightly with his chest. *Did I just do that on purpose? I did. I damn sure did. And I liked it.*

"So this is a table," she said. He'd already said that, obviously. She sipped her beer and noticed that she felt a little buzzed. How many beers was it now, anyway? That six-pack was supposed to last her all week.

"Big enough to seat twelve. The wood came from a barn they razed to install a pool." He leaned over the plank and ran his fingers lightly over the surface. "See how the grain is raised here?"

"No."

"Give me your hand," he said.

Kyra held out her hand; he took it and pressed her fingers lightly to the plane of the wood, sweeping them across the surface. "Feel it?"

She was feeling something all right, and she was pretty sure it wasn't the grain. "Yes."

He let go of her hand. "People pay crazy money for that raised grain. I'd be surprised if the clients who commissioned this even know what they've got."

"Where are the legs?"

He pointed to a pedestal next to one of the sawhorses.

Kyra leaned over his arm to have a look. "Nice," she said, nodding at the carved piece of wood.

"Thanks," Dax said. He moved his arm and himself away.

Okay, she'd gotten too close, so sue her already. Was it her fault that she was a single mom with an extremely limited social life and starved for physical contact? Okay, yes, it was technically her fault, but surely the statute of limitations had to be running out on that one. Was it her fault that he happened to be an astonishingly sexy grouch? Nope.

He was squinting at something on the thick plank, flicking it off with his finger.

The thing was, Kyra hadn't been with a guy in so long, and her supergrouchy neighbor, who was maybe a little off in the mental department, was really very hot. *Hot* hot.

She walked around the end of the sawhorse and set her beer down on the corner of it. She shoved her hands into her pockets to keep from doing something stupid with them, like twirling her hair around a finger like Ruby did. She turned her back to him and looked at Number Two. "You live here by yourself, huh?" she asked. He didn't answer. She glanced at him over her shoulder.

He was watching her now, holding the beer loosely between two fingers. "No."

"No?" she asked with surprise and turned around to face him.

"Otto lives here, too." He pointed to his dog and received two thumps of the tail for it.

"Oh yeah, of course," Kyra said. "You and the dog."

Dax gave her a tiny bit of a smile and tilted his head to one side. "You don't have to say it like that."

"Like what?"

"Like I'm a shut-in with a therapy dog."

Kyra smiled. "If the shoe fits."

He smiled, too. And then he began to move toward her. "Here's the thing about that, Kyra," he said, saying her name for the first time, and wow, did it ever trickle down her spine when said in that low-timbre voice. He was moving slowly, his gaze, dark and intent, locked on hers. The closer he drew, the more Kyra felt a little like bacon on the inside, everything sizzling. *Is he going to kiss me? He is totally going to kiss me.* Kyra was a little nervous, and a little hopeful, and yeah, a little crazy. But she kept smiling, because suddenly kissing The Grouch seemed like the perfect idea.

But when Dax reached her, he swept her beer up off the sawhorse and pressed it into her chest. His gaze fell to her mouth, and he said, very softly, "Otto couldn't be a therapy dog if his life depended on it. He's too lazy." He smiled, lifted his beer, and drank. "Thanks for the beer," he said, tapped his bottle against hers, and stepped away.

Kyra blinked. He hadn't kissed her, but he'd looked at her with those gray-blue eyes, and her heart was pounding like a jackhammer right now.

He bent over and picked up sandpaper from the ground.

Kyra drank more beer, then walked around to his side of the plank and squatted down, picking up a sheet of the sandpaper. "Where are you from?"

"Teaneck."

Teaneck, Teaneck. She tried to think of something to say about that, but in her buzzed head, she had nothing. "Here." She handed him the sandpaper. When he took it, she made sure her fingers brushed against his. Awkwardly—because she had to reach for it, but she managed it. And then she dropped her hand to the ground before she toppled over, because apparently she'd had more beer than she realized.

Dax gave her a slow, droll smile. He rose up, reached for her hand, and pulled her up.

The help was much appreciated.

"Can I ask you something?" he asked.

She noticed he was still holding her hand. "Yes." *Ask me if I'm single. Ask me to come inside. Ask me anything.*

"Are you flirting with me?"

Kyra's eyes widened. *Except that.* What was that old saying? If you have to ask . . . Heat flooded her cheeks almost instantly. Good God, she was so bad at this. She deflated. She sighed. "Sort of."

Now he smiled fully at her, and it was surprisingly warm. He let go of her hand and tucked a bit of her hair behind her ear. His gaze flicked down the length of her and up again. "I'm flattered," he said. But that was all.

Oh Jesus, how embarrassing.

"Thanks for the beer. I need to pick up around here. I've got an early day tomorrow."

Mortifying! She'd tried to flirt, she'd been called on it, and now she was being sent home like Ruby, like a little girl who had crawled over the fence when she wasn't supposed to. Her face was on fire with humiliation, but somehow Kyra smiled and said, "You can't fault a girl for trying."

"Nope," he agreed, smiling fondly at her now, as if she were someone's pesky little sister.

She reached for his bottle.

"I've got it," he said.

"I wouldn't dream of leaving this here. I recycle."

I recycle? God, Kyra, go home and go to bed.

"Good job," he said, and handed her the bottle.

He really did have a nice smile, the kind that could make you all melty on the inside. She began to move away from him, walking backward, not ready to lose sight of that smile quite yet. How come she'd never noticed it before? Oh, right—because he hadn't used it. "Okay, well," she said, her gaze still on his mouth. "See you around." She gave him a funny little wave that was totally unnecessary and kept moving backward, the dog escorting her as if to make sure she removed herself from the property.

"Kyra?"

"Yep?" she asked, hopeful that maybe he'd changed his mind.

"You're about to—"

She hit the fence and scraped the back of her leg. "Got it," she said. She climbed over and walked forward, trying her damnedest not to sprint back to Number Three in complete humiliation.

Chapter Eight

"Can you work a double?" Randa Lassiter asked when Kyra showed up for her shift Friday.

"Yes!" Kyra said instantly. "Well, I think—let me call my babysitter."

"Okay, but do it quick. If you can't, I have to find someone to cover Nyree's shift tonight," Randa said as she returned her gaze to some paperwork she had spread on the bar.

"I'll be back in two shakes," Kyra said and hurried back to the area where the staff stored their things during their shifts.

Deenie was there, primping before the mirror. "Hey," she said.

"Randa asked me if I could work a double!" Kyra almost squealed. "I just have to convince Mrs. Miller to agree." She dug her phone out of her purse and held up two crossed fingers to Deenie.

Deenie responded by crossing her fingers, too.

Mrs. Miller answered after the first ring. Kyra could hear the TV blaring in the background. The day started with *Good Morning America*, then slid into soap operas, then the Judge Judy–type shows, and of course *Dr. Phil*, and then the news. Kyra imagined that a big bowl of oatmeal mush resided in Mrs. Miller's head with all the television she watched. "Hi, Mrs. Miller! Listen, my boss asked me if I could work a double—"

"No," Mrs. Miller said curtly before Kyra could get the question out.

"Please," Kyra begged her. "I need this. I could make some serious extra money."

"I don't care. Six o'clock is my quitting time. I already told you my husband likes his dinner on the table."

"If I can work this shift, I can get the TV fixed," Kyra said hopefully.

"You can't get that TV fixed, that thing is damn near as old as me. What you need is a *new* TV, and you ain't gonna make that in one night's tips."

Kyra closed her eyes. She had to think—she really needed this extra shift. Deenie touched her arm, and Kyra glanced up at her friend. Deenie pointed to herself.

Kyra held up a finger to indicate she'd be a moment. "Mrs. Miller, I'm begging you."

"Beg away, but it still ain't gonna happen. I leave at six." She hung up on Kyra.

Kyra stared at her phone. "I can't believe it!" she exclaimed angrily. "She hung up on me!"

"I'll do it," Deenie said.

"Do what?" Kyra asked, distracted.

"I'll keep Ruby tonight."

Kyra gasped. "You *will*? Are you kidding? Don't kid me, Deenie!"

"Not at all. I love that kid. I can take her over to Megan's. She invited me over, anyway."

Kyra suppressed the tiny part of her that took note *she* had not been invited to Megan's. Or that she really didn't want Ruby anywhere near Megan, especially when she wasn't there to protect her from vegetables and judgments. But on the other hand, she couldn't pass up this opportunity. She threw her arms around Deenie. "Thank you so much! I really need the money."

"I *know*," Deenie said with a laugh.

"I'll call Mrs. Miller and tell her," Kyra said.

♦ ♦ ♦

It was settled—Kyra was getting her first night shift at the bistro, and it couldn't have come at a better time. The last few days had been a real snoozefest, and tips had not been great. But today they were slammed. It was a surprise, too—Randa had only scheduled Kyra and Deenie to work the floor, and the two of them kept bumping into each other at the wait station. "This is so crazy," Deenie said at one such bumping. "Did a bus pull into town or something? I don't care if they did, I am making some great tips today. A guy at a one-top left me twenty." She picked up her wait tray. "Can you grab table fourteen?" she asked. "A two-top. Randa just sat them, but I'm swamped."

She ran off before Kyra could tell her she was swamped, too. Kyra picked up her tray, delivered drinks to table three, then hurried to the front of the bistro and table fourteen. She was reaching for the pen behind her ear when she noticed who was sitting at table fourteen. Her heart dropped and her cheeks flooded with embarrassment all over again.

No wonder Dax wasn't into her—he was seeing someone.

He hadn't noticed her yet—he was studying the menu as if it were a treasure map. But the woman he was with smiled up at her. "Hi," she said perkily.

She was pretty, with honey-blonde hair that hung like a silky sheet, and green eyes. She was wearing a blue shirt tucked into a dark skirt and high heels. Kyra tried to remember the last time she'd worn high heels. "Hi," she said. "Can I, ah . . . can I get you something to drink while you look at the menu?"

"I don't know," the woman said. "Dax? What are you having?"

"Water," he said and glanced up. He started when he saw Kyra, physically shifting in his seat. His glanced around her, almost as if he thought it was some kind of joke and someone was going to jump out and tell him he'd been punked. "Ah . . . hi," he said carefully.

"Hi," Kyra said. She waited for him to say something. Maybe, *"Hey, cute date, this is my neighbor."* But he didn't say anything. He seemed to be actually avoiding her gaze.

Kyra looked at his date. "For you, ma'am?"

"I'll have iced tea," she said. "Unsweetened."

"Be right back," Kyra said and whirled away, hurrying through the crowded restaurant with her heart beating wildly with embarrassment. What was *that*? Jesus, she couldn't believe she'd tried to flirt with him last night! She couldn't believe she'd been hoping to kiss him and maybe even have sex. And really, why had she been hoping that with some guy she hadn't even liked until a day or two ago, and did it really matter? Because here was Supergrump, ordering water (buzzkill), on a date with a very pretty, bubbly woman (he didn't deserve).

The exact opposite of Kyra Kokinos. *"I am such an idiot,"* she whispered under her breath.

She grabbed their drinks, picked up an order from the kitchen that was ready to go out, and returned to the floor, delivering the food first and then reluctantly lugging the drinks to table fourteen.

Dax didn't look up when she set the drinks down. He seemed a little antsy. Was he *embarrassed* of her? Why else would he not acknowledge her? Should she say something? Maybe she'd mention last night. *"Hey, Dax, last night was sort of weird, huh?"* Why was he embarrassed, anyway? She was the one who ought to be embarrassed, which she was, thank you—but why him? Was it because she was a waitress? Because she'd tried to hit on him last night? Supergrump was all dressed up, wasn't he? His hair was combed, he was clean-shaven, and he was wearing a pressed, white-collared shirt tucked into jeans that looked almost new.

"What would you like for lunch?" she asked brightly, looking right at him, silently daring him to pretend he didn't know her.

His date, who was cheerfully perusing the menu, said, "I can't decide between the roasted beet salad and the spinach salad with the duck confit. What do you recommend?" She looked up at Kyra.

"Either of those choices is excellent, but the duck confit is one of our signature plates." It was also the most expensive.

"Hmm," she said and tapped a fingernail against her lip. "What are you having, Dax?" she asked.

"Burger."

Of course. A meal he could get anywhere, along with that glass of water. What a great date! Kyra was actually beginning to feel sorry for the pretty girl.

But the pretty girl laughed and closed her menu. "That sounds wonderful. I'll have the same."

Pretty, cheerful, and agreeable. Here was a woman who knew how to date properly. Kyra was impressed.

"Cooked medium? Does that sound good to everyone?" she asked.

"Sounds perfect!" the date chirped.

"Yep," Supergrump said and carefully straightened the silverware at his elbow.

"Coming right up," Kyra said and walked away. Maybe he was worried that she might say something to his date. What would she say? *"I tried to hit on Dax last night and failed miserably. Would you like some fries with that burger?"* Well, whatever the reason, she was going to make sure she gave them the white-glove service. In other words, she was going to drop by more than was reasonable.

She put in their order, bused a table, returned a man's pasta because the sauce was "too salty," then went back to Dax with a pitcher of water in one hand, a pitcher of tea in the other. "Refills?" she asked brightly.

Pretty Girl had hardly touched hers. "I'm good," she said.

Dax's glass was almost empty. Kyra reached across him and tried to make eye contact, but he wasn't having it. She filled up the glass and set it down right in front of him. "Just let me know if you need anything else. Condiments. Extra napkins. A side dish or two."

Pretty Girl laughed again. "I think we're all set, don't you, Dax?"

"Yep."

Pretty Girl was probably counting down the minutes until she could get the hell out of here. She probably wasn't used to talking to a wall, which was essentially what she was doing. Well, Kyra was going to help her out. She was going to get those burgers out to them pronto so they could end this lunch.

When the burgers were ready, Kyra garnished them—big pickle for Pretty Girl, gherkin for Supergrump—and returned to table fourteen. "Look, I'm back!" she said loudly, and carefully placed a burger before Pretty Girl before slapping the other down in front of Dax. "Now, what can I get you? Mustard? Ketchup?"

"None for me, thanks," Dax said, looking at his burger.

"I'll have some mustard, please," Pretty Girl said as she began to doctor her burger.

Kyra leaned to her right, took the mustard from an empty table, and placed it in front of Pretty Girl. "What about steak sauce? Our sous chef makes the steak sauce, and it's delicious."

"Oh, that sounds really good," Pretty Girl said, looking at Dax.

He slowly lifted his gaze to Kyra. His eyes were dark. "No, thank you," he said carefully.

"Suit yourself," Kyra said with a shrug, and glared right back. "I'll be back to check on you."

She waited what felt like an uncomfortably long time before she returned to their table. Pretty Girl had, predictably, eaten only half of her burger. She was telling Dax something that was making her giggle. Dax was listening politely, his mouth cocked up into a half smile, the sort she'd seem him cast in Ruby's direction. His plate was clean. He might have even licked it.

"How are we doing?" she asked. "Box this up for you?"

"No, thank you," Pretty Girl said. "It was delicious, but I just couldn't take another bite."

"I know, they're huge," Kyra said in girl-on-a-date unity. "Looks like you had no problem polishing it off," she cheerfully remarked to Dax.

He folded his arms across his chest. "Nope."

Kyra picked up their plates. "So did you two lovebirds leave room for dessert?"

Pretty Girl squealed with laughter, her face flushing. "We've only just met!"

"No way!" Kyra said. "You look like you've been together a long time."

Pretty Girl laughed again, her gaze sliding to Dax. "Well, I hope we know each other a long time."

"I guess we'll take the check," Dax said.

"Really? I wouldn't mind coffee and a dessert," Pretty Girl said. "That is, if you have the time."

"Oh, I bet he does," Kyra said. "We have apple pie with ice cream, a peanut butter cheesecake, and the house favorite, molten lava cake."

"Molten lava cake!" Pretty Girl exclaimed. "What's that?"

"It's a cake with a gooey chocolate center. They put it in the oven until the chocolate oozes out of it. Like lava." Dax actually grimaced, but Pretty Girl clapped her hands. "Wonderful!"

Kyra winked at her. "Two spoons?" she asked, waggling two fingers in Dax's face. "Two coffees?"

Dax leaned away from her fingers. "Sure," he said and shot a look at her.

Kyra returned a few minutes later with the dessert, which was the size of a small dinner plate, and the coffees. By now the lunch crowd had started to thin. Kyra cleaned off a few tables and straightened things in the wait station, then joined Deenie at the bar. Dax and Pretty Girl were bowed over their shared dessert. Pretty Girl was laughing.

"They look happy," Deenie said idly.

"You know what? That's my neighbor," Kyra said. "The one I was telling you about."

Deenie gasped and punched her in the arm. "Get out! That gorgeous hunk of man is the asshole? And he's in here with Heather Patterson?"

"You know her?"

"She works at the library. I've met her a couple of times at the Green Bean. But what is *she* doing with that guy? Girl, if he's your neighbor, you need to get *on* that," Deenie said and punched Kyra again.

Kyra grimaced and rubbed her arm. "He's obviously unavailable, Deenie. Plus he's not the friendliest guy in town."

"Then maybe you really need to go out with my friend Phil," Deenie said. "He's a great guy."

This was a running theme between the two of them of late, Deenie mentioning Phil every other day. Kyra had resisted—she had Ruby, it wasn't as if she could *date*. But seeing Dax in here with Heather Patterson had convinced her. If *he* could get a date, surely she could. "You know what? Okay," she said.

Deenie actually gasped with delight. "You *will*? I'm texting him after our shift is up. Hey, keep an eye on Farmer Jones over there for me, will you? I'm going to take these glasses into the kitchen." She picked up a tray and disappeared through a swinging door.

Wait—what had she done? Kyra didn't know if she was ready to go out on a date or not. She glanced at the lovebirds at table fourteen. Dax was holding up a finger in the international sign of *bring the check*.

Kyra pulled out the check and placed it on a silver tray, then sashayed across the room. She laid it down squarely in front of Dax, lest Pretty Girl have any doubts about who should pick up the tab.

But Pretty Girl knew what she was doing. She made no move for it. She smiled at Kyra and ignored the check entirely. "Thank you so much! It was really good."

"Oh, I'm *so* glad you enjoyed it," Kyra said sweetly. "I hope to see you two again. By the way, you make a great couple." The moment she said it, she felt a strong bump against her foot. Had Dax just *kicked* her?

"*Thank* you," Pretty Girl said. She was putting on lipstick now as Dax reached into his back pocket for his wallet. Kyra wondered what had happened to her and lipstick. She used to wear it—when had she stopped?

Dax picked up the silver tray, threw down a card, and shoved it at Kyra.

"Be right back!" she said with great cheer.

She returned the processed bill to Dax and Pretty Girl, who were now the only people in the restaurant. "It was *great* having you here," she said to him and smiled serenely at Pretty Girl. "You two ought to walk down to the lake. It's so pretty today, isn't it? I would if I could."

"You know, she has a point," Pretty Girl said hopefully to Dax.

"Thanks again," Kyra said and walked away, smiling smugly to herself.

She joined Deenie in the closing out of the lunch rush, made sure Deenie had thirty dollars to give Mrs. Miller, then went out to collect the bill from table fourteen. She looked out the window—there was no sign of Dax's truck or anyone on the street. She wondered where the two lovebirds had gone. She turned around and headed for the wait station and happened to glance down at the bill, realizing that Dax had probably tipped her. She would be furious if he hadn't, embarrassed if he had. Lord, but she was a mess.

But what she saw made her stop cold.

Dax had left her a hundred-dollar tip. Like some damn charity, he'd left her *one hundred dollars*.

Oh, no. No, sir. *No, no, no.*

Chapter Nine

Dax thought he was dreaming when he heard the *tap tap tap* on his door. He lifted his head and blinked and then looked around. Everything was as it should be—Otto snoring at the foot of his bed, the light from the streetlights near the lake weakly filtering in through his curtains.

He'd imagined it. He punched his pillow, then resettled.

The knock came again, only this time it was loud and insistent. Otto leapt from the bed, barking and sliding across the hardwood floor as he tried to get out of the room and head for the front door to rip someone's head off.

The pounding came again, and Dax felt a slight panic. No one came knocking on a person's door in the middle of the night except the police or home invaders. What time was it, anyway? He glanced at the clock. Half past twelve.

The knocking came again, and he shouted, "Just a damn minute!" He groped around, trying to find something to clock this person with. Finding nothing in the bedroom, he marched through the kitchen, saw some tools on the kitchen table, and grabbed a crowbar.

"This had better be good," he muttered.

Otto was scratching at the door, barking. Dax had to lean around the damn dog to push aside the drapes and peer out. It was dark, and he could only make out a figure. And while he couldn't see the person's face, he knew it was Mrs. Coconuts.

He flipped on a light and yanked open the door. "What the hell?" he demanded, taking note of Mrs. Coconuts's blazing eyes. In fact, if those lovely teak eyes had been guns, he'd be lying in a pool of blood right now. Otto chose that moment to leap up and plant his paws on the screen door. Stupid dog would have taken the shot for him. Dax shoved him aside. "What's wrong?" he asked and pushed his fingers through his unruly hair. "Something happen to the kid?"

"You want to know what's wrong?" she snapped and slapped a hundred-dollar bill up against the screen door. "*That's* what's wrong."

He looked at the bill. Then at her. "It's called a *tip*."

"It's called *charity*," she said. "And I don't want your stupid charity. Open the door."

"Excuse me?"

"Open the door! Open it right now or I'll put my foot through it!"

He didn't think she was really capable, but he pushed the screen door open. Otto burst out with so much force that she was knocked backward, almost falling, but she grabbed onto the screen door, then used it like a slingshot to propel herself inside. She awkwardly slapped that bill against his bare chest and held it there. "I wanted to stuff it in your pocket and tell you to take a flying leap, but since you don't have any pockets . . . take it."

He glanced down and remembered he was wearing nothing but boxers. He fixed his gaze on her and all her craziness and covered her hand with his. "Okay."

"All right."

"Let go and I'll take it."

She yanked her hand free, then turned to go.

"I was trying to help," he blurted. That's all he'd meant by the tip. He hadn't known she was waiting tables until he saw her at the bistro, and he'd thought of how much he imagined waitstaff made, and how the kid had wanted that purple octopus bath toy, and he'd left a big tip.

But Mrs. Coconuts whirled around so fast when he said it that it startled him. "By leaving me an unreasonably large tip? How exactly was that helping, other than contributing to the Kyra Kokinos charity? And why didn't you *acknowledge* me?" she demanded. "You acted like you've never met me—or couldn't stand the sight of me."

"I didn't act like that," he scoffed.

"*Yes*, you did. You know you did. Why?"

Dax didn't know how he'd acted to Kyra. He'd been too uptight about Heather. "I was on a date."

Her eyes narrowed. *"So?"*

"Why didn't you say something if you were so concerned about it?"

"I don't know—maybe because you would hardly even look at me?"

Dax shrugged, feeling a little out of his depth here. Being on a date seemed a perfectly reasonable explanation to him. He wasn't supposed to look at another woman while he was on a date, was he? Especially not one with a dark mane of hair and arresting eyes and an ass with the perfect amount of bounce. He feared he might get unreasonably hard just thinking about it.

"Are you embarrassed by me?" she asked.

"What? *No*," he said. Where did she come up with that?

"Then why?"

He sighed. He dragged his fingers through his hair. *Why* was a difficult question to answer. All he knew was that when she'd looked at him like she had last night, he'd felt things stirring in him that he didn't want to stir. He'd been sort of intrigued, sort of shocked, sort of scared, and the truth was, he still felt that way. He didn't want . . . complications. He didn't want to feel anything for her, and yet he couldn't seem to bury the tiny shoots of feelings growing in him. Today at the bistro, he'd been confused about being confused and had felt very uncomfortable looking at Kyra while he was on a date with Heather. "I didn't want you to be . . ." He whirled his hand around. "You know."

"No, I don't know."

Neither did he, but he went with it. "*You* know," he said again.

She blinked. But then something sparked in those lovely eyes, and they narrowed dangerously. She said, in a low voice that probably set off male alarms across East Beach, "You thought I'd be *jealous*?"

Jealous? Was she crazy? Well, yes, she was—but there was no way she should be jealous of Heather.

"You thought that I would be *jealous* of a girl because she was at lunch with *you*?"

She shoved him in the chest with what looked like a supreme amount of effort on her part, but which barely registered on him.

"Calm down," he said.

"If you want me to calm down, then don't you dare patronize me!"

"Patronize." He snorted. "I'm not patronizing you, Kyra. You're acting crazy. You seem a little volatile." He was grasping at straws, trying to figure a way out of this while his body was trying to figure a way in.

Kyra gasped. Her eyes sparked with so much fire that he was amazed she didn't torch Number Two to the ground. And then she lunged at him. Dax had a split second of believing she was going to choke the life out of him, and he moved to grab her arms in case she had that in mind, and then he was kissing her.

He was kissing her, and oh God, it was good. It was more than good, it was *hot*. She was all lips and tongue and fingers raking through his hair, and he was all hands and mouth and hard. He was lit up like a holiday display, colorful heat flashing and glittering in his veins. This wasn't just a kiss, this was an unexpected explosion of senses, and it was about to be an explosion of *him*. Dax was seconds away from pulling her shirt over her head, but the moment he realized he was on the verge of doing it, he swayed backward.

At the same moment, so did she. But not without one last shove at his chest. They stared at each other, their breathlessness in sync. "Holy shit," she muttered.

Holy shit, Dax thought.

"I have to go." She whirled around and flung the door open and tripped over Otto, who was patiently waiting to be readmitted to his den.

Dax didn't move. He listened to the sound of her soft-soled shoes flapping down the porch steps. It was a moment before Dax realized that Otto was sniffing around his bare feet. He looked down and saw the crumpled one-hundred-dollar bill.

Dax scratched his head. He picked up the bill, shut the door and locked it, then went back to bed. But he didn't sleep. Nope. His body was thrumming, wondering what the hell was up, wondering why he'd bailed before it had been satisfied.

♦ ♦ ♦

It seemed like he'd only just fallen asleep when the teeth-clenching grind of an old engine woke him up. *Ruuuummmp. Ruuuuummmp. Ruuuummmp.*

Dax groaned. He pushed himself and got out of bed, pulled on some jeans, which he didn't bother to button all the way, slipped his feet into some sandals.

He walked outside, Otto darting out ahead of him, loping down to the lake for his morning swim. Dax made his way across the lawn. He leapt over the fence and headed for that damn car.

She saw him coming. He knew she did because she slowly bowed her head until her forehead touched the steering wheel. Like she was giving herself a much-needed pep talk. Like she didn't want to see him. Too bad—he wasn't listening to that grind anymore, and it wasn't his fault that she'd gone bonkers and kissed him. He knocked on the window. She hesitantly rolled it down. He braced his arm on the hood of her car and leaned down. "Aren't you getting tired of this car-grinding business every morning? I know I am."

"It just needs to be primed a little," she said. "Sorry."

"It's way past needing to be primed. Pop the hood."

"That's okay—"

"No, it's not okay," he said. "This car is depriving me of some much-needed beauty rest. Open 'er up." He punctuated that with a slap on the top of her car.

Kyra muttered under her breath, but she pulled the hood latch.

Dax opened the hood and had a look. The battery cables were corroded and the battery was a Walmart special that looked a little old. If he had to guess—obviously he had to guess, but he was pretty good at this sort of thing—he would say the starter needed to be replaced. He shut the hood.

"What?" she said. She'd come out of her car and was standing beside him.

"You need a new starter."

"Noo," she said instantly, swaying backward, her eyes closed. "Please tell me that's cheap."

"It's not cheap. You're talking two to three hundred dollars."

"Ohmigod," she whimpered.

"For the part. Labor will run you another buck fifty."

Now the blood drained from her face. "You have to be kidding."

"I wouldn't kid about a starter."

"This is a freaking disaster!"

Dax looked at her hair, loose around her shoulders, and her plump, rose-colored lips. And her shirt, which fit quite tightly and left nothing to the imagination. He thought about that very unexpected kiss. It was a little crazy, but if a man could get past the unexpected craziness, that kiss was pretty damn hot. So hot that he said, "I can do the work if you can get the part."

"What?" She looked up from her car. "You know how to replace a starter?"

"It's not that hard. I learned it in the army."

"You were in the *army*?"

She didn't have to say it like she thought it was beyond the realm of all possibility.

"Okay, thanks. I'll take that under advisement," she said. She was moving back to the driver's door. "But I have to go to work now, and as you have clearly noticed, it takes a little bit to get it to start."

"Look," Dax said, "you've got a handful of times left on that thing. Better you get it fixed now than find yourself stuck somewhere with the kid in the car. I'll take you to work, and I'll pick up a starter and fix your car. Then I'll pick you up. You can pay me back after work."

"But four to five hundred dollars?" she said and began to chew on her bottom lip. "I don't have that kind of money right now."

Dax hadn't had to worry about five hundred dollars in a long time, but he remembered what it felt like, and he sympathized with her. "Just buy the part," he said. "I'll fix it for free." This offer, he realized, was as much of a surprise to him as it was to her.

"What? No, no, no," she said, shaking her head. "That's nice of you to offer, but I don't want to owe you anything."

"I know. I get it. But you just said you don't have five hundred dollars lying around."

She winced. "Yeah, well, I'm actually a little short, seeing as how I'm having to hand back tips."

His eyes narrowed. "If you'd kept that tip like I told you, you'd be halfway to a new starter." This was the thing about his neighbor—she could be so damned attractive and sexy and appealingly quirky, then do something ridiculous, like throw away a one-hundred-dollar tip.

She opened her mouth—to argue, he presumed—and he quickly threw up a hand to stop her. "But you didn't, and now it's in my wallet and not coming out. So I guess it's settled, isn't it? Get your stuff. I'll be waiting for you in the truck."

She began to chew on her lip again as she considered it, and Dax couldn't take his eyes from that lip. He wanted to kiss it. He wanted to kiss her. He wanted to do all sorts of things to her that were too absurd to even contemplate. He was going to fix her starter like he fixed her door, then be done. But this time he meant it—*done*. As in no entanglements.

"Okay," she said, nodding. "Okay. It would be much appreciated if you can drop me off, but I'll get a ride home."

"Whatever," he said. "Let's go." He walked away before he kissed her.

He didn't know how long it took to get someone's work stuff together, especially when they'd seemed in such a hurry, but he bet five minutes passed before Kyra showed up and opened the passenger door. She tossed a backpack and a tote bag full of books onto the floorboard, then climbed inside. "Thanks," she said sheepishly. "This is surprisingly nice of you."

"Not *that* surprising," he muttered.

Kyra shrugged a little. She crossed one leg over the other. Then she tucked hair behind her ears. Then she folded her arms tightly across her middle and turned to the window.

"I can be nice," he added, a little miffed that she didn't seem to believe it. "Contrary to the popular opinion in Number Three."

"That's not fair. Ruby likes you," she said to the window.

Now he was curious to know the full opinion of him in Number Three. He turned his head to back out and wondered why she was wound up as tight as a spring. "Your body language says you'd rather ride in back. Is there something you'd like to say?"

"Nope," she said quickly. "I'm just . . . I have a lot going on."

He put the truck in drive and looked at her again. She still wouldn't look at him. "All right, I'll lay it out there—are you thinking about last night?"

"No," she said instantly and vociferously.

Oh, she was thinking about it, all right. Well, that made two of them. He was supposed to call Heather today, which he didn't really want to do to begin with, but Kyra's kiss had given him mountains of second thoughts. He couldn't imagine sweet, bubbly Heather kissing like that. He couldn't imagine sweet, bubbly, talkative Heather ever launching herself at him like Crazy Pants Kyra had.

He stole another look at his passenger. She had not unwound herself.

All right, he was man enough to admit it—he wanted another kiss like the one last night. But bigger. And more explosive. Mind-bending. But he wouldn't do it, because he definitely was not getting involved with someone who got that wound up about a big fat tip. Or who lived right next door. Just say, for argument's sake, that they kissed again. And maybe it wasn't as great a kiss as last night's, and there she was, living right next door. That would be awkward. Or say it was even better than last night. And there she was, still living next door, only then making him want more.

Then again, what if he decided to date Heather? He wasn't exactly leaning that way, but what if? Kyra would still be next door, and they'd have this kiss thing between them, and she'd see Heather going in and out of his cottage, and she would wonder what was going on, and he'd have to tell her.

Or maybe he could invite her and the kid, and the McCauleys, to a barbecue and introduce them to Heather. That way Kyra would get that he was dating Heather. Problem solved.

God, no, he was *not* having a barbecue. What the hell was the matter with him? And he was *not* going to date Heather, was he insane? "Do you like barbecues?" he blurted.

Her head snapped around. "What?"

"I asked if you liked barbecues. Not that I'm going to have one. Last thing I'd do. But do you like them? I mean, would you go to one if you were invited?"

Her brows dipped. "What the hell are you talking about?" she asked irritably.

He noticed the color in her cheeks was high. "You *are* thinking about last night."

"No, I'm not!" she said loudly. "I'm thinking about money, if you must know."

"Okay. So you're thinking about last night *and* that Benjamin."

"Who?"

"The tip."

"I am *so* not thinking of that tip," she said, twisting toward him now. "You don't get it, do you? I would go live under a bridge before I'd take that tip from you."

"That seems like an extreme reaction for a waiter to have toward a tip," he said as he turned onto Juneberry Road.

"The *tip* was way over the top, Dax. Anyway, I don't want to talk about it. I said what I had to say."

"And you punctuated it with a kiss," he said, although he wasn't entirely certain who had done the punctuating. "That's what I call returning a tip." He winked at her.

Wow, a wink, too? Dax didn't know who he was right now, or why these words were coming out of his mouth. Or why he thoroughly enjoyed the way she huffed when he said it and sank deeper into her seat and stared out the window to avoid looking at him. He felt like a kid on the playground, pulling her hair. It was bizarre but oddly satisfying.

He didn't say any more than that on the way into town, and she sure didn't. He pulled up in front of the Lakeside Bistro and leaned over her to have a look out the window. "It doesn't look open."

"It's not," she said. "I usually do laundry in the morning."

"Don't know how I forgot that. So what are you going to do?" he asked, and pictured her sitting on a bench like a vagabond with her two big bags.

"Don't worry about it," she said curtly. She flung open the door, grabbed her things, and said, "Thanks for the ride."

"Kyra?" he said before she could slam the door.

"What?"

"Just for the record, *I'm* not upset that you launched yourself at me." For the record, he did know why he said that. He wanted to mess with her a little bit because her fluster was charming the pants right off of him. And she didn't disappoint him—she gasped and her eyes flew open wide. And then narrowed. "You are delusional!" she said and moved to shut the door.

"Wait," he said.

"What?" she demanded.

She looked good with a little color in her cheeks, he thought. Hell, she just looked good. Really good. "I need your keys."

She threw her backpack onto the seat and began to rummage through it. Things were flying out of it. Bills. Grocery lists. Used tissues. Makeup brushes and two plastic toys.

"You just had them. You woke me up grinding the engine, remember?" he said.

"I don't know what I did with them. They're here, I know they are."

"Check the pockets," he said.

She paused and cast a withering look at him. "Are you kidding me right now?" She gestured with both hands to her backpack. "What do you think I'm doing?"

"Don't tell me you lost—"

"Nope," she said and triumphantly held them up. She tossed the keys at him and began to stuff things into her backpack. When she had it all secured, she slung it over her shoulder and stepped back. "Again, thanks for the ride. And for taking care of my car. I'm still mad at you, but I really appreciate it."

"My pleasure. It seems the least I can do after that kiss."

The way she slammed the door, rattling his whole truck, made Dax smile.

♦ ♦ ♦

He left her stewing on the sidewalk and drove on. He picked up the part he needed, grabbed a coffee at the Green Bean, then went back to Number Two to get to work. Her car was old and some of the bolts were hard to get undone, but he managed it.

Naturally, Ruby visited while he worked. He saw her feet approaching in her light-up cowboy boots, then her head appeared, upside down, the tails of her red hair dragging in the dirt. "What are you doing?"

"Working."

She squatted down. "What's that?"

"A car. Don't touch."

"But what are you *doing*?" she said, and sat on her bottom, sliding one leg under the car.

"Stay out there, Ruby Coconuts. I'm fixing it so your mom will have a car. What does it look like?"

"My mom hates this car."

"Seems like an okay car to me."

Ruby crisscrossed her legs and began to dig in the dirt with a stick. "She hates it because my dad was in a car crash. His car hit like, four cars. And then it went off a bridge."

Startled, Dax looked at her. "I thought your dad was a cat trainer in Africa."

"He *is*," she said, as if one did not negate the other. "The crash happened before. They had to cut off his legs."

Huh. Dax tried to picture how many Americans without legs were training big cats in Africa. He was going to go out on a limb here and guess exactly zero. "He doesn't have any legs," he said skeptically.

"No. But he has a skateboard."

"Well, sure," Dax said. "How else is he going to get around? Okay, kid, go play."

"Okay!" she said and hopped up. He watched her boots disappear from view. He didn't know if she went inside or not, because he knew how to fix a door, and he'd fixed the one on Number Three but good.

As he continued to work, he grew more curious about Ruby's dad. Did she see the dude at all? What was he, a deadbeat dad who couldn't cough up some money to fix Kyra's car? Was Kyra divorced? Working on a divorce? Maybe she'd never married.

It made him think of himself. His child would make an entry into this world in the next couple of weeks. A baby—children—was the one thing he'd wanted out of life, and it was about to happen, at long last. And yet his own pride kept getting in the way of truly enjoying this moment in his life. Because he had a hard time swallowing the fact he was going to have to share this child with Stephanie. Frankly, he could hardly imagine sharing a child with Ashley after what she'd done to him, but he didn't have any choice in that. He didn't know what to expect, but one thing was certain—his kid would never have to make up stories about him, no sir. His kid would know *exactly* who and what his father was.

Ruby had not gone inside, as it turned out, because she appeared a few minutes later and dumped the many rocks she'd collected on the drive next to where he was working.

"We are not going to play with rocks right here, right now," he said and pulled himself out from under the car.

Ruby stood up, too. She was tapping her fingers together, over and over, her gaze fixed on the engine under the open hood. Dax watched her a moment. He'd seen her do this before, sort of zone out, her hand moving, her gaze fixed. "Ruby?" he said.

It was as if she didn't hear him. She didn't look at him but kept staring at the engine, her fingers moving.

Dax dipped down. "Ruby," he said and touched her arm. Nothing. Was she having a seizure? He was reminded of a call he'd gone out on in Teaneck. The emergency was an unresponsive child, but when they'd arrived four minutes after the call came in, the kid was running around the yard. "Hey," he said and squatted down.

Just like that, Ruby looked at him and said, "I'm building a rock castle. You wanna see it?"

She'd checked out for a few but then reappeared. "Not unless it's big," he said. "I'm not wasting time on a tiny castle."

"It's *big*," she assured him.

His phone began to ring, and Dax stood up, pulled the phone from his pocket. "Maybe later, Ruby Coconuts. I've gotta work. Now get out of here." He winked at her and answered his phone without looking. "Hello."

"Hey, stranger!"

Jesus, it was Heather. Dax had said he'd call her and hadn't yet. "Hi, Heather." A stranger? He'd seen her yesterday.

"I was just wondering about you," she said. "I was in Black Springs this morning and ran into an old friend. She told me about a new jazz club that opened there, and I thought, I know who would like that."

"Who?" Dax asked.

She laughed. "*You*, silly! What would you think of trying it out sometime?"

What would he think of checking out a jazz club? That he'd rather stick hot needles in his eyes. Why was she calling him, anyway? He was supposed to call her. Weren't there any rules to dating anymore? A guy was the first to call, everyone knew that. A guy calls three times, and then it's open season.

"Well, I—"

"I probably caught you off guard," she said before he could answer. "Just think about it and give me a call. Are you having a good day?"

"So far."

"Great! Listen, I really enjoyed our lunch."

Somewhere in the distance, Dax heard Otto barking. "Ah . . . yep," he said.

"And I . . . I look forward to hearing from you," she said quite cheerfully.

What was Otto into now? The damn dog wouldn't stop barking.

"Right," he said. He wasn't sure how to end this call, but he was pretty desperate to do it. He wasn't ready for Heather yet. He had to gear up, get his game face on.

"Okay, well . . . talk to you later?" she asked.

He was relieved she was going to end this call for them. "You bet. Bye for now." He clicked off the phone and stuffed it in his pocket. What was he doing, again? Right, he was almost finished with that car, but first he had to get Otto out of Mrs. McCauley's garden. But when he turned toward the Victorian house on the hill, he realized that Otto's barking was coming from the lake, not the McCauley house. He turned around, moved from in front of Kyra's car, scanning the lake in search of his dog.

He spotted him—Otto was on a rock, his butt in the air, his tail wagging furiously. And there, next to him, was Ruby Coconuts. She was crouched down, and it looked like she was holding a stick.

Dax scanned the lakeshore. No one around but Otto and Ruby. He glanced back at Number Three. Through the open screen door, he could hear the TV. He jogged over to tell the woman that Ruby was down at the lake, but when he walked up on the porch, he saw the old bag in a reclining chair, fast asleep while some game show blared.

"Hey!" he shouted. The woman startled awake. "Your kid is outside," he said and pointed toward the lake. He glanced back and his heart seized—Otto was crouched down on the rock, his head over the side of it, pointed toward the lake, and Ruby was nowhere to be seen.

Dax leapt off the porch and ran, his stride as long as he could make it. It seemed to take forever to cover the roughly fifty yards between the cottages and the lake, and by the time he reached the rock, Otto had gained his feet and was barking again. Dax raced around the rock, saw Ruby flailing in the water.

He jumped in—thank God the water was really shallow here—and grabbed her up, holding her tightly to him, her head against his shoulder, his arms firmly around her body. She wrapped her legs and arms around him and started to cry.

His heart was beating as wildly as hers. He clung to her in relief as he climbed out of the water. He paused to give Otto a scratch behind the ears and a "good boy." When he was on the beach again, he caressed Ruby's crown and asked, "What were you doing down there, Coconut?"

"It was a *dragonfly*," she sobbed.

"Ah, a dragonfly," he said, still caressing her head, still swallowing to get his heart to stop pounding. He continued on, walking up the shore with her, trying vainly to catch his breath. He kept picturing what he might have found had he not been out front—a little girl floating facedown in the lake. The vision made him feel sick.

The babysitter had managed to get off her butt and was hurrying toward them as fast as Dax supposed she could go, considering her girth. She stopped running when she saw Dax carrying Ruby up from the lake, and braced a hand against her knee to catch her breath. "She's not supposed to be out there," she said between pants.

Dax walked past her, hardly able to look at her. "Get me some clothes for her," he said curtly. He wasn't going to say any more, because he thought he might take her head off if he did.

"What are you going to do?" the babysitter asked as she hurried to keep up with him.

She had not even asked how Ruby was, had not tried to comfort her, and Dax was a boiling egg about to explode. "Ruby's going to hang out with me today."

"What? You can't do that!"

"Sure I can." He paused on the drive in front of Number Three. "If you have a problem, I'll give Kyra a call."

The woman frowned. "Carrie ain't going to fire me. She doesn't have another option."

That remark infuriated him. The old bag showed absolutely no remorse for what had nearly happened. Ruby could have *drowned.* "Okay. Then maybe I'll call the police," he said.

"No, don't call the police!" Ruby wailed. "I don't want to get in trouble!"

"Just get me some clothes for her," Dax said angrily.

The woman pressed her lips together and marched into Number Three. She returned a few minutes later and thrust some clothes at Dax. He caught them with his free hand.

"You haven't heard the end of this, buster," she said.

"Are you kidding me?" Dax asked incredulously. He turned around and walked away from her. She was the second woman in his life he'd wanted to punch in the mouth.

He, Ruby, and Otto crowded into his cottage. Ruby was still whimpering. Dax set her down then squatted in front of her. "Look, Coconut, you're okay. Stop crying."

She nodded and sniffed.

"Go in there and put these on," he said, pointing at his bedroom door. "You can put on your clothes, can't you?"

"I have to put my clothes on every day."

"Okay. Well, you can understand my confusion, since you never have your boots on the right feet."

She looked down.

He gestured for a foot. She lifted it, and he yanked off the boot, grimacing as water spilled on his clean floor. He took off the other one and stood up, holding the boots in one hand. "Go put the dry clothes on, then bring me your wet clothes."

"What are you going to do with them?"

"I'm going to put them in a sandwich and eat them."

She looked at him very studiously. "You can't eat clothes."

"No?"

Ruby shook her head.

"Then I guess I'll hang them out to dry. And then I'm putting you to work, Coconut. You're going to be my helper."

She gasped. *"Yay!"* she said, and just like that, her blues were banished. She took the clothes from him and ran into his bedroom to change.

"Yeah, you think it's all cookies and cream right now, but just wait 'til I'm through with you," he called after her.

"Awesome!" she shouted back.

Dax walked out onto the porch to deposit the boots, then put his hand against the porch railing and drew a deep breath. He wished he could banish the blues as easily as that little girl could, but his heart was still trying to jackhammer out of his chest and his belly still churned with the nausea of imagining what might have happened if he hadn't been close by.

He didn't know quite what to make of her mother, but Dax wasn't going to let the coconut out of his sight anytime soon.

Chapter Ten

As far as bad days went, this one ranked near the top, and God knew several had already crowded up there. Add the awkwardness of having kissed Dax—*what sort of temporary insanity was that?*—to her humiliation in having to accept his offer to fix her car because she was, as usual, *broke*, and now the news that Deenie's friend Phil had passed on the offer of meeting Kyra, she was batting a thousand.

Talk about feeling like the scourge of society.

"He doesn't want to even *meet* me?" Kyra asked Deenie again, just to make sure she understood correctly.

"It's not that he doesn't want to *meet* you," Deenie said, although she'd said, *He said thanks, but he'd rather not meet you.* "It's just not a good time for him."

"Wow," Kyra said. "Wow." She was sort of hoping. Actually, hoping was too soft a word. Since last night, she was praying for any alternative that would keep her from doing things like banging on Dax's door after midnight and then kissing him like a desperate head case who hadn't had sex in about . . . forever.

But Dax was seeing someone else. She had *waited on them*, for God's sake.

"What's the matter, he doesn't like children?" Megan asked, her elephant ears having overheard the conversation.

"It's not that, either," Deenie said, squirming a little. "It's just not an ideal dating situation for him."

"Ah," Kyra said. "You mean because I am a single mother."

"That is *such* bullshit," Megan said, and pointed a giant spoon at Deenie, who instantly threw up her hands as if she were being held at gunpoint. "So are single mothers not allowed to date?" she demanded. "Is that it? And what kind of cretin doesn't like children?"

"You're taking this way too hard, Megan," Deenie said. "Phil likes children. It's just . . ." She sighed, then glanced sheepishly at Kyra. "He doesn't want that complication in his dating life right now."

"By 'that complication,' I take it you mean Ruby. He doesn't want an adorable six-year-old in his life right now," Kyra said bitterly.

"Well?" Deenie asked. "Can you blame him?"

"Yes! I can blame him! Six-year-olds are a lot of fun, and now I feel like an idiot, and it was *your* idea, Deenie," Kyra reminded her.

She was deflated by this news, and it made her feel a little unlovable, but she was definitely not surprised. She already knew that there weren't a lot of hot guys out there dying to get in the pants of a single mom with a bit of a paunch and Barbie dolls strewn all over the backseat of her piece-of-shit car. She knew that, so why was she mad at Deenie? Because Deenie had to go and mention the dude to begin with and get Kyra's hopes up.

"It's ridiculous," Megan said and angrily began to stir something in a big metal pot. "I have a friend who has three-year-old twins, and every time she starts dating a guy, it's like they spend one Sunday with them and they're like no, I'm out, I can't with this kid thing. It's disgusting."

"Okay, to be fair, in that case it could be the three-year-old twins," Kyra said.

Megan gave her a sharp look. "Children are the purest, most wonderful creatures on God's earth. I would think you'd be on my side, Kyra."

"I *am* on your side. But Ruby was a handful at three years old. I can't imagine two of her and trying to date. I'm just saying."

"I don't think you should just accept this lying down, Kyra," Megan added as she dumped a creamy liquid into the pot.

"You're right," Kyra said as she tied on her apron. "I'll hunt him down and demand he date me or else."

"Why not?" Megan asked pointedly. "How else will he know what he's doing is so, *so* wrong?"

"Maybe I can tell him," Deenie suggested. "I'll text him—"

"God, please don't," Kyra said. She picked up her tray. "The only thing worse than being rejected, sight unseen, is to have your friend call and beg for you." She went through the swinging door between the kitchen and the dining room and went to work. Phil or no Phil, she needed to earn some money.

They had decent traffic for lunch, thank God, because that car repair was going to put a serious dent in Kyra's bank account. When her shift was over, Kyra bought supper for her and Ruby from the bistro—pizza, another nutritional fail, and if she wasn't sure of it, Megan mentioned it—then bummed a ride home from Deenie. They drove by the bank on the way to the cottages so Kyra could get the money to pay Dax for her car repair.

When they arrived at Kyra's cottage, her car was sitting in the same place she'd left it this morning.

"Is it fixed?" Deenie asked as Kyra gathered her things.

"I hope so," Kyra said. She pushed the car door open and climbed out. "Thanks, Deenie."

"You're welcome. Giving you a ride was the least I could do after the Phil thing. I didn't want to say it in front of Megan and risk a volcano, but I know this other guy—"

"No!" Kyra laughed. "I'm good, Deenie. I swear it."

Deenie shrugged. "Just trying to help a sister out. Okay, call me if you need a ride tomorrow. Now I'm going to go hunt Phil down and lecture him about judging single mothers. I'm doing it for Megan." She wiggled her fingers at Kyra and backed out of the drive.

Kyra juggled her bags and the pizza and started up the steps of the porch. Just as she reached the landing, Mrs. Miller stepped out of the cottage, her utilitarian shoulder bag and her lunch box slung over her arm.

"Hi," Kyra said. She smiled. Mrs. Miller did not return her smile. "Everything okay today?" she asked as she put the pizza on a folding chair before unloading her book bag from her shoulder.

"The usual," Mrs. Miller said.

Kyra looked around her. The usual was Ruby bouncing out of her room or the cottage to greet her. "Where's Ruby?"

Mrs. Miller stuck her hand out for her money. "Next door."

Next door? That couldn't be good. Kyra reached into her backpack. "With Dax?"

"Whatever his name is," Mrs. Miller said. "And that dog."

"Uh-oh," Kyra said as she pulled out a wad of bills. "Is there something I should know? Why is she over there?"

"He said it was okay," Mrs. Miller said stiffly and inched her hand a little closer to Kyra.

Kyra counted out thirty dollars and handed her the money. Mrs. Miller snatched her hand back quickly and stuck the money into her purse, adjusted her lunch bag, and stepped around Kyra. "Righty-oh, have a good evening," she said and moved carefully down the porch steps. "You need to get that TV fixed!" she said on her way to her truck.

Kyra groaned. She needed to do a lot of things, and that TV was not high on the priority list.

She watched Mrs. Miller back out of the drive, then looked across the lawn to Number Two. There was no sign of Ruby or Dax. She hoped he wasn't holding her daughter hostage for something she'd done, because Kyra was tapped out—she didn't have any ransom money. She dragged her fingers through her hair and steeled herself. She left her things on the porch and jogged down the steps and across the lawn to Dax's cottage.

The dog was barking from somewhere inside before she even made it up the steps. The door swung open and Ruby peered out from behind the screen door through her blue glasses. She was wearing pink shorts that were much too small for her and a pajama top with a unicorn galloping across a field of flowers. Her hair was in two pigtails that were tied in a big knot on top of her head.

"Hi, Mommy!"

"What did you do to your hair, pumpkin?"

"Dax said it was in the way."

Oh no. "Of what?"

Ruby shrugged and stuck her finger in a tiny tear in the screen. "He was painting something, I think."

Kyra pushed Ruby's finger out of the tear in the screen. She was almost afraid to ask what had happened that had forced him to pile Ruby's hair on top of her head and bring her into his house to begin with. "Where is Mr. Bishop?" she asked as Otto crowded in beside Ruby at the screen door. A thought suddenly occurred to Kyra. "Oh shit. He's here, right? You're not . . . you're not in his house *without* him, are you? Because I know you wouldn't do that, Ruby."

"You said a bad word," Ruby declared.

"I'm right here," Dax said and appeared behind Ruby, wiping his hands on his T-shirt. A form-fitting T-shirt, Kyra certainly couldn't help noticing, and one that was covered in sawdust and curious black marks that looked almost as if he'd been run over.

"Ah . . . hi," she said, feeling suddenly sheepish. Why did the man have to be so damned good-looking? "Okay, let me have it. What'd she do?"

"That lady didn't tell you?" he asked and leaned over Ruby to open the screen door. The dog bolted outside, and Ruby would have, too, but Dax caught her with a hand to her shoulder. "You're not going anywhere," he said and pulled her back. "Come in," he said to Kyra.

"When you say lady, do you mean Mrs. Miller? Because she didn't say anything," Kyra said. "Why, what happened?"

Dax glanced at Ruby. So did Kyra. "Ruby?"

"Come in, come in," Dax said.

Kyra reluctantly stepped across the threshold. This was not going to be good, she could feel it. He still had his hand on Ruby's shoulder. Kyra just hoped it wasn't a superexpensive fix. "Look, whatever she did, I will pay for it, and she won't bother you—"

"She fell into the lake."

Kyra's breath froze in her throat. That didn't make sense—how could that have even happened? She'd obviously heard him wrong. "What?"

"She was chasing butterflies," Dax said.

"Not butterflies. *Dragonflies*," Ruby corrected him.

"Dragonflies," Dax conceded.

A million questions flitted through Kyra's brain at warp speed, but she couldn't voice them—she had no breath. Her heart wasn't even beating. She was being assailed by a horrible image of Ruby floating facedown in that lake.

"There was no one around," Dax said. "She was out there alone, unsupervised—"

"But how did she . . . did she cry?" Kyra asked, nearly choking. "Did she scream?"

"Otto was with her. He barked an alarm and I saw her."

"Oh my God," Kyra said. She pressed a hand to her belly. She felt sick. She felt faint. Ruby was not a good swimmer. She usually splashed around the shallow ends of pools. "*Oh my God*," she said again.

"Don't . . . it was very shallow where she fell—hey, hey, are you all right?"

Kyra hadn't even realized she was sinking until Dax caught her and pulled her back up to her feet, steadying her with a hand on her waist. "Do you need to sit down?"

"No," she said, although she was nodding. "Oh God," she said. "Oh my God." What kind of mother was she? She'd gone for cheap day care and had put her daughter's life in danger. She *knew* Mrs. Miller wasn't watching Ruby very closely, and yet she'd kept her. It made her sick. "It's my fault," she wheezed, still unable to fully catch her breath.

"Yours?" Dax scoffed as he helped her onto a leather armchair. "It's not your fault, Kyra. It's that woman's fault. She was asleep in front of the television."

"No, no, it's mine," she said and looked at Ruby, who appeared completely at ease. She reached for her, catching her by the arm and pulling her into an embrace, wanting to both strangle her for going down to the lake after being told a thousand times not to, and never let her go again.

"Don't do that to yourself," Dax said. "She's fine, she's all right. And she's never going down to that lake again without an adult, isn't that right, Coconut?"

"That's *right,*" Ruby said, her eyes blinking up at Kyra through her glasses. "I promise."

"Oh, Ruby," Kyra said and buried her face in her daughter's neck. "Ruby, Ruby—I don't know what to do with you. But I don't know what I'd do without you, do you know that?"

"You're pushing all the air out of me, Mommy," Ruby said into Kyra's shoulder.

Kyra reluctantly let her go. She ran her hand roughly over Ruby's head and around the big knot of hair, then looked up at Dax. "*Thank* you," she said, her voice thick with emotion. There was no way to convey her gratitude.

"Don't mention it."

"Don't *mention* it? You saved my daughter, my car, gave me a ride to work . . . God, this is embarrassing," she exclaimed as she enumerated all that he'd done in the last twenty-four hours. She raked her fingers through her hair, wanting to assure him she wasn't the burden she appeared to be but at a loss to believe it herself. She found her feet and stood up. "I need you to know that I'm really not this kind of neighbor. I mean, obviously I have been exactly this kind of neighbor, but it's a fluke—really."

He smiled a little. "I'm not sure what I'm supposed to take away from that."

"I've just had a string of really bad luck."

"Mommy, look at Otto's bow."

Kyra turned away from Dax's gray eyes. The dog was standing at the screen door, wearing an enormous cloth bow around his neck. She wondered how she'd missed that before.

"Dax made it from one of his shirts," Ruby said and opened the screen door like she lived in Number Two, and frankly, Kyra wouldn't be surprised if Dax casually mentioned that Ruby had been spending an awful lot of time here.

The dog sauntered inside, presented his head for petting by Ruby, then flopped down with a burp and began to lick his paws.

"I'm not supposed to use the take measure."

"Tape," Dax muttered and glanced at Kyra. "She was going to tie it around his neck. That shirt was the only substitute I had."

"Just how long has she been here?"

He shrugged. Glanced at the clock. "Since about eleven."

Good God, it was even worse than she thought—Ruby had been at his house all day. "I'm . . . stunned."

"I wasn't going to leave her with that woman after the lake incident."

"Dax . . . thank you. I'll just add babysitting and the T-shirt to the long list of things I owe you."

Dax looked down. He rubbed his nose and squinted toward the window. "It's okay, Kyra. I like cars. And I like coconuts."

"*I'm* not a coconut," Ruby said, and began to hop up and down, exciting Otto.

"I don't know how I'll ever make it up to you," Kyra said. "But look, I have the money for my car next door, and I also have a pizza."

"Yay! I love pizza!" Ruby cheered.

"And I've got some beer," Kyra added. "Can I at least feed you some pizza?"

"Come over, come over!" Ruby said excitedly. "I can show you my toys!"

Dax shook his head. "I don't want to see your toys."

Ruby kept jumping as if she hadn't heard or didn't care.

"Don't you want some pizza?" Kyra asked.

He looked at her, considering the offer, his eyes settling on hers and making her feel a little glittery inside in spite of the nerves she was still feeling after hearing about Ruby's fall into the lake.

"I promise not to ah . . . attack you, if you're worried about that," she said, shooting a sidelong glance to Ruby.

"Hmm," he said.

"We'd love for you to come . . . but maybe you have a date?"

His gaze narrowed. "Just so happens it's a rare night without a date," he said. "So yeah, I want some pizza."

Kyra was absurdly pleased and tried to suppress her giddy little smile of relief but failed. "Well, come on, then."

The three of them trooped over to Number Three, Otto pausing to mark his territory every few feet, Kyra with her hand wrapped firmly around Ruby's. But as they walked around the front of her car, Kyra suddenly stopped, holding her arms out so that Ruby and Dax couldn't pass her. There, on the porch steps, was the pizza box. Upside down.

"What *happened*?" she cried.

"Did you, by chance, leave your pizza outside?" Dax asked.

"Yes!" Kyra said. "I put it on the chair, right there," she said, pointing to the folding chair on her porch. Her bags were still there on the floor of the porch, next to the chair.

"Great," Dax said. "I'll be smelling that damn dog all night."

Kyra jerked around to him. "You think Otto did this?"

"We're not going to have pizza, Mommy?" Ruby asked in a whine.

Kyra had forty dollars left over from her tips today that she'd planned to put toward some new work shoes, but after what had happened today, she would gladly put off getting new shoes. "We're having pizza," she said. "I'll order it."

"*I'll* order it," Dax said. "It was my dog—"

"Like hell you will," Kyra said.

"Mommy, you said *another* bad word."

"I might say another one," she muttered and marched up the porch steps, swiping up the pizza box as she went, and grabbed her purse to get her phone.

Five minutes later the pizza was ordered, Kyra had opened a couple of beers, and she was surreptitiously kicking toys and articles of clothing under her couch and behind a chair, privately vowing to start straightening the house every morning before work. While she quickly picked up, Ruby talked. And talked. And talked some more.

If Dax was put off by the toys strewn everywhere and Kyra's homework stacked on the kitchen table, which she had to shove aside to make room for the pizza, he didn't show it. He did, however, pick up a dried, blackened banana peel between finger and thumb, holding it away from him, and walked it to the trash, which, by some miracle, was not overflowing.

Kyra then darted into her room, and like a quick-change artist, she ditched her work clothes and pulled on a sundress. When she returned to the kitchen, Dax's gaze meandered down the length of her and back up again, and Kyra's thoughts went straight to the idea of his hand following the path of his eyes, and she turned around, pretending not to notice. "Any trouble with the car?" she asked.

"Nope," he said and sipped.

"It's running?"

He cocked his head to one side and gave her a look that suggested he was slightly insulted by the question. "Army, remember? You're all set for transportation." He put down his beer. "Look, Kyra, it's none of my business . . . but I think you ought to get rid of your babysitter and go with someone new."

Well, of course she should, and she was definitely going to explore a better option. But she didn't want to explain to Dax how stuck she was between the proverbial rock and hard place with child care. She had a little less than two months before school started, and then she wouldn't need child care. "You're one hundred percent right," she said and left it at that, because Ruby had appeared with a selection of Barbie dolls that she periodically tortured and mutilated.

She spread them out on the kitchen table.

"I hope you don't think I'm going to play dolls," Dax said. "I'm a boy."

"Boys play with dolls," Ruby said.

"No, they don't."

"Yes, they do," she said, giggling. "You can have Starlight," Ruby suggested, pushing a Barbie whose hair had been brushed into a wild array of synthetic fiber, then chopped unevenly the day Ruby got hold of scissors. Starlight had also lost most of her clothes.

"Starlight," Dax said, sounding a little appalled. "What is she, a dancer?"

Kyra shot him a look, but Ruby said, "She's a teacher."

Dax pushed Starlight back to Ruby. "Looks like she's enjoying her summer vacation."

Ruby agreed that she was, and that she was going swimming today. She picked up Pinkie, who Kyra knew had a rough backstory. "Ruby, sweetie, put your dolls in your room now. We're going to eat pizza soon," Kyra said.

"Pizza!" Ruby exclaimed as if this was the first she was hearing of it. She gathered her dolls, dropping one, then another, then all of them when she reached to pick up the first dropped doll.

Dax sighed wearily, then squatted down and picked up the dolls and arranged them in Ruby's arms so she could carry them.

He was so patient with Ruby. He was so kind to her. Kyra was touched.

When Ruby ran out of the kitchen, Dax picked up his beer, noticed Kyra looking at him, and said, "What's that look?"

"I think you like her," Kyra said.

"Do not," he said and drank more beer. "Where's the pizza?"

She smiled and picked up her wallet. "I think I hear him now." She walked out to meet the delivery guy.

They sat around her small kitchen table, eating pizza, watching Ruby pile her toppings onto the side of her plate, then pull the cheese off her slice. She did more talking than eating in spite of Kyra's best efforts to get her to be quiet and eat. But Ruby's exuberance was very hard to tame. It was as if they'd never had company . . .

Oh, right. They rarely had company.

Ruby was eager to explain to Dax that she was going to be in first grade, and that Taleesha, her friend, who had *three* ponytails, would be in first grade, too. But maybe not in her class. She had not yet learned geography would keep Taleesha from attending her school in East Beach. "That's how they do it in first grade," Ruby explained.

"I know how it works," Dax said and helped himself to another slice.

"Have you ever been in first grade?" Ruby asked, seemingly impressed by this.

"Nope. Just heard about it." Dax took a bite.

Kyra laughed. She was enjoying this evening, which in some ways was a bit astounding. She hadn't expected this from Supergrump, but the way Dax treated Ruby filled her heart with happiness—those two had clearly connected on some level. Kyra was beginning to think that maybe the three of them could be friends after all. She didn't mind that—she imagined an easy friendship between neighbors. Friday nights they'd share a beer and pizza. Maybe Sunday she'd be out washing her car and he'd come over to chat. Ruby could play with the dog, and they could watch the sunset. Something normal like that.

Kyra liked the idea of normal.

When the pizza had been devoured, mostly by Dax, it was time for Ruby to go to bed. If Ruby's own mother had had her fill of the constant chatter, she could imagine that Dax was more than done with it.

Kyra helped Ruby put on some clean pajamas, then set her up with some coloring books and her favorite stuffed animals. "I didn't brush my teeth," Ruby said.

"I know. I'll be back. But right now, I need you to stay here while I talk to Mr. Bishop."

Ruby looked at her coloring book. She began to flutter her fingers, sort of tapping them together, as if she couldn't decide which color to start with.

"Ruby? Did you hear me? Stay in your room."

Ruby didn't answer.

Kyra clucked her tongue. "I'm speaking to you, Ruby Ellen."

Ruby dropped her hand and looked at the window. "I didn't brush my teeth."

"I know. I just told you I'll be back, but I need to talk to Mr. Bishop first. *Stay here.*"

"Okay, Mommy," she said and reached for an orange crayon.

Kyra returned to the kitchen and discovered Dax had cleaned up the pizza mess and collected the beer bottles. "You didn't have to do that," she said.

"I kind of did," he said with a lazy smile. "Thanks for the pizza. That saves me from having to heat a frozen dinner."

He looked like he was going to leave, and Kyra wasn't ready for him to go yet. "Thank *you,*" she said.

Dax held up a hand. "You have to stop thanking me. You've said it, I get it, but you're saying it too much."

"I can never say it enough, not after what you did today. Will you at least stay for one more beer? It's so nice tonight. We could sit on the porch if you like."

He pondered the invitation. "Sure," he said.

Kyra smiled with that tiny rattle of giddiness in her again. "Just give me one minute, will you? I'm going to get Ruby's teeth brushed and put her to bed."

He nodded; Kyra practically dashed to Ruby's room. Ruby had colored half a page orange and had just started in on green. She protested when Kyra pulled her up to brush her teeth and wash her face, but she was tired and came along willingly, then sank into her bed and closed her eyes without complaint.

Kyra returned to the kitchen. Dax had already gone outside. She got the beers—her last two, she noticed, and mentally calculated when she could go for groceries again—and went out to join him. She pulled her two folding chairs up to the railing, and they sat and propped their feet on it, both of them staring out at the lake and the kaleidoscope of color the setting sun cast on the surface.

Neither of them spoke at first, but after several moments, Kyra couldn't stand the empty air around them. "So," she said very casually, "what's your story, Dax Bishop?"

"Haven't got one."

She laughed. "Everyone has a story. Like, do you have any siblings? Where are your parents?"

"I have a brother," he said. "He's in the army and stationed in Germany right now. My parents are in Phoenix. What about you?" he asked.

"It's just me and my dad," she said. "My mom died when I was twelve."

"Wow, that sucks," he said. "Car wreck?"

"Brain tumor," Kyra said. "Cancer."

He winced. "I'm really sorry, Kyra."

She smiled softly. "Thanks. It's been a really long time now, but I still miss her so much."

"Where is Grandpa?" he asked.

"Florida," she said on a sigh. "Tampa area."

Dax took a good drink of his beer, then began to peel the label. "Mind if I ask when your husband died?"

"My what?"

He looked up from his work on the label. "Your husband. Maybe I read too much into Ruby's story of a car wreck and amputated legs and how he now rides a skateboard to train big cats in Africa, but I figured the car wreck might have been real."

Kyra didn't know whether to laugh or cry. Laugh, apparently, as she suddenly had to bite one down. In fact, she doubled over trying not to guffaw.

Dax grinned. "It's the skateboard, isn't it?"

"My daughter has a very vivid imagination," Kyra said and couldn't help the laugh that escaped her. "Her father is very much alive. Or at least according to Facebook, he is."

Dax looked surprised. He shook his head. "For the record, I didn't buy the cat training."

Kyra laughed.

"You're divorced?"

"No, not divorced," Kyra said. She always hated this part when the subject of Ruby's father came up. "I've never been married. It was one of those things—I met her father at a destination wedding in Mexico. I knew him for a total of like, three days."

Dax's expression remained impassive, but nevertheless Kyra could feel herself coloring. "What can I say? It was a superfun weekend," she said, trying to sound light and airy. "But . . . he failed to mention he was engaged."

"Yikes," Dax said and turned his gaze to the lake.

"It's embarrassing," she admitted. "But, you know . . . life happens."

"It sure does," Dax agreed. "I take it he's not involved with Ruby?"

"Nope." Kyra drank more beer.

"Does she know he exists?"

"She knows about him," Kyra said. "It's hard to explain to a child, you know? I've told her that sometimes daddies don't live with their kids for whatever reason. But of course it's hard for her to understand, and I guess she fills in the gaps." Kyra looked away from him, remembering the times Ruby had asked her pointedly about her father. *Can he come visit? Does he know my name?* She'd tried to be as truthful as she could, but she guessed Ruby would always have questions. When she was older, maybe she'd understand.

And then again, maybe not.

"Can we please talk about you again?" she asked, feeling uncomfortable with the topic. "So you've been in the army, and you are a furniture maker."

"I was a paramedic in there, too," he said.

"Really! Where was that?"

"Teaneck."

Kyra didn't really know where that was, other than somewhere near New York. "How'd you end up in Teaneck?"

He put down his beer bottle on the porch and looked at Kyra. "My wife wanted to move to the area."

"Oh," she said. "A wife."

"Ex-wife."

"How long?"

"That I've been divorced? Or that I was married?"

"Both."

He glanced down. "Both a while."

He obviously didn't want to talk about it, and Kyra found the silence between them a little awkward. She could talk about Josh, offer him up in the spirit of situations gone bad. But the truth was that it had taken her several years before she could explain the situation without feeling a little sick, and now she just felt ashamed.

Dax's phone beeped. He fished it out of his pocket and looked at it. "Great," he muttered and shifted his gaze to Kyra. "I need to go."

Kyra wondered if that was Pretty Girl.

He stood up. She did, too.

He paused and looked at his phone. "Maybe I should get your number in case . . . in case something comes up again," he said.

"Good idea," she said and put out her hand for his phone. He tapped into his contacts list and handed the device to her. She typed *Kyra the Neighbor* and entered her number before handing it back to him.

He stuffed the phone in his pocket. "Thank for the pizza and the beer," he said. He smiled a little and shoved his hands into his pockets.

"You're more than welcome. Thank you—"

"No more thank-yous, remember?" He started down the steps.

Kyra smiled, far too brightly. "Thanks for the car—oops, I forgot. Oh geez, wait, Dax!" she said suddenly. "I forgot to pay you." She darted inside to her purse, and when she returned to the porch, Dax had gone down to her car. Kyra joined him there and held up the money. He moved as if to take it from her, but Kyra yanked her hand back. "Before I hand this over, I'm going to need some proof that the car is working."

"I like that," Dax said, nodding. "Always make sure you got what you paid for." He opened the car door, got in, turned the ignition, and it started right away without a single grind. Frankly, it purred.

Kyra gasped with delight. "It's like Christmas," she said. "A new car."

He shut down the car, got out, closed the door, and held up her keys. "That put you back two seventy-five," he said.

Kyra counted out the cash and handed it to him. He folded the bills and put them in his pocket. Kyra put her hands on her keys, but he didn't let go—his thunder-blue eyes locked on hers. One corner of his mouth tipped up in a droll smile. Kyra could feel things stirring in her, swirling around. Lustful, yearning things. She could feel a little heat tingling under her skin and her own smile slowly emerging.

Dax let go of the keys and brushed her hair from her face. "You're looking at me in that hungry way again."

"Am I?"

He nodded and caressed her cheek with a knuckle.

"Well, don't worry. I'm not going to kiss you."

"Yeah, well," he said, shrugging before he slipped his hand to her nape, "I'm going to kiss you."

His lips softly met hers. His tongue moved along the seam of her lips, then slipped into her mouth. It was a simple kiss, but it was so erotic to Kyra that she had to grab his waist to keep from flittering away.

He caught her chin in one hand and angled her head so he could deepen the kiss, and a sizzle began to creep through Kyra's body. That kiss was a shock wave of desire, electric and pulse-pounding, and her body was revving up, ready to take off.

He pushed her up against the car and slid his leg between hers, pressing against her. Kyra made a sound in the back of her throat that was really a desperate cry for sexual release. She was kissing him like she'd never been aroused in her life until now. Her skin was flush, and the air was slipping out of her, making her feel heady. She was rising up on her tiptoes to return his kiss with all that want, holding his head in her hands now. She forgot that she'd promised she wouldn't kiss him, forgot that he was dating someone else, forgot that she had only a half hour ago imagined how their neighborly friendship might unfold . . . but not like this.

There was *nothing* like this, and boy oh boy, she was going to lose her mind.

Dax tasted and felt so damn good, and she was imagining how he would feel inside of her, and she was certain this was going to lead to some of the best sex of her life—

And then Dax lifted his head. He ran his thumb over her lip, then her cheek.

She sucked in air, trying not to pant. "That . . . was much better than last night," Kyra said. "I mean, if you're judging kissing on a technical scale."

"Agreed."

"So . . ." she said, still staring into his eyes, "is this a thing?"

Dax chuckled. "Nope." He tucked her hair behind her ear.

"I didn't think so," Kyra said. It was crazy how much she hoped it would be the start of a thing. It was like a spigot had been turned on in her, spewing desire and wanting this guy to stick around. Not just tonight, but for . . . longer. Days, maybe. Weeks and months. Kyra really liked Dax. *Really* liked him. She adored how he treated Ruby with respect and affection. She admired how he was a no-nonsense but tender kind of guy. And she damn sure liked the way he kissed. She would probably make herself raving mad thinking about how much she'd like whatever else he wanted to do with her.

Dax softly tugged on her earlobe, then dropped his hand and started across the yard. "Don't forget to fire that old woman," he called over his shoulder.

"Yep," she said dreamily, but she was certain he didn't hear her.

She was going to do something about that old woman, but first she was going to have a bubble bath and imagine all the places that kiss might have gone while she soaked.

Chapter Eleven

He had to stop kissing that girl, that's all there was to it. Now, because he'd kissed her, and he'd kept thinking about kissing her, and he'd been off his game, Dax had managed to get himself stuck hosting a small barbecue. He'd rather guide a canoe over Niagara Falls, but that's what happened when a woman distracted a man—he said and did dumb things.

It happened the day after that kiss. He was up early. He hadn't slept well because he'd been thinking about it all night. And he had some furniture to deliver that morning and was worried the varnish hadn't dried.

He stopped in at the Green Bean to devour a bear claw and read the morning paper, starting with page one and then concluding with the MLB box scores, none of which he retained thanks to Kyra and her lips, then headed over to John Beverly Home Interiors.

He pulled around to the back just as Wallace was arriving at work in his red roadster. Wallace was wearing bright yellow pants today with a pink polo shirt, a belt with pineapples dancing across it, and boat shoes. It was a little blinding.

Wallace lowered his mirrored Ray-Bans to look at Dax. "What a treat for my morning eyes," he said. "Wouldn't I like to wake up to *you* every morning."

"Yeah, well, the feeling is not mutual," Dax said.

"So *cruel*," Wallace said, smiling. "What'd you bring me, handsome?"

"A dresser," Dax said. He opened the gate of his pickup and brought it down, putting the drawers in so Wallace could inspect it.

"Beautiful," Wallace said as he ran his hand over the top.

Not only had Dax cut a top with wavy edges, he'd distressed the whole piece to give it a rustic look. People up here liked that look in their lake houses. As if they'd salvaged their furniture from pioneers.

"It looks like a piece right out of *Alice in Wonderland*. Or *The Wild Wild West*," Wallace said.

"Huh," Dax said, looking at the piece again.

"Either way, I adore it, as usual," Wallace said and sighed longingly as he glanced at Dax again. "To think of all that talent bound up in the body of one tight T-shirt. Come in, let me write a check."

As Wallace retreated to the office to cut the check, Dax examined a vase with some paper hydrangeas, his thoughts drifting back to last night. He was so distracted by those thoughts, so caught up in remembering how her mouth had felt against his, and her body had felt against his, and how much he'd liked it, that he missed the approach of Janet and didn't see her until she popped up right in front of him. *"Well?"* she demanded. "How was your date?"

The kiss business was bad—Dax had forgotten all about Heather.

When he didn't answer immediately and effusively, Janet punched him in the arm. "Come on, Dax—how'd you like Heather?"

"She was nice," Dax said. Maybe he should ask Wallace to start mailing his checks to him so he wouldn't have to come in at all.

"She really liked *you*," Janet said, waggling her eyebrows at him. "She said she was hoping you'd go with her to this new jazz club in Black Springs Saturday. I told her I was sure you're free."

"Why would you say that, Janet?" he asked, annoyed.

"Because I'm sure you are," she said with an indifferent shrug.

"Well, I'm not."

"Why not?" Janet demanded.

Why had he ever let himself be talked into this mess? "I've got a thing Saturday."

Janet stared. And then she laughed. "You don't have a *thing*. Come on, Dax, don't make me laugh. You don't have anything but that dog. You shouldn't be so shy. You have to get out there and meet people—"

"I'm having a barbecue, that's why," he blurted before Janet could browbeat him into a jazz club.

Janet gasped. And then she laughed harder.

"What is so funny?" Beverly McCauley Sanders, the owner of the shop, came in through the front door as Janet was practically writhing on the floor in a skirt that was just too short.

"Dax is hosting a barbecue!" Janet wailed.

"What?" Wallace screeched as he came out of the office with a check.

This was Dax's own damn fault for having opened his mouth. "What's the big deal?" he asked irritably. "I've got new neighbors. I'm being . . . neighborly."

The three John Beverly employees looked at each other. And then howled again.

"What?" Dax demanded irritably.

"Don't mind them," Bev said soothingly as she fought to contain a huge smile. "Where are you having this barbecue, sugar?"

"At my place."

"In your hobbit hovel?" Wallace squealed with delight.

"It's not a *hovel*, it's cozy. And it's a small barbecue," Dax said defensively. "Just some folks living near me."

"You know what?" Bev asked. "John and I will be at my mom's on Saturday. We'll come by, too." Bev's mom and dad were Mr. and Mrs. McCauley, who, he'd also forgotten, would be included in the general *folks living near me*. Dax should have thought of that complication, but no, he'd turned his head to mush by kissing a very attractive woman.

"We'll all come by!" Janet said.

Dax began to panic. "That's not what I had in mind."

"It's not a big deal, sweetie," Bev said, waving her ring-heavy fingers at him. "Just throw some more dogs on the grill. I'll bring my famous potato salad."

"It's not famous," Wallace said. "It's right out of Betty Crocker."

"I don't have a grill," Dax said.

Wallace gasped. "What is this, some sort of Boy Scout cookout? Hot dogs on *sticks*?" He pressed a hand to his throat.

"It's a small group," Dax said.

"Darling, you still have to have a grill," Wallace said. "I have a tabletop grill. I'll bring it. But I am *not* eating hot dogs. Do you know how processed they are? We need turkey burgers."

"I can bring turkey burgers," Janet said.

"This is really not what I had in mind," Dax said again, sounding pretty hopeless even to himself.

"Don't you worry about it," Bev said and gave him a pat to his cheek. "It's going to be fine. It's a barbecue, not brain surgery. Shall we say four?"

"Sounds perfect," Janet said.

"Great! Now, let's get to work!" Bev said and whirled around, her silky tunic swirling with her.

That's how Dax was stuck with planning a barbecue for Saturday. He hadn't actually grilled anything in years, and he hadn't exactly had people over in at least as long. This was going to take some planning. He'd have to make a list or something. He'd have to get things he'd never use again, like pickle relish and charcoal.

He returned to Number Two and sat in his truck, thinking about this damn barbecue and the predicament he'd gotten himself into. But he had to hand it to himself—he'd given himself the perfect excuse to see Kyra again.

The jury was out as to whether this captivation was a good idea or not. Dax didn't feel like his heart had quite healed from the split with

Ashley. He didn't feel like he had the strength to go through it all again. But there was something about that woman with the dark hair and the nutty little kid that had gotten under his skin. So Dax screwed up his courage, pulled out his phone, and scrolled through his contacts. There it was: *Kyra the Neighbor*.

He texted, Having a barbecue Saturday. Small group. You and coconut free? He stared at the text, wondered if he ought to edit it, and chewed on that a moment until he got impatient with himself. Once a guy started editing texts, that was it—he was hooked. It had been a couple of kisses, goddammit, not a date. This wasn't a life decision, this wasn't a commitment. It was a damn barbecue. He punched Send.

He waited.

And waited.

Approximately two hours after he'd sent the original text, his phone pinged. He pulled it out of his pocket. Yes, she wrote. Thanks! We'll bring cookies.

Dax smiled. Otto's tail began to thump. He looked at the dog staring up at him from his sprawl across the kitchen floor. "What are you looking at?" Dax demanded, and went back to work designing a new hutch.

Chapter Twelve

It figured that the one time Dax would host a barbecue, it would rain. It rained all day, on again, off again, and kept him guessing whether he'd have to cram five people into Number Two.

It felt a little as if God was messing with him.

At three o'clock, miraculously, there was a bit of sunshine over the lake and a break in the clouds. Maybe God had had his chuckles for the day and was going to cut Dax a break.

Dax went outside to make a picnic table. He spaced three sawhorses, then laid a couple of planks of pine across them and nailed those together.

He was unrolling the felt when he heard a small coconut shout, "*Hey!* What are you doing?"

He looked over his shoulder; she was hanging upside down on the fence.

"What are you doing?" she shouted again.

She must have thought he was deaf, because she was always repeating her questions in a very loud voice. "Making a table," he said. "Does your mom know you're out here?"

"No. I'm not supposed to get off the porch."

There was no logic in that little red head. "Go ask her if you can come over and help me. Then get over here and help me."

"Okay!" Ruby flipped off the fence and darted off.

She was back a few minutes later, climbing over the fence, tumbling down the other side, then racing across the lawn in her light-up boots, her ponytail waving like a flag behind her.

"Mommy said I could come," she said breathlessly. "She's putting makeup on her face and it's taking a *really* long time."

"Put your hand right there and hold this down and don't move," he said, pointing to the felt at one corner of his makeshift table.

Ruby did as he told her so Dax could staple the felt. "I have a new dress. See? It's yellow."

"Yeah, I see. Stop talking and hold this corner down," he instructed her.

Ruby didn't stop talking, of course not. She asked why he was using felt. She asked if they could cover the sawhorses with it. She asked if Otto knew how to shake hands because her friend Taleesha's dog shook hands, and what did barbecue mean.

Dax told her if she didn't stop talking he was going to cover her and Otto in felt and turned back to his task. Otto whimpered. "Not you, too," he said, and glanced around to see what the fool dog was looking at now.

The fool dog was looking at Ruby, his tail swishing anxiously. Ruby's eyes had taken on a glassy look, and her fingers were moving in that strange, fluttering way Dax had noticed before.

"Hey, kid," he said and snapped his fingers before her face.

Ruby didn't respond.

Dax sank down onto his haunches before her. He put his hand on her shoulder. "Ruby," he said.

She blinked rapidly and her eyes refocused on him.

"Are you feeling okay?" he asked.

"Uh-huh."

"Did anything just happen?"

She nodded.

"What happened?"

"Otto licked my hand," she said.

Otto was licking her hand at that very moment.

"I guess that makes you a lollipop," Dax said.

Ruby giggled. "I'm not a *lollipop*," she informed Otto as she petted his head.

He'd noticed the petit mal seizures in Ruby a few times now. It didn't concern him, exactly, as he knew from his training that it wasn't unusual for some young children to have tiny epileptic episodes, otherwise known as absence seizures. Most children outgrew them in adolescence, and most were not harmful. Generally the child wasn't even aware that it had happened—just like Ruby.

Nevertheless, while he supposed Kyra knew, he thought he ought to mention it to her just in case. If for some reason she didn't know what was happening to Ruby, she needed to have the kid checked out on the slim chance it was related to something else.

Dax finished covering the felt with a plastic tablecloth he'd picked up at Eckland's. At a quarter to four o'clock, which Bev had designated as the hour of his barbecue, the skies began to darken. Dax sent Ruby home to clean up. He went inside to change his clothes. He'd pulled on some clean jeans and a crisp, blue-collared shirt when the skies opened up.

"Freaking fabulous," he muttered.

At five after four, the first car arrived in his drive—it was a Mercedes, and four doors swung open, and four people dashed to his front porch. Janet, Wallace, Wallace's significant other, Curtis, and . . .

Jesus, it was Heather.

Dax was going to kill someone. He thought he'd start with Janet and then move on to Wallace. Maybe include Curtis just for being associated with Wallace.

At the same time he was opening the door to those four, glaring at Janet, frowning at Wallace, greeting Curtis and Heather with a thin smile—he wasn't a complete hermit—he heard a "Yoo-hoo" from his back door. In walked John and Bev Sanders along with Mr. and Mrs. McCauley and a toddler he'd seen at the McCauley house on occasion. Otto was beside himself with glee, barking and jumping and wiggling around like he'd never met people before this very moment.

The child, as it turned out, was the McCauleys' great-grandson, Ethan. They all crowded into the front room, chattering loudly about the weather, and the beans Mrs. McCauley had brought with her, and how Mr. McCauley was shocked—*shocked*—that Dax was hosting a barbecue, but had invited some of the new renters all the same, and John said that Dax's good table saw was taking up too much space, and with Wallace's direction, he and Mr. McCauley began to maneuver the thing out onto the porch. As they spilled out on the porch to shove it into the corner, Kyra and Ruby appeared, dashing across the lawn. Kyra was holding a cardboard box over her head and a plate in her hand. Ruby had on a hat.

They bounced up the steps, where Kyra set the box down, then shook out her long, dark hair. "Hey!" she said cheerfully. "Great day for a barbecue, huh?"

She'd spruced up for his barbecue. She was wearing makeup that made her eyes leap out of her head, and had donned a summer halter dress that showed off her fantastic legs. She was equal parts sexy and cute . . . maybe more sexy than cute. Okay, so sexy that Dax was having trouble keeping an eye on his prized table saw.

She smiled as if she was slightly concerned and slightly amused, and Dax realized he was staring at her. "Is that your idea of an umbrella?" he asked, averting his gaze to the box.

She laughed. "Poor girl's umbrella."

"Mommy, there's a baby in there," Ruby said, peering through the screen door.

"Really?"

"There's enough people in there to field two soccer teams," Dax muttered.

"Dax, darling, are you going to introduce us?" Wallace had appeared at Dax's elbow and was eyeing Kyra with great interest.

"Can I go inside, Mommy?" Ruby asked.

"Just a minute, pumpkin," Kyra said, and to Wallace, she smiled, juggled her plate of cookies—God help them all—and held out her hand. "Kyra Kokinos."

"Wallace Pogue." He said it as if he were the grand duke of East Beach, and took her hand and bowed over it. "I'm what you might call Dax's best friend."

"I would not call you that," Dax said flatly.

"His love interest, then."

"I definitely wouldn't call you *that*, either," Dax said, a little more firmly.

"I'm a little surprised Dax would have a best friend or a love interest," Kyra said, and winked at Dax as Ruby grabbed her hand and tugged on it.

"I want to go inside, Mommy."

"Is it okay with you if I put these in the kitchen?" Kyra asked, waving the plate under his nose.

He thought maybe he ought to ask her to leave the cookies on the porch in case a biohazard team had to be called, but said, "Sure."

He watched her walk inside, Wallace gallantly holding the door open for her and crowding in after her. Dax made sure his table saw was unhurt, then followed the others.

Wallace was making all the introductions when Dax stepped into a crowded living room. Janet and Bev had already closed in on Kyra like a pair of vultures and were sizing up the juicy parts as if they meant to feast later.

"Hey!" Heather said, sidling up to him. She rose up on her tiptoes and surprised the hell out of him by pecking him on the cheek. "Hope you don't mind that I tagged along with Janet," she said. "When she asked if I'd come, she *swore* to me that you would be okay with it. I probably should have texted you to ask."

She probably should have, because Dax wasn't okay with any of it. However, it was a little late to complain about it. "Don't give it another thought," he said. "Glad you could make it."

She beamed. Maybe he shouldn't have said that.

"Can I help you with anything?" she asked.

"Ah . . . no, thanks," he said, distracted again—Wallace was chatting Kyra up in a manner that smelled like trouble. "It's only hot dogs. Wallace!" he said. "Did you bring that grill?"

Wallace very deliberately turned away from Kyra. "Yes, I did, sweet cheeks, but if you haven't noticed, it's raining."

"We can put it in the oven!" Janet announced as if she were living there, too.

"Just give it a minute," Dax said. "It'll clear out."

"Weather station says rain all night," Mr. McCauley said. "I told Sue that we ought to bring you all up to the house, but she said it was your party, not hers."

"I'll just put these burgers in the fridge," Janet announced. "We'll give Dax's theory a chance to play out, and if it doesn't stop raining, we'll put them in the oven."

Dax didn't know where to start—with the fact that it wasn't Janet's place to decide? Or that his fridge was so full of hot dogs there might be an issue? He didn't want Janet rearranging things after he'd spent twenty minutes shoving everything into it. He decided to go with the more practical problem of fridge space and stepped forward before Janet could take over his kitchen. "I got this," he said and took the platter of burgers from her and went into the kitchen.

Ruby and Ethan and Otto were under the table. Ruby was explaining to the toddler that she'd trained Otto to shake. The only contribution to Otto's education that Ruby could possibly claim was to have helped hone his begging skills.

"Okay, don't be mad," Janet said, startling him—Dax hadn't heard her come in. "But Heather had nothing to do, and I couldn't stand the thought of her home alone while we were all over here having fun." She opened his fridge. "She made a sheet cake. Isn't that nice? She's a really good baker. I think you should turn on the oven and let it warm up."

"What are you doing?" Dax asked.

"Helping," Janet said, and as she leaned into his fridge, Bev and Heather squeezed into the kitchen.

Janet suddenly squealed. She came out of the fridge with his platter of hot dogs and held them out before her as if offering them to the hot dog gods and said, "Are you *kidding*?"

"No. Stand aside."

"You must have fifty hot dogs here, Dax!"

"So?" He didn't care that they were processed meats and would offend everyone. They were easy. And they were good. He dared anyone to disagree with that.

"Do you think we'll all eat five hot dogs?"

"I want five hot dogs!" Ruby shouted, sticking her head out from beneath the table.

"Okay, that's it," Dax said. "Everyone out. I've got work to do, and I've got this. Janet, put down the dogs and back away. Beverly and Heather, it would be great if you could step back into the living room. And you three," he said, bending over to peer under the table, "go into the back bedroom to play. You know where it is, Coconut. Lead the way. Skedaddle. Get out of here."

"Otto, too?" Ruby asked, climbing out from underneath the table.

"Otto, too," Dax said and whistled. Otto hopped out from underneath the table and sauntered in and around the many legs in the kitchen and into the crowded living area, where Dax could hear Wallace's voice rising above the others'.

"All right, the rest of you," Dax said, pointing at the door before grabbing the platter of hot dogs.

Ruby ran, shouting at Ethan to follow her, which the kid did, toddling along as fast as he could. Bev and Janet were reluctant to leave but departed with a lot of grousing and *just trying to help*s. Dax was so annoyed with everything that he failed to notice Heather had not heeded his direction and was still in the kitchen. Now she, too, was looking in the fridge. "I think we can get all of it in there," she said.

"I've got it."

"You must be used to doing things on your own. But there's nothing wrong with accepting a helping hand, you know." Her smile twinkled at him.

He was not going to win this battle, he could see. "Fine. Put my dogs back," he said and thrust the platter at her.

Heather laughed too loud and too long as she took the platter from him. She bent over to slide it into the fridge, then straightened up. "What about the burgers?"

Dax stepped up beside her to study the contents of his small refrigerator. He was calculating the number of items that would have to be moved when Heather turned and put herself directly between him and the shelves. Which meant she was standing very close to him, her head tilted back, her lips pursed in a smile of amusement.

"Tell me the truth, Dax. Is it jazz? Or is it me?"

"Pardon?"

"I mean, which is it that you don't like? Jazz? Or me?" Her smile deepened with the certainty that it couldn't possibly be her. Her gaze slipped to his mouth, like she wanted him to kiss her.

He did not want to kiss her, didn't want any part of that. He was already in enough of a bind from kissing, and that was kissing he'd wanted to do. "I didn't say that."

"Great! Then maybe we can plan a date, just the two of us. How about Wednesday night?"

"Ah . . ." She'd caught him off guard, and Dax had to think about how best to say it—

"Is that a yes?" she purred.

"Hello?"

Kyra's voice drifted over the top of the open fridge door, which was blocking his view of her.

"Yes?" he said quickly, and stepped back from Heather.

Kyra bent her head around the fridge, her eyes darting with surprise between him and Heather. "Oh! Hi," she said hesitantly. "I hope I'm not interrupting."

"Nope," Dax said instantly.

"A little," Heather said pleasantly and poked him in the ribs. "He's a little shy," she said.

"Oh. Hmm," Kyra said and winced a little. "I, ah . . . I was going to put these down somewhere, but I don't see . . ." She glanced around the kitchen, still holding the plate of lethal cookies.

Heather stepped around Dax, her hand trailing along his waist as she moved. "I can help you. What have you got there?"

"Cookies. My daughter and I made them."

"That's so *sweet*," Heather said. "She's such a cutie. You know, you look really familiar," Heather said as she took the cookies from Kyra. "Have we met?"

"Ah . . . I waited on you and Dax at the Lakeside Bistro."

Heather blinked. *"Oh,"* she said. "You sure did, didn't you? I didn't know that you knew Dax."

"Oh, I . . . not really," Kyra said, without looking at Dax. "I mean, we're neighbors, that's all. New neighbors. Very new."

"Huh," Heather said. She sounded, Dax thought, a little put off. "What's your name?"

"Kyra."

"Well, I'm Heather. We sure appreciate you bringing cookies."

Who was *we*? And why was Heather thanking Kyra? Why did everyone seem to think this was their house and their barbecue?

Heather put the cookies on the last empty bit of counter space and smiled a little coolly at Dax.

"What's happening in here?"

Now Wallace was popping in, Curtis crowding in behind him. "Have you decided what to do about this barbecue, Dax?" he asked. "Curtis and I are *starving*."

Curtis held up a bright blue insulated box. "What should I do with this? I hope you don't mind, Dax, but I brought some crudités."

"What?" Dax said absently, wondering where he was going to put that box.

"Crudités. It's raw vegetables—"

"I know what it is," Dax said gruffly. "I meant . . . *why*?"

"Why? Because I am watching my figure." Curtis sniffed. "I'm just going to arrange them on a platter and take it out there," he said, pointing to the living room. "Do you have a platter?"

"No."

"No?"

"I have a plate. Or a cutting board. You choose."

"Oh my," Curtis said, sharing a side eye with Wallace. "Well, I guess the cutting board will have to do." He slanted another look at Wallace. "I *told* you to bring the dish."

"That enormous platter that looks like a cabbage leaf? Look around you, Curtis—there is no *room*," Wallace said.

"Speaking of room, there isn't enough seating, either."

This opinion was offered by Janet, who had returned to the kitchen and was pushing in behind Wallace and Curtis. Dax felt cornered now, trapped against the sink next to Heather.

"I have some folding lawn chairs," Kyra offered. "I could run and get them."

"Perfect!" Janet said.

"That'd be great. Let's go," Dax said.

"You don't have to come—"

He cut Kyra off before she denied him an out. "You'll need help carrying them," he said and gave her a look that he hoped conveyed she was not to argue under any circumstance.

"Maybe Wallace could go," Heather suggested.

"Me?" Wallace exclaimed, flattening his palm against his chest.

"I'll do it," Dax said. "Come on." He began to bulldoze his way through the crowd, sort of hustling Kyra along ahead of him and trying not to ogle her butt as he did.

"You're going to get wet," Kyra warned him as they went out of the kitchen.

"It's not that bad," Dax said. To those in the living room, he announced, "We're going to get chairs."

"Chairs! Why didn't you say so?" Mr. McCauley asked and tugged absently on his very large ear. "I've got a shed full of folding chairs for the occasional wedding or what have you. I'll just go up and get a few."

"Stay right there," Dax said. "Kyra's cottage is closer."

"Well, hurry up, will you? My knee begins to ache if I stand too long," said John Sanders.

"For heaven's sake, John," Mrs. McCauley said. "I told you to sit on the couch."

Dax nudged Kyra to hurry it up. She dipped around John and Bev McCauley and made it to the front door. Dax was right behind her. He leaned around her for the door—catching the scent of her hair as he did—and yanked it open.

Kyra didn't go through the screen—she stopped in her tracks, and Dax plowed into her back. He guessed Kyra had come to a halt at the sight of the rain, which had turned into a full gully washer. He winced a little at the thought of dashing across to her cottage in that.

But then he saw the real reason for her halt—there were two elderly people standing on his porch in rain ponchos.

"Hello!" the woman said. She was holding a bowl of cantaloupe.

Dax was busy trying to work out who they were and didn't respond right away.

"Are you Dax?" the woman asked.

"I am."

"Well, thanks for inviting us! We're Sid and Mary Branson."

"Okay," he said.

"We just pulled into Number Six this morning," Sid Branson said. "Mr. McCauley told us you were having a welcome-the-neighbors barbecue tonight. Thanks so much for inviting us. We're going to be here for a few weeks before heading on down to Florida. We're just taking our time and seeing the country and meeting folk."

"I saw the family in Number Five getting things together," his wife added. "They ought to be here in a few minutes."

Dax looked at Kyra. She looked at him. He could tell she was trying very hard not to laugh. "I'm Kyra Kokinos," she said and pushed open the screen. "My daughter, Ruby, and I are in Number Three."

"Squeeze on in," Dax said. "You might want to stand out on the porch if you prefer to breathe. We're going to get some extra chairs."

Mary Branson brushed past him. "We brought cantaloupe!" she announced to everyone in the living room.

With the Bransons now taking up the last of the air in the living room, Kyra and Dax stood on the top steps of the porch and looked through the sheets of rain to Number Three.

Dax sighed. "I guess we—"

Kyra leapt off the porch and ran. And she was fast, too. Dax ran after her, catching her at the bottom of her steps and seizing her by the waist, dragging her up with him.

When they were under the covered porch, Kyra laughed. "Not that bad? Look at you! You look like you just crawled out of the lake."

"So do you." Her thin summer dress was clinging to her, and Dax had trouble tearing his gaze away from her figure.

Kyra glanced down. "Great. I just bought this dress," she groaned.

"It's nice," he said. "Really . . . nice."

"Thank you. You know what else is nice? Your girlfriend. Come in and I'll get you a towel."

"She's not my girlfriend," Dax said loudly as he followed her inside.

Kyra had disappeared into the hall. She reappeared a moment later with two pink towels and pushed one up against his chest. "She thinks she is," she said and let go. She wrapped the other towel around the ends of her hair as she walked into the kitchen.

"Well, she's not." He followed her.

"You don't have to try and convince me, Dax. You don't have to explain."

He frowned at her. He pointed a finger at her. "Stop that."

"Stop what?"

"Smiling," he warned her.

Her smug little smile only widened. "Am I smiling?"

"Like a fat cat." He moved closer and used his towel to dab some of the rain off her cheeks.

Now her smile was a grin. "I'm not going to stop smiling just because you say so."

"Will you at least stop talking about Heather?"

"I'm *not* talking about her. Why does the mention of her name make you so nervous, anyway?"

"You know what makes me nervous?" he asked as he dabbed the water from her shoulders. "*You.* I'm scared to death you're going to kiss me again."

"Big baby. You didn't seem to mind it when you kissed *me.* I thought you really *liked* it. In fact, you sort of—"

"God," he said and pulled her into his body and kissed her.

He didn't mean to go all-in, he really didn't. He didn't want to have all those confusing feelings and emotions come rushing at him the moment his lips touched hers, but he was gone before he even realized what was happening. Her lips were soft and wet and so damn arousing. He was hard almost instantaneously, and he pressed that against her like a caveman.

That should have been her signal to back away, to run, but Kyra's arms went around his neck, and she pulled his head down so she could kiss him back.

They engaged in a ferocious kiss, harder than the storm outside, harder than hickory wood. But it was weird, because it was a soft kiss, too, the kind that dissolved a man.

Dax grabbed Kyra's thighs and lifted her up, setting her on the kitchen table. He heard something crackle beneath her, heard something else hit the floor. He stood between her legs, pressing against her. He wasn't sure where he was going with all this, but he suddenly couldn't get enough of her. He was burning to touch her, and he slid his hand into the V-shaped neckline of her dress and filled it with her breast.

Kyra's kiss deepened. She was feeling this thing between them, too. Dax moved his hand to the hem of her wet dress and moved up, slipping his fingers beneath her panties. Holy shit, she was wet, and he was on his way to bursting with desire. He hadn't touched a woman in a very long time, and it made him slightly dizzy. He wanted to put her on her back on this table, logistics be damned, and pump into her like a madman. But he also wanted to hold her and kiss her ears and her nose and the hollow of her throat.

He settled for swirling his fingers around and over and in the folds of her sex, because Kyra was making tiny little sounds in the back of her throat, and if there was one thing other than being inside her that revved his engines, it was knowing that he was capable and adept, apparently, at giving her pleasure.

She squeezed her thighs around him and began to pant. She tore her mouth from his and dropped her head to his shoulder, gasping. Dax intensified his efforts and knew she was enjoying it when she bit the hell out of his shoulder in an attempt not to cry out.

"Oh my God, oh my *God*," she whimpered.

Dax tried not to puff up with pride. After all that had happened with Ashley, there had been a moment or two that he'd wondered if maybe he'd lost his touch, but clearly, he still knew how to rock it—

Kyra suddenly pushed him hard, and he staggered one step back. "What?" he asked, startled. In general, he didn't think women shoved men away if the man was rocking it.

"Are we crazy?" she said, still panting, and hopped down from the table.

He didn't see what that had to do with anything. "Jury's still out."

"I'm serious! You have a house full of company. My *daughter* is next door."

"Yeah, okay," he said, holding up his hands. He didn't feel crazy. He felt . . . he felt alive. He felt like a man again. He felt like he mattered, like he cared, like he could lift this little house up and twirl it on the tip of his finger. But he said, "Fair point. I get it. But . . ."

"But what?" she asked impatiently as she arranged her very luscious breasts in her very sexy dress. "This is insane."

Was it really so insane? Had he been out of touch with himself and his own desires and feelings for so long that he didn't know what was real anymore?

Kyra stalked the three feet to the back door, where he could see she'd jammed three aluminum lawn chairs between the fridge and the wall.

"But what if I didn't have company?" he asked, trying to feel her out. "What if your daughter was, say, with a babysitter? Not that woman who comes to watch your TV, but a legit babysitter. Would it be so insane?"

Kyra paused. She glanced at him from the corner of her eye. Her cheeks were enchantingly pink. She pulled a chair out and shoved it at him. "You shouldn't ask complicated questions when we're in a hurry."

Dax took the chair. "Is it complicated?" He meant it sincerely. He needed to know. He was confused, uncertain about what was happening inside him right now.

"Isn't it?" she asked as she yanked another chair free.

"I guess if you think sex is complicated," he said, thinking out loud. "I don't think it's complicated. I have a pretty good feel for it. I go right in and get down to business and everyone is happy."

Kyra blinked. Then she laughed. "That's so *sexy*, Dax."

"You have no idea," he said in all seriousness. Maybe that's all this was, an intense need to have sex. Maybe he was assigning feelings and ideas and desires to plain ol' lust. "I'm just saying, it's not so complicated."

She shoved the second chair at him with such force that he dropped the one he was holding.

"It's not complicated, huh? What about Heather?"

"Okay, that's it," Dax said and dropped the second chair so he could take Kyra's fool head between his hands and kiss her again. Only this time, he kissed her very slowly. He wanted to savor it, because damn it, her lips were so soft, and he wanted to make sure the name Heather never came out of her mouth again. He did not want to think of anyone or anything but Kyra.

She touched his face, quite tenderly, then slid her hand to his shoulder and pushed a little until he broke the kiss. "We have to get back."

"We're going back . . . in just a minute," he said and kissed her again.

She sighed, and she let him kiss her some more, and just when he was getting into it, when he was thinking of unzipping her dress and walking her into a bedroom, she pushed him back again. "Seriously, Dax. Ruby will wonder where I am."

"Fine," he said, disgruntled. Every muscle, every fiber, every vein was on the verge of erupting into a massive barrage of confetti, after which, he was certain, there'd be nothing left of him. What a rotten time to have a barbecue. Really, was there ever a *good* time to have a barbecue?

He picked up the chairs. Kyra tried to take one from him to carry, but Dax wouldn't let go, forcing her to look up at him. "You never answered my question. If it was just you and me, if this was any other time, would this be insane?"

"Honestly?"

Did he want honest? He wasn't sure about that. But he did want to know in a very bad way. "Yes." He steeled himself.

"If it was just you and me . . . I would rip your clothes off."

Dax blinked. He felt a peculiar little flutter inside that went straight to his groin and made him hard all over again. He smiled broadly. "Well, all right, then."

She poked him in his overinflated chest. "So is this a thing *now*?"

He didn't know what the hell was going on, if this was a thing or not, but it was good. "I don't know," he said. "But it's damn sure a 'moment.'"

"A 'moment.'" She nodded, as if she liked the sound of that. "I don't know what to think about you, Dax Bishop."

"Feeling is entirely mutual, Kyra Coconuts."

She smiled as she yanked one of the chairs free of his grip and walked to the front door. "Are you coming?" Dax realized he hadn't yet moved. Before he could answer, Kyra was already out the door.

When they reached the porch of his cottage, Wallace was standing there with Curtis, his arms folded across his chest. "What took you so long?" he demanded, eyeing them both suspiciously.

"The chairs were behind some boxes I haven't yet unpacked," Kyra said with a flick of her wrist. "Here you go," she said, shoving the chair at him.

Wallace studied her closely. "Hmm," he said and shifted his narrowed gaze to Dax.

"Dax?" Mrs. McCauley had stepped out onto the porch behind Wallace. "The natives are restless. Are you going to get the food started? Goodness, look at all the leaves the rain has brought down," she said and shook her head. "I'm as grateful as the next person for rain, but my husband tracks all those leaves across my front porch." She smiled at Kyra. "I'll just have to get my little helper on it. Ruby's very good at sweeping."

"She is?" Kyra said. "She's swept your porch?"

"And my kitchen," Mrs. McCauley said, laughing. "She comes around about once a day to see if I have any cookies. Sometimes I put her to work for that cookie."

Kyra looked genuinely surprised, and Dax wondered how she could be so surprised. The coconut wandered the neighborhood like a nomad.

"Oh, it's no problem," Mrs. McCauley said. "She's such a lovely little girl. I enjoy her company and her very vivid imagination, too. She claims her father is a policeman, and that *you* train monkeys."

"Her father is a policeman?" Wallace asked.

"No," Kyra said. "And I've never seen a real monkey that wasn't in a zoo. I'm so sorry, Mrs. McCauley. I didn't know she was visiting you every day."

The screen door opened with such force that it caught Kyra by the arm and forced her back into the table saw.

Heather emerged, holding a blue Solo cup. "There you are!" she said to Dax, ignoring Kyra entirely. "I was just telling Janet that I finally convinced you to come with me to hear some jazz in Black Springs."

"You did?" he asked, confused. "No, I—"

"Dax!" Heather said laughingly. "We were talking about it in the kitchen, remember?"

What he remembered was that the last thing she said was *is that a yes*, and then he'd answered *yes* to Kyra. Good Lord, he had to end this.

After what had happened between him and Kyra in the last twenty-four hours, Dax was not even mildly interested in Heather.

"Have you ever been, Wallace?" Heather asked, heading off any disagreement before Dax could make it.

"Are you talking about *this* Dax? In a jazz club?" Wallace asked, pointing at Dax.

"I didn't say—" Dax tried, but Heather was too quick for him.

"You should totally go," she said to Wallace. "They're a lot of fun."

"Maybe I will," Wallace said. "And bravo to you for getting the Lone Ranger out of the cottage." He beamed at Dax. "I mean, what else has he got to do?"

What he had to do was build a scaffold across two oak trees down by the lake so he could hang himself, that was what. He looked around for Kyra, but she had disappeared into the house with Mrs. McCauley.

He was more than a little annoyed that the "moment" he'd had with Kyra had been almost ruined for him by Heather and her damn jazz club.

How had he gone from living without the complication of women to suddenly being utterly bewildered by two of them for very different reasons?

Chapter Thirteen

Kyra was stuffed full. She usually didn't eat so much, but she'd been more than a little disconcerted by that unexpected, sexy, surprising interlude in her kitchen with Dax, for which she'd been totally on board until she remembered all the people waiting for them to return. And then she'd come back to Dax's cottage and reality had seeped in, and she didn't know what that interlude had meant, or what a "moment" was, and she'd never been the type of girl who could politely nibble her way through stress. Nope, she was an all-in kind of eater.

Now she could hardly breathe in a dress that had not been too tight only an hour or so before. No one showed any sign of going anywhere—they all seemed to enjoy a claustrophobic baked-burger-and-hot-dog barbecue—but Kyra decided it was time for her and Ruby to go.

"So soon?" Wallace asked.

"I'm working a brunch shift tomorrow," Kyra said. That was the polite excuse. The real excuse, besides being on the verge of exploding, was that she couldn't bear to watch Heather fawning over Dax another moment.

"I don't want to go yet," Ruby said.

Of course she didn't—the family from Number Five, the Caldwells, had a boy and a girl around Ruby's age, and Ruby had been leading the pack.

"It's getting late," Kyra said and put her arm around Ruby's shoulders.

Ruby wrenched out of Kyra's loose embrace. "I don't want to *go*," she said again, and the tears appeared, and Ruby sank to the floor like a sack of bricks, refusing to move. Kyra had to pull the punishment card in front of everyone, threatening a loss of privileges if she didn't get up and move. So Ruby sobbed and stomped her way to the door and made sure the screen door slammed behind her.

Kyra was as startled as she was embarrassed. That was a rare display of temper from her usually happy little girl. "She's tired," Kyra said.

"Sure, sure," Janet said sympathetically.

No one else said anything. Not even Diana Caldwell, who Kyra thought might have had her back in this. But then again, her kids weren't flailing around on the ground. Kyra said a quick good night and thanks, waved to Dax with a quick thanks! then rushed out of the cottage without saying anything more. Like *what's going on here*, or *are you kissing Heather like that, too*, or *what does that mean, a "moment,"* or any other of the many questions that had drifted through her head while she chowed down on some hot dogs.

It was also worth noting that Dax did not follow Kyra out to ask any of his own questions, either. She didn't know if that was because he didn't have any, or if he was so engrossed in yet another of Heather's stories that he failed to notice her departure.

Kyra was annoyed with herself. This was what she did every time a man showed any interest in her. She'd analyze it to death, and then she'd get that slightly desperate feeling that this was her last and only chance at love because she had a kid and a lousy job. She marched Ruby across the wet grass, reminding herself that regardless of what had happened in her kitchen, only two weeks ago she'd thought Dax was repugnant in a very handsome but grouchy way, and suddenly she was worried that he liked Heather better than her.

She was so caught up in her own cycle of thoughts that she didn't realize Ruby was still pouting until she ran into her room and slammed the door.

"Be that way," Kyra muttered. She glanced around her house and sighed at the clutter. She picked up some clothes and shoes and began to put things away while she let Ruby think about it, and about fifteen minutes after their arrival home, she knocked on Ruby's door with a stack of clothes in her arms.

Ruby opened the door. She was apparently over her mad, because she smiled and held up a picture. "These are my new friends. That's me," she said, pointing, "and that's the girl, and that's the boy. And the little boy. And Otto."

She'd drawn some very colorful blobs. "What are their names?" Kyra asked.

Ruby shrugged. "I don't remember."

"Okay, sweetie, it's time to get ready for bed," Kyra said and handed her some pajamas before moving to her little dresser to put away the rest of her clothes.

"So listen, Ruby," Kyra said as Ruby struggled out of her dress. "There's something I want to ask you. Mrs. McCauley said you visit her every day."

"Not every day, Mommy," Ruby said, and pulled on her pajama top.

"How many times?"

"A lot."

Kyra groaned to the ceiling. "You're not supposed to go up there, remember? I don't want you bothering people. They have jobs and things to do, and they don't have time to talk to little girls every day. I want you to stay home with Mrs. Miller so she can keep an eye on you."

"She sleeps a lot," Ruby offered. "More than you." She put on her pajama bottoms.

Jesus, it was even worse than Kyra thought. "Still. You need to stay at home with Mrs. Miller. I'll talk to her about sleeping so much." And a lot more. "Okay, let's get those teeth brushed," she said and ushered Ruby into the bathroom. Ruby hopped up on the booster stool before the sink and studied herself in the mirror.

Kyra turned to the door, then glanced over her shoulder at Ruby. She was still studying herself, her fingers fluttering in that weird way. "Brush your teeth and get in bed, and I'll read you a story."

She moved on, picked up another armload of crap—all hers this time—and carried it into her bedroom to put away.

When she finished, she went back to the bathroom, but Ruby was gone. Kyra found her on the living room floor with her Barbies. "Did you brush your teeth?"

"No."

Her daughter sounded matter-of-fact and not the least bit apologetic. "I told you to brush your teeth!" Kyra snapped. "I'm too tired for this tonight, Ruby. Get in there," she said, pointing in the direction of the bathroom, "and brush your teeth!"

"I didn't know I was supposed to!" Ruby cried, wounded by the admonishment.

"Because you don't *listen*."

"Yes, I do!" she said tearfully.

"Don't argue with me, just please brush your teeth."

Kyra waited until she heard the water running, then scooped up the Barbies and returned them to their place in Ruby's room.

When Ruby finished brushing her teeth, she ran into her room and flung herself into bed, rolling away from the door and putting her back to Kyra.

Kyra sighed. "Do you want a story?"

Ruby shook her head.

That was all right with Kyra. She didn't feel like reading some stupid bunny-on-a-mission story right now.

She turned out the light and retreated to the bathroom to brush her own teeth. When she'd finished her nightly routine, she flopped onto her bed.

Her thoughts were immediately flooded with that kiss. *That damn kiss* . . . She felt so sex deprived. The want of it was eating her brain right now, feasting on all her common sense. She even considered taking Dax up on his really ridiculous offer—what was it he said? That he got in and got the job done, something like that, something so completely unappealing that Kyra had to smile. She should have been offended, but she wasn't. At this moment, getting the job done didn't sound so bad . . .

Yeah, and then what? What happened after their mutual itch was scratched? Would it be weird between them? Would they go back to being neighbors? Would it be a friends-with-benefits thing or something more? What did she want it to be? Did she want more? She liked Dax, she liked him a lot, but she was juggling so many things right now. Did she want to juggle a relationship, too? Or was this a physical thing with a lot of gratitude for his help piled on top?

She sighed and rubbed her belly. She was starting to feel a little queasy and rolled onto her side and drifted to sleep with a mountain of hot dogs slipping into her last thoughts.

♦ ♦ ♦

The next morning, Mrs. Miller walked into the house and deposited her lunch bag and purse on the kitchen table as if nothing had happened the last time she was here.

Kyra was ready for her. "Good morning."

"Morning."

"I heard about the lake," Kyra said. "Were you going to tell me?"

"Tell you what? That the kid fell in?"

Kyra was shocked the woman would belittle what had happened. "She was unsupervised and she could have drowned!" she said angrily. "She's a little girl, Mrs. Miller. I am paying you to watch her."

Mrs. Miller's expression turned hard and cold. "Just what are you saying, Carrie?"

"It's *Kyra*. I'm saying that you're not supervising her, and she almost drowned—"

"She didn't almost *drown*," she snapped. "The water where she fell in might have come up to her knees."

Kyra gaped at her. Did Ruby have to drown for her to be alarmed by it? Did she think it was okay that a kid just ran wild over the neighborhood? "That's not all. I saw Mrs. McCauley, too," Kyra said.

"Who?"

"Mrs. McCauley, my landlord. She lives in the big house on the hill," Kyra said, pointing in the direction of the McCauley house.

Mrs. Miller shrugged. "What about her?"

"She said Ruby comes up there almost every day. *Alone.*"

Kyra didn't know what she expected—a denial, perhaps—but Mrs. Miller's expression didn't change at all when she said, "It's not every day. And so what if it is? Those people like it."

"I can't believe you," Kyra said angrily. "You act as if there is nothing wrong with letting Ruby do what she wants! I'm *paying* you to keep an eye on her. She's only six. She could get hurt, or stolen—anything could happen."

Mrs. Miller snorted. "You don't like it? Hire another babysitter."

Oh, she was going to hire another babysitter, all right. And she should have done it right then, too, just fired her on the spot . . . but Kyra really needed to work the brunch shift. "I'm asking you respectfully," she said, shaking now.

Mrs. Miller opened her lunch bag and took out a cinnamon roll. "Asked and noted," she said and sat her lazy ass down on one of Kyra's kitchen chairs.

Kyra stormed out of her cottage, muttering to herself.

She was racked with guilt on the drive to work. How could she leave her daughter with that woman for even one more day? But how could she not? She had to work, she had to pay rent, buy food, and she and Ruby needed shoes. She had to get something else lined up, but she needed time to do it. It wasn't as if affordable child care was falling out of the sky.

She'd talk to Deenie, see if she could maybe watch her tomorrow while Kyra sought out child care.

Kyra's tumble down the path of guilt didn't end at work. Deenie wasn't working the brunch shift, but Megan was. And as usual, Megan was ready to gab as Kyra prepared the table setups. "What did you do this weekend?" she asked.

"Ah . . . we went to a neighborhood barbecue."

"Barbecue! Brisket?"

"Hot dogs," Kyra said absently.

"Gross," Megan said. "You know your daughter could choke on hot dogs, don't you? You should *never* give hot dogs to a kid."

"She's six, Megan. She's not two."

"Not to mention they're totally carcinogenic," Megan added, sounding annoyed.

"Hot dogs cause cancer?"

"Please," Megan said and put her hands together as if she was about to recite a prayer. "*Please* don't feed Ruby hot dogs. They're just so unhealthy and so unsafe."

"Ohmigod, I'm losing my mind right now," Kyra said irritably. "It was a *hot dog*, Megan! It's not like I fed her something tainted!" She picked up her tray and went into the dining room, miffed that Megan was always commenting on her parenting . . . and yet hearing that drum of guilt in her again. Was it really so bad to let Ruby have a hot dog every once in a while? Was this a new rule that all the other mothers knew about and she didn't? Couldn't be—Diana Caldwell's kids had hot dogs, and she seemed like she'd be the sort of mom on top of things like that.

It was Megan. Somehow Megan always made her feel like a huge parenting fail. It was the way she said things, so full of conviction and judgment. Well, Kyra had enough judgment of her own on her plate. She would never get over the fact that Ruby had fallen into the lake. But she was not going to add hot dog guilt to it.

She made good money during the brunch shift and was out quicker than usual thanks to Chip, another waiter, who told her he'd take care of their joint cleanup work. "I need a little extra time on the paycheck," he said. So Kyra headed home.

When she turned onto the private road that ran in front of the cottages, she saw Mr. and Mrs. Branson sitting on the porch of Number Six. They each lifted a hand and waved.

Kyra waved back.

The Caldwell kids were playing outside Number Five. Someone had pitched a pup tent for them, and just as Kyra was coasting past, she saw a redheaded child pop out of the tent and run after one of the kids up to the door of the cottage. Kyra stopped. She backed up. She put the car into park, got out, and walked up to the front door of the cottage. She hadn't even reached the door when it swung open and Ruby emerged, holding a Popsicle.

Kyra stared at her. "What are you doing here, Ruby?"

Ruby took a big lick of the Popsicle. "Playing."

"Oh, hey, Kyra!" Diana Caldwell filled the doorway behind Ruby. "Look what we found," she said cheerfully and settled her hands on Ruby's shoulders.

"*Found* her?"

"Well, I guess she found us. She saw the kids in the yard and came over to play."

"By any chance did her babysitter ask if it was okay for her to come over?" Kyra asked and glanced at Ruby.

Ruby avoided her gaze with some studious licking of that damn Popsicle.

"Oh, was she with a babysitter?" Diana asked. "I'm sorry, I assumed you were home."

Kyra's pulse began to pound in her temples. She was going to explode with frustration. But she preferred to explode on Mrs. Miller and not Diana Caldwell, so she forced a friendly smile. "Thanks so much for looking after her. I'll take her home now."

"She's welcome to stay—"

"Oh, I think she's had enough fun for a day," Kyra said, reaching for Ruby's hand. "We need to get going." She waved at Diana as she walked Ruby out to her car. She put her in the backseat, then got in front and handed Ruby a napkin that had fallen out of some fast-food bag. "What were you doing over there?" Kyra asked.

"I was just playing," Ruby said, still avoiding her gaze.

Kyra took a breath and put the car in gear. "It's not your fault, pumpkin, and I'm not mad at you. But I need to know—did you ask Mrs. Miller for permission to go?"

"No," Ruby said. "She was asleep."

Okay, that was it. Kyra might lose her job, but she wasn't leaving Ruby with this woman one more moment.

When they reached the cottage, Kyra grabbed her things and her daughter and walked her up to the porch steps. "Will you please go to your room and finish your Popsicle?" she asked. "I need to talk to Mrs. Miller about some grown-up things."

"I'm not supposed to eat in my room," Ruby reminded her.

"I know, I know . . . but I'm giving you permission to do it this one time. Okay?"

Ruby shrugged indifferently, slurped on her Popsicle, and went into the house, skipping through the living room. She stopped in the kitchen, held up her treat, and said, "I got a Popsicle!" And then she skipped off to her room.

Kyra put her things down and walked into the kitchen. Mrs. Miller had her purse over her shoulder, her lunch bag on the counter beside her. She stuck out her hand before Kyra could speak. "Thirty bucks," she said, as if anticipating things were going south.

"Nope," Kyra said and shook her head, then folded her arms. "I am not paying you to sleep."

"What's that supposed to mean?"

"I found her three houses from here, Mrs. Miller. I don't know if you even realized she was gone! And after what happened the last time you were here, it's unbelievable to me. She could have been in the damn lake again, do you realize that? Did you hear anything I said this morning?"

Mrs. Miller slowly lowered her hand. She picked up her lunch box. "Don't you get all high and mighty with me," she said. "I come here regular as sun and make sure your kid doesn't burn down the house. That's all you're paying for, missy. You want someone to hold that girl's hand and take her swimming? Then pay a decent rate."

There were so many things Kyra wanted to say, but she dropped her arms and walked to the screen door and opened it. "Please leave. You're done here."

"*I'm* done here?" Mrs. Miller said loudly as she came through the door. "Go ahead, blame me because you're cheap. But that's not my problem, it's yours. I don't know what you think I'm gonna do for thirty bucks, Miss Priss, but that ain't enough to entertain a kid."

Mrs. Miller had no idea where Kyra had come from in her life, or how she'd struggled to make it by herself with a baby, or the horrible jobs and hours she'd endured just to keep Ruby. She was shaking with fury so badly that she could hardly breathe. "Get out," she said.

"Not without my thirty dollars I won't."

Kyra leaned over and grabbed her backpack. She pulled thirty dollars from it and thrust it at Mrs. Miller. "Get *out*."

"Gladly." Mrs. Miller stuffed the money into her purse. "I hate this place, anyway." She marched down the steps and to her truck. Kyra walked out onto the porch to watch her and assure herself that the woman actually left. And with nearly every step to her truck, Mrs. Miller called out some choice opinions of Kyra.

Kyra was still shaking, her heart slamming into her chest with rage and frustration, her hands digging into her waist. She watched until Mrs. Miller had pulled out and gunned her truck down the road.

Only then did Kyra realize what a bind she was in.

"Everything okay?"

Dax's voice startled her, and she jerked around to the sound of it. He was at the corner of her porch, wiping his hands on a greasy rag. "How long have you been there?" she asked.

"Just a moment," he said and came around to the steps. "I saw the two of you and it didn't look good. I thought you might need some help."

"Then I guess you heard her describe what sort of mother I am."

"What I heard was a crazy woman yelling obscenities."

Kyra sighed heavenward. "Yep. Well, I'm now officially babysitterless."

"You'll find one."

"It's not that easy. I—"

Her phone rang. Kyra fished it out of her pocket. The number was the Lakeside Bistro. She held up a finger to Dax and took the call.

"Hello?"

"Kyra, glad I caught you." It was Randa Lassiter.

"Hi, Randa."

"So listen, James called in sick. Can you cover tonight's shift? I know you just got off the brunch, but I need a server, and Sundays are one of our busier nights."

"Oh, ah . . ." Kyra quickly debated it. Of course she'd finally get a night shift at the moment she fired the babysitter. But Kyra wanted the work; she really needed the money. And who knew if she'd be able to take any shifts next week now that she had no child care? She glanced up at Dax, who was casually waiting. "I would love to. But I need to line up a babysitter."

"I don't have a lot of time," Randa said.

"Right . . . can you hold on a minute? I might have a solution." Kyra covered the phone with her hand.

Dax's eyes narrowed. "No," he said.

"Dax! Please! I need the money. I may not be able to work at all next week until I find a babysitter."

Dax was still shaking his head. "I'm not a babysitter, Kyra."

"Just this once," she begged him. "I'm in a bind here."

He looked caught, and Kyra felt a twinge of guilt for having caught him. "I mean, unless you're going to the jazz club tonight," she said, giving him the out.

He frowned. "No jazz."

"Sunday nights are really busy," she said. "I could make some good money."

Dax groaned heavenward. "What time?" he asked, his voice full of resignation.

"Thank you *so much*," Kyra said earnestly and took her hand from the phone. "I can do it, Randa!"

"Great! Be here by five?"

That was an hour and a half from now. "Yep. See you then." She clicked off and smiled at Dax.

His gray eyes moved over her face. "Don't smile at me like that, woman."

"Why not?"

"Just don't." He put his hands on his hips and looked to the ground. "A guy can only take so much."

She walked down the steps to him and dipped down a little so she could look him in the eye. "I can't thank you enough," she said sincerely.

"That's true, you can't. But you keep trying." He lifted his head and looked at her in a way that made her skin tingle all over. Like she was the Popsicle.

"Do you want me to bring her to you?" Kyra asked.

"Nope. I'll hang out here. That way she's got her toys. And you probably need half a dozen things fixed in that cottage you don't even know about."

Kyra was smiling again. She really liked this man. A lot. But she sincerely wished that she didn't need so much of his help. "You're a good guy, Dax. This is yet another bind you're helping me with. I owe you."

His gaze flicked to her mouth and lingered there. "You do. And I'm going to collect."

Now, in addition to the tingling, she felt a little light-headed. She would like nothing better. "Promise?"

"Yep." His eyes turned a very sexy shade of smoke—hot and intense and locked in on her. She could feel the heat rising in her skin, her pulse beginning to race.

"Well, okay," she said. "I, ah . . . I better get ready to go." She started to back up the steps.

Dax silently watched her, his gaze still fixed on her. She was so turned on by the idea of him collecting his debt that her heart was jackhammering wildly with anticipation. "About an hour?" she suggested.

He nodded.

Kyra turned around and darted into her house before she did something like lunge at him to rip his clothes off and risk missing her shift.

Once inside, she walked quickly to the kitchen and braced her hands against the tabletop, taking deep draws of air. Work was the furthest thing from her mind right now. She'd never had a man look at her like that, with such ferocious desire. Never. And she'd felt it just as fiercely.

"Mommy, what do I do with the stick?"

Ruby had appeared at the kitchen door, and the remnants of the Popsicle had dripped down her dress and were all over her mouth.

"Oh, wow," Kyra said, her thoughts slowly swimming to the surface of her reality. "We better get you cleaned up. Guess what?"

"What?"

"I have to go to work and Dax is going to babysit."

Ruby gasped. "Awesome!" she shouted.

Yes, it *was* awesome, and Kyra couldn't wait for her shift to be over so she could pay that debt.

Chapter Fourteen

The night went by in a whirl—the bistro was so crowded that people waiting in the bar area spilled into the dining area. It was one of Kyra's most successful shifts yet—she made enough money that if she did have to miss work this week, it wouldn't ruin her. That only strengthened her resolve to get on night shifts . . . which, she realized, was in direct opposition to her equally strong desire to be home with her daughter. But she couldn't help thinking of what she'd be able to do for Ruby if she doubled or tripled her tips on a daily basis. She might even start saving for a house.

Kyra was exhausted by the time the bistro closed for the evening, and drove home yawning most of the way. When she pulled into the drive, she noticed her front door was open and soft yellow light was spilling out of the screen door. She gathered her things, locked her car, and walked up to her cottage. As she climbed the porch steps, she could see Dax and Ruby at the kitchen table. What was Ruby doing up? Hadn't she mentioned what time to put Ruby to bed? God, no, she hadn't—she'd been too busy trying not to grin like an idiot around him.

Ruby's head was bent over a piece of paper, and Dax was sitting in a chair across from her with his legs stretched long. There was something different about his hair that Kyra couldn't quite make out.

She opened the screen door and stepped in. "Hello?"

"Mommy!" Ruby dropped her crayon and sprinted for Kyra. She threw her arms around Kyra's legs and grinned up at her.

"Hey, you fixed your hair," Kyra said and kissed the top of her daughter's head.

"We made our hair like Taleesha's."

"We did?" She glanced up as Dax ambled to the door between the kitchen and living area and braced his arms against the frame overhead. That thing she'd noticed in his hair was tiny little pigtails. Three of them. *"Oh,"* she said, her voice full of awe.

"Dax did mine and then I did his," Ruby explained. "He doesn't have much hair, so his are tiny. I painted his fingernails, too, Mommy. You know, like you let me do to you sometimes."

Dax silently held up a hand, his fingers spread wide, so that she could see the paint job Ruby had done. It looked as if the tips of his fingers were bleeding.

"That's . . . festive."

"I painted some of Otto's, too, but he didn't like it and he left."

"Fled," Dax said over her head.

"And look, Mommy," Ruby said. She let go of Kyra and rocked back on her heels.

"What?"

"My *feet*," Ruby said.

Kyra glanced down at Ruby's pink cowboy boots. The ends had been split away from the soles, and her toes were peeking out. Kyra gasped. "What happened?"

"Dax made them so they didn't squash my feet anymore. They were *squashing* me."

"If they're too small, we should get you some new—"

"No, I like *these*," Ruby said and rocked again.

"Well, you two have certainly had an eventful evening."

"You could say," Dax said.

"Thanks," Kyra said. "And sorry for . . . the makeover. Come on, Ruby. It's way past your bedtime. Run in and brush your teeth, and I'll come in a minute."

Ruby walked on her heels out of the living room.

"I'm really sorry," Kyra said to Dax, wincing a little. "I forgot to tell you what time she goes to bed."

"Don't apologize. I didn't have to agree to any of it," he said, gesturing to his hair.

"Yes, you did. I know how persistent she can be if she wants something."

"She's six. I could have taken her if I had to."

Kyra smiled gratefully. "Let me get her to bed."

"Yep. I'll just go—"

"Please don't," Kyra said. "I brought you something." She held up a plastic bag.

"Food?" he asked hopefully.

"Eggplant parm. Are you hungry?"

"Starving. Ruby made me a sandwich, but it was inedible."

Kyra smiled sympathetically. "You have to toss those in the garbage when she's not looking. Look, I brought this, too." She put down the bag and withdrew a bottle of one of the bistro's top-dollar wines from her backpack.

Dax looked at the bottle, then at her.

"It's wine. *Good* wine. The kind I can't afford."

"I noticed," he said.

"I hope you like it, because I kind of made a deal with the devil for it."

"Oh yeah?"

"Bar cleanup duty, three times in the next week, for a ten percent discount."

Dax grinned. "I like your deals," he said approvingly. "I'm not sure it's a good deal, but I like it."

She grinned. "Just give me ten minutes."

It was past eleven, and although Ruby was bubbly and full of the news of what she and Dax had done all evening, she was unsteady on her feet. Her eyes closed almost the moment her head hit the pillow.

Kyra ducked into her room and hastily changed out of her work clothes, putting on a summer dress. She pulled her hair out of the required bun and shook it loose, then returned to the kitchen.

Dax had taken the pigtails out of his hair and the food out of the container. He'd found two paper plates on top of her fridge. "It smells delicious," he said.

Kyra opened the wine and poured two healthy servings. They settled at the kitchen table after Kyra cleaned off the drawings and crayons. "Cheers," she said, lifting her glass.

Dax touched his glass to hers, then picked up his fork.

"Ruby had the time of her life," Kyra said before she tasted the wine. "She could hardly stand she was so tired, but it was *Dax this* and *Dax that*. If a six-year-old can be in love, I think she is."

He laughed.

"You're really good with her," Kyra added. "It's not easy, I know. You could have put her in front of the television and she would have been fine."

"I didn't mind," he said with a shrug. "Gave me something to do." He ate a forkful of the eggplant.

Kyra ate a little, too, wondering if she had ever dated anyone who got on so well with Ruby. Well, no, because she could count on one hand all her dates in the last six years, and none of them had been around Ruby except briefly. Still, of all the men she would have guessed would be good with Ruby, Dax wasn't one of them. "Have you ever thought of having kids?" she asked curiously.

Dax's face instantly changed. He looked like she'd just asked him if he'd ever thought of murdering someone.

"What did I say?" she asked guiltily.

"Nothing."

It was obviously something. "Okay," Kyra said slowly. And here she was, feeling all warm and fuzzy about how well he and Ruby got along.

"It's just that I'm about to be a father."

Kyra looked up so quickly that her fork missed the plate altogether. "You *what*?"

"Surprised? Yep, my ex is due any day now."

Kyra put down her fork and cast her arms wide with surprised jubilation. "*Dax!* Congratulations! Why didn't you say so?" She lifted her wineglass in toast. He halfheartedly lifted his and resumed his meal.

His ex-wife was *pregnant*. That must be so exciting. But . . . as Kyra thought about it, she realized that meant he must have ended their marriage while his ex was pregnant. *"Oh,"* she said without thinking.

"Oh? What does *oh* mean?" he demanded.

"Nothing," she said, shaking her head more than was necessary. Except that she had a funny feeling in her stomach. She thought so highly of him—she would hate to know he was the kind of guy to leave a woman high and dry with a pregnancy. And if he was, well . . . that put a whole new spin on things, didn't it? She could hardly tolerate one man in her life like that, and definitely not two.

"It's something," he said and put down his fork.

"I was just doing the math, I guess."

"I'm not the kind of guy who's going to leave a woman when she's pregnant with my baby, if that's the math you're doing," he said flatly.

Kyra blanched. Was she so obvious? "I didn't mean that. I'm sorry, I don't want to pry—"

"That's what everyone thinks, you know. But that's not what happened. I *wanted* kids. And she . . . well, she used my sperm after we separated." He winced, then waved his hand. "It's complicated." He seemed exasperated and wounded all at once.

"Everything is complicated when it comes to breakups," she said.

Dax's jaw clenched. "Not like this," he said low. "We were trying." He focused on his plate, then breathed in so deeply that his shoulders lifted with it, then let it go. "But . . . she had other ideas about who she wanted to be with."

Kyra was shocked. That was a startling admission from her neighbor, and suddenly she saw him in a completely different and sympathetic light than moments before. She knew what that felt like. She knew how disheartening and lonely it could be, and her heart went out to him. "That sucks," she said softly. "I guess I know better than anyone how much that sucks."

He nodded.

"Why didn't she use the, ah . . . the other person's sperm?"

Dax snorted and drank more wine—a lot more. "Because the other person doesn't produce sperm."

Kyra had to work out that puzzle. "Oh, I get it," she said after a moment. "He's sterile, right?"

Dax groaned, then sighed to the ceiling as if this was all very difficult. "There is no *he*, Kyra," he said, then lowered his gaze to her. "Ashley left me for a woman, okay? God, I hate dancing around the truth, so there it is. My wife left me for a woman and then used my sperm to have a baby." He swiped up his wine and drained the glass, then put the glass down before Kyra could even grasp what he'd just said. "I better get going." He stood up.

"No!" She stood up, too. "You haven't finished your meal, and I told you what I had to promise to get the wine. Sit down, Dax—I'm not making any judgments of you, if that's what you think."

He laughed ruefully. "You don't have to, Kyra—I've made them all. I've beaten myself up every which way to Sunday." He shoved a hand through his hair. "Now I am waiting for a child, a *son*, who I want more than air, and I don't know what kind of role I'll have in his life. I mean, how it will all work. I just know that at the very best, it's going to include those two and me."

"Have you talked to her?" Kyra asked.

He laughed again. "Oh, I've talked to her. Ashley thinks we can all be one big happy family and raise the baby together. She doesn't seem to get or care how I feel about that. Honestly, that's the problem—I don't really know how I feel about it. I don't want to fight Ashley, because I know she'll be a good mom. But neither do I want to pretend it's all okay with me and spend any time with her . . . significant other," he bit out. "I don't know what the answer is—I just want my son."

"Is the significant other so bad?" Kyra asked.

Dax chuckled. And then he told her of how his ex-wife had hooked up with Stephanie. How Stephanie, a dour, sharp-tongued woman, had worked alongside him, and then had continued to work with him even after the truth came out. He admitted how humiliated he'd been and how he'd begun to realize he was the laughingstock around Teaneck.

Kyra was fascinated by such a salacious story, but she could feel Dax's anguish. He had loved his wife, had wanted a family, and had been blindsided by all of it. She suddenly understood the gruffness, his desire to keep to himself, to keep people at arm's length.

"So there you have it," he said at last. "The sad story of Dax Bishop."

"You're too hard on yourself," she said.

He grunted. "You don't know what it's like to wake up every day full of anger and regrets and so many freaking questions that it makes your head spin."

"I don't?" Kyra pushed her plate away and planted her arms on the table. "You *do* realize I am living hand-to-mouth because of one weekend, right? I have a college degree. I was working at *US Fitness* magazine, and I loved that job. I mean *loved* it. I had goals, *lofty* goals, and being a mother wasn't part of the equation. In fact, a baby was so far removed from what I was about that I even went so far as to make an appointment for an abortion."

Her eyes instantly began to burn with unshed tears when she said those words. It happened every time she thought of how close she'd come to not having Ruby. "I can't imagine my life without Ruby, you know? I love her more than anything in the world, and I can't believe I almost didn't have her. But I was this close, Dax," she said, holding up a forefinger and thumb.

To his credit, Dax did not look appalled or shocked—he looked concerned. And compassionate. "I'm so sorry you went through that." He reached for her arm and squeezed it affectionately.

Kyra told him about how it had happened. The fabulous weekend in Puerto Vallarta, then being ghosted by Josh, and Josh's panic when he found out she was pregnant. She told Dax she'd not known what to do, especially with her mother gone from her life and her father's less-than-supportive attitude. He was an old-school type who had been more concerned about how much it might cost *him*. She told Dax that had it not been for Brandi, who had gone with her that day to her appointment, she might have gone through with it. But Brandi had held her hand and had said, *"I'll help you, Kyra. You're not alone. I'll help you."*

It was the tiny shred of hope that Kyra had needed to cling to. She told him how she'd decided she'd give her baby up for adoption, but by the time she gave birth, she couldn't possibly let her go. And how Brandi *had* helped her. Through the first year of Ruby's life, Brandi had been there for Kyra. But then her new husband had gotten a job in LA, and Kyra couldn't afford child care or rent in New York, and she'd kept moving farther and farther out in search of jobs and affordable housing. She told him how she'd ended up in East Beach, and for the first time since Ruby was born, she wasn't lying awake every night worrying about how she'd put her finances together that month. And how she thought a career in real estate might be the thing that would finally give them breathing room, maybe even allow her to get a house for the two of them.

When she'd finished telling him everything, he seemed contemplative. "I'm sorry," she said. "I didn't mean to unload on you."

"I'm glad you told me," Dax said, and he smiled.

Amazingly, so did Kyra. She'd never told anyone the full story—too afraid of being judged for what she'd done, she supposed—but it was kind of freeing to say it out loud. She'd made a mistake, and it had been a hard lesson—it was still a hard lesson—but it was the best thing she'd ever done. She could honestly say she wouldn't change a thing.

Dax leaned forward. He touched her chin. "I'll keep her."

Kyra didn't understand. "Keep who?"

"Ruby Coconuts. I'll keep her," he said. "I'll babysit while you're at work."

Kyra gasped. Her heart swelled with affection. "Ohmigod, when did you get to be so *nice*? That . . . that is a very generous thing to offer, Dax, and I can't tell you how much it means to me. But I can't let you do that—"

"Sure you can. I'll put the kid to work. If she keeps my dog out from under my feet, it will be well worth it."

"No, I can't let you do that. She needs a *lot* of attention. She'll be underfoot as much as Otto." He had no idea what he was offering, but Kyra did. She would not subject him to a rambunctious, yard-wandering, talkative six-year-old. "I won't take advantage of you like that. She needs to be with a babysitter who can focus on what she's doing, and I know I can find one. I went cheap the first time around, but I never will again, I don't care how much it costs, I'll find something appropriate and *safe*—"

"Hey," he said and cupped her face with one big hand. "Take a breath, Kyra."

She obediently gulped a breath.

"Listen to me . . . I'll keep her until you can arrange something else. Or until school starts. It's not that big a deal."

"It is."

"It's not," he said, shaking his head. "Ruby likes to help. It will be fine."

She ought to protest, to refuse his offer, but once again, Kyra was overwhelmed with gratitude. He'd just offered to save her from yet another bind. She'd never realized how many binds she constantly found herself in until someone came along to help her unbind. She looked into his eyes, which she'd once thought were so dark and distant and now seemed so kind and caring. "You keep saving me," she said. "Doesn't that get old?"

"I'm not saving you, I'm helping you. Isn't it nice to have someone to lean on for once?"

He had no idea. She was so overcome with emotion that at first she could only nod. "Yes, it is. And you know what else?"

"What?"

"I so want to kiss you right now."

His smile, slow and sexy, burned right through her. He leaned back in his chair and opened his arms. "I'm sitting right here, baby."

Kyra wasn't very graceful in her lurch across the table, and in fact, she managed to knock over his empty wineglass. But Dax caught her and dragged her onto his lap before she destroyed the kitchen. She pushed her face into his neck and kissed him as she wrapped her arms around him. "You have surprised me in so many ways," she said. "I'm overwhelmed right now."

"Don't think about it," he said, his breath warm and soft on her skin. "Just kiss me."

Kyra kissed him. He twisted her around, bending her backward to kiss her more thoroughly. A shiver of desire quickly turned liquid in her veins, and her thoughts began to race toward what he'd said yesterday—he knew his way, he knew how to get in and get it done.

She pushed up and slid off his lap. She grabbed his hand and pulled him to his feet. Dax didn't question her, but let her lead him down the hall to her bedroom. Kyra pushed him inside, then carefully closed the door so as not to wake her little sleeping beauty. She turned around and faced him.

The two of them stood a moment, staring at each other. The air around them felt highly charged; it was as if a thousand words passed between them, the mute but mutual agreement that they both needed this, and in a bad way.

"Do you have any protection?" he asked quietly.

She nodded.

That was it, the only thing either of them needed, because they reached for each other at the very same moment.

Dax put her on her back on the bed and crawled over her. He stared down at her, his eyes darkening in the soft, pink light of an outside street lamp that illuminated her room. His mouth looked luscious to her, like candy, and she raked her fingers through his hair before pulling his head to hers. She didn't think about what this meant, if it was more than a moment, if she was ready for it or not. The yearning in her was so strong and explosive that she leapt headlong into it. She was staggered by how much she needed him right now, both physically and emotionally—but she would worry about that tomorrow.

His hands and his mouth were moving across her body as their clothes came off, a piece at a time. Kyra had to bite her lip to keep from whimpering with joyous agony when she saw him without his clothes—he was a Greek god, a powerfully built and perfect man. The fire in her began to rage, and there was no way to extinguish it except to take him inside her.

The sex was erotically chaotic as their hands and mouths and limbs tangled together. Her skin felt almost singed in every place his mouth touched her, sizzling right off the bone. She moved her hands in trails down his body, exploring and arousing him. Just the scent of him, all spicy and woodsy, drove her wild. When he looked at her, she felt desirable—she was not a single mother working long hours and trying to study for a real estate license in this bed—she was the woman she'd once been. She was young and vibrant and enthusiastic and beautiful.

He moved down her body, to her breasts, ravishing her with his mouth and his hands.

Kyra's breath grew shorter. She was inflamed and impatient, ready for all of it. She'd moved well past lust, well beyond reason. But she also wanted to move slowly, to savor it. And yet she pressed and moved provocatively against him, demanding more with her hands and mouth.

When Dax at last sank into her, the weeks and months and years of leashed desires began to ebb away from her. She had forgotten how exquisite the feel was of a man inside her. She'd forgotten how powerful she felt when he was moving against her. His body, his attention were like salve to an old wound.

As he stroked her with his body and his hands, Kyra moved with him, pressing harder and faster until she cried out in the tsunami of her release as the desire flooded out of her. She was aware of his release, aware of the heavy weight of him as he collapsed partially onto her. But it was several moments before she could swim to the surface of her consciousness and open her eyes.

He was looking at her, his expression soft and even affectionate. He brushed hair from her face and smiled. "Well, hello, Kyra Coconuts."

"Hello, you," she said and wrapped her arms around him.

At that moment, Kyra didn't care what happened tomorrow, or the day after that. She had gone so far down the rabbit hole of desire and tenderness that she didn't think there was any way out of it for her now.

Kyra liked that idea. She liked it a lot.

Chapter Fifteen

At half past three in the morning, Dax sprang up the steps of his cottage with more energy than was reasonable.

Otto was lying outside the door, and he lifted his head as Dax approached. He did not, however, wag his tail as was his habit. "Don't get your panties in a wad," Dax said and opened the door. Otto slipped inside and halted just at the threshold so that Dax had to step over him. "Look, I know you don't like it, but I'm entitled to be a man every now and again," Dax said and bent down to scratch the dog's head.

Otto wasn't buying it. He sashayed off in the direction of his dog bed.

Dax went into the kitchen for a glass of water. He was parched after that magnificent romp. He looked out his window at the tiny bit of light glowing through Kyra's kitchen window. He'd left her in her bed, wearing a T-shirt and some thong panties that she'd pulled on at the last minute. Her hair was all over the place—thick, rich, black Greek hair. He didn't know if she was actually Greek, but that's the way he thought of her now—a Greek goddess.

It had been a good evening. A spectacular evening. He was privately pleased to discover that he still knew how to ride that bike, but more than that, he was in awe of how he'd been moved by her response to him. She'd been all-in, an eager participant. He thought of how routine it had been between him and Ashley in the last year of their marriage, and the two trysts Dax had had since then were more about sex than anything else. But with Kyra . . . there had been something unexpected and intense about it. Dax wasn't sitting on his invisible shelf high above the rest of the world any more. Tonight he'd tumbled right off and had landed in soft, gooey happiness.

He went to bed smiling.

Otto woke him the next morning, whining to go out. Dax stumbled out of bed and opened the door and was surprised to find Ruby. "How long have you been standing there?" he asked.

"I don't remember." Her hair was in a long braid down her back and she was wearing overalls. "Mommy said to tell you that, um . . . we're, um . . ." She paused to pet Otto.

"Spit it out, kid," Dax pressed her.

Ruby's fingers began to flutter, and Dax realized he'd forgotten to mention the seizures to Kyra. He squatted down and touched Ruby's face. "Wake up, Coconut."

She blinked rapidly, then managed to focus on him. "Mommy said we'll bring you something from the store if you want. Do you want ice cream?" she asked hopefully.

He laughed. "No. Tell your mom I'm good. I've got all that I need."

"Not even ice cream?"

He couldn't help his smile. "Yeah. I want some ice cream. What kind should I want?"

"Chocolate."

"I want some chocolate ice cream."

"Awesome!" she said, thrusting her fist in the air. She whirled around, leapt off the porch, and landed on all fours, then bounced up and began to race toward her house. "Mommy! He wants *chocolate* ice cream!"

Dax walked out onto the porch and looked over at Number Three. Kyra was standing on the steps. She waved. He waved back.

Yeah, he was going to like this. A lot.

As it turned out, Kyra didn't have to work today, and they ended up in neighborly companionship during the afternoon. Ruby went back and forth between their cottages. Kyra brought Dax some iced tea she'd made. Dax finished a piece he was working on and put it in the truck, then invited Ruby to ride along to the John Beverly shop. Ruby was thrilled.

"You don't have to do that," Kyra said. She was wearing loose jeans and a gauzy white top and had her hair tied back with a bandana. She looked like she'd just walked back from the market on Mykonos Island and could not possibly have been more attractive to Dax.

"I know I don't have to. But I need a helper, and you need to study."

She smiled, her eyes sparkling with what he interpreted to be affection, and it rained glitter inside him.

"I'm making spaghetti for Ruby tonight. Will you at least let me feed you?"

"Meatballs?"

"Are you kidding? Of course meatballs. Did you think I was some sort of bizarre health nut?"

He laughed and couldn't help himself—he stroked her cheek. "I think you're a beautiful nut."

"Stop it," Kyra said sheepishly, blushing. But she was obviously pleased with the compliment—her smile was luminescent. She turned to go inside but said over her shoulder, "Hurry back, okay?"

Oh, he was going to hurry.

At John Beverly Home Interiors, Wallace eyed Ruby as she hopped out of the truck, then Dax. He frowned. "I wouldn't let Janet see that child if I were you."

"Too late," Dax said and nodded toward the shop door. Ruby had already disappeared inside. She'd been chattering about bath toys since they left the cottages.

Wallace looked over the pull-up chair Dax had made. "We need more consoles," he said as they went inside for the check. "The two we had sold before we could put them on the floor. You're becoming quite the furniture guy around town, did you know that?"

"No," Dax said.

He did not get to hear more about what a stud he was in the furniture field, because Janet met them at the door from the storeroom into the showroom, her hands on her hips. "Are you kidding me, Dax? What's going on here?" she asked, jerking her thumb over her shoulder. "Isn't that your neighbor's little girl?"

"Ruby, put that down," Dax said, and Ruby returned the candlestick to the display table. He shrugged and said, "She's my helper."

"Helper my ass," Janet said. "I know what's going on, Dax, I'm not stupid. You do know that Heather thinks you have a date Wednesday."

Dax snorted. "I don't think so—"

"You *do*. You told her you'd go."

"I didn't . . ." He sighed. "I didn't tell her I would go. I was answering someone else when she asked me, and she misinterpreted—"

"She is counting on it, Dax. She bought a new dress!" Janet made it sound like Heather had donated her kidney to him.

Great. "Okay, Janet. I'll handle it."

"You better," she said, pointing a finger at him.

He collected his check and Ruby and got away from Janet as fast as he could. As they headed home, he realized he would have to call Heather and break a date he'd never made. If he'd learned anything from this experience, it was that he would never, *never* let anyone set him up again. People tended to get a little bit too invested in it.

That evening there seemed to be a lot of chaos around the preparation of dinner. Kyra tried to cook and bathe Ruby at the same time, while Otto tried to take a bath with Ruby. Dax made himself useful by repairing a loose doorknob and a window that wouldn't latch. Twice, he noticed Ruby's seizures, but Kyra was talking and Ruby was talking, and Kyra seemed not to think much about it.

He figured she knew about them. Of course she did.

The spaghetti was standard fare, but the real treat was the conversation around the table and the delight with which Ruby squealed every time Otto would lick her. The dog had staked out his claim underneath the table, monitoring the floor closely for any food droppings.

Dax was a little surprised by how much he enjoyed the evening, but moreover, he was reminded of his truest desires. This was exactly the sort of scene he used to envision when he was married to Ashley. Somewhere along the way, he'd let that dream drift away from him and rarely thought of it now. This evening had brought it all back to him, and he realized that he still wanted it.

After dinner they played a game with Ruby until just before bedtime. As Kyra was putting the game away, Ruby had another petite seizure.

"Okay, come on," Kyra said. She didn't remark on the seizure, and honestly, Dax couldn't say if she'd noticed it at all. He reminded himself to speak to her about it after Ruby was in bed. He sat on the couch and listened to their voices as Kyra read her daughter a story, and Ruby interrupted her with questions.

Was he crazy to be thinking about this long-term? Had he allowed himself to return to an old, but failed, fantasy? Maybe it wasn't a fantasy. Maybe this thing between them could actually work. Dax felt a little foolish for even thinking about it after a couple of pseudodates with Kyra, but he was comfortable, and he was astonishingly happy. After all this time since Ashley had laid her bombshell on him and destroyed his good humor, he did not want to lose that.

He heard Ruby's door close, and then Kyra appeared. She leapt across the tiny living room and landed on his lap, straddling him, and then began to kiss him.

"Hey," he said between kisses. "There is something I need to tell you."

Kyra lifted her head and stared down at him. "Already?"

He laughed. "It's not bad."

She sighed with relief. "For a minute there I thought I made you my signature spaghetti and meatballs and you were going to tell me it's been swell, but."

"Please," he said gravely, "I would *never* do that on spaghetti night."

She laughed. "So then what are you going to tell me?"

He kissed her again. "Just in case you should hear about it, I'm breaking a date with Heather I never made."

She pushed herself up completely, bracing her hands against his chest. "With Heather, huh?"

He nodded. "We had a miscommunication, and she thinks I agreed to go. I didn't."

Kyra slid off his lap. "Hey, you don't have to explain," she said and pretended to pick up the game she'd already picked up. "I mean, I knew you were dating her, and we were having a 'moment,' so please don't feel like you owe me any explanation."

"Wait—what are you talking about?" he asked, feeling suddenly and annoyingly anxious.

"That's what you called it, remember? A 'moment.' And I . . . I took that to mean that it's mutually beneficial as long as it's mutually beneficial."

"That makes no sense. Who thinks that way? I never meant that." He reached for her hand and made her drop the game box. "Does this," he said, gesturing between the two of them, "feel like a 'moment' to you?"

"No. It feels like a thing," she admitted. "Are we having a thing?"

He pulled her down onto his lap again. "What do you want it to be?"

Her gaze settled on his eyes. "I don't know," she said, then instantly shook her head. "No, that's not really true. I *do* know. I want it to be a thing."

Dax drew a deep breath. Before he could respond, she said, "Is that the wrong thing to say? I'm out of practice here, and I know I'm not supposed to jump the gun, and I know I'm supposed to be coy and play hard to get, but I want it to be a thing, Dax. I would really like to see where this goes between us, because I have a feeling it could be amazing. So if you don't want it to be a thing, now is the time to pack your dog and go."

He chuckled softly and ran his hand roughly over her head. "I want it to be a thing, too."

Her eyes widened with delight. "You do?"

"Yes."

"So . . . we're a thing?"

"We're a thing," he said and smiled at the craziness of it all before he kissed her. He wrapped his arms around her, and he kissed her, and she sank into him and kissed him back.

They eventually and quietly made their way to her bedroom, and Dax found himself floating in that space between conscious thought and blissful release again. He didn't know why her, what it was about Kyra Kokinos that drove him to such heights of pleasure, but the sex felt almost new again. It was different and exciting, and he was . . . damn it, he was falling for her. Plummeting, really.

The thing was, he thought later, when he'd untangled his arms and legs from her, that he was old enough and wise enough to know a good thing when he saw it, to know when someone's pieces fit so well with his. Maybe the infatuation would fade away, but Dax didn't care at the moment. He was enjoying this too much. He'd been dragged out of his cave and into sunlight, and he wasn't going back in by overthinking it.

At a quarter 'til midnight, he reluctantly climbed out of her bed. He could see that Kyra was tired, and she had to work in the morning. He pulled on his jeans and T-shirt while she watched him with a sated smile on her face. "Oh, by the way," he said casually, "I've been meaning to ask—I assume you've had Ruby's seizures checked out?"

"Her what?"

Dax looked up from the buttoning of his jeans. "The absence seizures she's been having."

Kyra frowned and slowly pushed herself up. "What are you talking about?"

Dax gaped at her. Was it possible she didn't know? "She has absence seizures," he said. "Have you ever noticed how she sort of zones out? She does that finger thing," he said, mimicking it.

"That's a habit. I know she zones out, but she's easily distracted, that's all."

Dax mentally congratulated himself for stepping into this with the finesse of a cow. He sank down on the edge of her bed as Kyra hastily donned her T-shirt. "Look, don't be alarmed. These things are common with some kids. They check out for a few seconds. Most of the time, they don't know it. Most of the time, they grow out of it."

"You're wrong," she said, shaking her head. "I would know if Ruby was having seizures. How would you know, anyway?"

"I've been a medic and a paramedic, remember?"

Kyra stared at him. Then abruptly climbed out of her bed and stacked her hands on top of her head. "Oh *shit*! Are you kidding? That can't be right—I thought it was a behavioral thing!"

"Don't panic," he said and tried to take her in his arms, but Kyra shook her head and batted his hand away. "It's a childhood thing she'll grow out of."

"You said *most* of the time."

Dax wondered why he'd said anything at all. "Like, ninety-nine point nine percent of the time," he said reassuringly.

"And the point one percent?" she demanded.

"That's why I asked. I just wanted to make sure you ruled out anything else, even though it is highly, *highly* unlikely that it's—"

"My mother had a brain tumor and she died," she said flatly. "I was twelve years old, and she *died.* And in the end, she had horrible seizures."

What a clod he was, blurting that out without thought. "No," he said sternly and took her by the arms, forcing her into his embrace. "No, no, no. If she had a brain tumor, you would know it. Calm down, Kyra. Just see her pediatrician, and he will put your mind at rest, I promise. There is nothing wrong with Ruby. She's perfect."

"She doesn't have a pediatrician!" she said tearfully.

He leaned back to look at her.

Kyra shook her head. "I have this horrible insurance, and we moved here, and I haven't done anything about it because my deductible is so high, and she's been good, she's been really good." Tears were sliding down her cheeks now.

"Jesus," he muttered. "I never meant to upset you. I assumed you knew. Look, we'll make her an appointment. I made some furniture for a pediatrician here in Lake Haven. I'll give her a call. It's going to be fine, Kyra. Don't worry, everything is fine."

She nodded and sniffed back another sob.

"Promise you won't freak out."

She nodded again.

She could nod all she wanted, but when he left it was clear she wasn't fine at all. She looked distant as she chewed on her bottom lip at her front door.

She was better the next morning when she dropped Ruby off, but still distracted. Dax tried to talk to her, but Kyra shook her head and pointed at Ruby.

"I understand," he said. "I'll make a phone call today and set you up, okay?"

"Thank you," she said. "Thanks for everything."

"Kyra—"

"Okay, pumpkin, I'm off to work," she said and leaned down to her daughter. "You promise to mind everything Dax says, right?"

"Right!" Ruby said. "Bye, Mommy!" She turned from the door and dashed into the kitchen, calling for Otto.

Dax watched Kyra get into her car and drive away. She didn't look back at him but seemed intent on the road ahead of her.

He watched her until he couldn't see her any longer.

He put Ruby to work washing dishes. But she was six, and she was more interested in playing in the suds and revealing every thought in her head. When she was done, Dax had to mop the floor. While he was mopping, Ruby followed Otto outside and into a flower bed. She came back covered in streaks of dirt. Dax had to hose her down in the yard while she squealed with laughter. He let her dry off with Otto while he worked in the shed.

At lunchtime, he put her to work making sandwiches—an art form she really enjoyed and was horribly bad at—and then sat her down in front of an old TV with a roof top antenna. He didn't have cable, and could only get one channel. So Ruby watched *Days of Our Lives* and seemed engrossed with it.

Dax took the opportunity to make a couple of calls. The first was to Heather.

"Hi!" she said with far too much cheer.

"Hi," Dax said. "So, look," he said and managed to end any hope of dating with all the panache of a caveman.

He next put in a call to the pediatrician he knew. She called him back within the hour and he explained his unusual request.

"Sure," she said. "I'll have my receptionist give you a call to schedule. Summer is slow—I'm confident we can get her in this week."

"Thanks, Nora," Dax said. "I really owe you."

"Make me another beer box and we're even," she said laughingly.

He could make a rustic beer box in a single afternoon, and he would do it in exchange for this favor.

After lunch, Dax oiled some wood for a new project while Ruby dug up weeds with his trowel. His phone rang, and he gingerly fished it out of his pocket with two fingers. He looked at the display and groaned, then punched the phone icon. "What do you want, Stephanie?" he said gruffly.

"Hello to you, too," Stephanie said, just as gruffly. "I thought you might like to know that Ashley is in labor."

Dax's heart seized. He turned away from Ruby and shoved a greasy hand through his hair, then grimaced and rubbed his fingers on his shirt. "She's early. How long has she been in labor?"

"She's only a week early. And she's been having contractions a little over an hour. We just got to the hospital."

"What am I supposed to do?" he asked, more to himself than to Stephanie.

"I don't have time to help you figure it all out, Dax."

"I meant, should I come now?" he asked curtly. The moment of dread had come—he couldn't imagine anything worse than standing shoulder to shoulder with Stephanie as they watched his baby being born. And he could guarantee Stephanie wasn't going to bow out of the experience. He would just have to shoehorn his way in.

"If you want, I'll call you when she delivers," Stephanie suggested, perhaps a little too hopefully.

Dax didn't say anything. He felt a little woozy, like he'd been in the sun too long. It suddenly hit him—this was his baby. *His baby.* His boy.

"Dax?"

"She's at Holy Name Medical Center?" he asked gruffly.

Stephanie sighed. "So you're coming."

"Of course I'm coming. This is my kid, Stephanie."

"Fine," she said irritably. "Yes, she's at Holy Name."

"I'll be there as soon as I can," he said and hung up.

He stalked off to the shed to calm down a little. He was momentarily distracted by the wall unit he was making for some socialite on the north end of the lake. “Rustic,” she’d said. “But not *too* rustic.” She’d touched her finger to his chest and smiled up at him.

“Not too rustic,” he’d repeated and had stepped far away from her reach. But now he noticed a gash in the pallet wood he was using and stepped closer to assess if he could sand it out. He spent a few minutes working on it, his hands moving by rote, his mind on Ashley giving birth to his son right now.

Forget Stephanie—Dax was wasting time. He could not imagine his son coming into this world and him not being there to witness it. He threw down the sandpaper and looked at his watch. Kyra should be back in an hour. He could make it to Teaneck in a little under an hour.

He walked out of the shed. “Coconut!” he called.

Ruby started and turned around. He eyed her up and down. “Let’s go clean up. Do you have a dress in that mess you call a room?”

“I have a red one,” she said.

“Go get it. And come right back here. We have some work to do before your mom gets home.”

Chapter Sixteen

Megan yelled at Kyra twice in the course of her shift for not picking up food. Even Deenie was frustrated when Kyra dropped a ketchup bottle and it shattered all over the wait station. "What is the matter with you?" she asked as she wiped off her shoes. "I just bought these!"

"I'm sorry," Kyra said, fighting back invisible tears. She was sorry, so very sorry. She was sorry she'd dropped the ketchup and she was sorry she was a marginal mom at best.

Deenie noticed Kyra's despair as she threw the paper towel she'd used into the garbage. "What's wrong?"

"Just having a bad day," Kyra said and avoided Deenie for the rest of the shift. She didn't want to talk about it, not yet. If she did, she might collapse with grief and guilt and worry.

Her tips were lousy, which came as no surprise, seeing as how she'd forgotten things, dropped things, left people waiting. She couldn't focus—all she could think was that her daughter, her beautiful, spirited daughter, was probably growing a giant cancerous tumor in her head because Kyra was too dumb to realize those little lapses in attention were medical and not because Ruby was absentminded.

She'd felt sick since Dax had told her. She'd tortured herself with recalling how many times she'd snapped at Ruby and accused her of not listening, when in reality Ruby probably had been having a seizure. She loathed herself for having let Ruby's pediatric appointments lapse. What mother did that? But she'd been busy and tired and she'd told herself she would get Ruby to a pediatrician before school started.

She finished her work in a miserable frame of mind and headed home. When she pulled into the drive at Number Three, Dax and Ruby came pounding down the porch steps side by side. Dax looked intent. He'd probably had his fill of Ruby after one day and had probably lost respect for Kyra when he figured out that she was completely inept when it came to her daughter. She got out of her car, prepared for whatever it was . . . but she could hardly look him in the eye.

Ruby, on the other hand, looked radiant. It was impossible to believe anything was wrong with her beautiful, vibrant little girl. "Hey, pumpkin, how was your day?" she asked, hugging Ruby tightly to her.

"It was *awesome*," Ruby said. "He washed me with the hose."

Kyra reluctantly let go of Ruby. "The hose?"

"I was really dirty," Ruby said.

Kyra risked a look at Dax. He seemed so anxious. On edge. "Is everything okay?"

"No," he said, and Kyra's heart sank. "My baby is on the way."

That news stopped the slide of her heart into the dark pit of despair. "Oh, wow, that's . . . that's *great*, Dax." She was happy for him. He would have a beautiful, healthy child. Kyra tried not to compare his new baby to her daughter, but she couldn't help it. Life felt so unfair sometimes.

She also couldn't help but wonder how this might change things between them. She knew how much attention a new baby required and how there was so little left over for anything or anyone else.

"Yep," he said and grinned. "But I'm in a rush." He nudged Ruby toward her. "There's a bunch of muddy clothes in a sack by the back door. I didn't know what to do with them."

"Got it, not to worry."

He was clearly eager to be gone, but he hesitated and glanced at Ruby. "I don't know if I'll be back by morning. I don't know how long—"

"I'm off tomorrow," Kyra said. "Please, don't think about it."

"You're off, great. I got you an appointment with the pediatrician tomorrow afternoon. It's at two, but that's the only slot they had." He held out a piece of paper with the information.

Kyra stared down at the scribbled note with the doctor's name and the time. "You did that?"

"I told you I would, Kyra," Dax said and touched her hand, tangling his fingers with hers. "I've got to go. Will you keep an eye on Otto? I fed him, but he'll be rooting around for something in the morning if I'm not here."

"Yes, of course."

Dax was already moving, walking backward. "His food is in the kitchen. Ruby knows how much."

"She does?" Kyra asked, looking at her daughter.

"I do, Mommy. I've fed him twice. He eats a *lot*. And then he burps."

Dax raised his hand, then turned around and strode quickly to his truck.

Kyra and Ruby watched him go, peeling out of the drive like a man whose ex-wife was having a baby.

Kyra didn't even have time to say thank you for the thousandth time.

♦ ♦ ♦

Ruby played with her Barbies that night and sent them on a whale-hunting mission in the bathtub. Kyra watched her closely—every time Ruby looked away, she was certain it was a seizure. She was imagining things—her daughter was not having a seizure every minute of every hour. She googled seizures in children and found *absence seizure*, like Dax had called it. There were various causes, according to the sites she looked at, but it seemed from what she could find that it was fairly innocuous. It was probably genetic. Ruby would probably grow out of it.

Except if she didn't. In rare cases, the seizure could be caused by something else. Something ominous . . . like a tumor.

And then there were the discussion boards. *My son was diagnosed with having absence seizures, but we asked for a second opinion and found a cancerous tumor. Always get a second opinion!!* Those few comments of doom stuck with Kyra.

When Ruby was brushing her teeth, Kyra saw it—Ruby's fingers started fluttering and she stared at the sink for several seconds. Kyra dipped down—Ruby's eyes were a little glassy and fixed on the sink. And then, as if a light switch had turned on, Ruby looked at her toothbrush and seemed to remember what she was doing. Her fingers stopped fluttering.

"Ruby? Did something just happen to you?" Kyra asked.

Ruby looked at her mother strangely as she put down the toothbrush. "What happened?"

Kyra smiled and tousled Ruby's red curls. "Nothing."

When Ruby was in bed, Kyra returned to her googling, this time delving deeper into the symptoms of brain tumors. She began to feel a bit better about things—Ruby had none of the symptoms associated with a growing tumor, and not all tumors resulted in seizures. Dax had to be right—if this was a brain tumor, she'd know it.

She felt calmer the next morning when she woke up. She looked out the kitchen window and noticed Dax's truck wasn't in the drive. She wondered how it was going, if the baby had been born.

When Ruby woke up, they went together to feed Otto. The dog was lying in the middle of the kitchen floor and didn't lift his head when he saw Kyra come through the door. But his tail began to wag when he saw Ruby.

Kyra thought about texting Dax but didn't want to intrude on this important moment in his life. She remembered when Ruby had been born, how besotted she'd been, how nothing else mattered but that tiny little being in her arms. She would not have wanted her neighbor texting her to ask how everything was going.

Kyra spent the rest of the morning trying to study, but thoughts about Ruby kept creeping into her head. The clock seemed to be moving in slow motion toward the hour of their pediatric appointment. But finally the hour came, and Kyra and Ruby headed to town.

At the doctor's office, Kyra filled out miles of paperwork about Ruby and handed over her insurance card. The receptionist typed some things on her computer, then looked at Kyra. "You have a very large deductible."

"I know."

"We take the co-pay up front. It's sixty-five dollars."

A king's ransom, but Kyra counted the amount out in bills.

The receptionist looked at the money strangely. "You don't have a card? We don't generally take cash."

Who didn't take cash? "I have a check card. Will that work?"

"Yes," the receptionist said. She might think the check card was better, but Kyra didn't. She tried to live off her tips and leave the money in her bank untouched. For emergencies. Like this.

At last they were admitted into the examining room. It was painted Pepto-Bismol pink, and there were shadow shapes of children around the walls. The pediatrician, Dr. Giannarelli, was a busty, gray-haired woman with a bun on top of her head and a pen stuck through it. She had an easy, comfortable way with Ruby as she examined her. "Well," she said when she'd completed the examination and was washing her hands, "Ruby looks like a very healthy girl. Can you describe the seizures to me?"

"She zones out. And she does this weird thing with her fingers," Kyra said, trying to mimic it.

Ruby, who was twirling around in the middle of that small examining room, watching the hem of her dress spin out, stopped and laughed at that. "I don't do that, Mommy."

"All this time I thought she was easily distracted and the finger thing was a nervous habit. I never thought . . ."

"Have you noticed any seizure behavior on the heels of a fever?" the doctor asked.

"No, I'm certain I haven't," Kyra said, not certain at all. "I mean, I don't remember any. It's been a while since she's had a fever."

"Ruby? Can you breathe really fast for me, like you're running?"

Ruby began to pant. "She runs around a lot," Kyra said, uncertain as to why Ruby was required to breathe quickly. Did the doctor think Ruby wasn't active enough? She realized that Dr. Giannarelli was frowning slightly as she watched Ruby and glanced at her daughter—Ruby had stopped panting, and to anyone else, it would have looked like she was distracted by the figures on the wall. But she was doing the thing with her hand.

Dr. Giannarelli snapped her fingers. Ruby didn't move . . . for a moment. Then she looked down at her hand, shook it, and began to twirl around.

The doctor made a note on Ruby's chart.

"My mother . . . my mother died when I was twelve," Kyra said. "She had a tumor in her brain. Brain cancer," she added, her voice cracking a little when she said those words out loud.

The doctor glanced at her.

"I mean . . . maybe it could be hereditary," she said.

"Ruby, can you hold your arms out like this for me?" the doctor asked, and said then to Kyra, "It is highly unlikely that this has anything to do with that."

"Then what is it?"

"I think it's probably epileptic childhood absence seizures—"

"Epilepsy!" Kyra repeated, alarmed.

"It's not as bad as it sounds," Dr. Giannarelli said. "Ruby has the classic symptoms of absence seizures, and in the majority of cases, the child outgrows them," she said, echoing what Dax had told Kyra. "But let's cover all the bases. I'm going to give you the name of a neurologist in Black Springs. See Carol on the way out, and she'll get you in quickly. Otherwise you might end up waiting a month or so."

Kyra's head was spinning. "Does it need to be quick? That sounds so . . . ominous."

"What does ominous mean?" Ruby asked.

"Important, sweetie," Kyra said and looked at the doctor.

"Quicker is better than later, isn't it? They'll want to do an EEG on her and check her brain's electrical activity. That also sounds worse than it is. Mrs. Kokinos, I'm sure it's nothing to be alarmed about," she said reassuringly. "But we want to rule out anything else. I'm being overly cautious here."

Kyra nodded, but she didn't know what she was nodding to. Her thoughts were so jumbled between the remote idea that she could possibly lose Ruby and chastising herself for being so fatalistic. She needed to be optimistic right now. Positive energy into the world, positive energy back. Don't borrow trouble, don't assume the worst.

"Come back and see me when you've checked in with Dr. Green," Dr. Giannarelli said. "We need to get her up to date on her vaccinations."

Kyra thanked the doctor, gathered her purse and the doll Ruby had brought, and stopped at the desk on the way out. The receptionist made Ruby an appointment with the neurologist in Black Springs for a week from the following Monday.

She took Ruby for an ice cream she'd promised on the way to the doctor's office. When they arrived home, it didn't look as if Dax had come home. But Otto was outside, sniffing around Mrs. McCauley's plants.

Kyra wished she would hear from him. At least let her know that his baby was okay. But she didn't see him that night, either, and agonized about whether or not she should text him. It had only been twenty-four hours since she'd seen him, only forty-eight hours since they'd declared themselves a thing. She didn't want to appear desperate. She knew he needed his space. She decided not to text him.

Kyra opened her laptop. She meant to study, but instead she went to Facebook and looked up Josh Burton, Ruby's father.

A couple of years ago, Ruby had gone through a phase of asking about him all the time. As Kyra had explained to Dax, she'd been as honest as she could have been with her. "Your daddy and I only knew each other long enough to make a baby. Sometimes that happens, and the daddy goes away to live with other mommies."

Ruby accepted that explanation, perhaps because it wasn't so unnatural in her world. As far as Kyra knew, Taleesha's father wasn't in the picture, either. But naturally, Ruby wanted to know if her daddy could come visit—*no, he lives too far away*. Or if she could call him. *Not this time. Maybe when you're older.*

It bothered Kyra that she didn't have a really good, age-appropriate explanation for Ruby.

From time to time, Kyra had looked Josh up on the Internet. She'd found him a couple of years ago, late one night when she'd been bored out of her mind and had gone on a social media hunt for him.

She looked him up again tonight. He was still living in Indianapolis, by all appearances. Still married to a woman who was the exact opposite of Kyra in looks and size. His wife was petite, with short blonde hair and a wide mouth. There were pictures of Josh and his wife on a boat, pictures of Josh with a bunch of guys, two of whom Kyra recognized from Brandi's wedding. A picture of him and his wife on a hiking trip in some scenic mountain location, and a picture of a steak on a plate. His page said he was employed by Castlemaine Industries.

Kyra would bet that Castlemaine Industries, whatever that was, had good health insurance.

She typed out a private message to him, telling him that his daughter had something wrong with her and she needed his help.

But she didn't hit Send.

She deleted it.

Josh had had no part in Ruby's life by choice. Even when Brandi had gotten in touch with him and showed him pictures of his newborn daughter six years ago, he'd been just as clear with her as he'd been with Kyra. *I'm getting married. This would ruin everything.* He wanted nothing to do with his daughter. Nothing.

The mere suggestion that Ruby could ruin anything made Kyra so angry. She just hoped her daughter never had to breathe the same air as someone who saw her as a problem.

At half past eleven, exhausted with the worry of the last two days, Kyra closed her laptop. As she washed a few dishes at the sink before bed, her phone beeped. Kyra's heart quickened, and she punched the button with her elbow to see the text.

You up?

It was Dax. Thank God, it was Dax. She smiled and quickly wiped her hands dry.

Yes. Baby okay?

Enormous. 9 lbs, 8 oz. A crier. You're probably not surprised.

Kyra smiled broadly. That's wonderful. She inserted a smiley face.

I'll be home in fifteen. Come over.

Oh, how she wanted to, but she glanced at the hallway door. Can't. Ruby.

Then meet me outside. Moon is full and night is gorgeous. Fifteen minutes.

K.

As soon as she sent the last response, she darted into the bathroom. She quickly combed her hair and applied a little blush, then changed out of the awful sweatpants she'd cut off a few years ago and wore around the house as very baggy shorts. She pulled on some denim shorts and a T-shirt, checked in on Ruby, then went out her front door.

She was sitting on the bottom step when Dax pulled into his drive. He got out, bent down to pet Otto, then lifted his hand and waved. She felt lighter seeing him, felt the anxiety of her day sloughing away. He walked across the lawn in the moonlight, Otto bouncing along behind him, tail wagging. As he neared her, he lifted a bottle of champagne and two plastic Solo cups.

Kyra gasped with delight. "Excellent!"

He popped the cork, poured two cups of champagne, and handed one to her.

"A toast," she said and lifted her cup. "To your beautiful, healthy son."

"His name is Jonathan," Dax said, his grin as wide as Kyra had ever seen it. "He's got a full head of hair. He weighed nine pounds, eight ounces, did I tell you?"

"What was she feeding that kid? He's a little bruiser."

"He's a healthy boy, all right," Dax said. He fished his phone from his pocket and showed her some pictures of his bundle of joy. Kyra exclaimed over them and beamed alongside him.

As Dax gazed down at the pictures, she asked, "How'd it go with the ex?"

"Who, Ashley? She was fine. It was Stephanie," he said and shook his head. "She wants to have the biggest balls in the room. I'm ashamed to admit that a few weeks ago I actually thought about not going. I didn't want that moment to be about Stephanie and Ashley."

"I get that," Kyra said.

"But then I realized I was letting her have a moment that belonged to me, and I forgot she was there. It's the best thing that ever happened to me, Kyra—I wouldn't have wanted to miss that experience for anything in the world."

Kyra understood completely. "How long was she in labor? You've been gone a really long time."

"Oh yeah?" he asked and wrapped his arm around her shoulders, then kissed her temple. "She gave birth at three thirteen this morning. I stayed for a few hours. On my way back to East Beach I went by a place that is selling some old barn wood." He wrapped a tress of her hair around his fist. "I should have called you, I guess, but I've been on another planet today." He drained his champagne.

"That's the best planet to be on," she said as he pulled her close.

"You know, I have tried to imagine this day, but nothing I thought came close to the real thing. It was amazing." He glanced at her sidelong. "That makes two extraordinary things to happen to me in the last week," he said and leaned in to kiss her.

Kyra sighed and melted into his kiss. It was the first time in two days she'd felt right, like she'd found a harbor from the rough sea in her head.

But he lifted his head and asked, "Hey, did you see Nora?"

"Dr. Giannarelli? I did. She said what you said—nothing to worry about. She referred us to a neurologist in Black Springs to have Ruby thoroughly checked out."

"That's great," Dax said. "I told you there was nothing to worry about."

"I know," she agreed. "But I'll still feel better once this guy gives her the all clear."

Dax kissed her temple, then poured more champagne for them.

Kyra swirled her champagne around in her cup, thinking. She really was feeling more optimistic about Ruby . . . but there was that small, dark, pessimistic cloud in her that she just couldn't shake. Everyone said it was nothing to worry about, and she believed them, and yet that tiny niggle of doubt kept creeping back in.

"Are you okay?" Dax asked.

"What?" Kyra realized he'd been watching her, and something cracked in her. "No," she muttered softly. "I'm not okay. I'm trying to be okay, I'm trying as hard as I can to be optimistic, but I'm not okay."

Dax put down his cup to wrap both arms around her.

She turned her face into his shoulder. "I'm a horrible mother," she whispered.

"Don't say that—"

"No, it's true," she said. "I'm always too busy. It never occurred to me her zoning out was anything but being a six-year-old. I can't tell you how many times I've scolded her for not listening. I wouldn't believe her that she didn't hear me. I've let her down in the worst way—"

"No, you haven't," he said sternly. "That little coconut is a great kid, Kyra, and she didn't get that way on her own. She's respectful, she's fun, she's happy, she has a great imagination. Don't try and convince yourself she's been neglected, because she hasn't. Stop beating yourself up. Shit happens."

"I want to believe you, but I know what it's been like these six years. Always working, always sticking her with people like Fern Miller . . ." She winced and shook her head. "It's a miracle she's turned out like she has," she muttered. "You'll find out what I mean now that you have your son."

Dax didn't say anything.

"Did I say something wrong?" she asked.

"No. Maybe. I don't know, Kyra, but I'm feeling a little uncertain about what I'm doing here in East Beach when I have a son in Teaneck. I can't wrap my head around it yet."

Kyra didn't know exactly what he meant by that, but she knew a lot of new, raw emotions surfaced when a new life was brought into the world. Love and devotion and the strong desire to never be away from that little person. She sighed and put her head on his shoulder and looked at the moon.

"All I know is that I want to be with my son," Dax said quietly.

Kyra's heart skipped a little. Of course he did. But selfishly, she hoped that didn't mean he was going to return to Teaneck. She couldn't imagine losing him now that she'd found him. She couldn't imagine that at all.

"I have some decisions to make," he said, and he put his arm around her again and leaned back against the steps with her and turned his gaze to the moon, too. "Don't listen to me. I'm just a new dad rambling right now." He grinned at her. "I like the sound of that. New dad."

Kyra liked the sound of it, too. She just wished the sound of "dad" was somewhere closer to East Beach.

Chapter Seventeen

It was amazing to Dax—a man who had eschewed society and women and life in general for the last year or so—how quickly he and Kyra came together and fit into each other's lives.

The few days following Jonathan's birth were some of the best of his life. He could actually say that—they were the *best of his life*. He had a son. He had a girl. He had a coconut who made him smile every day, a feat he would have thought impossible just a few short weeks ago.

For the first time in months, Dax forgot his heart was broken.

Ashley was great about sending him pictures and texts about Jonathan. He hadn't asked for that, and he truly appreciated it. He wanted to be there with his son in the worst way, and he went to visit as often as he could. But he had to finish the massive table he'd been working on for Wallace, and there was Otto to take care of. But when he wasn't working on that table, he was staring at pictures of Jonathan or listening to the fanciful theories presented by Ruby Coconuts about squirrels or birds or dogs or whatever had caught her eye that day.

The little girl with the long, curly red hair had grown on him, that was for sure. Sort of like the old tree up on Juneberry Road that had grown around a fence post and practically swallowed the post in its trunk. He had to give the little twerp credit—she had come over the fence and wormed her way into his life when he wasn't looking.

Most days, while Kyra waited tables and he worked on his furniture, Ruby got dirty. She and dirt were magnets. Maybe because her favorite sport was digging or planting sticks. Mr. McCauley came by a couple of times and took her on his landscaping rounds with him—maybe to keep her from digging up something important—but whatever the reason, Dax was grateful for the break. Even though he found Ruby easy to babysit, at the end of those days he watched her, he was tired. He didn't know what it was—maybe having to be constantly alert or maybe the need to engage in constant conversation when he was so out of practice. He couldn't imagine how tiring it would be to have to clothe her and bathe her and make sure she brushed her teeth or picked up her toys or read her books and talk more about Barbies at the end of a long day.

He had developed a healthy respect for the life of a single parent.

Neither he nor Ruby could wait for Kyra to come home each day, albeit for different reasons. Inevitably, Kyra would shake her head at the sight of both of them. "If I didn't know better, I'd swear the two of you have been mud wrestling." And then she'd take over, freeing Dax from the responsibility of Ruby.

That's when the day really lit up. Dax loved being with Kyra; it was so easy between them. One night he made a picnic for Ruby and Kyra and took them down to the lakeshore. He and Kyra laughed about their most embarrassing high school moments while they ate turkey sandwiches, and Ruby threw rocks into the lake that Otto would swim out and try to catch.

The next night they drove to the fancy resort at the other end of Lake Haven. Because Dax made and delivered furniture to some of the houses on the high-dollar end of the lake, he knew the resort hosted free summer concerts. That night they threw out a blanket and the three of them sort of dog piled onto it and gazed at the stars while they listened to music.

Later, as Dax and Kyra lay tangled in her bed after making love, he asked if he could take Ruby to see Jonathan.

Kyra came up on an elbow, her hair spilling over him like water. *"Really?"*

"He's home now," Dax said. "I can't wait to see him again."

"I'm off work on Sunday," she suggested. "Can you wait until then? You don't want to take Ruby with you, Dax—you know how hyper she can get."

"She gets hyped up like any kid." He played with the ends of Kyra's hair, brushing them across her nose. "I have a good working relationship with the coconut. We could run a business together. She knows when I say cut it out, I mean it."

Kyra smiled. "Well, *that's* impressive. You'll have to teach me your trick," she said, and leaned down to kiss him.

"She'd have fun," Dax said. "And I could use the company."

Kyra's hand was sliding down his leg, distracting him. "As long as you understand what you're in for."

"I do."

"That will give me a chance to study," she said, contemplating. "I'm getting really close to being ready to take the exam."

"That's great," he said and rolled on top of her. It amazed him that he could be hard again, but Kyra had that effect on him. His hand drifted down her side, to her thigh. "How sleepy are you?"

"On a scale of one to ten?"

He kissed the corner of her mouth.

"A two."

"That's my girl," he muttered and realized, as he kissed her and his hands began to roam a body that was becoming so familiar to him, that he was very attached to the idea of having a girlfriend.

Yes, he damn sure was.

♦ ♦ ♦

The next day he and Ruby set off on their adventure to see Jonathan. Ruby peppered him with questions on the forty-five-minute drive to Teaneck until they pulled into the drive of the old Cape Cod he and Ashley had bought a very long time ago.

He paused in the drive, peering out the windshield. Someone had painted the red brick green. He could only imagine who'd had that brilliant idea.

"All right, here we go," he said. The words were barely out of his mouth before Ruby was out of the truck, hopscotching her way to the front door. Dax scrambled to get there before she did, grabbing up the gift he had for Jonathan.

The front door was open and the glass storm door was the only thing between them and his baby. Ruby pressed her face against the glass to see in. Dax rang the doorbell. A moment later he heard what he imagined was a thundering of thighs coming down the stairs.

"Don't ring the doorbell!" Stephanie hissed as she came down. When she reached the door, she sighed. "Well, if it isn't Shrek."

Dax glared at her. "Did you gain a little pregnancy weight, too, Steph? You're looking a little paunchy there."

Stephanie looked as if she was going to say something but happened to see Ruby. "Who's this?"

"I'm Ruby Kokinos," Ruby said. "Not Coconuts. *Kokinos.*" Apparently she thought this was a mistake all adults made now.

"Hi, Ruby," Stephanie said. She unlatched the door and opened it.

Ruby didn't wait to be asked but scooted past Stephanie and into the house.

Stephanie watched Ruby with surprise as she walked over to the couch and plopped onto it. She shifted her gaze to Dax. "Dating a little young, aren't you?"

"Shut up. She's my neighbor's kid. Where's my baby?"

"*Our* baby is upstairs with Ashley," Stephanie said. "But you both have to wash your hands first." She pointed to the half bath in the hall.

"You don't have to point. I know where it is," Dax said. "Come on, Coconut. Hands."

When he and Ruby had both cleaned their hands, they returned to the living area. All the furniture Dax had made was gone—probably sold dirt cheap on Craigslist—and in its place was some IKEA stuff that made him want to put his fist through the brick wall. He'd worked hard on this house. He couldn't believe Ashley put up with this new design aesthetic.

"Come on, let's get this over with," Stephanie grumbled and led them up the narrow staircase to the second floor and the master bedroom.

Dax could hardly look at the bed, onto which Stephanie promptly put herself, stretching out as she smirked at him. Ashley was in the bedroom's small sitting area. Dax had added shelves and a counter for diapers and baby things when he and Ashley had planned for this to be a nursery. They had both wanted the baby close.

Ashley was sitting in a rocking chair with Jonathan at her breast. She'd cut her hair short, like Stephanie's, and Dax hated it. He thought of Kyra's long black hair and her smiling eyes, and he recognized, looking at his ex-wife now, that he did not feel the twinge of regret for his old life that he usually felt around her.

"Who is this?" Ashley asked, smiling at Ruby.

"She's my friend," Dax said.

"My name is Ruby. I'm six," she said.

"Wow, six, really?" Stephanie asked. "Do you and Dax go to the same school?"

Ruby laughed while Dax glared. "He's too big to go to school. Can I look at your baby?"

"Give me just a minute," Ashley said and took the baby from her breast. To Dax, she said, "What's going on?"

"Ruby is my neighbor," he said. "She's keeping me company today."

Ashley stood up. "Here he is," she said and put the baby in Dax's hands.

Dax felt a jolt of electricity go right through him. He felt it every time he held his son, like he was shaking. But he wasn't shaking. He was just sizzling with pride and love and hope. His son was so small. So *small.* He had a curly patch of dark hair on his head, and he was holding a tight little fist by his face. Dax was mortified to get so misty-eyed as he gazed down at him.

"Isn't he beautiful?" Ashley asked.

Dax was incapable of speaking and only nodded. He dipped down onto one knee so that Ruby could see him.

Ruby leaned over the baby, studying him closely. "Can I touch it?" she asked.

"It's a he," Dax said. "His name is Jonathan. And yes, you can touch him very gently."

She carefully laid her finger on the baby's cheek, and the baby squirmed. "He's supersoft."

Dax smiled and stood up. "Stephanie, would you take Ruby downstairs?"

"To do what?" Stephanie asked, sounding annoyed.

"Steph, honey, will you?" Ashley asked sweetly. Dax's stomach turned—that's the way she used to speak to him.

"Fine," Stephanie groused and got off the bed. "Come on, kid."

Dax had the fleeting thought that next time he'd have Ruby make Stephanie some cookies. They would be perfect for her.

As they went out, he heard Ruby ask if they had a swing.

"Not yet," Stephanie answered. "But we're going to get one soon. I'll show you where we will put it."

Dax and Ashley were alone for the first time in months. He gazed at the woman he'd once loved. She didn't look the same anymore. She looked like another woman entirely.

Ashley smiled at him. "I can't believe it, we finally made a baby," she said and stroked Jonathan's crown. "You made a beautiful son, Dax."

"Yeah," he agreed. He didn't think he had so much to do with it, but rather that God had smiled on him—Jonathan was the most perfect baby he'd ever seen. He stroked his little cheek, then gave him his pinkie to suck. "I want to be part of his life, Ashley," he blurted.

"I know," she said.

"No, I mean in a big way. Not just some part-time gig."

"Really? That's wonderful," she said and put her hand on his arm. "I'm grateful for that. I want him to know his father. Will you stay at Lake Haven? Or will you come back to Teaneck?"

"I don't know," he said, looking at Jonathan's cherubic little face. "I have to figure things out, but I'll make it work somehow."

"*We'll* make it work," she said.

"What about Numbnuts?" he asked, jerking his head in the direction of the bed.

"Dax," she said disapprovingly. "Stephanie will be fine with it."

Dax gave her a dubious look.

"Okay, she won't be fine with it," Ashley admitted sheepishly. "But she understands—she'll make it work, too."

"How can you be so sure of that?"

Ashley smiled serenely. "Because she loves me and she loves Jonathan. She wants what is best for the both of us."

Dax supposed that was at least one thing he had in common with Stephanie. But it was the only thing.

He and Ruby stayed another half hour. Stephanie walked them out when they left. She stood on the stoop, her hands shoved in her pockets. "So I guess you'll be back," she said.

"Yep."

"I *knew* it," she muttered. "Okay, well, I don't want to hear a word about this house, Dax Bishop. I know you did everything, but I've got some skills, too."

Dax laughed. "No, you don't."

"Doesn't matter what you think. We bought you out."

"I won't say a word." He extended his hand to her in a gesture that surprised even him.

Stephanie grabbed it in a strong grip and shook it. "You know, Dax, I wish that—"

"Don't," Dax said. He didn't want to hear any platitudes from her, no *can't we all just get along* bullshit. He would never get over the fact that his coworker had gone behind his back and pursued his wife.

"You don't know what I was going to say," she said.

"I don't want to know. We've got a kid now, Stephanie. Let's not speak about the past and move forward. Deal?"

Stephanie shrugged. "Deal."

♦ ♦ ♦

Kyra was up to her elbows in workbooks when Dax and Ruby arrived home. Dax was starving and offered to take them for burgers. They drove into East Beach, to his favorite burger joint. They sat outside on wooden picnic tables, and while Ruby rattled off every detail of their excursion—including how many red cars they saw—Dax imagined Jonathan at six years old, wiggling around in a seat, ketchup on his face, glowing with the excitement of an outing.

He didn't know how he was going to be a dad in a crowded parental unit, but he knew, as he sat there watching Ruby, that he wanted it more than anything he'd ever wanted in his life.

He and Kyra and the coconut spent that weekend together, swimming in the lake, giving Otto a much-needed bath, and best of all, lolling around in bed Sunday morning while Ruby slept.

On Monday Kyra took Ruby to see Dr. Green in Black Springs while Dax drove to Teaneck to see Jonathan. When they met up later, Kyra was all smiles. "Dr. Green says he's ninety-five percent sure it's the absence epilepsy and it's no big deal. But we're having some tests next week to confirm."

Dax was relieved that Kyra seemed to have packed away the guilt she'd been carrying around. She was bubbly again, digging through her backpack as she talked about the trip and what she had to do this week.

She made dinner that night, "the first of many thank-yous," she announced. She cooked fish and made potatoes au gratin and a salad. After dinner the evening was so pleasant that they took a walk. The four of them—Otto festively attired in a pink bow—stopped in to say hello to the McCauleys. At the Caldwells', Kyra and Dax talked to the grown-ups while Ruby and the Caldwell kids chased butterflies.

They returned home, Dax and Kyra holding hands, talking about their week, watching Ruby run with Otto, her red hair flying behind her, her pink cowboy boots lighting up with every step she took.

Dax took Otto to Number Two and fed him while Kyra put Ruby to bed. When he strolled back across the lawn, he sat on the front porch steps to watch the moon rise above the lake while he waited for Kyra.

He felt remarkably content. *Remarkably.* He didn't feel that strange restless feeling he'd had before meeting Kyra. He didn't feel anything but happiness and peace. This was what he'd always wanted. He'd never expected to find it this way, but somehow he'd stumbled into this near-perfect little family unit. The thing that would make it perfect was adding Jonathan to it.

Dax was going to make it work. He'd never been more determined about something in his life.

He didn't hear the screen door open, thanks to his expert skills at installing a pneumatic hinge, and jumped a little when Kyra put her hand on his shoulder. She leaned over his shoulder, nibbled his earlobe, and said, "Ruby is asleep."

She slipped her hand into his, tugged him to his feet, and led him to her bedroom. She closed the door, then pushed him down onto his back on the bed.

"What are you doing?" he asked.

"Sssh," she whispered. "Don't wake the kid."

Dax smiled and pillowed his head and watched with rapt attention as Kyra performed a striptease for him, even swinging her bra over her head. She wasn't a great dancer by her own admission, but that was the sexiest, most arousing dance Dax had ever seen in his life. Hell, he couldn't imagine what she might have done to make him want her more . . . not until she climbed on top of him and kissed him. He definitely wanted her even more.

"What a great day," she sighed.

"Better than great," he agreed. He could hardly fathom it, but somehow, Kyra had managed to chisel her way past the hard shell he'd erected and turn him to mush.

As Dax was losing himself in her again, sliding into her body and giving himself up entirely and letting himself go completely, he thought, *This is it. This is the real deal.*

Nothing could come between them. He was generally not a believer in relationships blooming so quickly, but honestly, as they moved together, each of them finding their release, their hands clasped, he couldn't see a downside. Not one.

Chapter Eighteen

On a bright morning more than a week later, Kyra kissed Ruby good-bye, waved at Dax, then got in her car, and drove to work, giggling. *Giggling.* She didn't know when or why the giggling had started, but she couldn't help herself.

She still couldn't believe this had happened to her. She couldn't believe that the guy next door had fallen into her lap and she was now falling for him—and hard. She was falling so hard she was going to splatter in one big, gooey, heart-shaped puddle when she landed.

Even more amazing was that Dax was falling for *her*. He hadn't said it in so many words, but he'd said things like, "I'm crazy about you two, you know it?" At times she would catch him staring at her, and he would have this dreamy look in his eyes . . . oh, yes, he was totally into a broke single mom with a six-year-old who wouldn't stop talking. This was not some one-sided, Kyra's-desperate-again kind of relationship—this was real.

She marveled at how perfectly it was all working out, as if the love gods had arranged it all for them. Dax played with Ruby in the evenings so she could study. She cooked for him—a heretofore only passable skill that had miraculously seemed to improve, even to the point that she was contemplating asking Judgmental Megan for some recipes.

Kyra arrived at work, donned her apron, and went into the kitchen to help Deenie prepare the setups for the tables.

Kyra said hello, then as casually as she might, she asked, "Megan, could you give me that sweet potato mousse recipe? It was so good."

Megan's head instantly whipped around. "Why?" she asked, eyeing her with suspicion. "Have you turned over a new leaf?"

As a matter of fact. "Maybe," Kyra said, smiling. "Will you please just tell me how to make it? Ruby would love it."

"I'm sure she would. It's loaded with sugar," Megan said with great superiority. "But I'm so thrilled your daughter will actually have some decent nutrition with that sugar, I'm tempted to make it myself and send it home with you."

That remark would have annoyed Kyra to no end only a few short weeks ago, but she was too happy now. Megan couldn't get to her. "Or you could give me the recipe and let me try."

Megan peered at her as if she suspected she was being punked. But she said, "Remind me at the end of your shift." She picked up a big bucket and disappeared into the cooler.

"Okay, that's it," Deenie said. "What is going on with you? You're asking *Megan* for recipes? Has an alien invaded your body?"

Kyra glanced over her shoulder to make sure Megan was still in the cooler. "You really want to know?" she whispered giddily.

"Yes, I *really* want to know."

"I'm seeing someone," Kyra said.

Deenie gasped. She punched Kyra's shoulder. "And you didn't *tell* me? Give me all the details. Do I know him?"

"You know of him," Kyra said. "It's my neighbor, Dax."

Deenie gasped again. "The asshole next door?"

"Did I say that?" Kyra laughed. "Yep, one and the same."

"No way! Keep talking."

Kyra told her everything. How he'd helped her a couple of times and she'd decided he wasn't really an asshole. How he was really cute, and great with Ruby. How it had sort of happened after he'd brought a date here, and how everything about her life was suddenly falling into place. She'd had time to study for her real estate exam. There was the small glitch with Ruby and the seizures—Kyra had told Deenie about that earlier—but everyone said Ruby would be fine, and Kyra believed everything really would be fine.

"I don't know, Deenie—it's just perfect. I can't believe it—I've always assumed I wouldn't have an opportunity like this, at least not before Ruby was in college, and boom, here it is." She beamed at her friend. "I am so happy."

"Wow," Deenie said, beaming too. "I kind of wondered after the Phil thing. I mean, I didn't know having a kid was such a buzzkill. Not that Ruby is a buzzkill," she quickly amended. "But you know what I mean. How is she, anyway?"

"She's great," Kyra said. "I took her for the tests the doctor recommended a couple of days ago."

"What kind of tests?" Deenie asked and passed a big can of salt to Kyra so she could fill the table salt shakers.

"She had an EEG, which reads the brain waves or something like that. And an MRI and a CAT scan."

"And?"

"And nothing," Kyra said with a shrug. "When the test results come in, I'll get the all clear, they'll put her on some medicine, and that's that. The doctor said she'll grow out of it. And you know, I hardly think of it now. The seizures are so quick, and she never even knows it."

"Still," Deenie said. "Poor thing."

Kyra nodded. "She's such a little trooper. I am so proud of her, I'm just busting at the seams," she said. "The worst was the EEG. Not because it hurt, but because she had to lie still for an hour and a half. Dax made her a little wooden dog, so she held onto that, and she did *great.* I thought the MRI and the CAT scan would freak her out, but Ruby thought it was cool. She said it was like being in a witch's cave." She paused and looked at Deenie. "Should I be alarmed that she thinks being in a witch's cave is fun?"

Deenie laughed.

Kyra truly marveled at her young daughter's poise. Ruby had done everything they'd asked of her, without complaint. But when Kyra was signing off on the last of the paperwork—and writing a check for her share of the procedure from her dwindling bank account, Ruby had tugged her shirt and had asked, "Am I sick, Mommy?"

"No," Kyra had said. "Remember how I told you they just wanted to peek inside your head?"

"But why?"

"Because sometimes you flutter your fingers and you don't see me."

"I *do*?" Ruby asked, wrinkling her nose.

"You do. And that's totally okay, you know. But the doctors want to make sure there aren't any elves living in there," she said and fluttered her fingers against Ruby's head.

Ruby giggled. "Elves can't live in your head."

"That's what *I* said," Kyra had assured her. "Want to get some ice cream?"

Any thought of the tests had flitted out of Ruby's head at that point, and she hadn't said another word about it since.

"I'm happy for you, Kyra," Deenie said as she picked up her tray. "Everything is coming together, and you totally deserve it."

The lunch shift flew by, and afterward, with the sweet potato mousse recipe in her back pocket, Kyra went to the Washeteria. Dax and Ruby had gone to see Jonathan today, so she had the entire afternoon to herself.

She returned to Number Three with a basket full of clean laundry—which now included Dax's laundry, as Kyra figured that was the least she could do in return for all he was doing for her. Before she put the laundry away, she picked up the living room. Dax had made Ruby a menagerie of wooden animals. A cow, a horse, a dog. It seemed like a new one appeared every day. Ruby carried them everywhere, and twice Kyra had noticed Ruby experiencing a seizure while holding one of the wooden figures. She thought it was interesting that Ruby's fingers would curl tightly around the toy instead of fluttering, as if part of her brain knew not to let go.

Kyra was settling down to study when she got the call from Dr. Green she'd been expecting. "Hello?" she asked cheerfully and grabbed a pen to jot down the name of the medicine she expected him to prescribe.

"Hold for Dr. Green, please," the receptionist said.

A moment later, the doctor said, "Mrs. Kokinos?"

It never seemed to matter how many times she circled *Ms.* on forms, the doctors' offices insisted on calling her *Mrs.* "Hi, Dr. Green. I was hoping you'd call soon."

"We got the test results back and I've had a chance to look at them," he said. "I'm going to refer you to a neuropathologist."

Refer her? Kyra wasn't expecting that. "A what?"

"It looks like Ruby has a small tumor," he said.

With those words, the world dropped out from beneath Kyra's feet. Dr. Green suddenly sounded as if he were at the far end of a tunnel. Something about removal and a biopsy, and the location of the tumor was good, which sounded so asinine to Kyra, but she couldn't say so, because she couldn't breathe.

"Mrs. Kokinos?"

Kyra found her voice. "What are you talking about?" she croaked. "You said you were sure!"

"I said I was ninety-five percent, but that's why we did the tests. Look, I'm still not too concerned. It's a very small tumor, and the location is such that it should be easily removed. But we need to know what we're dealing with, so we need to have it removed and get it biopsied."

A wave of nausea came over Kyra so suddenly she thought she would vomit right there. A memory, so deeply buried she hadn't thought of it in years, came roaring back to her. *We need to know what we're dealing with.* That's what her mother had told her. That was the reason, she'd told Kyra, that she was going to the hospital.

"Ohmigod," Kyra whispered. *"Ohmigod."*

"I know this is not the news you were expecting to hear, Mrs. Kokinos, but please don't panic. We don't know what this is, and it might be nothing at all. No matter what we find, we have all sorts of treatments available to us. Now, I'm referring you to a place that can see you Friday. It's in the city, but they are the best. I've already sent the films."

The best. Did that mean she'd have to sell her car? "I don't . . . I don't understand," she said and rubbed her forehead. So many dangerous thoughts were suddenly pinging around in her head.

"Mrs. Kokinos, I am still very, very optimistic," Dr. Green said.

That was supposed to comfort her? Going from certain it was nothing to optimistic it wasn't anything did not sound like a good thing to her.

"Do you have a pen?" he asked.

Kyra took down the information. Dr. Green invited Kyra to call with any questions. "Anytime, day or night," he said.

"Thanks," she said weakly and hung up the phone. She still couldn't catch her breath—her heart was beating painfully in her chest. She stacked her hands on top of her head and walked a tight circle around her kitchen, trying to suck in air. A flurry of images of Ruby went by—her daughter in a surgery gown. With tubes sticking out of her. In a casket that happened to look just like her mother's casket.

That image forced Kyra into a chair. She braced her hands on her knees and bent over, trying not to pass out. Kyra had lost her mother when she'd needed her most—she never dreamed she could lose her daughter, too.

"No!" she shouted and slammed her fist down on the table. She would not lose both her mother and her daughter to brain tumors, she would *not*. She'd do anything she had to do—

Kyra suddenly opened her laptop and clicked on her banking app. She had thirty-six hundred dollars in savings. That was all she'd managed to save in the last six years, and she hadn't even scratched the surface of her health insurance deductible.

She went to a government site to see if she could get Ruby on Medicaid, but their quick calculation box said that she made too much money to qualify. How ironic was that? They were living hand-to-mouth, and yet she made too much money. Kyra's chest began to feel even more constricted, and she wondered if she was having a heart attack. She willed it to stop—she had to be here, she had to be strong for Ruby. She stood up and walked in a circle again, her mind racing, then went back to her computer and opened Facebook.

Josh Burton. He had to help her. There was no longer any choice for him.

She found him on Facebook again. There he was, his latest picture of him and two guys he'd tagged—one with the same last name—fishing on some lake. It was grossly unfair that he could enjoy some simple pleasure like fishing while his biological daughter was growing a fucking brain tumor. Kyra had let the man off the hook all these years, and until this moment she'd been okay with that. But she was going to pull out every stop for Ruby, and if he had health insurance, she needed it.

She googled him. Several Josh Burtons came up, three in Indianapolis. But there was only one Josh Burton at Castlemaine Industries. She searched Google records, clicked on every link she could find having to do with Josh Burton of Indianapolis and Castlemaine Industries. She was about to pay for a subscription to one of the record-searching sites that would give her a phone number and address, but before she did that, she went back to his Facebook page one more time to make sure she had her facts straight. And when she clicked on *About*, she saw something that she'd missed, and it startled her. Josh's mobile phone number was displayed. Apparently, he'd not locked that information when he'd entered it.

It was a gift from heaven.

Kyra grabbed her phone and dialed the number. It rang three times and a woman answered.

She jerked back, almost as if she'd been struck. "Ah . . . I'm sorry, I must have the wrong number."

"Who are you trying to reach?" the woman asked pleasantly.

"Josh Burton?"

"He's right here," she said. A moment later, a man said, "Hello?"

A visceral shiver ran through Kyra at the sound of his voice. The years sloughed away, and several forgotten memories crowded into her head.

"Hello?" he said again.

"Josh," Kyra said and cleared her throat. "It's Kyra Kokinos. I really need to talk to you."

Chapter Nineteen

Ruby Coconuts wanted to stop at McDonald's on their way back from Teaneck. "Mommy never lets me go there," she said, pouting.

"Maybe next time," he said.

"But we *always* go to McDonald's when we visit the baby."

Dax snorted. "Your math doesn't add up, Coconut. This is only the second time you've seen Jonathan. You haven't gone enough times for always."

Ruby didn't say anything, and Dax glanced at her in the rearview mirror. Her gaze was fixed on the window, but she was holding her hand up at her chest, and the fingers were fluttering. Dax wondered if it was his imagination that the seizures were growing more frequent or if he just noticed them more now.

She suddenly looked at him. "Can we go to McDonald's?"

"McDonald's, huh?" It was odd, he thought, how sometimes Ruby stepped back in time after a seizure instead of picking up with whatever she'd been doing. That didn't seem to fit with what he knew about absence seizures.

"We *always* stop at McDonald's when we visit your baby."

"I hope they teach you math in school," he said.

"I want chicken nuggets," she said.

"My life lessons are falling on deaf ears," he said and pulled into McDonald's.

By the time they made it back to East Beach, Dax was in a jovial mood, eager to tell Kyra that Jonathan was eating like a little oinker and was sleeping through the night. He would also report that Ashley made him change a diaper today, which, Dax could proudly admit, he got right on the first try. He was going back on Sunday. Ashley had mentioned Stephanie would be playing soccer all day, and in spite of his and Stephanie's quasi truce, Dax definitely intended to take advantage of that time without her hovering nearby.

When they pulled into the drive of Number Two, Ruby flung open the door and leapt from the car. Otto pushed his way out of the screen door and bounded down the steps to her, his tail wagging furiously, happier to see Ruby than the man who fed his useless ass every day. Ruby didn't notice Otto loping behind her as she raced toward her house, her long ribbon of red hair streaming behind her and the few functioning lights of her boots blinking with each step. The plastic toy she'd received in her Happy Meal was already forgotten, left behind in the passenger seat.

Dax picked it up and went inside.

In the kitchen, he carried Otto's water bowl to the sink to refill. He happened to look out the window and saw Kyra standing on her porch, looking in the direction of his cottage. He smiled . . . but then he noticed the way she was hugging herself. He had a shiver of premonition—something was wrong, he could sense it.

Dax put the dog's bowl down and went out the back door. He began to walk across the lawn, and when Kyra saw him, she ran. She leapt off the porch steps and ran, halting herself at the fence a few steps ahead of him.

His alarm bells began to sound—she'd been crying.

"Kyra?" He reached for her, cupping her face. "What the hell?"

Kyra glanced nervously over her shoulder and said, "She won't come out, I don't think—I put her in front of the television."

"Ruby?"

"She has a tumor, Dax. A *tumor*."

That word—the sound of it grotesque—didn't really compute with him. He stared at Kyra, waiting for her to take it back, to say *tremor* or *tutor*, or anything but that word. But Kyra didn't take it back. "What?" he asked dumbly.

"She has, like, a growth," she said, gesturing wildly at her head. "A tumor."

"Kyra, you're not making sense. She has absence seizures, not a . . . not that," he said, unable to say the word. He had an insane urge to laugh, but his heart was beating too hard for that. "Tell me what they said."

"He *said* he was ninety-five percent certain, but now he's only *optimistic*, and there is so much he said that I didn't understand because I couldn't *breathe*—"

Dax was stunned, but Kyra looked like she was going to collapse. He hopped over the fence and grabbed her before she could, wrapping his arms around her and holding her tightly to him.

She sobbed into his shoulder.

"Don't cry," he said roughly, stroking the back of her head. "Please don't cry. We'll get to the bottom of it, I promise. Calm down, catch your breath, and tell me everything."

She nodded and wiped her face on his shirt. They perched on the fence as Kyra told him her conversation with the doctor, her voice monotone, her expression desolate.

Dax was devastated. He thought of that bright little girl and couldn't imagine anything really *wrong* with her. It made him feel sick. And furious. He wanted to rip a tree from the ground and throw it in the lake. He put his arm around Kyra's shoulder and squeezed. "Look, it sounds dire, but it may not be."

"Please, don't say that," she said morosely. "Everyone said it was nothing before, and I believed them, and look what happened. My God, I am so scared."

"I know," he said and held her tighter. "So am I."

"I don't know how I'll pay for it. I'll have to sell my car and my grandmother's opal—"

"Hey, hey," Dax said. "Don't get ahead of yourself in finding things to worry about. First things first—you're going to see a neuropathologist on Friday, right? Let's see what that doctor says and then think about next steps."

"I already took the next step. I called Josh," she said, as if she were announcing something important.

"Who?" Dax asked, confused.

"Ruby's father," she said, and a tear slipped from her eye that she hastily wiped away.

Dax was stunned by her admission—he hadn't thought of that loser since Kyra first told him about the circumstances of Ruby's birth.

"*He* has insurance, I know he does," she said bitterly. "It's only fair, right?"

"What did he say?"

Kyra shook her head. "First, he had to call me back. I guess he was with his wife. He said that his wife didn't know about Ruby, and it would destroy his marriage, and he couldn't tell her. But that he would send me five thousand dollars to help." She snorted. "Like that's going to do it. My dad lost everything paying for my mom's care, and they had insurance."

"Had you talked to him before today?" Dax asked curiously, still trying to put the pieces together.

"What? No," she said morosely, shaking her head. "I haven't spoken to him since before Ruby was born. I found him on Facebook."

"He's never helped you." It wasn't really a question, but more a confirmation of what Dax thought he understood.

Kyra snorted and folded her arms across her middle. "Helped me? Not one bit. He made it pretty clear when I found out I was pregnant that he didn't want her. I should have forced the issue, but I didn't want him around if he didn't want her, you know?" She buried her face in her hands. "God, I'm such an idiot. I *knew* what it was like to be a single parent. I watched my dad work all the time just to make ends meet. Why didn't I insist that Josh do his fair share? She'd be on his insurance now, and I wouldn't have to worry." She lifted her head. "I can't stop thinking about all the mistakes I made that are going to cost my daughter now."

"Hey," Dax said sternly. He put his hand to her chin and made her look at him. "You didn't do anything wrong, Kyra. You didn't put that tumor in her head. You made the best decisions for her that you knew to make at every step of the way, and you can't fault yourself for that. I won't let you."

It was clear she wasn't listening—she was spinning. "I don't know what I'm going to do. What if she needs surgery? What if she needs more than that? What if she needs therapy, or a lot of medicine? I have the *worst* insurance."

"All I know is that right now, today, you have to get it together, Kyra. Ruby doesn't know what's coming down the pike, and she needs you at one hundred percent."

Kyra stared at him. For a moment Dax thought he'd crossed a line. But she nodded in agreement and dropped her gaze. "You're right. You're absolutely right."

He picked up her hand and held it. "I'll go with you to the biopsy."

"You don't have—"

"Don't even say it," he warned her. "I'm not going to let either one of you go through this alone. We'll see what they say and figure it out from there."

Kyra looked up, her expression hopeful and grateful at once. She squeezed his hand. "You will?"

"Of course I will. Everything's going to be okay." It had to be, because Dax couldn't bear to think of the alternative. But the rage of impotence was brewing in him. How could this happen to such a beautiful little girl?

How could this have happened to them all?

Chapter Twenty

Dax was right, Kyra decided. She couldn't spend another moment beating herself up with bad-mother guilt. For Ruby's sake, she had to focus on the positive. So she picked herself up and clung to the fact that Dr. Green was still optimistic. That was her new mantra—optimism in all things.

But privately Kyra couldn't stop comparing Ruby's situation to her mother's. She even called her dad one night, needing to commiserate with someone else who understood. It had been months since she'd talked to him—they'd drifted so far apart over the years that now their only communication seemed to come around the holidays.

"Haven't heard from you in a while," he said when he answered the phone.

For the record, Kyra hadn't heard from him, either. "I have news," she said.

Her dad was silent as she told him about Ruby: the seizures she didn't know were seizures. The tests, the tumor.

When at last he did speak, he asked, "Is it hereditary?"

"I don't think so. The doctor said probably not. But I . . . what do you think?"

"I guess it could be."

Kyra squeezed her eyes shut. What she really wanted was for her father to tell her that it was impossible, that everything was going to be okay. She didn't know why she thought he would give her that, really—he'd never been able to assure her, not even when she was twelve and had needed his reassurance so deeply. "I don't know what I'm going to do, Dad," she said quietly.

"You're going to put one foot in front of the other, that's all you can do."

"Yeah," she said.

"I'm sorry this happened," he said and then changed the subject. He began to talk about fishing, which seemed to be the only thing he did these days.

Kyra took his advice and worked to keep one foot in front of the other. But she was distracted, plagued by so many what-if scenarios.

For two days, she and Dax both went through the motions. They had dinner together. They walked along the lakeshore and watched Ruby and Otto run ahead, picking up things, discarding things, chattering about nothing and everything.

When Friday finally rolled around, Kyra was up before dawn. She would miss a good shift today, traded to Deenie for her Monday shift.

Dax was all smiles when he showed up on their porch to escort them into Manhattan for Ruby's doctor appointment. If she couldn't put up the necessary front, he would do it for both of them.

"Where are we going?" Ruby asked. She was dressed in a yellow dress with bumblebees embroidered in dizzying patterns. Kyra had put her hair in a high ponytail. She had on her pink boots and looked adorable.

"To the doctor, sweetie."

"For me?"

"Yes, you."

Ruby frowned. "I've already *been* to the doctor. Why do I have to go again?"

"Guess what?" Dax said. He was leaning against the door frame, and Kyra was momentarily struck by how strong and confident he looked. She wanted to sink into his arms and bury her face against his chest.

"What?" Ruby asked.

"We're going to McDonald's today."

Ruby gasped. "We *are*?"

"We always go after a doctor visit."

She giggled. "We don't *always* go," she said. But she walked out the door and down the steps to Kyra's car.

An hour later Kyra, Dax, and Ruby were in a glass high-rise in midtown Manhattan, in the offices of the neuropathologist, Dr. Mehta. After what felt like an interminable wait in the waiting room, they were finally shown into an examining room.

Dr. Mehta reminded Kyra of a mad scientist. She was short, wore a white lab coat, and her short hair, streaked gray, looked as if she'd been shoving her fingers through it all day. She carefully reviewed Ruby's films as Ruby played with Kyra's phone, then performed a cursory examination of her.

"Well," Dr. Mehta said when she'd finished examining Ruby and Ruby's attention was focused on Kyra's phone once more, "let's start with the good news. The growth in Ruby's head is quite small."

Kyra sat, waiting, immobile. That was not good news. She didn't care how small it was, it didn't belong there.

"That's good," Dax said.

"That's very good," Dr. Mehta agreed. "It's an easier surgery."

"Surgery," Kyra slowly repeated. Of course she knew it would require surgery, but she needed to say it aloud.

Dr. Mehta fixed a dark, brown-eyed gaze on Kyra. "We're going to want to get it out of there, obviously, and have it biopsied. It's on the cerebellum, just behind her ear, which is easy to reach. I think we have an excellent chance of getting it all."

"Then what?" Kyra asked.

"Then, depending on what the biopsy reveals, we'll hopefully need only to monitor her for seizures and keep an eye on her to see if it comes back. Often, these types of growths in kids don't come back."

"And . . . if you can't get it all? If it's malignant?" Kyra asked flatly.

"Well, then we'll have to talk about radiation and maybe chemo," the doctor said. "Even if it's benign, if we can't get it all, we would not want to risk a malignancy."

Kyra said nothing, processing that news.

"I don't understand any of this," Dax said. "She had the classic symptoms of absence seizures."

Dr. Mehta nodded. "Focal seizures can look exactly like absence seizures," she said. "It's not common, but it happens. This is all good news, Mrs. Kokinos. If your child has the misfortune of being diagnosed with a brain tumor, this is really the best of all possible worlds. I'll have my surgical coordinator get in touch with you to go over insurance and procedures. We'll want to get another MRI before the surgery to see if anything has changed. Sound good?"

No, it sounded like a nightmare.

Dr. Mehta moved to the door. "Take all the time you need," she said.

When the doctor had gone out, neither Kyra nor Dax spoke, both of them lost in thought, both of them staring at the bland tile floor. Ruby came around and stood in front of Kyra, and when Kyra looked up, she started—Ruby looked furious. "Mommy, you said I wasn't sick," she said accusingly.

Kyra didn't know what to say. "I don't think you're sick, pumpkin," she said, cringing inwardly at her lie. "But the doctors want to make extra sure."

"Can't you just tell them I'm not sick?"

She swallowed. "I can, pumpkin, but they want to make sure. Because if you are sick, they want to make you better."

"I don't like the doctor," Ruby said.

Kyra reached for Ruby and drew her into her embrace. "I know. I don't like any of this, either. I *hate* it. You know how bad I hate it? I want to stomp it into the ground like we stomped on the mud patties last week."

Ruby smiled a little. "I made a *huge* splat."

"Yes, you did."

"Can we go to McDonald's now?" Ruby asked.

"Yes," Kyra said and ran her hand over Ruby's head. "You bet." Today Ruby could have whatever she wanted.

"Yay!" Ruby said and ran around Kyra to pick up Kyra's phone. "Can I play on your phone until we get there?"

"Yep." Kyra stood up and looked at Dax.

He reached for her hand and gave it a reassuring squeeze. It was all he could give her. There was nothing in this world that could possibly make this better for any of them except for that tumor to disappear.

♦ ♦ ♦

Kyra had to hand it to Dax—over the next few days he did everything he could to cheer them all up. He made Ruby a set of furniture for her Barbies that she thought was the greatest thing to be produced in the history of toys. He made Ruby and Kyra homemade pizza Saturday night and produced an expensive bottle of wine.

"You've been holding out on me," Kyra had said when she looked at the pizza. "Who knew a guy like you could make a pizza like this?"

"You have no idea of the depth of my talents," he'd said.

"I think I have an idea," she'd said, winking at him.

Dax laughed and glanced at Ruby. "What do you think, Coconut, is it okay if I kiss your mom?"

Ruby looked up from her dolls. "Why?"

"Because I like her. I like her a lot."

"I *know* you like her," Ruby said and looked at Kyra.

"I like him, too," Kyra said. "Do you like him?"

Ruby giggled. "Is he your boyfriend?"

"Ah . . ." Kyra glanced sidelong at Dax. "Yep. He is my boyfriend."

"Then okay," Ruby somberly agreed. "Kiss her."

Dax wrapped his arm around Kyra and kissed her squarely on the lips for the first time in front of Ruby. And then he bent down, grabbed Ruby up, and kissed her, too, while she writhed and laughed and said, "Don't kiss *me*! I'm not your girlfriend!"

Sunday, they went to the movies, Dax's treat.

"You're doing too much," Kyra said. She knew he was trying to help, but it was beginning to feel like charity.

"Stop counting," Dax said and shoved a big bucket of popcorn at her. Kyra wasn't feeling so indebted as to protest popcorn. But she was aware that it was too much, that she'd sprung too much on this man too soon in too short a time. It wasn't fair. None of it was fair, but it especially wasn't fair to him.

Kyra took another day off work and went back into the city to meet with the surgical coordinator, who basically explained that anything short of cutting into her daughter's head wasn't an option. They reviewed Kyra's sorry insurance and all the things that were covered. Then they reviewed all the things that weren't covered. The bottom line was that no matter how many procedures were covered, it was still going to cost Kyra a pretty penny. She would sell her soul if she had to, but the question of where she would possibly get the money she needed weighed on her.

Forget studying—it was impossible for her to concentrate. So Kyra funneled her restlessness into work as much as possible. For the first time since she had moved in, her cottage was spick-and-span. She worked as much as she could at the bistro. She was able to pick up an extra shift or two and made up some of the money she'd lost to missed shifts because of doctor appointments.

And then the call came. In three weeks Ruby was required to get a follow-up MRI. The surgery was scheduled about a week after that, and Ruby would have that horrible tumor removed.

Kyra didn't know how she'd endure it, and she was grateful to have Dax to lean on. She didn't know how she would ever make this up to Dax. She didn't know if it was even possible. But she was so grateful to him for his support, so indebted.

Too indebted. As much as she needed him right now, their budding relationship felt dangerously out of balance.

Chapter Twenty-One

There had to be another pair of pink cowboy boots in the universe, and Dax was determined to find them. Ruby's toes were sticking out the ends, and one of the boots had stopped lighting up at all. So one afternoon he piled his trusty sidekick into his truck—the two-legged one instead of the four-legged one—and headed to Black Springs to find them.

It turned out that pink cowboy boots with lights were not as common as Dax had assumed. But he did manage to convince Ruby that a pair of tennis shoes with Velcro straps and lights might be a suitable substitute. They walked through a very long aisle of pink and purple shoes, none of them acceptable to the coconut until she suddenly gasped, screeched, "Elsa!" and begged for them.

Elsa, Dax learned, was a character in the Disney movie *Frozen*, and Ruby seemed more than a little perturbed that he didn't know it. He reminded her that there were a lot of things that she didn't know, either, and he didn't hold that against her.

She wasn't listening because she was studying every facet of those damn light-up tennis shoes.

This little shopping excursion was, under normal circumstances, the last thing Dax would want to do. He despised shopping in all its forms, and especially with a female, even if that female was six. But it had been a welcome diversion from the constant emotional tug-of-war in him—the worry about Kyra and Ruby, the elation of having a newborn son.

He returned to the cottages and delivered Ruby to Mrs. McCauley, who had invited her to help make a birthday cake for one of her grandchildren. Why anyone would willingly ask for Ruby's help in the kitchen was beyond Dax, but Ruby was excited. "Remember," he said as he walked her up to the big Victorian house on the hill, "you need to include *all* the ingredients."

"Maybe we can put M&M'S in the cake. Taleesha's mom makes cupcakes with M&M'S in them."

When they reached the door, Mrs. McCauley was waiting for them.

"Her mother should be home in a couple of hours," Dax said.

"That will be perfect," Mrs. McCauley said. "It takes time to create great cake art for my granddaughter."

"How old is she?" Ruby asked.

"Well, the truth is, I forget how old any of them are, but I know it's Mia's birthday because I wrote it down." She winked at Ruby and took her by the hand. "Don't worry about us, Dax."

Well, that was impossible.

He walked down to his cottage, but as he neared it, Kyra's Subaru pulled into the drive at Number Three. As he walked across the lawn, Kyra stepped out of her car. She was wearing red pencil jeans and a sleeveless denim shirt. Her hair was pulled back into one long tail. She had on huge, dark sunglasses, and as he couldn't see her eyes, he couldn't determine her mood. She looked like the tourists who strolled up and down Main Street.

She waited for him, leaning against the fender of her car. When he reached her, Dax took the sunglasses from her face and studied her.

"What?" she said, brushing her fingers across her cheek. "Do I have something on me?"

"Nope. I just needed to see your face. I thought you were at work."

"I was. I left early to go check on some things."

"What things?"

She smiled a little. "Money things." She pushed away from her car and started toward the cottage. "Where's Ruby?"

"She and Mrs. McCauley are making a cake," he said, following her. "What money things?" he asked.

"Oh, nothing. I went by social services," she said. "I thought maybe there was some program, something to help me with the cost of Ruby's care." She glanced over her shoulder. "There's not. And surgery is expensive."

Dax walked with her into the kitchen. "But you have insurance."

Kyra snorted. "Crappy insurance. A huge deductible and a low ceiling of maximum expenses. You know . . . the cheapest I could find. And I actually make too much money to qualify for aid. How ironic is that?"

"How much money do you need?" he asked.

"A lot. I'm looking at at least ten thousand in out-of-pocket expenses. And then there are things that aren't covered, like any psychotherapy she might need because of the trauma, and some of the rehabilitation."

Dax felt lucky to have good insurance. It cost him a small fortune, but it was excellent coverage, particularly for out-of-pocket expenses, and . . .

And why didn't I think of this before? I have excellent insurance.

The idea that just occurred to him was ridiculous. Really far out there. He looked at Kyra as she sifted through some bills on her kitchen table. God, but she was beautiful. The last couple of weeks had been so tense he'd forgotten to notice.

She glanced up and smiled, her gaze questioning. "What? I know, you're going to tell me to quit being such a sad sack, right?" Her smiled turned rueful. "I'm working on it, I swear I am."

"That's not what I was thinking."

She waited for him to explain. Dax had to think of how to say it.

Kyra tucked a strand of hair away from her face and laughed a little. "You're worrying me now. You look so serious."

"I was thinking that I have excellent insurance."

She nodded, but her expression didn't change. She didn't get what he was saying.

So Dax said it again. "I have *excellent insurance*."

Kyra's expression changed to surprise. "Dax . . ."

"Just hear me out, okay?" he asked. "What I'm about to say is for Ruby's sake. You and I could get married, and I could put her on my insurance. It's against the law now to deny her coverage. She would be covered. You wouldn't be out so much money."

Kyra was shaking her head before he'd finished his sentence. "*No*, Dax. I can't let you do that."

"Why not?"

"Why *not*?" she echoed incredulously. "Haven't you done enough for us? Don't you see how you're always bailing me out? I won't let you sacrifice everything for us. I won't do it."

"It's for Ruby—"

"I don't care. It's not fair to you."

"Look, we've been great together, haven't we? It could work. And it would be a huge help to you."

"We've only been together a *month*. You're talking crazy."

"Let's assume it could be great," he said. "But if it's not, okay, we divorce when she's in the clear. But the point is, you don't have to worry about money or coverage and you can concentrate on being there for her."

"You don't get it, Dax," she said, sounding frustrated now. "I don't *want* you to save us. I want to be an equal, not an anvil around your neck, and so far Ruby and I are the anvil that just keeps getting heavier."

He didn't agree with that. He'd been happy to be needed for a change, and he was disappointed in her adamant rejection of his idea. "We're talking about your daughter's health, Kyra. Not your idea of what this relationship should look like."

Kyra laughed. "You think you can shame me? Get in line. If anyone should be helping me right now, it's Josh Burton, not you. If I have to, I'll get a lawyer. He needs to pony up." She picked up a towel and began to wipe down her countertops with a vengeance.

Dax watched her. He felt weird. Like maybe he'd read this situation with Kyra all wrong. Like he'd forgotten all about his broken heart when maybe he should have been tending the cracks. "Getting lawyered up to go after a man who hasn't seen his daughter could take more time than you have."

"Maybe. Maybe not," she said. She put down the towel and turned around, folding her arms across her body. "Dax . . . I can't thank you enough for being there for me. I have needed you so much—but I think maybe I've needed you too much."

"What's that supposed to mean?" he asked, frowning.

"I'm not sure," she said and glanced down a moment. "But the balance is all wrong between us." She risked another look at him. "I need to think about it."

Alarm bells began to sound in Dax's brain. This thing between them, this amazing, wonderful thing, felt as if it was suddenly in danger of exploding. "Okay," he said with a shrug, as if he didn't care, which couldn't be further from the truth. "But the offer stands. Think about it." He glanced at his watch. "I need to get some work done." Not true. He just needed to get out of there. He stepped around her and walked out of her cottage. And he kept walking all the way to his house without looking back. What was wrong with helping her when she needed him?

Why did it have to be equal? Life wasn't equal. Life was ups and downs and it wasn't *equal* for anyone.

Dax had a frozen meal that night, one he found deep in his freezer and the first he'd had in a few weeks. Funny how one's dining habits changed when one was part of a couple.

After that unsatisfying meal, Dax wandered around his cottage. He was too at odds with himself to work. He took Otto for a long walk along the lakeshore, where he debated with himself over and over again. Had he lost his sense of how to be in a relationship? Was he wrong about what he'd felt between him and Kyra? Had it all been wishful thinking on his part? Or was Kyra simply running scared? Yes, what had happened to them was a lot to digest after only a few short weeks of being an item, he got that, and Kyra had raised valid points . . . but Dax thought there was something deeper to them, something that allowed them to hopscotch over the insecurities.

Whether he was wrong or right, he felt some uncomfortable rumblings in his heart. It was scooting back on its shelf, clinging to the wall at its back in fear of falling and shattering on the cold stone floor of truth.

He turned in early because he couldn't work and he couldn't read. But his sleep was shallow, his mind plagued with doubts. Nevertheless, he was asleep when a sound startled him awake. He shot upright and reached for something to swing.

"Dax, it's me," Kyra whispered.

His heart was pounding, and he eased back against the headboard of his bed. "What the hell? You scared me, Kyra. I could have hit you."

"I'm sorry. I didn't mean to scare you, but it seemed weird to throw rocks against your window when your door was standing open."

"My door was standing open?"

"Wide open."

"No wonder that damn dog didn't warn me you were here," he said and sighed. "Wait—what are you doing here in the middle of the night? Is everything okay? Is Ruby—"

"She's asleep." Kyra climbed onto the foot of his bed and started to crawl her way up his body, straddling him. And then she was on his lap, her hands braced against his chest. "Does the offer still stand?"

He studied her in the dim light. He didn't know if they were still out of balance, but he covered her hands with his and said, "Yes. Absolutely."

"It's a weird offer," she said and leaned down to kiss his cheek.

"Don't care." He caressed her, his hand moving over the pajama bottoms that felt like liquid silk beneath his hand.

"It's insane if you would take two seconds to think about it."

"What's your point?" he asked gruffly.

She kissed his other cheek. "I want to tell you that I love you, Dax, but I won't say it. Not yet, anyway," she said and nibbled his ear. "Because I don't want you to think I am telling you I love you simply because you bailed me out. *Again.* That's not why."

He tried to look at her, but she moved to his neck. "Do you love me?" he asked.

"I just told you," she said, her voice light. "I can't tell you that." She moved down to his chest, trailing her tongue and lips across him. "But I accept your marriage proposal." And she kept moving down his chest, to his hips, dragging his boxers down with her.

Dax sank back into his pillow. He was smiling for obvious reasons—and gasping with sheer delight when she took him in her mouth—but it wasn't just the physical pleasure. Someone had opened a window in the heavens, and the sun was shining bright in that dark room. Dax hadn't expected to be happy that Kyra would accept his offer of sudden engagement, but he was. In some strange way, this unusual arrangement felt right to him, like it was supposed to happen this way. He'd done something good for a change.

And he was shockingly happy about it.

Chapter Twenty-Two

Kyra was getting married.

She still couldn't believe it, and sort of floated through the next day, marveling at how her life had spiraled and flipped and somersaulted into this engagement. She was equal parts happy and worried and confused and certain . . . but she could not deny that after last night in Dax's dark room, when he'd made love to her so tenderly that it made her heart ache with longing, she'd felt something inside her move off center.

She couldn't pinpoint the moment when she'd changed her mind about his offer, or what had made her kiss Ruby's forehead while she slept and then slip out of the cottage last night. But it had happened during her conversation with Mrs. McCauley.

After Dax had left yesterday afternoon, Kyra had walked up to Mrs. McCauley's to fetch her daughter. Mrs. McCauley was marginally aware of the issues with Ruby's health, and she'd asked why Ruby was talking about doctors.

Kyra told her landlord the truth, spelling out certain words like *surgery* and *tumor* so that Ruby, who was otherwise preoccupied with putting icing on their cake, wouldn't take note of the conversation.

"Oh dear," Mrs. McCauley said and caressed the top of Ruby's head. "Oh my. That must be overwhelming for you."

"Look!" Ruby said, displaying the mess she'd made on one side of the cake.

"That's beautiful, sweetie," Mrs. McCauley said.

"It is overwhelming," Kyra admitted. "I can't stop thinking about it."

"Well, of course not," Mrs. McCauley said. "Do you have any family to help you?"

Kyra shook her head. "Just my dad in Florida, but he . . . he's not much help."

Mrs. McCauley nodded. "Don't be afraid to lean on your friends."

Kyra snorted. "I lean too much as it is."

"What's that?" Mrs. McCauley said. "You seem quite self-sufficient to me, Kyra. Trust me, I have a granddaughter named Skylar who is someone who leans too much, and I swear that girl can't tie her own shoelaces without someone's help. No, you have a good head on your shoulders, and you work for what you've got."

Kyra smiled. "Thanks." She wished it was as simple as working for what she had.

"Now, Dax, there's a good friend," Mrs. McCauley said a bit slyly.

Dax was more than that—he was her knight in shining armor. "He's been very helpful," Kyra agreed.

"He kissed Mommy," Ruby announced.

Mrs. McCauley arched a brow. "He did, did he?"

Kyra blushed. "Ah . . . he's been great, he really has," she said, bypassing the kiss remark. "But I feel as if I am taking advantage of him."

"Can't take advantage of someone unless they allow it," Mrs. McCauley said. "You have to look at it from his point of view. He's been alone for a long time, mean as a snake, and with no one to talk to but that flower-digging dog."

"Otto," Ruby offered.

"Otto," Mrs. McCauley agreed. "No one can live like that for long, Kyra. Everyone needs a purpose, a reason for getting up. Maybe he found that in you and Ruby."

She hadn't really thought of it that way. "But that doesn't make it fair," she said.

"For heaven's sake," Mrs. McCauley said and clucked her tongue at Kyra. "What's fair in this world? Seems to me that man has some pretty broad shoulders, if you ask me."

Maybe Mrs. McCauley was right. Maybe it wasn't such a bad thing to let Dax help her in this way. And maybe . . . maybe there was a small part of her that wanted this thing between them to go on forever. She really *did* love him.

She couldn't believe it. She couldn't believe she was actually going to marry him for insurance.

◆ ◆ ◆

Deenie *really* couldn't believe it.

Kyra had asked Deenie to meet her at the municipal park where she'd brought Ruby to play for the afternoon. It felt like madness to keep this news to herself, and Kyra desperately needed to tell someone, *anyone*. She thought—okay, she *hoped*—that Deenie would reaffirm her decision to take Dax up on his offer when she'd explained it all.

But Deenie didn't do that. She frowned, and she frowned deeply. "That is the dumbest thing I ever heard, Kyra."

Kyra's bubble instantly began to deflate. "It's for the insurance."

"What is it for him?"

"I don't . . . I think he just wants to help." She thought about what Mrs. McCauley had said, that she and Ruby were his purpose, but in the glare of Deenie's disapproving look that sounded silly.

"Wow, you sound so certain," Deenie said sarcastically.

Doubt began to creep into Kyra's thoughts. She could probably google it—*what does it mean when a guy offers to marry you so you can use his insurance?*—and find all kinds of reasons to assure her this was a bad idea. Maybe she should have done that before she'd crept into his bed or so excitedly texted Deenie. But Kyra shook that off—she *knew* Dax. Mrs. McCauley was right—he wanted to help. Kyra wasn't gullible—she knew what she was doing.

"That's insurance fraud, anyway," Deenie said as she examined her lipstick in a compact mirror.

"Is it?" Maybe Kyra didn't know so well what she was doing.

"*Yes!* You can't marry someone just to use their insurance and then *divorce* them."

Kyra hadn't said anything about divorce. She had very specifically *not* said anything about divorce because of her hope that this horrible awful nightmare would turn into a fairy tale and that maybe, just maybe, it could really work. She'd heard crazier stories, people who didn't know each other and married, and somehow it had all worked. Hell, the TLC network dedicated show after show to improbable unions. And what about the Bachelor franchise? It could happen. She wanted to argue this with Deenie, but she wasn't getting a conciliatory vibe off her friend.

"And what if he's really into you and this is his way of sealing the deal? Then you're just taking advantage of him."

The heat of shame crept up her neck. But Kyra *wasn't* taking advantage of him. She and Dax clearly understood one another. Didn't they?

Deenie was frowning at her, and Kyra had to consider that maybe they didn't understand each other. After all, wasn't she already beginning to treat him differently? Wasn't she treating him with deference because he was saving her daughter, instead of the way she might treat a boyfriend? This morning, when he'd wanted to take Ruby to see Jonathan, hadn't she said yes because . . . because she didn't want to displease him?

"I don't know, Kyra," Deenie said and stood up, hooking her purse over her shoulder as she glanced at her watch. "It just sounds really crazy to me."

"What am I supposed to do, Deenie?" Kyra exclaimed. "My daughter has a brain tumor—"

"I'm sure there is a way you can get help without getting married. This just smacks of desperation." She peered down at Kyra. "Wait—you're not doing this because of Phil, are you?"

"Phil! What are you talking about?"

"Do you maybe think this is your chance to be married?"

That remark hit Kyra squarely in the gut. "*No!* Jesus, Deenie, give me a little credit! I'm not desperate like that! This is about Ruby, and that's all."

"Is it, really?" she asked, then glanced at her watch. "Look, I gotta go." Deenie leaned down to kiss Kyra's cheek. "I'm sorry if I upset you. But if I won't say it, who will?" she asked cheerfully and winked. "See you tomorrow."

Kyra nodded, her head still spinning from the conversation. She'd thought this meeting would be fun. She'd thought they'd talk about dresses and venues and who should come. Jesus, Deenie spoke to her like she was living in a fantasy land.

When Deenie left, Kyra turned her attention back to Ruby. She was annoyed with her friend. This was not a winking matter. This was not a girlfriends-talking-about-boyfriends conversation. Okay, maybe she'd started the conversation that way, but really, this was serious, and Deenie shouldn't have dismissed it so readily. This was *deadly* serious.

And yet the conversation left Kyra feeling a little funny. Like the universe had pitched forward and she was leaning back to keep from falling.

The confusing vacillation between loving Dax and worrying that she was using him trailed Kyra like a tail for many days afterward. Their routine returned to normal: Dax watched Ruby while Kyra worked, and Kyra cooked dinner for him and took his laundry with her every morning. Once or twice, as she watched the clothes go round and round in the washer, she wondered if she and Dax had assumed their roles in preparation for a fake marriage, and it was nothing more than that. If she was completely honest with herself, she might admit there was something else that was bothering her—Dax had not said how he felt about her. Yes, he was attentive and kind and—give the man props—wonderful in bed. But he hadn't *said* he loved her or was falling in love with her.

And as if the burden of her guilt wasn't heavy enough, Kyra felt even more guilt for wanting him to say anything more than he already had. What more did she need from him? He'd made a grand and selfless gesture, and now she wanted him to spice it up by declaring deep feelings for her after only a short time dating? Now *that* was unfair.

Kyra was making herself crazy.

But she'd set the wheels in motion, and all of this angst and uncertainty was just going to have to work itself out, like that knot in her shoulder she sometimes got from carrying trays. They had the marriage license. Dax was on the hunt for someone to officiate. They sat Ruby down together and explained to her that Mommy and Dax were going to get married so they could help Ruby together. "Help me what?" she asked.

"Do all the doctor stuff," Kyra said.

Ruby blinked. As Kyra expected, Ruby didn't really understand the importance of marriage in this context. In fact, she shrugged and said, "Okay. Will we all live here?"

"Maybe someday," Dax had said before Kyra could respond. "But for now, we like having two cottages."

They hadn't actually decided that. Frankly, they'd been so busy with everything else, they hadn't really discussed the living arrangements. "Me, too!" Ruby said. "All my toys are in this house."

Kyra glanced at Dax. He shrugged a little. When Ruby ran off to get another doll, Kyra said, "We're going to keep the two cottages?"

"We've got enough going on, don't we?" Dax said. "It's not like we have to make that decision right now."

Well, no, they didn't . . . but she wondered about it.

But in the meantime, they'd agreed to marry the week between Ruby's MRI and the start of school. The week after school started, Kyra was taking her real estate license exam.

All the wheels were moving in the right direction for Ruby's sake, and Kyra couldn't ask for more.

In the meantime, Kyra kept a close eye on her daughter, looking for signs that her seizures were worsening. She agreed with Dax that they were more frequent. The next MRI couldn't get here fast enough.

The other issue that occupied Kyra's thoughts was an old and familiar beast—her finances. She was finishing up her real estate coursework, and she owed the last installment of the cost of the course. Her savings account was on oxygen. Short of picking up more shifts, she wasn't far from needing to borrow money. Every day she checked her mailbox for the money Josh had promised to send, but it didn't come.

That he hadn't followed through on his promise infuriated Kyra, and one afternoon she called his number. It rolled to voice mail. *Hello, you've reached Josh Burton. Please leave a number* . . .

"Josh," she said. "It's Kyra. You said you would send some money to help me and I haven't received it. Just in case you lost the address, I'm going to text it to you. Please," she said and winced when her voice cracked. "Please help me with this." She meant to hang up with that, but paused and said, "I haven't asked you for anything in seven years, and believe me, I wouldn't now if it wasn't an emergency. This is important, Josh—*really* important. She's your daughter, too." She hung up, and with a sigh, she tossed her phone into her backpack. She didn't expect to hear from him.

♦ ♦ ♦

The following weekend, the Caldwells left and took Ruby's playmates with them. Mr. McCauley, who had come to trim the hedges in front of Kyra's cottage Sunday afternoon, announced that the Bransons were leaving at the end of the week.

"Who am I going to play with?" Ruby complained.

"This is what happens at the end of summer," Mr. McCauley said. "The summer people leave and the year-rounders settle in for the long off-season."

"Guess what?" Ruby said to Mr. McCauley. "Dax made a baby bed for my new doll."

Kyra, who was in the hammock enjoying a couple of hours before studying, turned her head. "What new doll, pumpkin?"

Ruby looked around. "Dax bought me a doll."

"He did?"

"He painted the baby bed white. It's drying in his shed and I'm not supposed to touch it until he says. He said you could make a mattress out of a towel, Mommy. Do you have a towel?"

"Probably," Kyra said and sat up.

Her screen door swung open, and Dax stepped outside wearing a red, frilly apron someone had given Kyra as a gift years ago.

Mr. McCauley eyed him from below the porch. "Taking up a new profession?"

"Got a new pasta machine," Dax said proudly and placed his hands on his hips.

Mr. McCauley laughed and picked up his clippings. "Don't give up on the furniture business just yet," he said as he wandered away.

"You're full of surprises today," Kyra said, standing up from the hammock. "How'd you learn to make baby beds and pasta?"

"What, you think my college degree is just for show?"

Kyra stilled. "You have a college degree?" she asked as Ruby darted in front of her to go inside.

He looked at her with amusement. “Didn’t I tell you? Yes, I have a degree in business.” He gestured for her to come in.

How did she not know he had a college degree? She had assumed he’d gone into the army out of high school.

“Here’s my doll, Mommy,” Ruby said, suddenly appearing before her and holding up a baby doll.

“She’s adorable!” Kyra said, and to Dax, “You didn’t have to do that. You *shouldn’t* have done that.”

“Why not?” he asked with a shrug.

“Why not? Because I don’t want her to think she can have whatever she wants just for asking.”

“Hey, Coconut, will you go next door and feed Otto?” Dax asked.

“Yes!” she said enthusiastically, and with her new doll tucked in her arm, she ran out the door. They could hear her call for Otto.

“So what’s the big deal with it?” Dax asked as he removed the apron. “Sometimes a kid ought to get something just for asking. And it’s not like I’m getting her a new toy every day.”

“The big deal is that I can’t afford to buy her toys except for special occasions, and you keep giving her things, and I didn’t know you went to college.”

Dax arched one brow. “And?”

“And . . . I wonder what else I don’t know.”

Now the other brow rose to meet the first. “Are you implying I’m hiding things from you?”

“No, of course not!” she said and rubbed her forehead, trying to form her thoughts, to make sense of the confusion. “Dax . . . what if there was no Ruby?”

“What?”

“What if Ruby was fine, or I didn’t have her. Would we . . . would we get married?”

Dax folded his arms. “I’m not sure what you’re asking.”

“Would we even be dating? Would we be us?”

"We *are* us," he said, his expression annoyed now.

She wasn't making herself clear. She was apparently incapable of expressing the doubts that she harbored. "You know what I mean," she said.

Dax considered her as he casually scratched his chin. "I don't know."

That wasn't terribly reassuring. In fact, it was terribly unsettling.

"Don't read too much into that," he said quickly. "You have to understand, Kyra—I never thought I'd marry again, and I think if things had been . . . normal . . . it would have taken some time to get used to the idea of marriage."

"So . . . you're doing this just to help Ruby."

He looked confused. "You know that."

"It has nothing to do with me."

Now Dax looked flabbergasted. He pushed away from the door and moved toward her. "Of course it has to do with you. I'm crazy about you—you know that, too. Look, if this hadn't happened to Ruby, I would have seen where it was going between us before I ever thought of marriage." He put his hands on her arms, caressing her. "It means everything accelerated with us because of her condition. It means all things being equal, I probably would have taken it slow, because that's my nature. But please don't doubt I offered to do this for you every bit as much as I did for Ruby."

He still hadn't said how he truly felt about her. Being crazy about someone is what people said when they were dating. Not when they were about to get married. "You're making a huge sacrifice, and people don't make that kind of sacrifice for no reason."

He looked slightly flummoxed. "Why are we having this conversation? I love that kid," he said.

If only Kyra could explain why. If only she understood why. All she knew was that things were happening so quickly, and she loved him, and she wanted him, but she didn't know if he wanted her in the same way or if he was on some humanitarian mission. Those were two very different things. He could say he loved Ruby, and for that Kyra was thankful, because she loved Ruby, too. But he obviously couldn't say the same to her, and she couldn't keep the doubts she had about his feelings for her from swirling.

"What is it?" he asked, bending down a little to look her in the face. "This isn't news to you."

"No, no, I understand," she said. "And I'm grateful—"

"I fed Otto!" Ruby shouted as she came running into the house. "He ate it superfast, and then he threw up on the floor."

"God," Dax sighed. He touched Kyra's cheek. "More on this later, okay?" He took off the apron and left her cottage to take care of Otto's disaster.

They dined on homemade pasta that evening, which they all agreed could use some work. After dinner, Dax went off to take care of some things while Kyra spent time with Ruby. She was in the middle of a story about a girl who lassoed a star and brought it to earth when she heard the faint sounds of Ruby snoring. She was curled around the baby doll Dax had given her.

She wished she hadn't made a big deal about the doll. She wasn't herself these days; she was twisting around in her own head.

She slowly stood up and crept out of Ruby's room, then returned to the kitchen to clean up. She was finishing with the dishes when Dax returned. He walked up behind her, braced his hands on the kitchen sink, surrounding her, and kissed her neck.

Kyra closed her eyes and leaned back against him. No matter what her doubts, no matter how exhausting the days and no matter how high her increasing anxiety, there was something so soothing and sure about his touch.

His hands slid up her sides and he turned her around. His kiss was intoxicating, his touch almost fevered. He wrapped his arms around her waist and held her aloft, walking slowly to her room with her as he kissed her. In her bedroom, they moved without words, both of them pulling and tugging at each other's clothing, one of them reaching for a condom. There were no words between them—the desire in them felt equal and frantic, and perhaps Kyra was reading too much into it, but she had the feeling that Dax was trying to tell her something.

Dax put Kyra on the bed and shifted on top of her. He stroked her face, then shifted, his fingers brushing against her breast. "You captivated me from the moment I saw you moving boxes into this cottage, do you know that?"

Kyra didn't know if she believed him, but she kissed him and slid her hands down his chest, over his nipples, to his abdomen. She nuzzled his neck, pressed her breasts against him.

"I wouldn't have offered to marry you if I didn't care about you," he said and slid his hand between her thighs.

Kyra closed her eyes and surrendered to his touch. Her desire for him was potent, and as his hands and his mouth caressed her, she felt herself beyond caring what any of it meant. She just wanted to be with him, wanted to feel him slide into her and to cover him with kisses of adoration.

He began to move in her, driving her to the brink, his strokes growing urgent. Kyra plummeted with her release, Dax right behind her. As their skin began to cool, she clung to him, unwilling to let go. If she let go, reality would seep back into this room. If she held him, she could pretend that this was what was supposed to happen between them.

But eventually Dax dislodged himself from her and rolled onto his back. He groped around for her hand, then tangled his fingers in hers. "I'm going to deliver that damn table tomorrow, then go and see Jonathan," he said and sat up. "What do you have planned?"

Kyra yawned, drowsy and sated. "Study," she said sleepily.

He kissed her, then moved off the bed. "I'll see you tomorrow evening?" he asked as he pulled on his jeans and zipped them up.

"I'll be right here," she said. She curled around a pillow and watched him dress. He leaned over her one last time to stroke her hair. "Are we good, babe?"

"We're good," she assured him. In that moment, she *was* good. This man was everything she could ever want, and she was too sleepy now to think about how he said he cared for her, and how that sounded like a line from a movie, spoken by a player who wasn't ready to commit.

Only in this movie, the player was committing a noble sacrifice to save a child. He was, truly, a hero.

Chapter Twenty-Three

Dax drove Kyra and Ruby to Black Springs for Ruby's second MRI. On the way home, he pulled into McDonald's, because Ruby said that's what they *always* did when she went to see a doctor.

This Friday, Dax and Kyra would be married on the lakeshore by a lay preacher whose wife would witness the ceremony. On Monday, Ruby would start first grade. On Wednesday, Kyra would take her real estate exam. On the following Monday, Ruby would have her surgery.

Dax was feeling optimistic about things in spite of the looming surgery. His adoration of Ruby had only grown. And even though things had been a little tense from time to time, he thought he and Kyra were good. Solid. He believed they'd come to a mutual understanding of how their relationship was unfolding. Whenever he felt a distance from her, it would magically disappear when they were in bed.

Yessir, their sex life was magic as far as Dax was concerned—they'd had some mind-bending experiences together, and every one of them had felt important or huge.

Yeah, he was feeling pretty damn good about the whole thing. Once they got past the surgery, he thought it would be smooth sailing. His idea—one that he'd not discussed yet with Kyra—was that the three of them would move to Teaneck to be closer to his son. He'd haul his furniture to East Beach from there.

This particular morning, Dax borrowed Mr. McCauley's trailer. With Mr. McCauley's help, he'd loaded the table he'd made for Wallace to deliver to the client's home on the other end of the lake. Mr. McCauley had offered to ride along and help unload the table at the other end. "I got nothing better to do this morning," the retiree said.

On the way to the south end of Lake Haven, Mr. McCauley chatted about how he was starting to winterize the empty cottages. "By the way, seems you and Ms. Kokinos are getting a little cozy," he said and winked.

Dax smiled. "You could say so. I'll let you in on a secret—we're getting married Friday."

Mr. McCauley's mouth gaped open. "The devil you say!" he said and slapped the seat beside him. "That was fast."

"It was," Dax agreed. "But when you know, you know." He didn't know why he said *that,* exactly, but he wasn't going to say anything about the necessity of the marriage for Ruby's sake. She didn't need her business all over town. They'd agreed to keep their arrangement quiet. Not a secret, exactly, but as Kyra put it, "without fanfare," at least until after Ruby had come through her crisis. "She deserves her privacy," she said.

Dax couldn't disagree with that.

After the surgery was behind them and Ruby was on the mend—she *would* be on the mend, Dax was sure of it—they would either host a celebration or go their separate ways. But Dax never thought about going separate ways. He thought about the sort of celebration he'd like to have. And he didn't consider telling a few close friends outside the bounds. Kyra's friend Deenie knew.

"Sue is going to have a cow, she damn sure is," Mr. McCauley said jovially. "She's pretty attached to that little girl."

"So am I," Dax said. "She has a way of getting under a person's skin and setting up house there."

"She has a way of getting in the plant beds. She's worse than your dog," Mr. McCauley scoffed and laughed. "Well, good for you, Dax, good for you. Couldn't happen to a nicer guy."

Dax didn't know about that, but Mr. McCauley's encouragement spurred him to make the same announcement later when he swung by John Beverly's to collect his check for the table.

"Just the hunk I wanted to see," Wallace said when Dax sauntered in. "The Lake Haven resort is renovating their lobby. They're looking for some unusual coffee tables. Are you interested?"

"Of course I'm interested," Dax said. If business kept building as it had, he was going to have to get a larger workspace.

"I have some photos to show you," Wallace said. "Wait here, and I'll be back with them and a check."

Dax waited. He glanced to the cash register counter and noticed Janet sitting behind it, her head in a magazine. This was the first time he'd ever entered the shop and Janet wasn't in his face. He moved closer, but she wouldn't look up from her magazine.

"Are you never going to speak to me again?" Dax asked. "Asking for a friend."

"What do you think?" Janet asked curtly.

"I think you need to give up on matchmaking and stick with interior design."

That remark caused Janet to throw down her magazine and stand up. She yanked down on her short skirt and said, "Why didn't you like her?"

"I like her," Dax said sincerely. "She's nice. But she's a little intense, Janet, I'm not going to lie. And . . . the truth is, I've had something else going on."

Janet snorted. "Don't tell me the waitress next door."

Why should he not tell her that? "As a matter of fact," he said.

"What's this?" Wallace asked, poking his head out of the office as he waved the check around. "You and that little dish next door? Really, Janet, you can't be surprised. He's practically adopted that little girl."

"Actually," Dax said, "you may as well know . . . we're getting married Friday."

Unlike Mr. McCauley, Wallace and Janet did not grin and slap the car seat. They stared at him in stunned silence. "*What* did you just say?" Wallace asked.

"I'm pretty sure you heard me, judging by how white you both are," Dax said and gingerly reached for the check before Wallace wadded it up in a fit of shock.

"Are you crazy? I think you're crazy!" Wallace exclaimed.

Dax thought about it a moment. "Don't think so," he said. "It's complicated, but there is a method in our madness."

"Dax!" Janet cried. She'd come out from around the counter. "You can't marry someone you just met."

"I didn't just meet her. I met her earlier this summer and we've been dating for a while now."

"No, you haven't! One summer is hardly long enough to know if you're ready to marry," Wallace said, going all superior on him. "What is the *matter* with you?"

"I like her." Dax said it without thinking and didn't fully realize what he'd said until Wallace and Janet exchanged a look of terror.

"What about love?" Janet demanded. "Don't you want to *love* the woman you're going to marry? Doesn't *like* seem a little like a few dollars short of a hundred-dollar bill?"

"I *do* love her," he said, flustered now. He felt a little weird about saying it to these two and never having said it to Kyra. He hadn't said it because he wasn't entirely certain what his feelings were. He was just supremely confident he *would* love her. He wasn't the kind to let doubts ruin a good thing, and he knew from the way they'd made love just last night that the basis for a good relationship, a good marriage, was there. He and Kyra just needed to relax and let it unfold.

"This is crazy," Janet said, throwing her hands up. "I always thought you were a smart guy, Dax, but after this, I have to say, I'm glad you dumped Heather."

"I didn't *dump* her—"

"Because I would hate to see her mixed up with crazy."

"Okay, all right, as usual, your comments on my love life are unwelcome and just flat-out wrong," Dax said. "Where are the pictures, Wallace? I need to get going."

Wallace was still staring at him like he'd suddenly sprouted an extra head. "I think you've finally lost your mind," he said, nodding. "We've lost you." He shoved a binder toward Dax.

Dax quickly reviewed the pictures of the decor and the sort of tables they wanted and got out of there as soon as he could. He didn't like the daggers Janet was staring at him or the way Wallace kept looking at him like he was some kind of mutant.

From there, he drove to Teaneck and was lucky enough to arrive just as Jonathan was waking from his nap. Ashley was in the living room with him. Stephanie was at work. Dax had memorized her work rotation so he knew how to avoid her.

"He's huge," Ashley said, beaming. "I can't feed him enough."

"He's going to be strong," Dax said and took the baby from Ashley. He couldn't help the idiot grin he got every time he looked at his son.

"You're so happy with him," Ashley said and curled her feet up under her on the chair. "I know how badly you've wanted children, and I'm so glad I was able to give you at least one child. In spite of the way it came about." She smiled sheepishly.

Dax didn't want to be reminded of what had happened between them. "Looks like I'm going to have another," he said to Jonathan.

"What?"

"I mean Ruby," he said and looked at Ashley. "Her mother and I are getting married."

Ashley's eyes widened. "Dax, that's wonderful! Oh my God, I am so *surprised.* When?"

"Friday."

"*Friday!* What are you talking about? Why so fast?"

He shrugged and looked at Jonathan again. "It's the right thing to do," he said vaguely.

Ashley uncurled herself, leaned across the space between them, and kissed Dax's forehead. "Congratulations," she said. "I hope you are happier than you ever thought possible."

Dax looked at his ex-wife. He believed she wished that for him. He didn't know if he could be *that* happy, but once again he was filled with confidence that if he could be driven to such heights, it would be with Kyra.

♦ ♦ ♦

It was half past six when Dax pulled into the drive at Number Two and noticed the strange car in front of Kyra's house. He got out of his truck and took a closer look. It was a rental. Whoever it was, he hoped they were on their way sooner rather than later—he'd bought an expensive bottle of wine today that he wanted to share with Kyra.

As he started toward the house, Kyra's door opened and a couple walked out ahead of her.

He waved; Kyra pointed to him and said something to her guests, then all three started moving in his direction.

As they drew closer, Dax's belly did a funny little flip. His instincts told him who that man was. He had red hair. Not as red as Ruby's, more of a strawberry blond, but red all the same. And as they reached him, he saw that the man had Ruby's blue eyes.

"Hey," Kyra said to Dax. She was nervous. "Dax, this is, ah . . . this is Josh Burton, and his wife, Liz."

Dax stared at Josh Burton, debating whether or not to put a fist through his face, for many reasons, but foremost for Ruby.

"Good to meet you," Josh Burton said, clearly not reading the signs. He offered his hand.

Dax shifted the wine bottle he was carrying to his left hand and forced himself to shake the bastard's hand.

"Josh and Liz are staying at the Lake Haven resort for a few days," Kyra said. She had her hands shoved in the pockets of her jeans.

"Why?" Dax asked bluntly, and ignored the way Kyra's eyes rounded with alarm.

"It's a fair question," Josh said breezily. "We're checking in on Ruby."

Checking in? Like she was a pet at a zoo?

"Anyhoo," Josh said, and Dax hated him even more for saying *anyhoo*, "Kyra, we'll pick you up tomorrow at nine?"

"Sounds good," she chirped in a voice Dax had never heard her use.

"Good to meet you, Dax," Liz said politely. "Kyra says you've been a great help to her during this very trying time."

"Someone had to be," Dax said.

"We better go, Liz," Josh muttered and avoided Dax's gaze.

Kyra didn't. She shot him a warning look, then walked Josh and Liz Burton to their rental car. She watched them pull away but she didn't wave. She just stood with her hands still jammed in her pockets until they'd gone around the turn. Then she turned around to Dax.

"What the hell?" he asked bluntly.

"He came out of nowhere," she said. "With a check. And his wife. Apparently it was all *her* idea." She shook her head as if she were mystified by it.

"But how? How did they know where to find you?"

"I texted Josh my address a week or so ago and asked him to send the money he'd promised."

"And they came here to deliver the money to you personally? From where?"

"From Indianapolis." She was standing so stiffly. "And they wanted to meet Ruby, of course."

His head was beginning to ache. "They came all this way, out of the blue, to meet the daughter he's refused to acknowledge for almost seven years? And Ruby? How did she take the stunning news that the man in her cottage was her African cat trainer, legless skateboarding dad?"

"She doesn't know who he is," Kyra said, her voice going soft. "I told her they were some friends of mine. That's all she knows."

"I don't get this, Kyra. I don't understand—"

"I'm as surprised as you are, Dax. Can we go in your house and talk about this?"

"Where is Ruby?"

"She's with Mrs. McCauley. Please, Dax—I need to sit down."

He sighed. "Yes, of course. Come in."

He walked up the porch steps with Kyra and opened the door for her, pushed Otto out of the way, and walked into the kitchen to deposit the wine. He had to brace himself against the counter for a moment, because he was reeling. When he'd gathered himself, he returned to the living room. Kyra had been sitting on the edge of a chair, waiting, but stood as he entered. She looked far too nervous, and Dax didn't like that. It was all he could do to remain calm. "What does he want?"

Her chin started to tremble. "To . . . to be a father," she said, her voice shaking.

Dax's heart stopped. He stared at her in disbelief. He thought maybe Ruby's dad wanted custody so he wouldn't be stuck with child support, but he did not believe for one minute that asshole had somehow found a desire to know his daughter.

"From the beginning he wouldn't acknowledge her because Liz didn't know about Ruby. Well, she found out. And when she found out about Ruby, and the tumor, she wanted him to do the right thing."

"Which is . . . what?" Dax asked as his pulse quickened.

"Basically, they want to put Ruby on their insurance and get her the best care possible."

Dax was stunned. His thoughts were spinning so hard he felt light-headed.

"This is good news, right?" Kyra said and took a tentative step forward. "It's like a gift from God, if you think about it. Suddenly Ruby is taken care of, and you and I . . . you and I can take our relationship slow, like you wanted. We don't have to get married."

Now Dax's heart felt like it was cracking. Why did she say it like that, they didn't *have* to get married?

"Dax?"

"Just give me a minute," he begged her.

"I mean, if we *want* to marry, we can do it for the right reasons."

He shot her a look.

"You . . . you were doing it for Ruby, which I so appreciate," she said, stacking her hands on her heart. "But I think we can both agree it's not an ideal way to start a marriage, with one of us beholden to the other."

Jesus, but he felt so raw, as if every nerve was exposed. "I never said you were beholden to me, Kyra."

"I know, I know," she said and reached for his hand. "But I *feel* beholden. How can I not?"

He pulled his hand free. She couldn't smooth this over with a kiss or a caress. "So this guy rides in on his white horse and that's it? You're going to let him in?"

"He is her biological father," she said quietly. "And he has great insurance."

"*I* have great insurance," he loudly reminded her.

"I know! And that's great!" she said, her expression too earnest. "If things progress with us, that's good to know, because who knows what sort of care she'll need in the years to come?"

She didn't want to marry him. That's all Dax could think. He was stunned by it, blindsided by it. He'd arranged everything, had told his friends. He'd just driven back from Teaneck full of hopes and optimism and *goddammit*, when would he learn? "Where are you going with them tomorrow?"

"To meet Dr. Mehta," Kyra said with a wince.

Dax could feel the slice of the dagger through his heart. He'd been with Kyra every step of the way until the phantom father showed up, and that was it. His services were no longer needed.

"The results aren't back, but . . . but they want to meet the doctor. Which I guess is understandable."

It wasn't so understandable to him. He felt adrift, untethered suddenly. He'd been planning and thinking, and he hadn't counted on something like this. He *wanted* to marry Kyra on Friday. He *wanted* the responsibility for that little coconut. It didn't seem so nebulous to him now, it seemed very much sewn into his heart.

"Please don't be mad," she begged him. "I just found out myself. They showed up here, they surprised me, and I was overwhelmed, and I haven't had time to really process it, but my God, Dax, after all this time, he's finally going to step up and do what's right for his daughter."

He shook his head in disbelief.

"Don't you want to be off the hook?"

"I'm not on a hook, Kyra. My feet are firmly planted."

Tears began to well in her eyes. She walked up to him and wrapped her arms around him and laid her cheek against his chest. Dax couldn't reciprocate. Not yet. The rug had been yanked out from beneath him for a second time, and he couldn't deal with her just yet. He had to think.

He pulled her arms down. "Just . . . just let me absorb this, will you?"

Kyra tried to caress his cheek, but he backed away from it. "Sure," she said, her voice soft and distant. She turned around and went out his door.

Dax didn't know how long he stood there. But he moved when Otto stuck his head under his hand, looking for affection.

"Yeah, okay," Dax said, and went into the kitchen to get the dog's supper. At least he could count on Otto.

Chapter Twenty-Four

This was what insanity must feel like, Kyra thought, a bewildering state where a person was so at war inside her own thoughts that she couldn't make a decision on even the smallest things. Kyra couldn't seem to grasp how to *do* the smallest things. As evidenced by the fact that Deenie had just pointed out her work shirt was inside out.

Kyra looked down at herself. "Wow," she said, startled by that. She'd put on makeup, put up her hair, and looked at herself in the mirror, but she'd been so distracted she'd never noticed the shirt.

"You're losing it," Deenie decided.

"Tell me about it," Kyra muttered.

"Are you nervous about the big day?" Deenie asked and nudged Kyra with her shoulder.

Kyra supposed she meant her wedding and not Ruby's surgery, which was the Really Big Day in her book. At least Deenie had come around since their talk at the park. She'd even apologized for being judgmental. *"I should have been more supportive,"* she'd said. *"I just wish you'd asked me before you said yes so I could have talked some sense into you, you know?"*

"The big day," Kyra repeated and shook her head. "No, I'm feeling crazed because Ruby's father showed up."

"Who?"

"Her sperm donor."

Deenie gasped. "Get out!"

"It's true," Kyra said with a shrug. "He pretty much dropped out of the sky and promised to fix everything for Ruby."

Deenie sank down onto a bar stool, dumbstruck. "You have to tell me this story."

Kyra did. And when she was done, Deenie sighed with obvious relief. "Well, thank God, right? At least now you don't have to get married."

"Right," Kyra said.

She didn't have to get married.

She didn't have to take advantage of Dax's kindness, to burden him with her problems.

So why was she sad? Why did she feel like she'd lost her best friend? Why did everything feel turned on its head?

Kyra really didn't want to marry Dax like this, under these circumstances. She wanted more equal footing. But since Josh had appeared and said he'd take responsibility, something had changed between her and Dax, and Kyra couldn't figure out what, and she didn't like it.

She didn't know how to fix it, and even if she should. Right now, all her energy was focused on getting through the surgery. That was the only thing that drove her. She couldn't possibly think of the future, or relationships, until she knew what was growing in her daughter's head.

The constant anxiety of waiting for the MRI results and the surgery put Kyra in a suspended state of agitation—every time she heard her phone ping, she dug it out of her pocket with the madness of someone who was hallucinating about bugs.

Dr. Mehta called when Kyra was on her way home from work Wednesday afternoon. Kyra pulled over to the side of the road. She could hardly hear the doctor, her heart was pounding so loudly in her ears.

"Well, we have the results," Dr. Mehta said. "It's very good news, Mrs. Kokinos. The tumor doesn't seem to be growing. So let's remove that growth, and then we'll determine if Ruby needs further treatment."

"Okay," Kyra said, relieved. "She's starting first grade on Monday. How long will she be out?"

"Well, that depends. If all goes well, she'll be out two to three weeks."

"And if . . ."

"If necessary, there will be ongoing treatment. Radiation, most likely. But we'll need the results of the biopsy. You and your pediatric oncologist will discuss that."

Kyra pinched the bridge of her nose between her fingers. She felt faint at the mention of yet another doctor. "Thanks, Dr. Mehta. I need to discuss this with Dax . . . and Ruby's father," she added reluctantly.

"Yes, of course. I spoke to Josh earlier today. He informed me that you are looking into surgical options in Indianapolis?"

Kyra's eyes flew open. "What?" She didn't know what startled her more—that Dr. Mehta had told Josh the results of the MRI before talking to her, or that Josh had assumed the surgery would be in Indianapolis.

"I think the two of you are smart to explore all options," she said. "There are some great facilities here and in Indianapolis. I know Ruby will be in good hands if that's what you decide, and since the tumor doesn't appear to be growing, you have a bit of time to make a decision. Give me a call later this week and we can discuss going forward."

Kyra thanked her and hung up the phone. She stared straight ahead, her fingers wrapped tightly around the steering wheel, her mind in a blind rage. How dare he. *How dare he.* She picked up her phone and called Josh.

"Hola," he answered, as if they were buddies. As if he was on vacation. As if he hadn't shown up out of the clear blue and taken over Ruby's life without consulting Kyra.

"You called Dr. Mehta," she said angrily.

"Ah . . . yeah," he said uncertainly.

"Why didn't you tell me you were going to do that?" she demanded.

"I was going to tell you when I talked to you. What's the big deal? I was just exploring what options we have, Kyra. And she'd just received the test results and filled me in. What's wrong with that?"

What was *wrong* with that? There was so much wrong that she thought she'd explode all over her car. But she said, *"Indianapolis?"*

"Of course Indianapolis," he said, sounding annoyed. "What did you think?"

"Well, I damn sure didn't think Indianapolis!"

"It has to be, Kyra. My insurance coverage is in Indiana. She has to be treated in one of my network locations to get the full benefit. And besides, Riley Hospital for Children is outstanding. Come on, you know how insurance works."

"No, I don't know how it works. I never use it because my deductible is through the roof. I don't know anything other than my daughter needs to have surgery to remove a brain tumor, and suddenly I have to move to Indianapolis? What about her school? What about my job?" *What about Dax?*

"Well," Josh said, "you're waiting tables here. I'm sure you can get a job waiting tables there. And Ruby hasn't started school yet. She'll be fine in Indy."

Tears, which Kyra hadn't even known were present, began to slide down her cheeks. Forget the logistics—she was scheduled to take the test next week. All that work, all that money. Forget that Ruby was supposed to start first grade next week. What about Dax? Just a couple of days ago, she was planning on marrying him Friday. And now she would just up and leave him? "This can't be happening," she said. "Why didn't you tell me?"

"I'm telling you now." She heard a muffled sound, and a moment later, Liz said, "Kyra? It's Liz. I know this is a lot to take in—"

"No kidding," Kyra said.

"But think of it this way—you don't have to live in Indianapolis forever. All you have to do is bring Ruby and get her treated, and then, if you want to come back to East Beach and your job at the Lakeside Bistro, you can. By the way, we ate there last night, and it was fantastic."

Kyra didn't give a damn about the bistro or how good the food was. Her life had just been upended *again*.

"I can't . . . I have to think about this," Kyra said, swallowing down her tears.

"Of course you do. Think about it, then give us a call. But the thing is, we need to make a decision quickly."

"I *know*," Kyra said.

She could hear Josh in the background, and a moment later, he was back on the phone. "Kyra, you have to be smart about this. You reached out to me because you couldn't afford her treatment. I can afford it, but you need to let me do it my way."

She'd never wanted to punch a man in the face as much as she did in that minute. *His* way? "Whatever, Josh," she said and hung up. Why did he have to remind her of her shortcomings? Why did Ruby have to be sick? They'd been good for so long, the two of them against the world. But Kyra would not have known about the tumor until maybe it was too late, had it not been for Dax. She never would have made it through the last few weeks if it hadn't been for him. And now she was supposed to leave him for Indianapolis?

But what galled her most, what made her feel sick, was that she couldn't take care of Ruby on her own. She had to rely on one of two men to save her daughter. She had to make absurd choices about her life because she didn't have the means to care for her daughter.

Kyra didn't go home right away, but drove to the north end of the lake, where no one ever went. She sat on a bench under an enormous cypress tree and stared out at the water for so long that she began to shiver. When she stood up to leave, she knew what she had to do. She thought it would be less painful if she cut off her right arm, but unfortunately, that wouldn't help anything.

Ruby was at her easel on the porch, drawing blobs that were supposed to be people, when Kyra arrived home. Dax was sitting on the porch steps, sipping on a beer.

"Hi, Mommy! I'm drawing a picture of you. See?" Ruby asked.

"Ah . . ." Kyra didn't see, but she nodded. "Yes, there I am, the one on the right."

"No, that's Dax. You're this one," Ruby said, pointing to another blob, and turned her attention back to her work.

"You're late," Dax said casually. "Long day?"

A swell of nausea rose up in her. "You could say that." She wished she could go back in time, to those days before Josh had shown up. Things hadn't been great with her and Dax since, because neither of them knew what to do with Josh. Dax had become distant. He was still very much present in their lives, but Kyra could feel the distance stretching between them a little more each day.

"I'm sorry," she said, and sat next to him. She crossed her arms on her knees and lowered her head a moment, emotionally exhausted. When she lifted her head, Dax put his arm around her shoulders, and Kyra sank into his side. "Dr. Mehta called with the MRI results today."

"And?"

"And . . . no growth."

"That's great news," he said as he caressed her shoulder. "So when is the surgery?"

"That's the thing. Josh's insurance is in Indiana."

She felt Dax stiffen. He removed his arm and took a long drink from the bottle of beer he was holding. "Yeah, and?"

"Help me out here, Dax," she pleaded. "What do you expect me to do? I'm between a rock and a hard place. I can take advantage of your kindness and hope that it all works out and we don't use up all your goodwill. Or I can put the responsibility squarely on her father's shoulders, where it belongs," she said, glancing over her shoulder to make sure Ruby was focused on her drawing and not listening. "The only caveat is that I have to move her to be treated. Which one am I supposed to choose?"

He looked down.

Kyra moved to her knees on the step below him, bracing her hands on his knees so he couldn't avoid her. "You can come with me, Dax," she said earnestly. "You can make furniture in Indianapolis."

"And leave my son? Leave the clientele I have worked to build?" He shook his head. "What about your real estate license? You've worked hard for that, too."

She'd thought about that. "I'll take the test. Then, when I come back—"

"Come *back*?" he scoffed. "Are you really coming back, Kyra? Have you honestly thought about that? What if she requires a long-term kind of treatment? What if you settle in and get a job and Ruby becomes attached to her dad? Will you ever come back?"

"Yes," she said adamantly. "I don't want to leave you," she whispered. But she knew, even as the words came out of her mouth, that she couldn't any more plan for a future than she could predict what would happen with Ruby. She couldn't even say what would happen tomorrow—there were just too many what-ifs.

"And yet you're thinking about it," he said dubiously.

"Because I have no choice."

Dax shook his head. "You have a choice. We had planned to get married Friday, remember? There's your other choice."

"A shotgun wedding that we'd be rushing into for the sake of your insurance," she said. "Which is so incredibly generous of you, Dax.

But it's not the best thing for us, is it? We could get married Friday and hope—*hope*—that it works out between us and that our relationship develops, because if it doesn't, I will have a daughter who may be facing radiation and is in love with you. And then what?"

He looked over her, to the lake.

"None of this changes my feelings about you. I still love you," she said. "But . . . but is this what you really want to do now that her father has stepped up? I'm just thinking of what's best for Ruby and for you and me." She wanted to assure him, but when she looked into his stormy blue eyes, she saw the same uncertainties in him she had been feeling. She saw hurt and confusion. "You have to admit, a marriage right now is not ideal."

He sighed and rubbed his nape. "Of course it's not *ideal*," he said bitterly and glanced at his hand. "So where does this leave us? We can't exactly date if you're in Indianapolis."

"I don't know," she said. "I don't know. All I can do is focus on Ruby right now. All I can do is get through this crisis."

Dax held her gaze for a long moment. She thought he would argue, but at last he put his hands on top of hers and said, "Yeah, I get it."

"Do you?" she asked and turned her hands palms up under his, squeezing her fingers around his. "Do you really understand?"

"I'm doing the best I can, Kyra. I'm trying." He put his beer aside and stood up. Kyra's hands floated away from him. "Ruby's had her supper," he said and started down the porch steps.

"Wait . . . where are you going?" Kyra exclaimed.

"To get a drink," he called over his shoulder and kept walking.

With every step he took, Kyra felt her heart shatter a little more, her breath grow a little shallower. She was overwhelmed with the despair of uncertainty. How could she know she was doing the right thing? How could anyone know what the right thing was in a situation like this?

♦ ♦ ♦

Kyra felt sick with fear that she'd ruined everything. She fretted how to tell Ruby that they were going to a new city and—the thing she hadn't yet told her—that she had to have an operation on her head. She fretted how to tell Ruby that Dax and Otto weren't going with them. Her belly churned with such anxiety that she couldn't touch the sandwich she made herself for supper.

There had been no sign of Dax since he'd walked off her porch—his truck was gone, and there were no lights in his house. A gloom had settled in over the lake that seemed to seep through the cracks into their cottage. Even Ruby seemed distant tonight. Kyra didn't want it to end this way—she didn't want it to *end*. Had she not been clear enough about that?

She put Ruby to bed but dragged her feet at turning in herself, hoping that by some miracle Dax would appear and tell her yes, he would move to Indianapolis.

She was kidding herself with that kind of fantasy. He would never leave Jonathan, any more than she would leave Ruby.

Kyra robotically went about picking up the house and the endless stream of clothes and shoes and toys. She made the kitchen sparkle. She cleaned Ruby's new sneakers.

And still Dax didn't come back.

At last she gave in to fatigue. She brushed her teeth and washed her face, then piled her hair in a knot on her head. She was on her way to bed when she heard the rumble of his truck. Her heart instantly began to race with anxious hope and a little bit of fear. She hurried to her front door and opened it, peering into the dark through her screen door. But she couldn't see anything and stepped out onto the porch, moving to the steps, searching in the near dark for him.

She spotted him then—he was standing on the lawn between their houses, his legs braced apart, staring at her. They stood frozen in that moment, each staring at the other through the inky light of night. Then Dax began to stride toward her. Kyra came down the steps tentatively, still unsure of his mood. But then Dax began to jog, and so did she, running to him, launching herself at him, wrapping her legs around his waist, her arms around his neck.

He hoisted her up and somehow managed to carry her up the porch steps and to her room, kissing her the entire way. It was feverish between them, as if they were in a race against time. Maybe they were racing against their own thoughts, because certainly Kyra's brain was filled with confusion and love and desire to the point she couldn't think clearly. She could only feel—it was pure sentience between them, it was urgent, and it was blind.

He moved like a wild man, his hands and his mouth everywhere and frantic. He kissed her cheeks, her brow, her breasts, her mouth. It was the first time she'd felt him out of control, and it ignited her. She wanted him to lose control, to take her and fill her up, to pound against the inescapable need she had for him.

Her hands skirted over every plane and bulge, every angle and curve of his body. She wanted this moment seared into her consciousness so that she'd never forget it. She didn't know how she could leave him, she didn't know how she would function without him. She didn't know if it was the end, or a postponement, or maybe, please God, a beginning, but she would knit it into her soul and her memory.

He abruptly lifted his head and looked at her. His gaze was probing, seeking something from her. There was so much sadness and despair in his gaze that Kyra felt it at her core.

Not the beginning, then.

"How did this happen?" he asked. She could hear the scrape of raw emotion in his voice and felt the same scrape across her heart. She didn't know if he was asking how they'd come together or how they were being rent apart. She had no answers. So she responded by taking his head in her hands and kissing him softly. A lover's kiss.

He growled as he slid into her. He began to move, his body pressing home inside her, gently at first, then harder and faster, almost as if his frustration had spilled into their lovemaking and was driving them both to an end.

A shattering end.

They lay spent by their emotions and the volatile sex, their limbs wound around each other, neither of them willing to let go just yet.

But eventually Dax stroked her arm and said low, "Otto and I are going to spend a couple of days down on the shore."

Kyra stilled. The warmth began to seep out of her. "When?"

"We'll go tomorrow. After I talk to Ruby."

The burn of tears began to build behind Kyra's eyes, but she refused to give in to them. She rose up on her elbow.

"Why tomorrow?"

"Is there a better time? Or would you rather I stick around and help you move?"

That remark pricked her heart. "No, of course not," she murmured. She understood him—he was hurt by her leaving, and he couldn't bear to watch her leave any more than she could bear to leave him. "I don't even know when we'll go," she said.

"Yes, you do," he said low. "You have to go now. Every day you spend second-guessing yourself is a day that tumor could be out of her head."

She didn't need the reminder—the thought of that thing in Ruby's head never left her. "I do love you, Dax. Do you know it? I love you so much."

He sighed into her neck.

The tears clouded her vision as she put her arms around his neck and held him close. "I'm so sorry we ended up here. I'm so very sorry."

"It's not your fault, Kyra. But I don't have to watch the two of you go."

There it was, then—the best sex of her life had just turned into the worst sex of her life. It was breakup sex.

Well, it worked—she felt truly and utterly broken.

Chapter Twenty-Five

Dax couldn't sleep. As loath as he was to leave Kyra, he couldn't just lie there beside her with the splinter of his heart cracking in his head.

As painful as it was for him, he really did understand Kyra's decision—what parent wouldn't? But it hurt in a way he'd not expected. There was a moment, a very brief and panic-inducing moment, when he'd almost blurted that he wanted to marry her no matter what. But he caught himself, and he didn't say it, because it wasn't exactly true. There was a part of him that was relieved that he wasn't swearing to honor and cherish until his dying day a woman he'd known a little more than a month. He wasn't certain about anything about the two of them, other than he believed he did love her, and he loved Ruby, and he was devastated by this sudden turn of events.

He returned to Number Three early the next morning. He was leaving, but not without speaking to Ruby.

The coconut was eating cereal, her feet swinging beneath her chair. Kyra was cleaning up the kitchen and tried to smile, but her expression was full of painful chagrin.

"Mind if I have a word with the coconut?" he asked.

Kyra pressed her lips together and glanced at Ruby. "I haven't—"

"I know," he said quietly. Ruby didn't know about her surgery. She didn't know anything other than she hated going to doctors' offices and she liked Barbies and dragonflies and Otto. "I'll be careful," he said.

Ruby looked up at that.

"Come on, Coconut," he said and held out his hand. "Otto and I want to throw some rocks in the lake."

"You *do*? You never want to throw rocks in the lake," she said, wide-eyed.

He couldn't imagine not seeing those big blue eyes every day, and looked away. "Well, I do today."

"Awesome!" Ruby said. "Can I, Mommy?"

Kyra's lips were pressed together again, as if she was trying to hold back words. Or a scream. Dax wouldn't have been surprised by either. She nodded.

At the lake, they threw some rocks, and Ruby howled with laughter each time Otto dived into the lake to try to catch one before it sank, then paddled back with eager anticipation of the next one. "He doesn't know they *sink*," she said, her voice full of incredulity.

"He's no genius," Dax agreed.

Ruby waited for Otto to reach the shore, then squealed when he shook his coat off next to her. She threw another rock.

There was no way to make this easier, so Dax blurted, "So listen, Coconut . . . I want to tell you something."

"What?" She threw another rock.

"I'm going away for a while."

Ruby stopped throwing rocks and turned around to him, her legs braced apart, her long braid hanging over her shoulder. She peered at him through the rims of her blue glasses. "Where?"

"Vacation."

"Why?"

"I've been working hard and I need a break."

"What does that mean?"

"It means I need time off from working." What he really needed was time off from life.

"Why can't you not work here? You can play with me. That's not working."

He smiled and tugged on her braid. "I need to go away, Coconut."

She studied him with a shrewdness that belied her youth. "Are you mad at Mommy?"

He arched a brow in surprise. "No. Not at all."

"Then . . . don't you like us anymore?"

Dax didn't know how it had moved so quickly from his taking some time off to questions about his feelings for her and her mother, but he was suddenly asea, swimming for any hold. "*Like* you? Listen, Coconut, I'm going to tell you something I've never told another little girl. I love you. Do you understand? I *love* you. So don't ever let me hear you say I don't like you, okay?"

"Then why are you going away?" she asked, and her bottom lip began to tremble.

Jesus. "Because sometimes things change, Coconut," he said and reached for her hand. "I wish they didn't have to change, but that's life, kid." He roughly pulled her into his embrace, unable to look into her face and see her disappointment. She smelled like lake water and honey and sunbeams. She smelled like summer and brightness and love.

"Are you going to take Otto and Jonathan with you?" she asked, her breath warm against his neck.

"Yeah. Someone has to feed them, right?"

"But . . . are you ever coming back?" she asked, her voice full of tears now.

Dax felt himself on the verge of breaking in two. "Yes, I'm coming back, Ruby—right here. I'll be *right here*." His voice was hoarse with emotion. God, but he loved this kid, and as tears began to cloud his vision, she began to squirm. "I can't *breathe*," she said very dramatically.

He reluctantly let her go. He let the coconut go.

Ruby seemed to accept the news and began to look for more rocks, chattering about how many of them there were. After she'd thrown a few more, he reluctantly returned her to her mother.

His good-bye to Kyra had been said last night for all intents and purposes, and neither of them seemed to want to rehash it. Dax tried to think of what else to say, but his heart was so full of many conflicting emotions that it seemed as if his brain was unable to function effectively. He could only gaze at her, imprinting her on his mind's eye.

Kyra shoved her hands into the pockets of her jeans. "I feel like someone died."

Dax nodded. "Yeah," he said. He felt worse than that. Like he was the one who'd died.

"How long will you be gone?"

He shrugged. "I'm going to spend some time with Jonathan. Then maybe do a little fishing."

She nodded. She came down off the porch steps and walked right up to him and wrapped her hands around his. "I'll call you and let you know what's up."

"That would be great," he said. "I'm going to worry about her. And you."

"Dax . . . I can't thank you—"

"Don't," he said sharply. The last thing he wanted to hear from her was a thank-you for loving her daughter. For loving her. His heart was cleaving for a second time, and he didn't want to be thanked for it. "Take care of yourself," he said and kissed her forehead.

And then he retreated. His heart went back into its box and slammed the door shut. He untangled his fingers from hers. "See you," he said and turned his back on Number Three.

The sixty feet back to Number Two were the hardest and longest walk of his life.

♦ ♦ ♦

After a couple of days holed up in a hotel in Teaneck so that he could spend some time with Jonathan, Dax ended up in Montauk on Long Island, where he hired an old salt to take him out on Fresh Pond for three days in a row to fish. Dax didn't really know much about fishing, and he sucked at it. Worse, Otto kept jumping out of the boat and disturbing the waters. Dax had to haul him back into the boat and leash him.

When the old man—Kirk was his name—figured out that Dax wasn't going to carry his end of the conversation, he turned to philosophy. Each day, he launched into a new lecture: Politics. Obamacare. Russia. On the last day of Dax's beach rental, old Kirk decided it was time to wax philosophical on affairs of the heart.

"Had more than one guest out here nursing a broken heart," he said. "You know the best way to get over it, don't you?"

Dax said nothing.

"You think I'm going to say fishing, but I'm not. I'm going to say a man's broken heart is mended when he jumps back into the pond. Not this pond, of course, but the lady pond. The thing about guys is, we're adaptable. Sure, we get attached, but I tell you what, when a good pair of tits and a fine ass come along, we can get over it. You know what I mean, there, Dax?"

Dax said nothing. As Kirk appeared to be single, and by the look of things had no prospects, Dax didn't think he was qualified to give advice. And besides, he wasn't finished brooding yet.

"Now, I don't know your problem, but I'm pretty sure that piece of advice would help you out. Lady pond, or, if you prefer, the boy pond. Whatever floats your boat—don't make me no difference."

Dax said nothing.

He was trying not to hate himself too much. His heart had untangled itself, and he realized he could be such a goddamn fool sometimes. There was a part of him that had felt a little out of control with his sudden marriage proposal, and once she'd ended it, he had scurried like a rat back to square one, where he felt safest. But nothing worth having was easy, was it?

After much reflection—too much reflection, maybe—it occurred to Dax that he might have done a little less *we'll develop our relationship over time* talk and a little more *I think I'm falling in love with you* talk with Kyra. The problem with that, he'd figured out, was that it was hard to admit as much to himself. There was a part of him that felt insecure, and feared that if he put his heart on the line like that, it would be broken again.

Yeah, well, he hadn't put his heart on the line, and look how broken it was now.

After a few days of Kirk's never-ending stream of advice, Dax headed back to Lake Haven.

Number Three was empty, as he knew it would be. Kyra had texted him the day they left. I wish you were here to say good-bye. Ruby has been asking about you.

That got him worse than anything.

Now that Dax was back in East Beach, the place felt ridiculously empty and secluded without Ruby nosing into his business. Without her mother slamming doors and waving across the lawn. Even Otto seemed depressed. He would go from one door to the other and lie down with a heavy sigh, his gaze fixed on something outside.

Dax started working on the coffee tables for the resort, but in his spare time he was making something else: a Barbie mansion. The front came off, and inside there were built-ins, a model kitchen, and bathrooms. Five Barbies could live in this house at once. It was probably too big, but he figured that many Barbies needed their space.

One afternoon, Otto started barking, and Dax walked to the door to see what the commotion was about. A family with canoes strapped to the hood of their enormous SUV was unloading at Number Four. It looked like they had four kids, maybe five.

Dax looked at Otto. "Just great. How long do you think it will be before one of those snot-nosed munchkins is over here?"

Otto wagged his tail with great delight. He obviously hoped it would be very soon.

On his wall, Dax had a calendar where he marked the days leading to Ruby's surgery. He'd texted Kyra to ask about it. Week after next, she'd texted back. There was a bit of a hang-up with red tape over insurance, but it's worked out now. Ruby started school. She loves it.

He'd studied that text, debating his next one. How are you? he finally texted.

Hanging in there. You?

He was miserable, that was what. He was walking through each day in a fog. Hanging in there, he texted back.

He thought about calling her and having a conversation, but he couldn't trust himself not to lose his composure, and besides, she had enough on her plate without having to cover old ground. He told himself the less he knew about Kyra, the more control he had of his emotions. But God, did he miss her. He missed them both so badly that sometimes it was a physical ache, like a flu in his bones.

Dax was grateful to the McCauleys for not mentioning the disastrous end of his short engagement. In fact, they didn't mention Kyra and Ruby at all, as if they sensed the mere mention of their names might cause him to combust.

Dax mentioned his need for a bigger workspace, and Mr. McCauley told him he had a barn on some property nearby. After looking at it, Dax made a deal to convert it into a new, larger workspace than his shed.

"Does this mean you're going to stay on at East Beach?" Mr. McCauley asked.

He wanted to move to Teaneck to be near Jonathan, and had even gone so far as to look at some properties online. But something was holding him back—he'd told Ruby he'd be here. *Right here.* And until he knew in all certainty they weren't coming back, he was going to stay here. "Maybe," he said. "For now, anyway."

"Well, that's fine with us," Mr. McCauley said. "We've taken a liking to you, son."

Wallace and Janet, however, were much less sympathetic when they learned the wedding was off.

Oh, but they went on about it. "What were you thinking, anyway?" Wallace asked. "I thought we were going to have to straitjacket you to keep you from being stupid."

"Do you want me to call Heather?" Janet asked.

And all sorts of nonsense that Dax ignored.

The only bright light in his life was Jonathan. His son was smiling now and holding his head up. "He's strong," Dax said proudly to anyone who asked. He loved that baby fiercely and would have walked across hot coals for that kid.

On one particular visit, he was lying on the floor with Jonathan, studying the baby's perfection as he lay on the floor on his belly, surveying the world around him.

"Are you okay?" Ashley asked.

Dax looked up in surprise. "Why?"

"I don't know. I just know you, and I know how you must feel right now."

He'd had to tell Ashley about Kyra and Ruby, of course, because he'd opened his fat mouth and let her in on his personal business. Ashley had been sympathetic to the demise of his hastily arranged, and hastily abandoned, wedding. "I'm fine."

It was a lie. The truth was that he couldn't stop thinking about Kyra. It had been a few weeks since they'd left, and his heartache wasn't getting better.

"You don't seem fine, Dax. You seem so sad," Ashley said.

Good God, were they really going to have this conversation? "Ashley, please—let me just enjoy my son, okay?"

Ashley sighed as if she were dealing with a recalcitrant child. She shrugged.

"If it were me," Stephanie said from her throne at the kitchen table, "I'd go get her."

Dax rolled his eyes. "Yeah, I know what you would do, Steph. You went and got my wife, remember?"

"No, you're not hearing me, jackass." She stood up and walked over to where he was lying on the floor with Jonathan. "If you love her, and you want her, then man up and go and tell her so."

"Have you heard anything that's been said the last two months?" he snapped. "She's in Indianapolis so her daughter can have brain surgery. *Brain* surgery. It's not the time or the place for that."

"Yeah, and why not?" Stephanie answered smartly. "You act like she's in China behind the Great Wall and you can't get to her. If that's who you want, Dax, you have to fight for it. Don't be a pussy."

"Steph!" Ashley protested.

"Thanks for your sage advice," Dax muttered.

But that afternoon, as he drove back to Lake Haven, he had to agree that maybe Stephanie was right—which annoyed him to no end, but still.

He figured he'd wallowed in his despair long enough. He didn't want to live like a sad-sack shut-in all his life. His feelings for the Coconuts hadn't changed, and maybe the wedding had been a bad idea, but it didn't change his feelings. He loved those two.

Maybe it was time to make a stand. But no matter what else, Dax decided his self-pity was coming to an end.

Chapter Twenty-Six

Ruby's surgery was a success, although Kyra found that hard to believe when her daughter came out of the recovery room with tubes coming out of her and half her head shaved. The surgeon had come to the waiting room where Kyra, Liz, and Josh were waiting and said, "We got it all."

He said a lot more than that, but all Kyra could hear was that they got it all, and the results of the biopsy would be available within a few days.

She texted Dax at some point during that very long day: Surgery over. They got all of it.

A moment later, her phone pinged. Thank God. I want to come and see her. Okay?

Okay? It was more than okay. It was the best news Kyra had heard since *we got it all.* It filled her with happiness. And hope. And longing, such indescribable longing. Yes. Yes, yes, Kyra texted back.

I'll be there Thursday.

Thursday! That was only a few days away. She wished she didn't look so puffy with all the carbs she'd been stress eating, but it didn't matter—Ruby would be so happy to see him. Maybe as happy as her mother, although Kyra doubted it.

Over the next few days, Ruby's recovery from the surgery took a little longer than expected—there was an issue with an infection at the surgical wound, and for two days she was fevered and uncomfortable. Thankfully, she was on the mend now.

Kyra spent every day at the hospital, sleeping when Ruby slept. At night she went to work at a diner on the interstate. It was the only job she'd been able to find in a hurry, and it was one of the worst jobs she'd ever held. Her plan was to keep it until Ruby was out of the hospital and back in school, and then find something that did not require working the vampire shift.

In the meantime, she counted down the days and hours until she saw Dax again. She missed him so much, so deeply, that she couldn't even think of words to tell herself how much. When she wasn't thinking of Ruby, she was thinking of him, imagining him puttering around the cottages, Otto following him around. She was remembering the way he looked at her, and his slow, sexy smile. She felt hollow without him—she knew now what all the love songs were about when the lyrics talked of emptiness. Were it not for Ruby, Kyra thought her heart would be completely barren.

On the morning Dax was due to arrive, Kyra was a nervous wreck. She had finished her shift and was getting ready to leave work. She had just enough time to change out of her uniform and spruce up, best as she could, in anticipation of seeing Dax. But as she was removing her server's apron, her manager, nineteen-year-old Tyler, told her she had to stay. "Maureen is late."

Kyra panicked. "But I have to go, Tyler. You know my daughter's in the hospital." Plus, it was imperative that she have time to change out of that polyester, yellow waitress dress she had to wear. She could never launder the bacon smell from it, and it scratched at her skin. She didn't want Dax to see her like this.

"You can't leave me shorthanded," Tyler said, looking just as panicked.

It was ten o'clock before Maureen deigned to show up. Kyra didn't bother to change, but headed straight for the hospital. Now she was worried that Ruby would be awake and wondering where she was. Ruby hated the hospital—it scared her.

Kyra could have called Josh to be there when Ruby woke up, but his fatherly instincts had quickly worn off once they'd arrived in Indianapolis. Apparently the few attempts Josh had made to connect with Ruby had left him frustrated. He seemed to think Ruby ought to be very happy to know him.

Honestly, Ruby didn't seem to like Josh much. Kyra had assumed when she told Ruby the truth about who Josh was that her daughter would be thrilled to finally know the man she'd wondered about all her life. Yet surprisingly, Ruby didn't seem very interested in him. She didn't sparkle when Josh was around like she'd sparkled in Dax's company. She seemed to view Josh with suspicion, like she didn't really believe he was her father.

Nevertheless, Kyra couldn't complain. Josh was doing his part with the insurance and expenses . . . well, *Liz* was doing his part.

Liz worried about Josh's relationship with Ruby. Liz worried about everything, thank God, or Kyra might have been fighting insurance issues all day. Liz did that for her. It was her way of helping, she said. Liz seemed like a genuinely good person to Kyra, and she thought that in another life, they could have been friends. Kyra now knew that Liz had discovered her text on Josh's phone, and when she'd discovered the existence of Ruby, and the truth about her situation, she'd put aside her own disappointments and had thought only of a six-year-old girl out there who'd needed their help. Liz was devoted to making sure Ruby got what she needed—it was Liz who had figured out how to add Ruby to Josh's insurance, Liz who had chased down the referral to their surgeon, and Liz who had taken care of everything when Kyra was too exhausted or focused on Ruby to do anything else.

"I wish Josh would try harder with Ruby, you know?" Liz had said to Kyra one day as they sat at the edge of the hospital bed while Ruby dozed.

"Ruby's not exactly letting him in," Kyra said. "I'm hoping she comes around."

Kyra guessed that part of Ruby's disdain for Josh was that she wanted Dax. She asked about him and Otto frequently. Kyra had finally figured out that even though Ruby had always wanted to know about her dad, Dax had come along and been that dad she'd been missing before she even knew Josh existed. Ruby didn't want to lose Dax, and she didn't want a different father figure. She didn't care that Josh was partially responsible for her being on this earth—she wanted Dax.

Kyra understood exactly how Ruby felt—she hadn't wanted to lose her mother, either, and when her father began to date again, she hadn't wanted a substitute mom. She'd wanted her mother. She still wanted her mother.

Kyra still wanted Dax, too, and drove like a maniac to the hospital. She hurried down the hall, waving to the nurses who were so wonderful with her daughter. How she would ever adequately thank the people who had taken such care of Ruby, she had no idea.

Ruby's room was at the end of the hall, and she could see Ruby sitting up in bed, alert and awake. She was talking to someone, and Kyra's heart began to race. He was here already? She quickened her step, and just as she reached the door of the room, Ruby said, "Mommy! Look what Dax brought me!"

Her heart stilled at first, because he was there, he was really there, standing in her daughter's hospital room like some storybook angel. He looked magnificent, and sexy, and Kyra's heart began to swell and work again. She couldn't draw a breath, much less speak, because her heart had leapt into overdrive and was beating so wildly that she was momentarily arrested.

Emotion scudded across his face, and his gaze locked on hers. He swallowed and said, in a rough, low voice, "Hi."

Kyra dropped her bag in the doorway. "Hi," she managed.

"Mommy, did you see?" Ruby asked, trying to lean over the bed.

Kyra tore her gaze away from Dax and looked down. A massive wooden house was at his feet.

"It's for my Barbies!" Ruby said excitedly. "*Five* of them can live there. But not Ken. Dax said he had to live next door with his dog."

Kyra lifted her gaze to Dax again, her heart beating like a high school drum line. "It's . . . it's *so good* to see you," she said, wishing her voice wasn't shaking as badly as it was.

He nodded. "Same here."

"I wanted to change clothes," she said self-consciously, running her hands over her uniform.

He shook his head. "You look beautiful," he said, and his eyes seemed to mist. He opened his arms to her, and Kyra walked right into them. She closed her eyes and buried her face in his neck. She felt like she was falling into a white, fluffy cloud—she felt at peace in his arms. Safe and comforted. Loved. God, how she'd needed him these last few weeks, had needed his strength and calm to wrap around her and hold her when no one else would.

"You smell like bacon," he said.

She laughed, then lifted her head and kissed him. She kissed him right on the mouth with all the longing she'd felt for him. His arms wrapped tighter around her, his fingers sank into her hair . . .

"Mommy!" Ruby complained.

Dax slowly let her go, his hands lingering on her waist a moment.

He talked to Ruby for a while until the nurse came around to change her sheets and pajamas. Kyra and Dax went to the cafeteria and sat across from each other in a plastic booth with two coffees that smelled burned and that neither of them touched. She asked about Jonathan and smiled with delight at the latest pictures of him. Dax told her he was thinking of getting a place in Teaneck to be closer to his son.

"Oh," she said. "Wow. That's . . . that's news."

He shrugged. "It's not that far from East Beach. I found a place that could function as a workshop."

His life, she realized, was moving on. Without her. Just like hers was moving on without him. The realization staggered her, and she helplessly swallowed down a lump of regret and sorrow. "Really? When?"

"I don't know," he said. "I'm not even sure if . . ." He seemed to rethink what he was going to say and suddenly reached across the table for her hand, took it in his, and held it tightly. "I have . . . God, I've missed you so much, Kyra," he said, his voice breaking a little.

"Oh." She gripped his hand. "I've missed you, too, Dax. I can't tell you how much I've missed you. And so has Ruby—she talks about you and Otto all the time."

He smiled. "She seems good."

"She's *so* good," Kyra said. "She's getting stronger every day. I really believe she's going to be okay. I mean, I still don't know the results of the biopsy, and they will monitor her for a while, but for so long I kept thinking it was my mother all over again. I don't think so now, and I feel more optimistic than I have yet. And you know what else? Not one seizure since the surgery."

"That's fantastic," he said. His eyes were roaming over her face, lingering on her mouth, on her hairline. It felt almost as if he'd forgotten the small details of her. "I've thought so much about her," he said, and his gaze settled on Kyra's eyes. "I've thought so much about you. I've thought about all the things I said, and mostly the things I didn't say . . ." He glanced down at the table a moment. "There is something I never told you, Kyra."

She panicked for a moment. "Oh God . . . what is it?"

"I love you," he said.

Kyra gasped softly. She wasn't expecting him to say that. Those three little words seized her, grabbing her up and holding her aloft for a moment before settling into her tissues.

"I should have told you in East Beach, but I . . ." He paused, shoved a hand through his hair. "I guess I'm a little rusty. And maybe a coward. But I love you."

She couldn't yet speak. The admission was wending its way around her heart, wrapping it slowly.

He gave her a lopsided, rueful smile. "Aren't you going to say something?"

She nodded. "I'm trying. But you've snatched the breath from my lungs, and my heart is beating like a jackhammer, and I can't even put words to how happy that makes me."

His smile deepened. "I'll take it. I know I'm a day late with it, but I thought you ought to know. I thought I ought to tell you that if I had to do it all over again, I wouldn't change a single thing. Except maybe letting you leave."

"I wouldn't change a moment of it, either," she said and swallowed, trying to take the nerves from her voice. She squeezed his hand. "I never would have left if I hadn't been forced to go. You know that, right?"

"But that's the thing, babe. You didn't have to go. Yeah, I said so at the time, but I've thought a lot about it. A *lot*. I've wanted to pick up that phone a thousand times just to hear your voice, but I wouldn't let myself. Because I needed to know if what I was feeling was real enough and strong enough to walk out on this limb."

"What limb?" she asked, confused now.

"I want to marry you," he said. "Not because of insurance, but because I love you." He leaned across the table, his gaze on hers. "I am crazy, over-the-moon in love with you. As insane as it is to want to marry someone after only a couple of months, I want to do it."

Kyra was dumbfounded. She didn't know what to say—she couldn't even think, she was so surprised and shocked. His admission was something she'd longed to hear but had assumed she had no right. She had yearned for him to feel this way about her but had convinced herself she'd ruined any chance at it. To hear it now was overwhelming. She needed to absorb it for a moment.

"You're not saying anything again," he said, a little nervously.

All Kyra knew was how much she loved this man, with all her heart, with every bit of her being, and how much she missed him and needed him. But marriage? She couldn't even grasp the idea of it.

"Do you still love me?" he asked.

She groaned. "My God, how I love you, Dax. More than anything, can't you tell? But I don't know what to say. Ruby is . . . this is not—"

"Hey, no one's proposing here," he said quickly.

"You just said—"

"I said I want to marry you. But I didn't ask you, did I? I'm not going to propose to you now, Kyra. Because I don't want you to think I'm proposing because I feel sorry for you and the coconut. I don't feel sorry for you, I feel *great* about you two. I'm just going to wait for the right moment, when you come back to East Beach."

Kyra was stunned. She felt almost on the verge of hysterical laughter. Happy, frantic laughter. This man loved her, and she was not expecting it, and she was feeling glittery and warm inside. And yet there were so many questions. She didn't even know if Ruby's tumor was benign, if she would recover completely. And her care team was *here*. Not in East Beach. "I don't yet know—"

"Nope," he said and held up his hand. "Don't say anything. I just told you, this is not a proposal. All I'm saying is that I'm going to propose to you. But I'll wait as long as it takes."

She grabbed his hands with both of hers. "Dax! You're not making sense."

"Yes, I am. Listen to me, Kyra—I'm going to wait for you at East Beach. And if you decide you don't want to or can't come back there, then so be it. I'm a grown man, I will understand. But at least I'll know

I didn't let you go without telling you how much . . . how much I *love* you," he said, his voice breaking again. "And how much I want to spend my life with you and the coconut. And Jonathan. And whoever else comes along. But I'm putting the ball in your court, babe."

"My God," she said and shook her head with confusion. "No pressure there, right?"

He smiled a little. "Would you rather I kept that all to myself?"

Kyra snorted. *"No,"* she said. God, no. No matter what else happened to her and Ruby, she would always have this moment in this antiseptic cafeteria in Indianapolis, and she wouldn't forget a moment of it. She wouldn't forget how huge her heart felt right now, overflowing with love and affection and pride. "What you just said is the most beautiful nonproposal speech I've ever heard in my life, and I'll never forget it," she said, pressing her hand to her heart. "I feel it in my heart. I'll keep it there forever. I love you, Dax. Even more, now," she said with a sheepish smile. "But there are still a lot of unknowns about Ruby's health. Even in the best-case scenario, there's a lot of aftercare involved, and she has her doctors and the nursing team here, and she's comfortable with them, and she needs to be closely monitored, and I can't risk the excellent health care she is getting here."

"I understand," he said.

"Do you? Because I would get in your truck right this minute and go anywhere you wanted to go, and be whoever you wanted me to be. I would. But I can't right now, and every waking moment has been about Ruby, and I've hardly had time to feed myself, much less think about the next day or the next."

"I know," he said sympathetically. "I get it. I honestly don't want you to think about this now, okay? I just want you to know that the door is wide open," he said and tapped his chest.

She'd already walked through it. He would take a piece of her with him today, because she was already in there. "You are the best thing that ever happened to us, do you know that?" she asked softly.

"I think I got the better end of the deal." He slid out of the booth and held out his hand to her. "Let's go see what the coconut is up to."

Kyra slipped her hand into his and stood up. But before he could turn away, she caught his chin in her hand and pulled his face around. She rose up on her toes and kissed him softly, with all the love and tenderness she felt for him brimming out of her. Nothing had changed for her except that once she had loved this man beyond measure. Now she loved him beyond reason.

But she didn't know when, if ever, she could return to East Beach.

Chapter Twenty-Seven

A few days after Dax returned from Indianapolis, he got a text from Kyra with a huge smiley face and the word *benign*.

He was so overcome with emotion at the news that he fell into a chair in his kitchen and buried his face in his hands . . . until Otto began to lick them.

Two weeks after he returned from Indianapolis, he got another text. This one included a picture of a gap-toothed Ruby. Her hair had been cut short to match where they'd shaved her head for the surgery. Kyra wrote, Ruby returned to school today and told everyone a pirate had scalped her. She attached a GIF of a woman drinking from a giant wineglass.

The coffee tables Dax made were so good that people were wanting copies. And then they wanted more—hutches, craft tables, dining tables, headboards. He was busier than he'd ever been. He never went to the Green Bean anymore, either—he went to Teaneck to spend time with Jonathan. He'd scouted out a few houses in Teaneck, a couple of workshops he could rent. But he hadn't yet pulled the trigger, because he'd promised two coconuts he'd be right here, waiting.

He worked all week, and on weekends, he and Otto drove around looking for unusual wood. They picked up pallets and drove by lumber yards, estate sales, and demolitions. He was so busy he didn't see any of the usual characters—Wallace had started sending a delivery truck to him so that Dax could finish all the work Wallace had lined up for him.

Kyra called him most weeks so that he could speak to Ruby. She said she'd found a job at an upscale restaurant and the tips were decent. He wanted to ask her what her plans were, but he didn't—he'd promised he wouldn't, and usually she was full of talk about Ruby's progress with the rehabilitation and the testing.

When she asked about him, he told her about his work and Jonathan. But his heart was aching—he wanted them to come home.

Ruby had her seventh birthday. Kyra texted him photos of her Barbie party, which Ruby had arranged in the massive house he'd built—and from the look of the photo, it took up most of the room in their little apartment. Kyra said that Ruby's doctor said her progress was good. But that's all she said.

Just before the holidays, Kyra called him. "Hey, how are you?"

"Good," he said. But he'd felt on pins and needles. He had a fear she was going to tell him she wasn't coming back to East Beach. "I'm getting ready to fly out to see my folks," he said, just so he could head off any bad news before he flew to Arizona.

"We just wanted to wish you a happy Thanksgiving," she said and put Ruby on the phone.

He and Ruby talked a moment—that is, Ruby talked and he said uh-huh a lot—and then she mentioned that they were going to her father's house for Thanksgiving. "We're going to eat a fried turkey!"

Dax's belly did a weird little flip when she said it. Not over the fried turkey, but the fact that she was spending Thanksgiving with her biological father. He was a fool to think he could ever compete with that.

"Oh geez, I should have noted the time," Kyra said, taking the phone back. "I'm sorry, I've got to get to work. Happy Thanksgiving!" she said cheerfully and hung up.

The texts continued to come—usually pictures of Ruby, usually asking for pictures of Jonathan—but Kyra said nothing about returning to East Beach. Not a single word.

Dax began to despair that she would. He wondered if she and he had been put into some kind of friend zone and he was too dumb to know it. It wouldn't be the first time the signs were all there and he hadn't seen them. Three months had passed since Kyra and Ruby left, and Ruby was in school and thriving by all accounts, and Kyra was working, and there wasn't any sign, not a single sign, that they were coming back to him.

He began to give himself pep talks. He'd said what he'd had to say, and he'd meant it, all of it. If Kyra wasn't coming back, well . . . he'd have to man up and face facts.

But he was crushed by it.

A week before Christmas, he was sanding down some wood in the shed to use in making a hutch when Otto barked, leapt up, and ran out the door. That was followed by the sound of voices and car doors slamming.

"Great. Neighbors." He tossed down his gloves and reached for a towel, then heard a young girl squeal with delight. "Down!" she said. "Down!"

His heart stopped beating. Just stopped, like it couldn't take any more surprises. He slowly put down the towel and walked to the open door of his shed in disbelief. There was a girl crawling under his fence. She had curly red hair, but it was short. And she was wearing the light-up shoes. Blue ones. With the face of a princess emblazoned on them.

Ruby Coconuts was suddenly on his side of the fence.

"Stop licking my face!" she cried laughingly as Otto attacked her with his tongue.

In the drive of Number Three was the Subaru, just as if it had always been there. And leaning into the open hatch was a backside he knew very well. She had on jeans and boots and a sleeveless jacket over a long-sleeved T-shirt. As she backed out, holding a box, her hair spilled around her face and her shoulders.

"Guess what?" Ruby shouted from the fence. "Mr. McCauley said we could live here!"

Dax was too stunned to speak. He looked at her, then to Kyra.

"GUESS WHAT?" Ruby shouted again, only louder.

"I heard you, Coconut," he said and made his feet move—stumbling, really—across the lawn to the fence.

"I mean, what are the odds?" Kyra asked cheerfully. "That Number Three would be available?"

He wasn't sure what was happening, but it felt like Christmas and New Year's and a shiny new table saw all rolled into one. "I, ah . . . I wasn't expecting you," he said uncertainly.

Her eyes were sparkling with delight. And love. He could see it. He could *feel* it. "I *know,*" she said pertly.

"Are you back? I mean . . . did you come back?"

She laughed. "I'm here, aren't I?"

"Could you maybe have mentioned it?"

She grinned. She looked antsy, and he had the idea she was going to explode with delight. "Nope. Ruby and I wanted it to be a surprise."

"Are you surprised? Are you surprised? Are you surprised?" Ruby asked, jumping up and down.

"Flabbergasted. You look like you've grown a foot, Coconut," he said and roughly grabbed her up, hugging her.

"I know, I'm seven now! Mommy said we're going to get married!"

Good God, his heart felt like it was going to burst open and spray rainbows all over that lawn. "Really?" he asked, looking at Kyra. "That's odd—I haven't asked your mom to marry me."

"Well," Kyra said giddily, "I meant if the offer still stands. Of course, I understood you to say the offer stands until I say otherwise. Isn't that what you said? Or did I hear it wrong?"

He didn't say anything. Frankly, he was afraid a tear might roll down his cheek if he spoke.

"Because . . . because I forgot to tell you something in Indianapolis," she said as Ruby ran off to have a look at the cottage. Kyra put down the box she was holding.

"Oh yeah?"

"I forgot to tell you that I love you so much that if you don't want to propose to me anymore, I will do something wildly outrageous about it, because I feel that strongly about it."

"Like what?"

"Like . . . lock you in a room with Ruby and her Barbies, for starters."

A small kernel of delight sprouted in his belly. "Doesn't scare me."

"Okay," she said, nodding, contemplating. Her eyes were shining brightly, and Dax thought he could see hope and a bit of worry in them. "Then I'll do something else. Maybe tie you up and cover you in honey and lick it off until you give."

The kernel of delight turned into a different sort of delight altogether. "Bringing out the big guns, huh?"

"Oh, that's only the beginning of my guns," she said.

"I'm impressed," he said. *And in love. Completely, utterly in love with this woman.* "What else?"

"Honestly?" Her nervous, giddy little smile faded, and he noticed she was holding the hem of her jacket in something of a death grip. "I would do whatever it took, Dax," she said quietly. "Anything. Because there is never going to be another you for us. No one will ever fill our hearts like you have. No one. Ever."

Good God, he was going to melt. Like a pat of butter, all over the grass—no one had ever said anything like that to him. "You'd do anything?"

She nodded. *"Anything."*

Yep, his heart was going to burst into rainbows at any moment. He sighed. "Weren't you a little smart-ass about it, making me wait without a single word? Not even a *hint*. I thought you weren't coming back," he said, reaching across the fence for her as Ruby galloped back to their side.

"I got here as soon as I could," she said, grabbing onto his arms. "Because guess what happened two weeks ago?"

"What?"

"Let me tell him, Mommy!" Ruby shouted. "The doctor said I can be a normal girl and go to school, and run, and swim, and whatever I want, and I don't have to go to the doctor anymore."

Dax looked at Kyra for confirmation.

She nodded. Her eyes were glistening with tears now. "She's got the all clear," she said, choking on the words a little. "She's to have biannual checkups, but there is no reason to expect anything other than a long and healthy life for her."

That news was the best thing Dax had heard since the birth of Jonathan. But there was still a question or two lingering in his heart. "You don't need his insurance?"

"Maybe. But it's a done deal—until my situation changes, he's covering her. Here. In East Beach. No matter the cost."

What was that Dax was feeling in his chest? His heart swelling like a balloon? "So . . . you're really here," he said, still disbelieving. "You've really come back for us."

"Dax . . . I came back in a heartbeat," she said. "I came back for us, for all of us, for you and me and Ruby and Jonathan and Otto. I came back for that nonproposal, because I have thought of it every single day since you made it. And I'll wait as long as it takes for you to make it, too. I'm here for good. I'm scheduled to take the real estate exam after the first of the year. Oh, and I'm on a sub list at the bistro. And I've got a place to live," she said, nodding toward Number Three. "I mean, who knows how long I'll have to wait for you to propose?"

"Who knows," he said and reached across the fence and slipped his hands under her legs, picking her up and swinging her over to his side. He kissed her. "Did you mean to torture me?" he muttered and kissed her. "Because it was hell."

"I meant to do it right," she said. "Equal footing."

He kissed her again, only deeper, with the swell of possibilities and love in his heart. With the joy and prospect of a new year, of a new beginning, of a family. He wished someone would kick him, just to make doubly sure he wasn't deep in a dream.

"Stop *kissing*!" Ruby cried and threw her arms around their waists, pressing her face into his side.

Dax laughed. He let go of Kyra, tousled Ruby's hair, then picked up the box. "Let's get you moved in. What do you two think about a pizza tonight?"

"Awesome!" Ruby shouted and raced up to the porch steps of Number Three in shoes that burst a flash of colors with each step, and with Otto loping behind her. She opened the screen door and went in.

The screen door slammed behind her, as apparently the pneumatic arm had been knocked loose. But this time, Dax laughed about it—it was music to his ears.

Epilogue

The following July Fourth holiday

It was only the second barbecue Dax had ever hosted. He still didn't believe in barbecues, but Ruby had made friends with the O'Reilly children in Number Six, and she was desperate to show off her new backyard fort. The McCauleys had put it up for their grandchildren, but Ruby had full use of it. Or rather, she had full use of it when Otto didn't walk up the plank and make himself at home. That old dog liked to lie there with his paws hanging out the door, his head propped against the side, watching the comings and goings on the lake.

Dax had bought a house in Teaneck over the winter, one near enough to his boy so he could see him every day, but one close enough to East Beach that he could see the coconuts every day, too. He still hadn't proposed, as the timing had not yet been right, and neither of them seemed in a hurry. He and Kyra had committed to each other, and that's what mattered. They were taking the time to know each other like a couple of sane people instead of rushing into anything.

Dax loved Kyra and Ruby more and more each day.

"I hate barbecues," Dax groused as he opened another package of hot dogs.

"It will be all right," Kyra assured him and patted his cheek. "Just relax."

She'd recently gotten a job with a brokerage in Black Springs and had sold her first house. It wasn't one of the million-dollar homes, but as she pointed out, "It's more money than I would make in three months at the Lakeside Bistro."

"How am I supposed to relax?" he demanded. "One of these bozos is going to complain about hot dogs, just you wait and see." He had grumbled about the barbecue since coming up with the idea, but the truth was that he was a little eager to show off Jonathan, who was staggering around like a little drunk in his red overalls.

The sound of a car door slamming annoyed Dax next. "And they're *early*," he said, as if someone had personally insulted him by being careless with the time.

The first people to arrive were Janet and her new boyfriend, Ted, who was interested in getting Dax to invest in some sort of deal he had with a golf club manufacturer. They were accompanied by Wallace and Curtis, who wore matching plaid shirts and jeans. Dax asked if they were worried about getting lost in the crowd. Wallace suggested Dax might invest in a wardrobe, period.

The McCauleys came walking down the hill together, John and Beverly close behind them. The new couple in Number One had come, too—Lola and Harry. She was a writer, and Harry built bridges, which Dax privately envied. Deenie had come with a couple of friends, but they weren't staying long, she announced. There was a better, hipper party happening on the other end of the lake.

Within twenty minutes, everyone in their little circle of acquaintances at East Beach had arrived, which made it perfect for what Dax had in mind, even if he did hate that what he had in mind had to include a barbecue.

They dined on burgers—veggie, thanks to Janet, beef, thanks to Kyra—chips, and a mountain of hot dogs that were most appreciated by the children who were running around. They drank wine and beer and told tall tales, and now, as the sun was setting, Dax invited them all to walk down to the lake so that the kids could play with sparklers.

"Sparklers," Wallace said. "That's so unlike you, Lumberjack."

"I was only thinking of you, Twinkletoes," Dax said, and Curtis laughed.

When they had all trooped down to the beach, Dax handed Jonathan to Mrs. McCauley, then walked to the water's edge. Otto trailed along and sat right in front of him, oblivious to anyone else. "I don't need your help, but okay," Dax muttered to him. He raised his arms. "Can I have everyone's attention?"

It took a moment—in fact, Kyra was talking to Deenie, and Dax had to call her out—but he finally managed to get everyone to look at him. "I won't be long. I just want to say thanks to all of you. You've made East Beach home."

"But you live in Teaneck now," Janet said.

"But this is where I consider home," Dax said. He hadn't counted on having to diagram his little speech for everyone.

"My God, are you getting *sentimental*?" Wallace asked, his hand going to his throat.

Dax sighed. "Okay, look. You all know that last summer I tried to marry Kyra Coconuts. She turned me down then, but I'm hoping that if there's an audience, she won't do it again."

Kyra gasped. Deenie squealed with delight. "Are you really doing this?" Kyra asked in a tone she might use if addressing someone about to jump off a roof. "I'd given up on you."

He was doing what he'd been dying to do since the day she and Ruby had pulled into the drive at Number Three for the second time. But he'd been patient. He'd let her see where this would go. He'd let her discover, like he had, that they were perfect for each other. And now he withdrew the ring from his jeans pocket and sank down onto his knee, almost falling over when Otto decided to move at the same moment.

Suddenly everyone was shouting. Good God, a man had never heard such a hue and cry. "Kyra, it would help if you would come a little closer," he suggested.

Deenie pushed her, and she stumbled out, wide-eyed, clearly surprised, which gave Dax a great deal of male satisfaction. "Will you please put me out of the misery of wanting to marry you already and marry me?" he asked.

She laughed a bit nervously, which was not the response he'd been expecting. He'd expected little whimpers and sighs and stars shooting out of her eyes.

"What's the matter?" he asked, frowning.

"I'm *excited*!" she said and laughed again. "Yes! *Yes*, of course I will," she said and fell to her knees in front of him, trying to push Otto out from between them, but the dog would not budge.

Dax was shaking as he put the ring on her finger. "This didn't go anything like I thought it would."

"Nothing about us has ever gone like we thought it would," she said, smiling up at him, her eyes glistening with unbridled happiness. "Why would it now? Oh my," she said, looking at the ring. "It's gorgeous, Dax. *You're* gorgeous." She wrapped her arms around his neck. "Do you know how happy I am right now? Delirious! I've never been as happy as I've been with you these last few months . . . but now? Today? I'm over the moon. I may keel over. And if I do, please know that I couldn't wait to share a lifetime with you." She kissed his cheek. "I love you, you old grump," she said and kissed his mouth.

Dax felt a little giddy himself. Butterflies in his belly, the whole nine yards. "Not as much as I love you, babe," he said as she kissed his cheeks and the bridge of his nose.

She wasn't listening now—Mrs. McCauley put Jonathan down beside them, and Kyra was squealing with delight and holding her hand out to show Deenie the ring, and then they were almost knocked into the lake when Ruby launched her small body at them and shrieked, *"You're going to be my daddy!"*

As if he hadn't figured that out. What a coconut that girl was.

About the Author

Photo © 2010 Carrie D'Anna

Julia London is the *New York Times*, *USA Today*, and *Publishers Weekly* bestselling author of more than forty romance novels. Her historical titles include the popular Desperate Debutantes series, the Cabot Sisters series, and the Highland Grooms series. Her contemporary works include the Lake Haven series, the Pine River series, and the Cedar Springs series. She has won the RT Book Club Award for Best Historical Romance and has been a six-time finalist for the prestigious RITA Award for excellence in romantic fiction. She lives in Austin, Texas.